HE

He felt h... ...g...ning to cramp. He reached down to release his weight belt, and his sense of speed increased as he started to kick furiously. His hands and fingers began to curl, and as he shot upward he felt the muscles throughout his body tighten and knot.

Pain blurred his vision as the gases behind his eyes pushed outward. The soft organs twisted in his body. Then his chest suddenly swelled to twice its size, cracking his backbone and shattering his rib cage.

Five feet beneath the surface, he screamed. But only bubbles and blood came from his mouth . . .

ACTION ADVENTURE

SILENT WARRIORS   (1675, $3.95)
by Richard P. Henrick
The Red Star, Russia's newest, most technologically advanced submarine, outclasses anything in the U.S. fleet. But when the captain opens his sealed orders 24 hours early, he's staggered to read that he's to spearhead a massive nuclear first strike against the Americans!

THE PHOENIX ODYSSEY   (1789, $3.95)
by Richard P. Henrick
All communications to the USS *Phoenix* suddenly and mysteriously vanish. Even the urgent message from the president cancelling the War Alert is not received. In six short hours the *Phoenix* will unleash its nuclear arsenal against the Russian mainland.

COUNTERFORCE   (2013, $3.95)
Richard P. Henrick
In the silent deep, the chase is on to save a world from destruction. A single Russian Sub moves on a silent and sinister course for American shores. The men aboard the U.S.S. *Triton* must search for and destroy the Soviet killer Sub as an unsuspecting world races for the apocalypse.

EAGLE DOWN   (1644, $3.75)
by William Mason
To western eyes, the Russian Bear appears to be in hibernation— but half a world away, a plot is unfolding that will unleash its awesome, deadly power. When the Russian Bear rises up, God help the Eagle.

DAGGER   (1399, $3.50)
by William Mason
The President needs his help, but the CIA wants him dead. And for Dagger—war hero, survival expert, ladies man and mercenary extraordinaire—it will be a game played for keeps.

Available wherever paperbacks are sold, or order direct from the Publisher. Send cover price plus 50¢ per copy for mailing and handling to Zebra Books, Dept. 121, 475 Park Avenue South, New York, N.Y. 10016. Residents of New York, New Jersey and Pennsylvania must include sales tax. DO NOT SEND CASH.

TRUK LAGOON

MITCHELL
SAM
ROSSI

PINNACLE BOOKS
WINDSOR PUBLISHING CORP.

PINNACLE BOOKS

are published by

Windsor Publishing Corp.
475 Park Avenue South
New York, NY 10016

First Pinnacle printing: June, 1988

Printed in the United States of America

For my father,

without whose love and support
I would never have taken
my first steps,
or reached my dreams

Acknowledgments

There are so many people I wish to thank it would easily take another book, yet certain ones need mention: My family and friends for unending support; Philip Alan Rosenberg, whose underwater photography set the seed of the story; John D'Angona and Bill Erwin, two ex-submariners who gladly allowed their brains to be picked of details; Dave Branconier, for his research; Stephen Moorhouse and Lourdes Vita, for their suggestions and editorial.

Special thanks to Ben Masselink, my mentor and my friend.

To the commanders and crewmen of the 52 submarines lost during World War II; Time has not diminished your gallantry.

There is a port of no return, where ships
May ride at anchor for a little space
And then, some starless night, the cable slips,
Leaving an eddy at the mooring place . . .
Gulls, veer no longer. Sailor, rest your oar.
No tangled wreckage will be washed ashore.

L. N. Jennings
"Lost Harbor"

PROLOGUE

Choukoutien, China, 1929

"Herr Doktor, Herr Doktor, Ich habe es gründen!" yelled the young man as he ran from the mouth of the cave.

The noon sun carved hard shadows into the ground as the doctor stepped from under the canopy. The temperature on his skin jumped immediately to 110 degrees. He turned, shaded his eyes with the flat of his hand, and looked up the footpath. His assistant had stopped and was now waving at him to follow.

The doctor wiped the sweat that began to form on his forehead. He picked up his wide-brimmed hat, set it loosely over his thinning red hair, and started up the steep path that led to the opening in the side of Dragon's Tooth Hill.

The trail had become well worn over the ten years the doctor had walked it. He usually worked at the cave site during the spring and fall, leaving the extreme hot and cold seasons to numerous assistants and colleagues. This allowed him time at the university to sort through the thousands of minute chips of rock and dirt that hinted at being fossils.

But not this year. It was now mid-July and he had been at the site since September desperately trying to find one indisputable fragment. Anything that could link the three-million-year-old tooth he had found here so long ago with the theories he had built around it.

"Where?" the doctor asked as he reached his assistant.

"In the small cavern off the main chamber's lower level," the assistant said, still somewhat out of breath. He drew his dusty sleeve across his face. "I think this is what we have been looking for, Doctor Hoffmann."

The two men hunched over, squeezed into the narrow crevice, and followed the tiny zig zag path into the darkness. After several yards, the walls of the cave separated, revealing a concert-hall-sized chamber lit by dozens of flickering torches. They began to climb down the series of bamboo ladders that connected the four major digs. Three were considered complete while the fourth had only been looked at over the last two years.

The doctor nodded to a few of the workers who looked up and smiled at him. *"Ni hao,"* he said, and they each rattled back some unintelligible Cantonese dialogue and lifted a sliver of rock for him to evaluate. The Chinese were the best workers, he thought, they dug from morning to night with more enthusiasm than most of his colleagues.

When the two men finally reached the bottom of the cave, the assistant took the lead. He moved toward a single torch by the far wall. Bending down to his knees, he crawled through a small opening and into another chamber. The doctor followed.

The minor chamber was only about five feet from rock ceiling to dirt floor, but its length stretched far beyond the light of the three torches that burned over the digging area. From the sand deposits between the rocks, the doctor could tell this was once a channel for an underground stream.

A young Chinese girl with a long braid of dark hair lying down the center of her back looked up as they entered. "Here," she said. She turned back to the dome-shaped brown bone and continued to dust the soil away with a soft brush.

"How much have you uncovered?" the doctor asked as he knelt beside her.

"Only a small piece, but there's more."

Moving close, the doctor pulled out his round gold-rimmed glasses and tucked them behind his ear. He took out a small needle from his breast pocket and began to scrape lightly around the edges of the fossil. Very slowly, he removed the encrusted soil as a surgeon would remove scar tissue.

As he cleared more and more dirt, he began to realize that this was not a fragment of bone, but a complete cranium. His heart started to pound hard in his chest and his hands began to shake with anticipation. He had to stop several times.

It took a total of nine hours, each of them working in turn to remove the sand and rock and the millennia of time that held the fossil. But finally it was free.

The doctor lifted the skull slowly from the rock. This was it. The supraorbital was intact, its brow ridge highly overstated as the doctor had suspected it would be.

He sat back on the dusty floor of the cave and leaned against the sharp-edged wall. He held the skull with both hands and inspected it under the torch light. Then, as the smile grew at the edges of his mouth, he looked up at his assistant and the young dirty-faced girl and nodded thankfully.

After so many years, *Sinanthropus pekinensis,* his Peking Man, had finally come alive again.

ONE

Norfolk, Virginia, 1986

From the night sky, the snow fell gently, unseen until it passed into the dome of light beneath the lamp. It drifted down from gray clouds in the cold windless air and landed silently on the water. Several waves, sent by a passing boat, slapped the steel pillars below the dock.

Commander Brian Bovan stood with his right foot atop a giant iron docking cleat, letting the snow fall around him. He bit hard on the end of his cigarette, trying to decide whether or not to light it. Finally, he tossed it into the bay and rubbed his face. The two days worth of beard below his thick mustache pulled at his wool glove.

He looked up at the huge silhouette. God, she's beautiful, he thought. From where he stood, he could see the conning tower and small section of deck that showed above the waterline. Three fourths of the *John Adams* still lay beneath the surface of the bay.

The nuclear submarine rested almost motionless except for a slight roll of her deck that caused the gangplank to slide forward and back in well-worn grooves on the dock, moaning gently. Her dull black hull held in the lights of the harbor while the surrounding bay reflected them in sparkles.

Brian invisioned her gliding through the sea at four hundred meters. She could be bright pink at that depth, it wouldn't matter, the eyes of the abyss were blind. There would only be a sense of her presence as she cruised silently.

Staring at the submarine, he knew he would never again feel her decks slant as she rose from the blackness and into the light of day. He wouldn't hear the rush of the sea leaving her ballast tanks nor the waves washing over her skin.

"She is a gem," Captain MacFife said as he stepped close to Brian.

Brian didn't turn. "You're up late," he said to his commanding officer, his ex–commanding officer.

"Couldn't quite sleep," MacFife said, looking up at Brian. He was a small man, made smaller by Brian's six-foot-two frame. And he was thin, so much so his face seemed only covered with a few layers of skin.

Brian nodded. He knew exactly how MacFife felt, though he wouldn't say so.

MacFife looked down at the water. Idly, he kicked a pile of fresh snow off the edge of the dock. It seemed to hover in the air before dropping into the dark harbor. "Damn it, Brian, I don't know what to tell you. I can't believe they didn't give you a command."

Brian turned to him, but MacFife was behind the mist of his breath. He looked back at the *John Adams.*

"Let it lay, Mac," Brian said.

"No. You're the best exec I ever had," MacFife said. "A bit cocky at times, but no question, you should have your own. You've earned it."

"Not everybody agrees, I guess," Brian said in a low voice. His eyes followed the outline of the submarine from bow to stern. Turning, he started to walk along the dock. He hadn't expected MacFife to be there, especially at two A.M. Brian wanted to be alone. He needed to be.

MacFife matched Brian's pace at his left shoulder. They stopped midway along the cement expansion that ran the length of the submarine.

"She's been good to us, hasn't she, Mac?" Brian said.

The two men were silent for a time, both within their

own thoughts as they stared at the weapon of war as if she had been their lover. Then again, she had. A steel maiden who beckoned them to release her lines and set her to sail. It was the lure felt by every submariner. Unlike the modern giants that crossed the oceans with crews numbering in the thousands, a submarine was more like the old wooden warships. One captain and one crew separate from the world until she docked in some distant port.

"It doesn't make sense," MacFife said finally.

"It doesn't have to," Brain said. "Does the repair crew know about the trouble in that ventilating duct in the missile room?"

"Why the hell are you worrying about that? Goddamn it, you just lost a career."

"Because it's important," Brian said flatly. "Whether I'm her exec or someone else is. The men need good air."

"It'll be fixed," MacFife promised. Then after a moment, "I just can't figure out why the hell—"

"It's over," Brian cut him off. The night was cold and MacFife's comments were making it colder. "All I've wanted, Skipper, was my own command. Nothing else, but now it's over. It's time to move on."

"I put in the highest recommendation for you," MacFife said as he pulled his coat tighter against the wind.

Brian didn't say anything. He pushed his hands into his coat pockets.

"You know," MacFife said. "I still think you ought to talk to Mills. It couldn't hurt, that admiral being a friend of your family and all." As soon as he said it, MacFife could see in Brian's dark eyes that for just that reason, he would never call on him.

Brian shook his head and looked back at the submarine as he rubbed his right forearm.

"Told you it would itch?"

Brian hadn't realized he had been scratching at the scar. Pulling his sleeve back, he looked at the two-inch square of healing tissue. "It's not that bad," he said.

17

"That was the prettiest one I ever saw," MacFife said. "You should have kept it."

"Well, I thought it was better to get rid of it."

"Why, plenty of captains have tattoos."

"So do a lot of civilians."

The words brought silence between them again as they stood in the winter night. A lone tugboat, its engine chugging deeply, revealed itself in a ghostly image as it moved downriver toward the Chesapeake.

"I'm sorry, Brian."

"No reason to be. It's the second time they passed me over for a command. Either I take a desk job or I'm out. Simple and sweet," Brian said, the muscles in his jaw tightening as he held his anger. "And I'm not one to push a pencil."

"Is there anything I can do?"

Brian looked into MacFife's narrow face. "No. I've got some loose ends to take care of on base, but that's it." He pulled off one of his wool gloves and adjusted his cap over his curly brown hair. "I'm going to head up north and see my mom. She's been sick the last couple of weeks."

"Sorry to hear that," MacFife said. "How about we head over to Farley's? I'll buy you a drink."

Brian shook his head. "Thanks, Mac, really. But I'm going to stay here a while longer."

MacFife understood. He brushed the snow off the top of his collar, it was beginning to melt into his shirt. He put his hand on Brian's shoulder and squeezed it hard. "If there's ever anything."

Brian nodded and forced a thankful smile. He would miss standing next to MacFife on the bridge of the *John Adams*.

"You know, Brian, it wasn't your record."

Brian looked up at the nuclear submarine for a moment, then turned to his commander. "Then what the hell was it, Mac?"

TWO

Rye Village, New Hampshire, 1986

"Let us pray," the priest said as he faced the crowd who had walked from the white towering church to the grave site. They gathered close to the casket. Beneath their feet, the frost-covered ground and frozen maple leaves crackled.

Catherine Bovan's coffin was chestnut red and shone bright under the lights of the church, but now it was dull in the reflection of the solemn winter sky.

Brian looked at the faces of the people who huddled near him and wondered when his mother had grown as old as her friends. When had her hair become so thin and gray, and when had she begun to walk in such small, unsure steps? The air smelled bitter of mulch and musty woolen coats.

"Let us pray. Lord Jesus Christ, the three days you lay in the tomb you made holy the graves of all who believe in you," the priest continued.

As Brian stood with his arm around his aunt Martha, he could feel her frail body shake as she cried. Her thin hand clutched his as she held her crocheted handkerchief to her eyes with the other.

"Give our sister peaceful rest in this grave, until that day when you, the resurrection and the life, will raise her up in glory. Then may she see the light of your presence, Lord Jesus, in the kingdom where you live for ever and ever," the priest said. Warm clouds of breath rose from the priest as he spoke.

"Amen," said the crowd together.

After a pause, the priest took the silver scepter from the small neatly dressed boy who stood beside him and sprinkled holy water over the casket. "Let us pray for our sister to our Lord, Jesus Christ, who said: 'I am the resurrection and the life. The man who believes in me will live even if he dies, and every living person who puts his faith in me will never suffer eternal death,' " the priest said, and then lifted the small brass cross from where it rested on the lid of the coffin near the arrangement of yellow jasmine, roses, and purple lilac flowers.

He sprinkled it with the water, closed both hands over it, and prayed silently. He stepped toward Martha, handed her the cross, and kissed her gently on the cheek.

"Today the Lord has taken someone very dear to us," the priest said, moving back to the front of the grave. "We will all show our tears today, but not for Catherine's death, for that is but a step into our Maker's arms.

"No, our tears are not for Catherine," the priest continued, "but for our own loss of her presence among us. We will miss her friendship and her kindness." Then he lowered his head and spoke in a low voice. "Lord, you wept at the death of Lazarus, your friend; comfort us in our sorrow. We ask this in faith."

"Lord, hear our prayer," everyone said together.

Brian sensed what the priest said was directed toward his mother's friends, most of them in their seventies. This must become a common event in their lives, he thought, until the funeral was their own.

Brian looked up and saw Admiral Mills walk up the path. A huge man, Mills carried his ever-present air of power on strong strides. He stopped a few feet behind the congregation and removed his cap, revealing the shaved dome of his head that was his hallmark. Under his heavy coat, Brian could see, Mills was in full dress uniform.

20

"You raise the dead to life, give our sister eternal life. We ask this in faith," the priest said.

"Lord, hear our prayer."

On the wet gravel road in front of the cemetery, no one noticed the white limousine pull slowly into the churchyard nor could they see the woman inside its dark tinted windows. Raising the Leica camera to her eye, she focused on Brian, catching him through its high-powered lens. She snapped off six frames, photographing as much of his face as she could from where the car stopped.

"Over there," the driver of the limousine said as he tapped the woman on the shoulder. She looked in the direction he pointed and saw Mills remove his coat and stand straight-backed at attention.

The woman focused her camera on the admiral and took several more shots. Then she leaned back in the thick leather seat and waited.

"Our Father, who art in heaven, hallowed be thy name, thy kingdom come, thy will be done on earth as it is in heaven. Give us this day our daily bread, and forgive us our trespasses as we also forgive those who trespass against us. And lead us not into temptation, but deliver us from evil. Amen."

"Amen," everyone said in one voice. Then they stood in a silence broken only by muffled crying.

"That concludes the services, thank you," said the neatly dressed boy as he stepped around the coffin. But for an instance, no one stepped away from the grave, Catherine's friends seeming unable to say good-bye. Then finally, the congregation began to thin as they moved toward the cars.

Brian leaned down and kissed his aunt. "I'll be over here," he said as her friends moved close and huddled around her with condolences and promises of companionship.

"Your mother was a fine woman, Brian. I'm truly sorry," the priest said as he shook Brian's hand with the both of his.

"Thank you. I hope you'll be coming back to the house."

21

"Of course I will," he said sincerely, and moved to talk to others who remained near the coffin.

Several more people approached Brian and expressed their sorrow and then their fondness for his mother. They were close friends and not-so-close friends, the gentle people of New Hampshire who still came to comfort neighbors even on cold winter mornings. Brian felt satisfied that his mother had not been lonesome over the years she had lived in the town.

A little girl who had been held by her mother was now running joyfully around the nearby headstones with a smaller boy chasing her. Both oblivious to their surroundings.

Brian noticed Admiral Mills's eyes were dry but red as he stepped next to him. "I really am sorry," he said, shaking Brian's hand.

"Thanks for coming, Tom," Brian said. "She, uh . . . died Wednesday night in her sleep," he said without looking at Mills. "The doctor was over earlier but there was nothing he could do."

"I knew Catherine before your father did," he said with a grin. "She lived two blocks over. I remember the three of us playing hooky from school and sneaking into the show together."

Brian smiled. He had heard all the old stories.

"I found out your mother was pregnant with you the day I went to tell her Douglas wasn't coming back," Mills said. "I was the one who had to tell her the *Seakrill* had been lost. God, Brian, I had wished your father had never—" he stopped. He turned toward him. "If there is anything, you only have to ask."

The old admiral brought so much fear to the officers that served under him, yet to Brian, Mills was the kindest man he had ever known. "Really," Brian said, "there's nothing."

"Brian." Frank Darvito walked quickly up to him. "My boy, I am sorry. She was a great lady, your mother," he said. "A kick in the pants, she was. I'll miss her."

Brian couldn't help but smile at Darvito. He had been

his mother's fix-it man, gardener, painter, and just about everything else from the first day she had come to Rye.

"How've you been, Franky?" Brian asked.

"Old, but I'm getting younger every day," he said, slugging him lightly in the shoulder. "You look as fit as ever," he said. "Hair is getting a little long, huh."

Brian turned toward Mills. "Admiral Thomas Mills, I'd like you to meet Frank Darvito."

Darvito snapped into a salute, "Sergeant Frank Anthony Darvito, U.S. 10th Armored Division. We were the first in Metz."

"And I was on the other side of the world with nothing firm to stand on but American steel," Mills said with a smile and a returned salute. "It's a pleasure, Sergeant."

"It's mine, Admiral," Darvito said, and then turned to Brian and looked over his dark pin-stripe suit, "So where's the uniform?" he asked.

Mills suddenly stood perfectly still, his eyes staring into the distance at nothing in particular.

Brian shifted on his feet, "Not today, Franky," he said.

"Well." Darvito took a step back. "It was nice meeting you, Admiral." He turned to Brian. "I think Martha wants to get back to the house before anyone arrives, but she hates that damn limo. I'll take her back in the truck."

"Thanks. I'll be there in a little bit," Brian said.

"You didn't tell them, did you?" Mills asked; his tone was direct.

"No. I haven't had the chance. She was sicker than I realized when I arrived and my aunt never asked. Probably thinks all my uniforms are at the cleaners."

"Well," Mills said. "I don't think it would have mattered to Catherine."

"I do," Brian said. "I think it would have mattered a lot."

Mills was quiet for a moment. "I made my own inquiry."

"I wish you hadn't."

"I wasn't going to say anything," Mills assured him. "But I had to find out if there was something I could do."

Brian sighed. "Okay, so what did you find out?"

"Nothing. They said it was under the committee's discretion who they give a command to and who they don't. No other explanation."

"I was blacklisted with no reason?"

"None that anyone would talk about."

Brian looked at Mills. "Any quesses? You know my record, Tom."

"What can I say?" Mills held out his hands.

Brian shrugged. "You're right. Nothing to be said, nothing to be done."

Mills put his coat back on. "Have you figured out what you're going to do?"

"Yes," Brian said. "I'm going to stand here until they lower my mother's coffin into her grave and then I'm going to stay with my aunt a few days. Beyond that, I haven't thought about."

Mills turned and looked directly at Brian, "I have to be in Washington this afternoon. Give my regards to Martha, will you?" the admiral said.

Brian nodded without looking at him.

Mills took a step and then stopped. "You know, Brian, I tried to be there for you when you were growing up."

"You were, Tom," Brian said.

"I know Douglas would have done the same for my family if I hadn't come back. But I never thought I could replace your dad, Brian. Doug was the best man I ever knew," Mills said, then he turned and walked back toward the dark blue sedan that waited for him.

Brian stood there until Mills drove away, then he moved to the grave site as the two men from the cemetery lowered the casket. Only a few people remained nearby talking quietly.

Brian scooped up a handful of the cold, wet soil and let

it fall between his fingers onto the oak lid of the coffin. Dust to dust, he thought.

"Commander? Commander Bovan?" she said as she stepped close to him.

Brian didn't hear her at first but turned as he felt her light touch on his sleeve. She was a thin Oriental woman, with spiderwebs of gentle wrinkles pulling the corners of her eyes. Her pepper-gray hair was uncommonly long for her age, but it gave her an air of youth. She was bundled in a heavy brown sweater and scarf against the cool morning.

She moved close and looked into his eyes, hers sparkling as she smiled up at him. Then suddenly, as if catching herself dreaming, she looked down at the coffin. "I'm sorry about your mother."

Brian looked at her; she came only to the top of his shoulder. "Did you know her well?" he asked.

"No," she said, "I didn't know her at all. I'm sorry, though. I think we could have been friends."

"I'm afraid I don't understand," he said.

"I've come to give you this," she said, producing a small package from her pocket.

As she handed it to him, she suddenly moved against him. Standing on the balls of her feet, she leaned up and kissed him on the mouth, her lips open, soft against his as they lingered there. Then she backed away. "Your eyes are as dark as his," she said softly.

His blood rushed hard throughout his body from the kiss. It shocked him, melted him, and then chilled him. Before he knew what happened, she had turned and moved quickly away to the white limousine. He could only stand there and catch his breath.

It wasn't until the car pulled out of the churchyard did he realize she had pushed the package into his hand. It was small and thin and wrapped in a cocoon of string. He leaned on a nearby headstone and pulled it apart. It was an envelope, its wrapping white from age. He read the fading letterhead on its upper corner.

COMMANDER IN CHIEF OF THE U.S. FLEET, PACIFIC: CINCPAC

He ripped the envelope open and pulled out a thin black leather notebook. Its cover was embossed with gold lettering:

Lt.Cmdr. DOUGLAS BOVAN
U.S.S. SEAKRILL, SS-231

Brian stared at the book. He ran his fingers over the cover and along its edges. Then he opened it and slowly flipped through its pages. Both in pen and pencil, the entries were dark and clear. From his mother's letters, Brian recognized his father's handwriting.

They were notes on repairs needed by the *Seakrill*, parts to be ordered, a crewman's birthday, and various other reminders. He turned to the last page as if beckoned.

12-30-43, *Pick Catherine up at airport. 1400 hrs. Party at*
Lou's tomorrow. 1830 hrs.
1-5-44, *Take Catherine to the airport. 0700 hrs.*
1-19-44, *Report to HQ, 0600 hrs.*
1-25-44, *Reorder shaft bearing for forward motor.*
Burky set sail. Shark preparing.
2-3-44, *Pick up orders.*

It was the last entry that made Brian weak. He looked at it again and then closed the book and stared blankly at the mosaic of gold and red fallen leaves under his feet. His mind raced and his heart pounded unsteadily as if off a beat.

February third, 1944. The day the United States Navy recorded the U.S.S. *Seakrill* as lost on patrol. The same day she was said to have sunk in an unknown position in the South China Sea.

26

THREE

Canton, China, 1942

Captain Itamuro tossed the small map onto the cluttered desk and leaned back in the heavily padded chair. Rubbing his eyes, he yawned. For seven hours he had been working on the best of three plans to move his men north and only now was the sun reaching the top of its noon crest.

He stood up. A feeling of excitement swirled within him. Today he was going to execute the officials of the small village to the east.

Like the owner of this estate, several families had received shipments of Western-styled furnishings from wealthy relatives living in the United States. It was an acceptance of Western influence and had to be dealt with severely. The executions, Itamuro knew, were an important practice and one he enjoyed.

He reached for the small cup of sake at the edge of the huge oak desk. It had gone cold, but he finished it in a quick swallow, its taste staying in his mouth.

Itamuro strapped his holster around his soft waist and set his khaki-colored hat over short gray hair, then he walked briskly out.

Moving down the hallway, he stopped where a young soldier was standing guard in front of one of the bedrooms. The soldier stiffened to attention as Itamuro entered the room.

The large bedroom, once lavishly decorated with Western-styled furniture, was now almost empty. Only the two U.S. Marine footlockers took space in the middle of the wooden floor. Itamuro smiled as he knelt down and ran his hand over one of the locker's olive-green lids. "You will bring me much honor," he whispered.

The two footlockers with their precious contents had come into Itamuro's possession after his garrison captured the Americans as they tried to leave their marine base and escape Canton. Reports of the imperial forces crushing Pearl Harbor had come too late for them to prepare for Itamuro's attack and his men had taken them without firing a shot.

From behind, Itamuro heard someone step into the doorway. He turned and stood.

Lieutenant Mikobuto saluted. He was a wiry man with wide, round eyes and a thick black beard. His thin body always seemed half hidden in his uniforms.

"Mikobuto-san." Itamuro waved for him to enter. "Come," he said as he bent back down beside the footlockers.

Mikobuto moved next to his captain.

"I don't know why Tokyo would care so much about these," Itamuro said, tapping the lid. "But who am I to question? The general is most pleased with us."

"With you, Itamuro-san. He is pleased with the way you captured the Americans," Mikobuto said.

Itamuro smiled. He opened the lid and pulled out one of the newspaper-wrapped objects from the locker. There were over two dozen such packages inside, each of a different size and shape. "But these are what he is excited about. He will send them to Tokyo."

Stripping it of the twine and newspaper, Itamuro held the dark brown skull up to the light. He stared at it. "Old bones." Itamuro shook his head again. "Boxes of old bones, monkey's bones at that, Mikobuto-san, but the Chinese would die for them."

"They consider these fossils national treasures. That's

why they were sent to the Americans to be smuggled out of Canton and kept until after the war.''

Itamuro suddenly laughed. ''But they didn't expect us to take the Americans, did they?''

Mikobuto also laughed. ''No, they did not.''

''And now their Peking Man will go to Tokyo,'' Itamuro said as he continued to look at the skull.

''Excuse me, Captain.'' Second Lieutenant Honma stopped at the entrance of the room. Honma was a small man, but extremely muscular, and his eyes could barely be seen over his high cheeks.

''What is it?''

''The men are ready to go into the village, sir,'' Honma said.

''Good.'' Itamuro handed the skull to Mikobuto. ''Lock them,'' he said, moving to the door.

As Itamuro stepped from the room, Honma stared down at Mikobuto. Their eyes locked onto each other's, but neither spoke as they listened to the sound of Itamuro's heavy boots leave the house.

''We've . . .'' Mikobuto began, but Honma raised his finger to his lips, silencing him. He looked quickly into the hallway to be sure the guard had followed their captain out to the yard.

He had. The hall was empty and they were alone. ''We must switch them tonight,'' Honma whispered as he stepped closer to Mikobuto. ''The freighter leaves for Sasebo in three days and her captain will not wait another.''

''We won't have the chance,'' Mikobuto said as he rewrapped the skull and set it gently next to the others. ''We have received orders to move north tonight.''

''Then the fossils will go to Tokyo. There won't be another freighter captain so easily swayed to carry such cargo. The Peking Man is going to end up in a vault in the Imperial Palace,'' Honma said.

Mikobuto shook his head as he stared at the footlockers. ''These are worth a fortune.''

''We have no choice.''

Mikobuto looked at Honma. "Somehow we will get them away."

Mikobuto sensed it would be a colder night than usual as he watched his men load their equipment onto the six diesel trucks. The wind had taken a chill from the mountains as the sun dropped below their crest. If he had been back in Okaya, Mikobuto would be sure there would be snow by morning. But in China, the wind seemed not so honest.

It was a few minutes past 1700 hours when Itamuro's jeep drove into the yard, its tires kicking up a fine dust almost choking Mikobuto. The truck carrying the two dozen soldiers he had taken into the village followed right behind.

When Mikobuto saw the smile on his captain's face and the woman in the back of the jeep, her hands bound, he knew everything went well.

Itamuro stepped down from the jeep as it rolled to a stop. "Are we on schedule, Mikobuto-san?"

"The garrison will be ready to leave before midnight, sir."

"Good, good." He smiled broadly as he watched two of his men lift the woman from the vehicle. She was plump with a round face, tight hidden eyes, and short chopped hair. Under her white silk dress, Mikobuto could see she had large soft breasts.

"A doctor's wife, what a prize, ay?" Itamuro said with a laugh. Then he ordered the men to take her to his quarters and she went without a struggle.

"As soon as you are ready to leave, Captain," Mikobuto said.

"We will leave as scheduled," Itamuro said as he walked toward the house.

Honma stepped up to Mikobuto. "We executed her husband and seven others," he reported.

Mikobuto nodded and looked back at the house as if he didn't hear. In a whisper, he said, "We will not have much time. You know what to do?"

Honma looked quickly about. "Yes, yes. But are you sure that—"

"Yes," Mikobuto said sternly. "Wait until you see me enter the house."

Honma said nothing but nodded.

For several minutes, the two men stood in the center of the yard and watched as the soldiers continued to load the trucks and pack the equipment. Finally, Mikobuto looked at Honma. "It's time," he said. Turning, he walked toward the front doors of the house.

The two soldiers standing on each side of the doorway stiffened to attention as he entered. If either of them had been watching closely, they might have noticed the change in his step as he passed them.

Once inside the house, Mikobuto automatically began to place the outer edges of his feet down first onto the wooden floor, allowing the rest of the sole to roll gently and absorb his weight.

Slipping silently into the second hallway, his movements became even more measured and calculated. He turned his right shoulder forward and stepped closer to the wall, his hand gliding lightly over it, the tips of his fingers on the smooth wood.

Farther into the house, Mikobuto's heart began to pound faster, but his breath remained steady. He moved through the office and then toward the double doors of the master bedroom. Stopping, he pressed himself close and listened.

Within the room, he could hear the rhythmic swaying of the bed and the moan of a woman. Turning the doorknob slowly, he timed the noise of the latch with that of the bed.

Itamuro clutched the woman's hair as he lay on top of her, thrusting his hips into the spread of her legs. Her face was contorted in pain and pleasure. With her eyes shut tight, she tried to twist her right hand free from where it was tied to the bedpost. Yet at the same time, her left reached down to his buttock pulling him closer, deeper.

In a single motion, Mikobuto moved quickly to the edge

31

of the bed, drew his knife from its sheath on his belt, and thrust it into the center of Itamuro's back.

Instinctively, Itamuro tried to push himself away from the woman, but Mikobuto pressed his hand against the naked man's back, forcing him down. He stabbed him again.

The woman opened her eyes but didn't scream. She grabbed the back of Itamuro's head with her free hand and pulled it down tight against her breasts. Itamuro continued to thrash about, trying to get away from her and face his assailant. But she locked her legs around his waist and held him as the knife came down again and again and again.

Mikobuto's blade snapped Itamuro's backbone and ruptured his left lung and heart. The captain's body shook violently in spasms until, finally, it stopped.

Then Mikobuto withdrew the knife, and handed it, almost casually, to the woman.

She stared at him as she took the weapon. Then she struggled to separate herself from the body, but Itamuro was still deep within her. She reached back and began to cut her right wrist free from the bedpost.

As Mikobuto drew his pistol from its holster and aimed, the woman turned and looked at him, and for an instance, her narrow eyes met his. He pulled the trigger as she began to scream.

The impact slammed her head backward. The bullet shattered her lower jaw as it entered, sending blood and bone onto the silk pillows and across the room. Mikobuto was satisfied she would reveal no truths about Itamuro's murder.

Quickly he moved to the dresser and took Itamuro's identical knife from its sheath. He slipped it into his own as the two soldiers rushed in.

They had heard the gunshot, and as they ran through the house, neither were aware that the two U.S. Marine footlockers and their precious contents were no longer in the other bedroom.

FOUR

Washington, D.C., 1986

Brian slid out of the rear seat and tossed the taxicab driver a twenty. He stepped onto the curb and slammed the door behind him, not waiting for the change. It was 4:45 P.M. by his watch. He pulled the collar of his overcoat up and switched his briefcase from his left to his right hand. Quickly he headed up the long tier of stairs to the side entrance of the national archives building.

It was a gray and windy day, and the white clouds that raced across the sky blocked the sunlight more often than revealed it. The remaining snow along 7th Street was black and dirty and piled into the corners where it was protected by shadows most of the day.

Brian pushed through the tall glass doors and entered the building. The large marbled entry on the first floor was empty this late in the afternoon. A uniformed guard stood in the corner near the doorway, pacing in small circles anticipating five o'clock.

Taking off his dark wool gloves and shoving them into his pocket, Brian followed the signs to the second floor. He found the door marked Military Service Records at the end of the hall, pushed it open, and stepped through.

"Empty around here today," Brian said as he moved up to the counter.

The young man sitting on the opposite side nodded without looking up. "What do you expect? Three-day weekend, most everybody takes off around noon," he said.

Brian looked at his name tag: Ted Gruil. It sounded like a name of a football player, yet it didn't fit the small man with the pasted-down black hair. Brian pulled out his wallet. "I'd like to see my files and my father's. Douglas Bovan, skipper of the U.S.S. *Seakrill* lost in February of 1944," he said showing him his identification card.

" '44," the man said, shaking his head. "Those are in St. Louis."

"They're not on the computer?"

Ted Gruil shrugged. "Maybe, I'll check."

"Thanks," Brian said.

"Let me get yours first," he said as he wrote down Brian's full name on a scrap of paper. "And what was the other name again?"

"Douglas Bovan, captain of the U.S.S. *Seakrill,*" Brian repeated.

The man wrote it down, then walked from the counter to one of the computer terminals at the rear of the office.

Brian unbuttoned his tan overcoat, moved to one of the brown vinyl waiting chairs, and sat down. He rubbed his eyes hard with his index finger and thumb. His head was throbbing, pounding at the temples.

He hadn't slept in the two days since the funeral. Thoughts and questions had been bouncing around his head as he searched every trunk, drawer, and old box that his mother had saved in the attic of the old house. He had gone through everything but found nothing that could give him a hint of how the Oriental woman could have gotten the notebook.

At the back of the office, Gruil waited as the small computer searched for Brian's file number. He tapped his fingers impatiently on the top of the black and white monitor. Finally, the screen came to life, but the readout wasn't what he expected.

34

BRIAN BOVAN: COMMANDER, U.S. NAVY
RESIGNED. ALL PERSONAL AND NAVAL
RECORDS SEALED UNTIL FURTHER
EXAMINATION.
CODE: 7-BLUE

Gruil whistled to himself. 7-Blue. He had never run across a 7-Blue before. He looked over at Brian, then back at the screen. The code told him that the name he had called up was someone highly knowledgeable with delicate information. Someone classified as a possibly high risk to national security.

But the seal on his records was the surprise. Gruil guessed Brian was under some type of investigation.

The clerk cleared the screen and walked to the counter. "Mr. Bovan," he said with heavy emphasis on the mister. "I'm afraid I can't release those files."

Brian got to his feet. "They're not in the computer?"

"Oh, they're there, I just don't have the authority to turn them over."

"Who does?" Brian could feel his headache increase.

"I'd guess the officer of records at the Pentagon. He'll probably be able to help you. But"—Gruil looked at his watch—"I doubt if there's anyone in the office now." He smiled. "You will have to wait until Tuesday."

"Who else can I talk to?" Brian said. He could feel himself starting to flush with anger but he was trying to control it.

"No one until Tuesday." Gruil smiled again and turned to walk away.

Brian reached over the counter and grabbed him by the arm. "Listen, goddamn it. Who do I have to talk to?"

"Hey, it's out of my hands, buddy," As he pulled away, breaking Brian's grip, Gruil lost his balance, caught his foot on the bottom of a chair, and fell to the floor. "You son of a bitch," he yelled.

Brian turned, picked up his briefcase, and stormed out of

the office. He walked directly from the building and onto the sidewalk. He turned north and started up the street. A taxi slowed, and Brian saw it but didn't bother to flag it down. He wanted to walk, needed to walk to clear his head.

Tuesday. He couldn't wait for Tuesday. There was one person he knew he could talk to before then.

"Thanks for meeting with me, Tom," Brian said as he followed Admiral Mills through the sterile white hallway. Brian felt awkward; his brown suit was wrinkled while the old navy man was dressed in starched white pants, a powder-blue polo shirt, and a wool V-neck sweater. Ready for a Saturday cruise on the Potomac, Brian thought, and wondered if that was exactly what he had taken Mills away from.

They walked down corridors lined with framed photographs of modern warships and military planes. Their footsteps echoed ahead of them as they entered the inner offices of the naval wing of the huge Pentagon complex.

"You said it was urgent, so I came over as quickly as I could," Mills said as he nodded and waved to the guard moving past them. "Where did you say you were staying?" Mills asked.

"The J.W. Marriott," Brian said.

"You should have called. We've always got an extra bed in the house," Mills said as they continued down the bleak Formica hallway.

Like most of the office doors, Mills's had a huge combination lock above the knob. The admiral spun it left then right and left again to the last number. Brian heard the inside mechanism release. He pushed open the door and they stepped in.

The admiral's own offices contained thick emerald-green rugs. Oil paintings of old galleons and other square-riggers at full sail were hung on the rich wood-paneled walls. The four rows of secretaries' desk were all cleaned and polished.

Each phone, notepad, Rolodex, and assorted paraphernalia were set in exactly the same place. Military precision, Brian thought as he followed Mills into his private office.

"So," Mills said as he walked around the back of his large oak desk and sat down. He motioned Brian to sit in one of the two red leather chairs in front of him. "What's all this about?"

Brian set his briefcase on his lap, opened it, and pulled out the black notebook. He leaned forward and handed it to Mills.

If years of military command had taught the admiral anything, it was the importance of control and composure. Yet at that moment, as he read the gold-embossed letters on the cover, the blood rushed away from his face and turned his cheeks white.

He opened the cover and flipped each page slowly, reading every entry. Then he closed the book and set it down. He looked up. "Where did you get this?"

"It was given to me at the funeral," Brian said flatly. He leaned forward, placing one hand on the edge of the desk. "Did you see the date of the last entry."

"Yes," Mills said. "I saw it." He shrugged. "Somebody found your father's old notebook. It was nice they gave it to you. You know, I had one similar to it but I can't find it anywhere. You should hang on to this, Brian, it's something you'll be able to show your grandchildren," he said, forcing a smile onto his lips.

Brian read through the evasion. "The date of the last entry, Tom. February third. The *Seakrill* was supposed to be in the South China Sea that day. You know it as well as I do. But this shows she was in Pearl Harbor," Brian said. "The records are wrong."

There was an urgency in Brian's voice and Mills could hear it. He was grasping, trying to make sense of what finding the book meant. If it meant anything.

"Brian . . ." Mills raised his hands. "That was a long

37

time ago and it was a big war. The records are not perfect, they never are. There's nothing more to it, son.''

Brian stood up and walked around to the back of his chair. "I tried to get mine and his files. I couldn't."

"Jesus, Brian. You only left the navy a week ago. They are probably still in the review board's office or en route back to the records building. Besides, you left a high-security position. Your files will probably never be released, even to you."

"Then what about my father's?" Brian asked.

Mills leaned back in his chair. "They are undoubtedly with yours," he said.

"Why?"

"Because they reviewed both," Mills said. "They look at everything, Brian. Having the command of a U.S. nuclear submarine is not an everyday thing. The navy doesn't just hand out its most important warship like popcorn at the theater."

"His records influenced the decision, didn't they?"

Mills shifted in his chair. Suddenly, he realized he was being backed into a corner. He looked straight at Brian and told him the truth. "Yes."

"How the hell could they keep me from getting a command?"

Mills swiveled around to the credenza behind him. Three crystal decanters rested on its oak top. He poured two tumblers of Jack Daniel's from one and cut the amount with water. "Here." He stood and handed one to Brian. "We both need it."

Brian took the glass and watched as Mills moved slowly across the office.

The old admiral stopped at the bookshelf, turned, and stared at Brian. He swirled the gold liquid in the glass as he spoke. "On February sixteenth of '44, our Hellcats began a two-day attack on Truk Lagoon in the Carolines. When the aerial photos from the raid were developed, they revealed a U.S. submarine moored to a Japanese freighter.

38

It turned out to be the *Seakrill*," Mills said. "At first, it was thought that she had been forced to surrender, but no records ever showed the capture of a Gato-class sub at Truk."

Brian sat back down in the leather chair. He didn't look at Mills but focused on the faceted glass in his hands.

Mills continued. "The photograph was kept under wraps and the *Seakrill* was listed as missing in action until the end of the war. Then, after further investigation found no other records of the Japanese sinking her, she was recorded publicly as lost on February third. But in fact, the U.S. Naval files listed her as turned over to the enemy by her captain, and Douglas was charged with treason."

"You don't believe that."

Mills sipped his drink; it warmed his throat but gave him no strength. "At the time, I believed what I was told, that they had been lost on patrol. I didn't know anything different from anyone else. Then there was an inquiry into your father's activities at Pearl. Several officers were questioned about who he knew and who he associated with outside the base, that type of thing. We were told he was up for a Navy Cross. I felt pretty good about that." Mills smiled. "We all did. He was one of the best submariners in the service.

"Then nothing. No Medal, no announcements, we didn't hear a thing about it. So I started asking around." Mills took another drink. "All I got was silence. Until finally one of the officers I knew from the inquiry board showed me Doug's files."

"And?"

"And that was when I found out about the photograph and the charges and how the seemingly harmless testimonies by his friends and fellow officers all built a case against him," Mills said. "Even what I had said about him drew the same conclusion. And believe me, I told only the truth."

Brian took a drink from his glass. It burned his tongue.

"You didn't know your father, Brian. I did. He was a hell of a guy, but he had bad habits. He was a gambler, an unlucky gambler in debt with the wrong kind of people in

Pearl. And he was a ladies' man with a partial eye for Asian women. And, son, during those times that was a habit that could get you into big trouble. So what else was I supposed to think?''

Brian looked hard at Mills. ''I don't know, Tom, but loyalty is the most important thing in a man, isn't that what you used to tell me? My father was your best friend, you told me that too.'' Brian stood up. ''You said war records could never be perfect, but you believed the Japanese records.'' Brian set his drink down and picked the notebook off the desk.

''What are you going to do?'' Mills asked as Brian turned toward the door.

''I don't know.''

''Brian, don't be stupid. It was over forty years ago. There's nothing you can do. Let it go, son,'' Mills said.

''Maybe you're right,'' Brian said as he stepped through the door. ''But that's something I'll find out for myself.''

Mills stood there for a moment staring at the door. Then he made up his mind. The past was dead. Buried. It wouldn't come back haunting, he thought. Unless someone went looking for it, disturbing the ghosts. A cold shiver rushed through him. He reached over, picked up the phone, and dialed.

Troy Merith again brought the high-powered Bushnell binoculars to his face and watched the traffic below. From a seventh floor room of the Willard Hotel, he could see the familiar Saturday-evening scene. A line of taxis pulled around the corner and in and out of the circular driveway of the Marriott, emptying out their passengers. All of whom were returning from similar tours of the national monuments. He imagined hordes of parents, exhausted from miles of history, walking into the hotel with sleeping children in their arms.

Merith was pleased. His team was in place in under an

hour. Maybe not a record, but it showed the up and coming agents what experience could do. There were short cuts to be taken when time was an underlying factor, and he knew every one of them. Invented some himself. Yes, he was pleased with his team.

Only one thing bothered him. Merith hated the Marriott. Of all the hotels in D.C., it was the worst for surveillance. Its bulbous facade stretched out over the driveway, blocking any clear view of the hotel's entrance. There wasn't a single point where both the front doors and the rooms could be watched.

The hotel forced him to place someone on the street and he didn't like that. It called for more personnel and it put them in the open. That made margins for mistakes, and Merith wouldn't have mistakes.

He focused on a black Dodge van parked catty-corner to the main entrance of the hotel. "Karen. Anything yet?" Merith spoke into the thin tube that ran along the side of his round face and hooked in front of his mouth. A third of the surveillance team was inside the van, hidden in its dark windows.

"Nothing," came the voice into his earphone.

Merith let out a sigh. He turned to Beckman, his partner. "Still nothing," he said, repeating what Beckman had heard over his own earphone.

Beckman didn't look away from the tiny screen of his mini television set. He nodded and glanced at his watch, then turned back to the *I Love Lucy* rerun.

"Doesn't that give you a headache?"

He was a large man, Beckman, with thin oily hair and a continual habit of scratching his groin. "Nope," he said simply.

Merith looked at the watermelon-mound under Beckman's maroon plaid shirt. Straight up from his sides and below his once muscular chest, it rose peeking at the fourth button. Then Merith looked at his own rounding physique. They were dinosaurs, he thought. Locked in rooms to watch the world pass by while the young and aggressive agents like Karen tackled down the villains.

"You have anything?" Merith asked him.

Beckman made a gesture of putting his hand up to his earphone. He listened for a second. "No. There was a handyman in the room for a few minutes but he's gone now. I checked him out through the scope, huge son of a bitch. I heard him make a call over the telephone. He didn't bother the bug, though; I still got a green light on the panel," Beckman said, gesturing to the electrical array of tape recorders and microphone receivers in the two silver Halliburton cases opened next to him.

Merith turned back to the window and looked into the hotel room directly across from them. It was empty. Quiet and empty and it was almost eight P.M. Where the hell could he be? Merith thought. He hated waiting for the first contact. Always had.

"Got him!" Karen said. Her voice was high with excitement and it tore into Merith's brain.

Beckman also heard her through his earpiece. He reached over and started one of the recorders. Their conversations would now be taped.

"Tan overcoat, brown suit, no vest, dark tie. Carrying a brown briefcase. He's alone and going directly into the hotel," Karen continued. "Should I follow?"

"Go," Merith ordered. "But only as far as the lobby."

"Okay," she responded.

From the tinted window Merith couldn't see Brian go into the hotel. He focused on Karen as she stepped from the rear of the van. At six foot, she was a big woman with a mane of black curly hair. But she was a good tracker, and even with her large frame she managed to blend into the crowd. Merith would use her as often as he could on his teams, knowing it wouldn't be long before she was moved up in the ladder of the CIA.

"You'd better call this in. Contact, Bovan. Time,

8:07 P.M.," Merith told Beckman. "The old man is going to want to know that he finally showed up."

Beckman switched off the television, leaned over, and picked up the phone from one of the cases. It automatically dialed. On the second ring, the other end was picked up. "This is Beckman and Merith. Got Bovan at the hotel at 8:07 P.M. Continuing surveillance."

"Thanks," the woman's voice said. "I'll transfer the message."

He hung up and turned his chair to a more comfortable position in front of the two aluminum suitcases. Adjusting one of the knobs, Beckman increased the sensitivity of the microphone near the hotel-room door. Then he looked over at Merith. "Ready and waiting," he said.

Merith didn't say anything. He was hunched over the telescope, also waiting.

"Room 755, please," Brian said to the young female clerk.

Her large breasts pushed against her white blouse and out from her dark brown coat as she reached for the key. "No messages, Mr. Bovan." She smiled as she handed him the flat plastic code key that unlocked his room.

He didn't acknowledge her but scooped the key from her hand and headed for the glass elevators. The first one to open spilled out a family of seven on their way to dinner. The two-foot-tall travelers with their parents pushed by him.

He stepped into the empty elevator, pressed the button for the seventh floor, and held the side rail as it shot upward. It went directly to his floor without stopping. The doors slid open and Brian stepped out and walked toward his room. Pushing the key into the lock, he turned the handle and opened the door.

As he began to step inside, Brian sensed the man behind him. But it was too late to turn. A huge arm wrapped around Brian's body and suddenly pulled him backward.

Yet it wasn't a violent assault, it was as if Brian was merely in his way.

With his opposite hand, the man gently closed the door. He released Brian, and without a word, he brought his index finger to his lips assuring silence.

Beckman turned sharply toward Merith. "I heard the key, then the door open and close. But now, nothing. I've got no sound in the room. What do you see?"

Merith didn't move at first. He concentrated on the telescope. "Nothing, damn it, I don't see anything." He stood up. "Karen, get up there and see what you can find. Don't interact," Merith warned her. "But see what the hell happen to him."

"Commander," the gentle voice whispered from the open doorway across the hall. "Please, this way."

Brian turned to see the Oriental woman slip back into the room. He looked back at the huge dark-skinned man who was smiling down at him, his lips forming a large fleshy crescent under a broad flat nose. The man motioned Brian toward the open door.

Brian turned and walked into the room.

FIVE

Honolulu, Hawaii, 1944

Captain Douglas Bovan stepped in through the front door of the officer's club. The room was smoke-filled and noisy with laughter and it felt good to Douglas to be there. He made his way around a group of loud sailors and headed for the bar.

Seeing an empty space between two pilots, he elbowed his way in and caught the bartender's attention with a wave of his hand.

"Evening, Cap'n," the bartender said, an unlit cigar dangling from his mouth.

Douglas nodded and pushed his hat back on his head. His dark hair, curling up under the band, was a little longer than regulation. "How you doing, Marty?" he asked.

"No complaints, not tonight anyway. Beer?"

"Yeah."

Marty filled a mug and slid it to him. Douglas paid with change from his pocket, took a drink, turned and looked across the club.

Two couples danced close to slow music in the center of the floor while a half-dozen impatient sailors waited at the edge for their turn with the nurses.

Walrus was there sitting alone in his usual booth near the

back. Douglas wiped the beer foam from his thick mustache and pushed away from the bar.

The club was crowded tonight. More than expected at this hour. But then Pearl was flooded with navy ships and the joke around the base was that there were so many in port that you could walk across the harbor. Scuttlebutt had it there were even more vessels off the islands.

As Douglas moved across the room, someone grabbed his arm from behind. Immediately, Douglas's shoulders tightened and he clenched his free hand into a fist. A good fight was always welcomed in this bar and Douglas wasn't one to hold from tradition.

He spun around. But the face he found behind him looked as if it had already lost a recent confrontation. "Don't grab me like that, Willy," Douglas said as he pulled his arm free and relaxed.

"Sorry, Bovan, but I've got to talk to you," Willy said, his eyes darting around, looking from face to face at everyone near him. Willy was even with Douglas's six-foot height, but had nowhere near his width. A skinny man with thick glasses, Willy had a mind for facts and figures. He was from some obscure office at headquarters.

"What the hell happened to your face?" Douglas asked, looking at Willy's swollen lip and black eye. His glasses were missing.

"Doesn't matter," he said, guiding Douglas to a corner where no one could hear them. "They told me to give you a message."

"What are you talking about?"

"The men from the ranch, Bovan."

"You've been to the ranch?" Douglas smiled. He couldn't image Willy betting on the cockfights.

"It's not funny, Bovan. I had to pay tonight and I didn't have all the money." Willy looked quickly around again. Then he lifted his right hand, and for the first time, Douglas saw two of his fingers were wrapped in white bandages.

"They pulled out my fingernails, the bastards," he said with a swallow.

Douglas lifted an eyebrow.

"You're making them look bad. They want their money or they're going to make you into an example." Willy's eyes wouldn't hold still.

Douglas looked hard at Willy. "Fuck them," he said.

"They mean it." Willy's voice was high.

"So do I," Douglas said. Then he nodded. He understood Willy was taking a chance warning him. "I'll be all right. You just watch out for yourself and take care of that hand, Willy," he said patting him on the shoulder.

"Don't cross them, Bovan," he said, and then disappeared into the crowd.

Douglas slid into the empty seat of the booth. Walrus looked up. "I thought you weren't coming tonight."

"We don't get the drive-shaft parts until tomorrow," Douglas shrugged. He sensed something was bothering his friend. "What's with you?"

Captain Walton P. Corton, or Walrus, as he was known for his large brown mustache and his less-than-trim physique, looked up from his empty beer mug. He shook his head in disgust. "I heard my sub is being assigned between Christmas Island and the continent."

"There's no Japs out there."

"It's going to be a long patrol." Walrus said. Then, as he looked beyond Douglas, his eyes lit up. "Margaret," Walrus called out over the music. He waved and began to stand.

Douglas turned slightly toward the door and looked out of the corner of his eye. He couldn't see her, but he knew who Walrus was waving at. There was only one Margaret on the base who would make his friend smile like that and she was the same woman, the only woman, who made Douglas cringe.

It wasn't just that Margaret O'Tullie was brash and headstrong, but she could talk for hours about nothing in

47

such a high-pitched voice that it reminded Douglas of a bad bearing. And worse, she was one of Admiral Nimitz's personal secretaries.

"Mind if we join you?" Margaret said as she plopped her slender, almost pencil-thin body into the booth and slid in beside Walrus.

"Not at all," Walrus said. He knew Douglas minded, but at that moment he didn't care what Douglas thought. With her short curly blond hair and green eyes, Margaret melted Walrus's heart and heated his groin.

Douglas didn't say anything but looked up at her partner, who waited patiently for him to offer his seat. He stood, realizing she wasn't one of Margaret's usual cohorts from headquarters.

The woman was only a few inches shorter than him, slender and dark, and Oriental. She smiled into Douglas's eyes as she lowered herself into the booth and glided across the seat. Her gently curved body was outlined in a black silk dress and her long legs were encased in silk stockings and lifted in high black heels. Douglas moved in beside her.

"This is Lai Ming," Margaret introduced them. "She's with the Chinese delegation in Honolulu. They're going to Washington next week," she said with excitement as if it was a special secret. "Tell them, Mimi."

"Mimi?" Douglas asked.

Mimi laughed softly, "It's a pet name that stayed."

"Tell them about Washington," Margaret pressed. "She might get to meet Roosevelt himself."

"No kidding?" Walrus leaned forward. But it was Douglas who he was amused with. His friend had not taken his eyes off the woman.

"No, no," Mimi said, slightly embarrassed, "I won't, but Ambassador Lee might. I'm only one of his translators and not a very good one."

"You are too a good translator," Margaret disagreed. "Your English is perfect. Better than mine in fact, and the

48

President will need a translator and they're going to pick you," she persisted.

Douglas caught only fragments of the continuing conversation as he looked at her. He watched as she drank the vermouth they ordered and smiled and laughed at Walrus's crude jokes. He noticed the smoothness of her skin above the high collar of her dress, its trail of woven buttons running along her left shoulder.

When most of the Oriental population on the island was trying to hide itself, Mimi accented her almond eyes with touches of makeup. Soft color on her bold cheeks and rose red on her full lips.

With a gentle motion, she pulled her long black hair over her right shoulder, leaned forward and rested her elbow on the table. She set her head in the palm of her hand and looked at Douglas. "You haven't said much, Commander."

"I've been listening."

"Are you always so quiet?"

"Not always."

"I guess being in the Silent Service you are used to having your guard up around strangers," Mimi said, not taking her eyes from his.

"It comes with the turf," Douglas said.

"Too bad," Mimi said, turning to Margaret and Walrus who were now wrapped in their own conversation. "Margaret," she interrupted, "I think we should be getting back."

Margaret reached over and twisted Walrus's wrist to see the face of his watch. It was half past ten. She sighed, *Already?*

Douglas put his hand lightly on Mimi's. "Dance with me first."

She looked at his dirty fingernails, chipped by rough attempts at cleaning. "Okay," she said. "One."

He led her to the center of the dance floor where two other couples were dancing close, swaying and turning

49

slowly with the music. Douglas slid his arm around her thin waist and pulled her against him. There was a gentle fragrance of lilies in her hair.

She leaned her head back and looked directly into his eyes. "You're just like Margaret described."

He laughed, "Oh?"

"Ya. Walton's a lot of fun and you're quiet and serious. She said that your dark eyes scared her."

Douglas looked over the top of Mimi's head and back at the table. "Besides Walrus, I never thought O'Tullie noticed anyone outside of sending them memos or orders," he said. He pulled back and looked at her. "Do my eyes scare you?"

"No, not at all," she said. The record stopped and they slowed their pace but neither let the other go. "I'll Never Smile Again" started and they matched their movements to its slow melody. "Margaret said that you're leaving on patrol this week. Do you know where to?"

"She told you that, huh?" he said, somewhat surprised that Nimitz's secretary would trust anyone enough to tell them such information. "No. I won't know my exact orders until we set sail."

"Must be scary being under the water like that," she said, her eyes leaving his as she stared over his shoulder. "The Japs trying to find you, you trying to sink them. Stupid, isn't it?" She looked back at him. "I mean, the war and everything."

"I never thought of it as stupid," Douglas said. "Just thought of it as a job. Going on patrol and trying to make it back."

"My parents were killed in '35 when the Japanese moved through our village. Killed them because they were teachers," she said as if proving the stupidity of it all by that single action of the enemy. "I was in Peking and didn't find out for six months."

They continued to dance; one couple sat down, two others joined them. "I'm sorry," he said finally. "I've never

50

really worried about my family. They're in New York and I guess the war seems so far away from them."

"I thought that too," she said simply and then released him and stepped back. "Thank you for the dance, Commander."

He nodded, feeling suddenly uncomfortable there in the club. It was a place where sailors hungered for laughter, for talk of anything but war. Where they looked for companionship after months of patrol, or for a last night of tenderness before setting sail.

But she didn't seem to notice the heavy smoke and harsh laughter about them. She had only looked at him, searching his thoughts and revealing hers as if he were an old friend. He followed her back to the table.

"Margaret, I really think we should be going," she said as she reached for her sweater on the seat of the booth.

"I suppose you're right. Well, boys, good night." She kissed Walrus on the cheek and stood up.

Douglas held the sweater as Mimi slipped into it. "I really am sorry," he said again.

She smiled. "I know," she said, and then followed Margaret to the front door.

Douglas dropped heavy into the booth. He took a long drink of his warm beer.

"What do you think of her?" Walrus said, leaning across the table.

"She's going to get you into trouble with Nimitz."

"Not Margaret, Mimi."

"What do you mean, what do I think of her?"

"Come on, Douglas. I know you. You got a weakness for them slant-eyed dames. And fuck, she's a looker, class all the way."

"Ya, she is at that."

"Great," Walrus said with a huge smile. "We're having lunch with them tomorrow. Margaret is fixing a picnic."

"A picnic? Shit, I don't have time."

"Make the time, old buddy. We'll both be leaving on

51

patrol in the next couple of days, and they're going to be long patrols."

Douglas rolled his eyes back and finished his beer.

It was hot by eleven A.M. Tropical hot and Walrus's khaki uniform shirt already revealed his body's wet reaction to it. He walked up to the gangplank of the U.S.S. *Seakrill* and yelled to Douglas. "Permission to come aboard?"

Douglas looked down from the conning tower. "No," he yelled back. "I'll be right there." Then he turned and finished giving Lieutenant Michael Albert his instructions. "Get Charlie to help Clancy on that forward engine. I don't want to set sail until I'm a hundred percent sure she's solid."

"Aye, Skipper," Michael said. Then he glanced over the rail toward the docks. "Holy cow."

Douglas followed his stare to the bright yellow Packard roadster as it pulled up and stopped on the dock alongside the sub. Mimi was behind the wheel with Margaret beside her. A half-dozen crewmen turned to admire the car and the women.

"I want a full report on our condition when I return, Michael," he said, pushing the clipboard into the lieutenant's hands. He slid down the ladder to the rear deck and crossed the gangplank.

"What a beauty," Walrus said as he ran his hand over the curve of one of the polished fenders.

Margaret popped out of the passenger seat. "This is going to be so much fun," she said as she slipped her arm through Walrus's. "Come on, we get the rumble seat."

Douglas slid in next to Mimi and shut the car door. "Morning," he said.

"Thanks for coming, Douglas. I thought I was going to be playing chauffeur to them all day," she said. Gone was her formal sophistication of the night before. She wore a simple white dress and only a hint of makeup. Her long hair was tied back with a pink bow. The freshness of what she wore made Margaret's green dress look like army fatigues. In the rearview mirror, she watched Margaret and Walrus crawl into the rumble seat.

"It's nice to get away from the base," Douglas said as he settled into the seat.

She smiled as she shifted into first and pulled slowly forward, weaving around the crates and trucks that lined the submarine docks. The guard at the main gate saw the Packard approach and waved Mimi past the line of stopped cars.

Under the broad Hawaiian sky, the sun and the warm wind seemed to clean the day, quenching them as they drove through town and out the narrow road that led east toward Barbers Point.

Douglas couldn't hear Margaret or Walrus over the wind as it whipped across the convertible but he could see them laughing. He looked at Mimi and watched the thin strands of her hair dance on her cheek and the rims of her sunglasses.

"How long have you been in Hawaii?" he asked her, his voice raised for her to hear.

"Only about a week. I've been making arrangements for the ambassador's trip to D.C.," she said. "I like it here."

The vegetation of the mountains along the road was thick and blanketed the hills in an endless color of green. On the opposite side of the road, the sea was calm except in the distance where the waves foamed white over the reefs.

Blue sea, blue sky, and green hills cut by a black road and a yellow Packard. The war was a million miles away, Douglas thought. At least for a few hours.

Finding a dirt path wide enough for the Packard, Mimi pulled off the main road and drove until it ended. As they got out, Walrus lifted the picnic basket off the luggage rack.

"Jesus, what did you girls make?" Walrus groaned as he carried the wicker basket down to the beach.

Douglas followed, carrying three bottles of white wine

and a smaller basket that Mimi had stressed he hold hori-zonal.

Margaret and Mimi led the way, and after four locations were passed over as unacceptable, the women decided on a patch of beach shaded by two high crossing palms.

Spreading out a red-and-white-checkered tablecloth, Margaret opened the basket and handed Mimi plates and silverware and the four wineglasses she had so carefully wrapped. "We've got fired chicken, potato salad, cheese and fresh pineapple and mango slices," she said.

"Now, this is paradise," Walrus said as he bit into a chicken leg.

"Walton," Margaret said with smiling exasperation. Then she turned to Douglas. "Mimi made sweets. Real Chinese pastries, glazed apples, and date rolls."

"Really," Douglas said as he sat on the edge of the checkered cloth and removed his shoes and socks.

"You sound surprised," Mimi said.

"No, it's just . . . I mean you don't look like the type to cook."

"Well, I am cheating. They are easy to make and the rolls should be served hot, but I think they're just as good cold," she admitted as she removed them from the basket Douglas had so carefully carried.

"Sounds great," Walrus said between bites.

Margaret scooped out a large helping of the salad and tapped it onto a plate. "Doug?" she held it toward him.

"In a minute, thanks," he said, standing. "I'm going to take a walk down the beach."

"Care if I join you?" Mimi asked, looking up at him, her hand covering her eyes against the sun.

"Nope," he said, helping her up with his left hand.

"Hey," Walrus called to Douglas, and tossed him one of the unopened bottles of wine. Margaret handed Mimi two glasses and the opener.

But Mimi hesitated and looked back at Douglas.

"Take them and come on," he said, heading toward the point.

"Don't hurry back," Walrus added, and Margaret slapped him playfully on the shoulder.

"They're funny," Mimi said, walking beside Douglas. The sand was warm on her feet and it felt good to her.

"They're like two high-school sweethearts. I never thought O'Tullie could act like that. I hope Walrus knows what he's getting into."

"What do you mean? Margaret is a nice girl and she's been a good friend," Mimi said, swinging the glasses in her left hand as she walked. "These aren't the easiest times to make friends if you're Chinese. Everyone thinks it's the same as being Japanese," she said.

"I meant it's not easy for a woman to sit and wait. And waiting for a submariner is even harder," he said. "O'Tullie has got to be crazy if she wants that."

"Is that why you sent Catherine back to the States?" Mimi asked, not looking up at him.

She caught Douglas off guard. He should have guessed Margaret would tell her he was married. "I suppose that was part of the reason."

"Well, there is no war." She stopped and sat down in the sand. "Not today, not for them." She looked back up the beach toward Walrus and Margaret, though she could no longer see them from where she was.

Douglas sat down next to her and she handed him the bottle opener and held out the glasses.

Douglas uncorked the wine and poured. It was too sweet, and at the moment he would have preferred a beer. "When do you leave for the mainland?"

"Friday morning."

"How about dinner Wednesday?"

She turned and looked into his eyes, "Thanks, but I have a party to go to that night with the ambassador."

"Oh." He took another sip of wine.

"But I do need an escort. That is, if you're willing to put

55

up with all the formal handshakes and how-do-you-dos," she said, smiling the kind of smile sailors dreamed of putting above their bunks.

"For one night, I think I could put up with that," he said. "That is, if you don't mind being with a simple lieutenant commander."

Mimi laughed. "Not at all," she said, tapping her glass with his. She leaned back and stretched herself over the warm, dry sand. "You like being a submarine commander, don't you?"

"My country's at war. And it's what I do best."

"And what did you do before the war?"

"Same thing. I've always been in the service, probably always will be. You?"

"You'll laugh."

"I won't," he promised.

"I was a scientist."

"You mean like looking through microscopes and cutting up little animals?"

"Not exactly, I was an anthropologist. You know, fossils and dinosaurs."

"Why'd you stop?"

"My country's at war," she said flatly. "The thought of that made my work less important. Funny,"—she looked up at the blue sky—"the research was my life for so long, then suddenly"—she shrugged and smiled—"it was like I had a calling to do something else."

Douglas didn't say anything. He nodded, knowing all too well what the war did. The way it changed you, the way you saw yourself, the way others looked at you.

He watched the distant waves as they continued their forever assault on the reef. Three seagulls flew in formation above the ocean and toward the harbor.

Finally, Douglas turned back and looked at her, but she had leaned back and closed her eyes. The wineglass rested on her stomach, balanced between two slender fingers.

He too stretched out in the sand, turned onto his left side

and studied her. There was something about this woman that drew him, made him want to touch. Something more than the sleekness of her arms or the texture of her skin. He had felt it before, once with his wife.

But that had vanished. A few months after marrying Catherine, he realized she was only a childhood sweetheart. They had made the wrong decision. She knew it too, but was too stubborn to admit it.

Douglas pushed the thought out of his mind, rolled onto his back, and covered his eyes with his forearm. Sleep came to him gently.

"Douglas." She nudged him gently. "Douglas."

He cracked his eyes open, one at a time.

She leaned over him, one hand on each side of his chest. "Hello," she said in a childlike voice. "Are you going to get up or do I have to carry you back?"

"Carry," he joked and then in one quick motion sat up, scooping her into his arms. "But who is going to carry who?"

"Ah." She put her hands on his chest but didn't push away. "We should really get back," she said as he leaned closer to her.

"You're right," he agreed, then he brought his lips to hers. She moved her hands slowly around to his back and pulled him close as they kissed.

After a moment, she released him. "Now who is crazy?" she asked as she reached up and moved a loose strand of brown hair from his forehead.

He smiled. "It's hard to wait for a submariner."

"Some people wait a lifetime for things they can never have. Patrols aren't forever."

"No," he said. Though, in the back of his mind, he knew some were.

As they headed down the beach, he moved next to her and slipped his hand into hers. They walked back in silence.

57

SIX

Washington, D.C., 1986

"Please close the door," she said politely.

Brian stepped into the room and shut the door softly. He tried to focus on her but she was a silhouette against the single light next to the bed.

"Please sit down," she said, motioning to the chair in front of the circular table next to the window. The woman flipped on the ceiling lamp, then pulled open the vertical blinds revealing the lights of Washington sparkling in the night.

"I'm Lai Ming, but call me Mimi, please." She lifted the coffeepot from the center of the table and filled two cups. "Cream and sugar?"

"How did you get my father's notebook?" Brian asked flatly.

She lifted the steaming cup to her lips. Then she looked up. "He left it in the back of my car when I drove him to the docks."

The shiver started at the base of Brian's brain and crawled slowly down his back. He moved to the chair across from her. "What day?"

"The third of February, 1944. They sailed out late that night," she said slowly. "Sometimes I remember it too well."

He could see in her eyes she was there again. "What do you want from me?"

"I want you to find the *Seakrill.*"

Brian studied her for a moment. "Why?"

Mimi looked out the window. The full moon was breaking through the clouds. With one hand, she twisted the end of her long braided hair that dropped over her right shoulder. She looked back at Brian, "To prove he is innocent."

"The records say—"

"They're wrong!" she snapped.

"How can you be so sure?" Brian asked.

"Because I sent him into Truk," she said, her eyes not meeting his. "It was my mission. I was the one who talked the ambassador into finding a submarine captain to make the rendezvous."

Brian stared at her. "What the hell are you talking about? Why would he agree to sail into an enemy base, especially Truk?"

Mimi set her coffee cup on the table. She wiped her hand across her cheek. The room seemed to be getting warm. She knew she had to tell him. Not everything. She couldn't tell Brian everything, she had promised she wouldn't.

But it had all been haunting her for so long, and now, it would be like telling Douglas the whole story. Somehow, finally saying she was sorry.

"Before the U.S. became involved in the war, I was working at the university in Peking. I was in charge of several anthropological finds. The most important being the fossils of the Peking Man."

"I've heard of them."

"At the time the Japanese were moving through my country and destroying everything. So I made a deal with the American ambassador to have them taken to the U.S. Marines based in Canton.

"Then, a few days later, the same day the Japanese attacked Pearl Harbor, they captured the U.S. base and took the marines prisoners," Mimi said. She stood and moved

59

to the window. "For safekeeping," she said, and her voice cracked. "I sent them to the Marines for safekeeping and I never saw them again."

"I still don't follow how this ties in with my father."

"In '42, the fossils came onto the black market. We were sure they had been destroyed or sent to Tokyo, but evidently some Japanese soldiers had found them and knew their value. They contacted the Chinese ambassador with a deal, a trade. Five million American dollars in diamonds for the two crates of fossils. My government brought me in immediately to get them back. At any cost, they said, it didn't matter."

"And the *Seakrill* was sent to make the trade." Brian was beginning to understand.

"Exactly. But it wasn't quite that simple. The U.S. Navy knew nothing about it. The so-called mission was a phony."

Brian looked hard at her, "No one knew?"

"Key people knew. People needed to make it work."

Brian leaned back in the chair and looked at her. "Why haven't you gone after the *Seakrill* yourself? You've had plenty of time."

"I'm not sure she's still in the lagoon," Mimi said, not looking at him.

Brian pulled at the corner of his mustache. "Mills said there was an aerial photograph that showed her moored to a freighter."

"The *Kuma Maru,*" Mimi remembered the ship's name.

"So you want me to find your precious fossils?"

"I want you to find the *Seakrill*. If you find the fossils, all the better. But if you want to clear Douglas's name, you have to find his sub."

"If she's there, it'd be the final proof he was a traitor."

"No. Douglas was given forged orders instructing him to enter the lagoon. They'll prove he wasn't a traitor."

Brian shook his head. "Forty years in saltwater won't leave much of those."

"They were kept in a courier's briefcase wrapped in oil

60

cloth. It was waterproof, Brian, and it's still aboard that submarine," she said.

Brian stared at her for a moment.

"If the *Seakrill* is in the lagoon, you have to find it."

"You only want the fossils," Brian said, his voice hard.

"That's precisely what I want. Since the day the Japanese took the Peking Man fossils, I've been searching for them. I honestly don't know if they were ever at the lagoon. Tomorrow I leave for Karachi, where I'm told there's a small shop with some unusual bones for sale. For me, Truk has to wait a little longer," Mimi said.

Brian looked at her. "How well did you know him?"

Mimi smiled at Brian, then she dropped her eyes like a shy little girl. "We spent that last afternoon together."

"What was he like?"

"He was strong and quiet, and more than anything else, he loved being a submarine commander." She looked into Brian's dark eyes. "That's what he was, a submariner. I knew him for only a few days but . . ." She didn't finished her sentence. "Here—" she lifted her purse from under the table. "Here's an airline ticket for Hawaii. It leaves tomorrow at ten-thirty A.M."

"I haven't agreed to anything."

"No, but I have a feeling the *Seakrill* is going to haunt you as it has me. One day you're going to have to go and find her. It might as well be tomorrow," she said as she handed him the ticket. "There is also a flight back to Boston International at that time. When you get back to your room, use the hotel phone to make the reservations for the flight home. The gates are close to each other, so it will be easy enough for you to slip aboard the one to the islands."

Brian laughed. "Slip aboard?"

"You're being followed."

"By who?"

Mimi shrugged. "I don't know, but don't let anyone stop you from getting to Truk," she warned.

61

"You're serious." He was suddenly unsure what was happening. "Who are you working for?"

Mimi steeped close and kissed him on the cheek. "I'll be in touch," she said, then she turned and left the room.

Brian let the hot water from the shower run through his hair and down his back. The combination of sweat and steam beaded on his face. He turned and rinsed the remaining soap from his chest and shoulders.

The blare of the radio met him as he stepped from the bathroom wrapping a towel around himself. He had seen it in a spy movie. With the radio volume on full, the music covered any noise or voice a hidden microphone might pick up. It was foolish, he thought, he was alone and was not about to start talking to himself.

He had pulled the curtain closed earlier, leaving his room dark except for the green light of the radio dial.

But the darkness was comfortable to him. As a submariner, he had performed most of his training blindly. At dockside and in forty-foot swells, and at sixty fathoms below the ocean's surface. Drill after drill, he had functioned without a spark of light. Practicing until instinctively he knew where every lever, switch, or button was located. Enemy attacks, electrical failures, fires, reactor meltdowns, missile malfunctions, they had all been simulated a thousand times in the blackness of a titanium hull.

The glow of the station numbers blurred as he spun it from jazz to the thundering beat of punk rock. Then he heard the sharp knock at the door.

"I've got a knock at the door," Beckman said as he leaned forward and increased the sensitivity of the microphone in the doorframe. "I'm telling you, he knows the bugs are there. No one listens to that goddamn music but my kids."

"Try to pick up the voice outside the door," Merith said, watching the expression of his partner's face. Where the hell had he been? Merith wondered. Thirty-five minutes missing from when Bovan stepped from the elevator until he finally walked into his room. The question was killing the CIA man. He didn't want to believe the young man with a perfect record could really be a threat to national security. But it was his job to find out.

In two steps Brian moved across the room, pressed himself against the wall next to the door, and listened. After a moment, the knock came again.

Brian looked at his watch. 9:45 P.M. He had given room service his suit, but even with a rush request and an extra ten dollars on the side, the hotel's cleaners said it wouldn't be ready until midnight.

The knock returned.

"Who is it?" Brian asked above the music.

"Commander Bovan?"

"Yes."

"I have a delivery, sir. Admiral Mills sent me."

Brian unlatched the door slowly, leaving the six-inch chain attached. Through the narrow opening, Brian saw the three stripes and insignia of a First Class yeoman. The uniform fit perfectly on the young red-haired man.

"What is it?" Brian asked.

"A package, sir, and a message," the yeoman said, moving his eyes back and forth trying to make certain the identification of the man in the room with the loud music.

"What's the message?"

"I'm to give this to you, sir, and tell you that he insists you return them to me after you have read through its contents."

"Slip it through the door," Brian told him. The yeoman hesitated, then handed the envelope to him. "Okay, now go downstairs and have dinner. Charge it to my room and I'll bring this down to you when I'm finished."

"Yes, sir," the yeoman said, and between the door and its frame, Brian saw the man snap into a salute.

Brian closed the door and locked it.

"The old man's not going to be happy about this," Beckman said as he looked up at Merith. "What do you think Mills gave him?"

Merith looked at his partner and sighed. He knew exactly what was in the package. "Hand me the phone, would you," Merith said with a grimace. "I have to make this call myself."

Brian moved to the table near the window. He shifted the shade of the lamp so it would shine against window blinds. Another cinema lesson; no silhouettes for the eyes across the street—that was, if Mimi was telling him the truth.

Unwinding the figure-eight of red thread from the flap of the heavy envelope, Brian hurriedly pulled the contents out. A single thick folder dropped on the table. It was his father's war records.

He opened it, skipped the first entries, and went directly to his naval records aboard the *Seakrill*. Buried in the middle of a paragraph from a statement by a CINCPAC commander was the date of the *Seakrill*'s departure from Pearl Harbor. Her last departure. February third, 1944.

The date jumped at him again as it had from the notebook. He turned back to the first pages of the report and skimmed over them. He read about his father's training in New London before the outbreak of the war, his first command of a World War I S-boat, and his transfer to the Pacific. It was all things he had heard in fragments while growing up.

Finally, he came to the thick hard-covered folder that

contained the transcripts from the board of inquiry into the loss of the *Seakrill.* As Mills had told him, there were several pages of interviews from naval personal at Pearl Harbor. Brian recognized most of the names; he even remembered some of the old captains coming to his house for dinner on one occasion or another. The good old wartime buddies, he thought.

He flipped to Mills's interview and read through it. There was nothing said Brian wouldn't have guessed at, although the interview was much shorter that any of the others.

The next page was the report from the OSS.

OFFICE OF STRATEGIC SERVICES
November 10, 1945

From: Director of Office of Strategic Services, Pearl Harbor

To: The Officer-in-Charge, Board of Inquiry, Loss of U.S.S. Seakrill

Subject: Lieutenant Commander DOUGLAS BOVAN

Enclosure: Summary of personal observation records

(NOTE: Observations of military personnel is part of normal O.S.S. procedure.)

Observations began October 12, 1942, with his transfer to CINCPAC.

Questionable activity started August of 1943. Subject was sighted several times at illegal cockfights held at a ranch on the north side of Honolulu. It was then discovered Lt.Cmdr. Bovan was in debt for several thousands of dollars with local loan sharks.

The report went on for several pages about his father's gambling habits. There were half a dozen reports of his activities with women, on and off the base.

But it was the last paragraphs that Brian read over and over.

Lt.Cmdr. Douglas Bovan was sighted numerous times in the company of one Lai Ming, assistant to the visiting ambassador of China. The day the Seakrill departed on her last patrol, Bovan was seen entering the Naval base with the woman.

"We spent that last afternoon together," Mimi's words came back to him. He shut the folder and pulled out the 8 x 10 black-and-white photograph.

It was the aerial photo taken over Truk Lagoon. Although somewhat blurred, its subjects could be seen on the black-colored water. Two ships anchored off a small curve of beach were engulfed in white specks of machine-gun fire as the Hellcats attacked.

Brian could tell that the one ship had just taken a direct hit. The ink-black smoke that billowed from its decks told the horror of fire.

The other, the one in the foreground, was still untouched by the onslaught. Brian looked closer at the image. Against its hull, like an irregular shadow, was the distinct outline of a moored submarine.

Brian looked at the second picture stapled to the first. It was an enlargement, the image grossly out of focus, but it made identification unmistakable. The large white numbers of the U.S.S. *Seakrill* were on the submarine's conning tower.

He turned the photograph over and read the handwritten note on the back. *U.S.S. Seakrill, SS–231 tied to Kuma Maru.*

Brian got up and walked over to the nightstand near his bed. From the top drawer, he took out a pen and one sheet of the hotel's stationery with the gold Marriott insignia across it. Placing the thin paper on the photograph, he traced over the images of the two ships and the curve of the shoreline.

Finished, he folded the paper in half, then folded it again

and rolled it tight. Walking into the bathroom, he slipped the paper into his toothbrush holder. He placed it back in his overnight kit.

Brian returned the photographs and the file to the envelope and rewebbed the flap. He dressed in his extra slacks and shirt and headed down to the restaurant.

As Brian stepped from the elevator he scanned the lobby. A young couple, newly in love, moved to check in at the desk. At 11:35 P.M. the gift shop was still open with only one customer. He headed toward the dining room.

"Got him in the lobby," Karen whispered into her concealed microphone as she flipped through the *Newsweek* on the magazine stand. "He's going into the restaurant."

The red-headed yeoman sat with his back to the door and at a table in the center of the main room. Only a few other people were seated at the remaining cloth-covered tables.

Brian dropped the package on the table in front of the yeoman. "Tell the admiral thank you," he said, then turned to leave, not noticing the tall woman walk slowly pass them.

The yeoman stood up, quickly swallowing his last bite. "Admiral Mills was hoping you would have lunch with him on Monday, sir."

Brian turned and forced a smile. "That'd be fine. Tell him I'll be at his office at 1200 hours."

"Yes, sir, and thank you for the dinner, sir," he said.

Brian nodded and walked from the restaurant. He picked his suit up at the valet's desk near the entrance, saving the teenage attendant a trip up to the seventh floor.

Again Brian turned on the radio as he entered his hotel room. He changed into his suit and repacked his flight bag. He picked up the airline ticket, pushed it into the breast pocket of his coat, and tossed the coat over a chair.

He piled the bed pillows against the headboard, switched

off the lights, and lit a cigarette. Then he sat back against the pillows and stretched his feet out over the unturned bed.

Just how he was going to switch gates, he hadn't decided. He really couldn't believe anyone was following him. But that didn't matter; he wasn't going to take the chance. He knew Mills had sent him his father's records to convince him to drop the whole thing. And that wasn't like the good old admiral. Nor was the expression on his face when Brian had handed him the notebook. It was as if a ghost had walked into his office and sat down before him.

Brian took a long drag from his cigarette; it dried his mouth. Whether Mimi was lying to him or whether Mills was, he knew the Chinese woman was right; he had to go to Truk. Only there would he find out the truth.

SEVEN

Truk Lagoon, 1986

Ty Wuun spit twice into his goggles. Reaching down, he rinsed them quickly in the warm water of the lagoon, then put them over his eyes and tied their leather strap behind his head. Placing his small rusting bayonet into the waistband of his trunks, he began to wade out into deeper water.

Instinctively, he looked up and down the beach. It was high tide in the tourist season at Truk, but there was no one. This section of white sand was still bare of young lovers or afternoon explorers who had set out from Moen. It was still pure and empty.

At 58 years old, Wuun's dark-tanned body was still thick with muscles but some corners had begun to sag from age. Loose folds of skin hung beneath his arms, his once broad chest now gave the impression of an old woman suckled by too many siblings, and his short jet-black hair was now limited to only a narrow strip over his ears.

But it was only the tropical sun that had taken the vision of youth from him. He was still strong, still quick, his brown eyes still sharp and piercing, and he still remembered all that the Japanese soldiers had taught him.

Wuun lurched forward and dove through the surf as a small wave rolled toward him. He swam powerfully over the reef and around the shallow outcroppings. Jeweled fish darted away as he approached; orange and purple coral polyps retracted at the vibrations of his movements. The water was warm and soft as it flowed over his body.

Barely breaking the surface with his swift strokes, Wuun took in an extra gulp of air and dove down. There was only one quick way through the jagged maze of stag's horn coral that lay in front of him. A small tunnel thirty feet underwater that extended the entire hundred-foot breach of the reef.

Finding it easily, he moved into its narrow opening. He pulled himself along, hand over hand, as he had done a thousand times since he was a boy. The sunlight that filtered into the tunnel danced about him, sparkling like the mirrored ball in the bar of the Blue Waters hotel.

In over forty years, this was the first time he had been called. And except for the checks that arrived monthly, he had almost forgotten about his agreement. Forgotten about the war, forgotten about the American he had shaken hands with. But last week it had all come back to him.

Wuun pushed away from the exit of the passage and kicked upward to the surface. As he broke water, he looked toward the center of the lagoon. In the distance, the small white skiff rose and fell with the gentle swells.

It looked like most of the boats from the harbor, sun-bleached and weathered, cracked decks and deserted by the vacationers who had rented them to escape to hidden paradises. They would leave the boats anchored alone, bobbing peacefully, waiting until it was time to return from exploring an uninhabited island or from diving one of the sunken wrecks.

But this skiff had not carried honeymooners. It had brought someone else to this part of the lagoon. It had been anchored here five days in a row and now was once again over the wreck of the *Kuma Maru*.

Wuun swam quietly as he approached the boat, his heart pounding faster as he reached up and grabbed the wooden rail. Effortlessly, he pulled himself out of the sea. He had been right, the skiff was deserted. He looked around, finding only miscellaneous diving gear. A single fin and a mask were in the bottom of a canvas bag; a scuba tank with its valve removed, leaned against the hatchway. These were extras, odds and ends of equipment now being used below.

Looking over the rail, Wuun found a thick nylon line secured to a stern cleat. It dropped vertically into the water. He knew exactly what was tied along its length. Replacing his goggles, he jumped back into the water. Two deep breaths and he grabbed the line and followed it down.

The scuba diver swam carefully through the engine room, avoiding the sharp edges of the rusting steel around him. At 160 feet below the surface, caution was always a forethought.

A diver could too easily become entangled in the twisted fingers of steel, or in fallen wires or piping. Or he could simply become lost in winding corridors. Death in the sea was as spontaneous as life and it knew no boundaries between sea creature and intruder. It would take who it wanted.

The diver drifted upward, leaving his tools behind. They would wait until tomorrow for him. Entering a hallway, he pulled himself along by the rail. He knew exactly where he was going as he kicked his way through the ship, moving like an astronaut in zero gravity.

His Dacor light cut into the darkness as he swam past the galley and up through the tilting stairway. He stopped and peered into the doorway of the operating room. Silt and sponges encrusted the map table with dusty browns and oranges.

He had crossed thousands of miles in this ship. He had worked, slept, and lived in the bowels of this steel cavern that was now home to fish and clams and coral.

He reached out and touched a hand rail he had once stood near. It was sad, he thought, that she would never set sail again and never reach her home port. She would remain here forever.

Over the past few weeks, he had dove the *Kuma Maru* several times to search her holds. In the forward hold a tank still waited its unloading. Near it, several crates of ammunition lay spilled across the deck. Most were caked into huge blocks encrusted with brown silt, their copper casings blue from the saltwater.

But like the stern hold, the forward had not been damaged by the attack. It was sound, and that wasn't what he wanted.

For the last two days he had tried to get into the amidship hold, but had found the mechanics' hatchway sealed tight with rust and the twist in the freighter as she came to rest on the bottom.

When he thought he could finally break the hatch free, his pressure gauge told him it was time to return to the surface. A thousand pounds of air was all he had left and it would be just enough for him to reach the fresh set of decompression tanks waiting on the line above. The hatch would have to wait until tomorrow.

Now he swam past the bridge and out on to the deck. Tied to one of the ship's cleats, he grabbed hold of the single nylon rope that led up through the green darkness to the surface. He followed the line upward.

Carefully he watched his ascent, measuring his speed with the tiny bubbles that escaped from his regulator. He checked his depth gauge and then the pressure gauge, all the while concentrating on the rate of his breathing.

As the green water began to lighten, he could finally see again the yellow of his gloves. He continued up the line, thankful that he had worn his black rubber suit. After an hour, even the warm tropical water began to feel like ice.

At 90 feet, he could see the outline of the single scuba tank dangling along the line above him. They were at the 40-foot mark, his first designated decompression stop.

He checked his pressure gauge; it was down to 200

pounds. Just enough air to reach the fresh set of scuba tanks, he thought. There he would switch tanks, clip himself to the rope, and hang for exactly 9 minutes. This would allow the tiny nitrogen bubbles that had built up in his muscles and tissues time to be released.

After, he would ascend to 30 feet and wait 19 minutes. Then to twenty feet, another fresh tank, and 33 more minutes of decompression. Then finally, he would rise to only ten feet and drift there for an hour and ten minutes until the last of the nitrogen had been dissolved from his body.

As he came to the first tank, it seemed like the hundredth time he had gone through the steps of decompression. Mechanically, he found the loop in the line and attached it to his belt with a steel clip. Sucking out the last bit of air from his tanks, he twisted out of their harness. He reached for the fresh regulator, pushed it past his numb lips, and breathed in.

It was the extreme effort of the breath that seized him. His muscles pulled to fill his lungs with air promised by the regulator. Quickly he grabbed the tank's pressure gauge. Its thin red needle rested on the zero mark. He was without air twenty feet from the next decompression stop and the next scuba tank.

He chanced a third breath, filling his chest with as much as he could manage. He grabbed the line, released the clip from his belt, and pulled himself toward the surface.

It was not the first time he had ascended 20 feet on a single breath. But those were times in training, under controlled conditions. Now he had to force himself to remember the rules of free ascent. He released a steady stream of bubbles from his lips and tried not to rise too quickly. The picture of nitrogen bubbles growing inside him, rupturing cells and popping veins, ran through his mind. He began to hum an old Japanese folk tune to keep calm. No longer was the water cold, nor did he watch the fish or the sun's rays dance about him as they cut through the depths.

His heart pounded in his throat and his eyes began to

water behind his mask as he stared upward searching for the tank. He fought the urge to check his depth gauge, fearing the panic that would surely kill him.

The burning in his chest began to grow as his diaphragm pulled at his lungs, the muscles in his throat choking him. The darkness began to close around him like the aperture of a camera lens. He envisioned himself breaking through the surface, gasping, choking, taking in sweet warm air. He forced the thought from his mind, shook his head, and continued up.

Finally, he could see it above him hanging from the line. Letting go of the rope, he took two strong kicks to the equipment. His hands grabbed the regulator, turned it, and pushed it into his mouth. He inhaled.

Nothing. It was empty, completely drained of precious air. He spit the regulator out and kicked toward the surface.

Now, all the training and rules of deep-water diving were blocked from his mind. Survival, the need of air by the body took control. There was only 20 feet of liquid between him and the surface. A distance he could run in fractions of a second. Twenty feet of oxygen-rich water that he could not use, oxygen his body could not absorb. With no breath, the distance became twenty miles.

Feeling his hands start to cramp, he reached down and released his weight belt. His sense of speed increased as he kicked furiously. His hands and fingers began to curl first as he felt the muscles throughout his body tighten and knot.

Pain blurred his vision as the gases behind his eyes pushed outward, his soft organs twisting within his body as he shot upward. His chest swelled to twice its size, cracking his backbone, shattering his rib cage.

At 5 feet below the surface of the sea, he screamed. But only bubbles and blood came from his mouth as his right lung exploded.

Now, the diver rose more slowly, buoyant by his rubber suit, his left leg kicking only in spasms. And the nitrogen bubbles continued to froth cold within his body.

EIGHT

San Francisco, 1986

.... I'VE GOT SOMETHING FOR YOU, GLASGO (SALT-
MAN). . . .

Martin J. Glasgo looked up at the top of his computer
screen and read the message. It was from Saltman. Always
from Saltman. That asshole never leaves me alone, Glasgo
thought. He typed in the command button and a capital V
on his keyboard to instruct the computer to retrieve the rest
of the interoffice message.

.... I'VE GOT SOMETHING FOR YOU, GLASGO. UPSTAIRS
JUST SENT A GOLD-CARD REQUEST TO PULL ALL OUR FILES
ON A GUY NAMED . . . HITO YOKAMATA . . . TELL ME
WHEN YOU HAVE SOMETHING. . . . (SALTMAN)

It was just like Saltman to blow everything out of pro-
portion, Glasgo thought. Gold-card only meant someone's
secretary's secretary had delivered the request in person.
But then that was Saltman's division, always thinking the
worst. Aliases, raincoats, and secret weapons in tiepins.

Glasgo wanted to go home. The 49ers were on against
the Chicago Bears tonight. He added the last few entries
into the Belgium file he had been working on for the past

three hours. Then he typed in the computer command that sealed the file and sent it back to the record banks.

A second later the screen went blank as the information was recorded and the small green square cursor flashed patiently in the upper corner of the screen.

He entered the name Saltman had given him and leaned back, his steel-and-imitation-leather chair groaning under his large bulk.

The TRV computer in the tall mirrored building overlooking the wharf instantly connected with its sister systems along the west coast and searched for the name. Then it linked itself to the east coast and to Europe, while simultaneously going on line with computers of friendly governments in the Orient and Middle East. It also connected with a dozen unfriendly governments who had yet to discover the CIA tie-in.

Hito Yokamata's file came on the screen before Glasgo could get his coffee cup from the desk to his lips.

YOKAMATA, HITOBUTO
FILE #3168–825
BIRTH DATE: June 28, 1923
BIRTH PLACE: Osaka, Japan
SUMMARIZED BIOGRAPHY: Born June 28, 1923, Osaka Japan, to MIKKO and SAKETO Yokamata, both deceased. Two sisters, HANNA and MEGOTO, both deceased. Brought to United States in 1927 with migration of family. Educated at Belmont High School, Los Angeles. Graduating class of 1939.

Returned to Japan in November of 1939 and enlisted in the Japanese Navy. Served until the end of the war as a lieutenant on Japanese freighter. Prisoner of war for six months after which he returned to Los Angeles. Married CYNTHIA DIPPERY on March 1, 1951.

Son, JOHN HITO, born May 6, 1953, and daughter, LESLIE HANNA, born August 25, 1956. Both raised and schooled in Los Angeles.

Wife and son deceased. Killed October 10, 1963, in an automobile accident.

Currently teaching as a professor of American History at the University of Hawaii in Honolulu, Hawaii.

Daughter now living in New York. (SEE BIO BELOW OR FILE #6003–711).

. . . FOR FURTHER INFORMATION SEE IN-DEPTH FILES BELOW . . .

A: HITOBUTO YOKAMATA
B: LESLIE HANNA YOKAMATA

(FOR DETAILED INFORMATION PLACE COMMAND LETTER IN APPROPRIATE POSITION)

_____ CURRENT RESIDENCE	_____ PHOTOGRAPHS
_____ PERSONAL BIOGRAPHY	_____ FINANCIAL STATUS

Glasgo read through the first page of the file. Then, using the flashing cursor, he typed an A on the Current Residence line.

The file came on the screen.

HITOBUTO YOKAMATA
CURRENT RESIDENCE FILE:
8654 Kahiku Road, Honolulu, Hawaii
_____ PHOTOGRAPHS   _____ BLUEPRINTS
_____ SURROUNDING STREET MAPS

Glasgo returned to the original file. Out of curiosity, he placed a B on the line to call up the photographs of Yokamata's daughter. The computer listed the types of photographs on file. He called up a head shot.

The screen went blank and then, after a moment, it came

on with the clarity of a television set. The computer displayed a photograph of Leslie Hanna Yokamata.

Glasgo hated Orientals. Hated blacks, Mexicans, Jews, and just about every other race. Although his mixed heritage twisted more like ivy than a family tree, he surrounded himself with the Irish. Mostly big-bosomed Irish with mounds of red hair who smoked, loved to drink, and were easy to get into bed.

But the face that stared at Martin Glasgo from him computer screen with deep almond eyes hit him like a hammer. Leslie Yokamata was the most beautiful woman he had ever seen. She looked directly at him, her eyes, only hinting at her Japanese heritage, rested on high smooth cheeks. Her nose was small, petite, and fashionably perfect for her face. Dark hair, undoubtedly closer to black in winter and lighter from the summer sun, hung down to the center of her upper arms. It was full and bellowed around her neck.

Glasgo hit another command, calling up a full-length photograph. This time it was a candid picture. Leslie was getting into a yellow taxicab; her thin body was accented in a sheer light-blue dress that clung to her torso and blossomed at the waist. Her hair was braided into a ponytail and showed under the brim of a wide hat.

It was a photograph taken by people hired by the agency. People instructed to be unseen, yet Leslie's head was turned toward the camera, her eyes peering into it. Perhaps she thought he was a tourist or a newspaperman, Glasgo guessed, trying to imagine the New York scene. The busy traffic, the people rushing, talking, yelling on the street. A hundred, a thousand people around her but she sensed him, sensed the camera, and at the right instant turned and looked directly into its lens.

There were girls like that, Glasgo thought, especially in New York. Girls who could hear the click of a shutter across any crowded room. Models, striving actresses, groupies all trying to be in front of a camera.

He went back to the first page of the file and put Leslie's

code on the personal biography line. The computer returned to its black screen and green letters.

LESLIE HANNA YOKAMATA
PERSONAL BIOGRAPHY:
   BORN: August 25, 1956, Los Angeles, California
   HEIGHT: 5'6"   WEIGHT: 115 lbs.
   EYES: brown   HAIR: Dark brown
   SEX: Female   MARITAL STATUS: Single

CURRENT ADDRESS: 45 West 10th Street, Apt #6,
                    New York, New York
Roommate: Terry Campton (FILE #7803–511)
BIOGRAPHY: Currently a member of the Letofsky Dance Company. Living in New York since 1978 where she attended the School of American Ballet.

Graduating Carson High School in 1974, she continued in performing arts at the University of California, Los Angeles until 1978 when she moved to New York.

Performs with several smaller dance companies and theatre groups during the off season of the L.O. Co.

She has had three long relationships (over one year) in New York. First with JAMES KANSON, 34, who is married and living Miami, Florida. Break-up caused by Kanson's return to his wife. Second, JON SCHUTTS, 26, still with the L.O. Co. Their relationship began when both joined the company in 1978 and continued until 1980. Break-up seemed to stem from her more rapid advancement in the company. Last was ERIC FRANKLIN, 36, lasted only nine months but considered substantial as they lived together in his penthouse apartment on Park Ave. for seven months. Reasons for break-up unknown.

A dancer, Glasgo thought; that explained her ear for cameras. She must be used to them.

The file was complete, even gave a cross reference for her roommate. He wondered what kind of files they kept on him. Shit, they probably know which side of my face I shave first in the morning.

. . . HAVE YOU FOUND ANYTHING ON YOKAMATA YET? . . . (SALTMAN) . . .

The message came across the top of the screen. "Damn," Glasgo said out loud. Then sent a message back to Saltman saying he was going over it now.

He called up Leslie's financial file and found she had saved about $2400. Just over $300 in her checking account. All her credit cards were paid to date except for a moving-company bill for $230. Out of Franklin's place, Glasgo figured. Nothing else seemed out of the ordinary.

He returned to the file summary and put an A on the financial line of Hitobuto. It, too, showed the usual. A few thousand dollars in his savings account at a Honolulu bank, less in his checking account, and the mortgage records of his house and his car, a dental bill outstanding.

But there was the file line at the bottom of the screen Glasgo had not expected..

_____ FINANCIAL STATUS: INTERNATIONAL

He debated calling it up as he stared at the screen. He looked at his watch. It was almost five P.M. He was going to miss the first quarter of the game sitting in traffic. But if he missed something . . . Glasgo called up the file.

MITSUBISHI BANK OF TOKYO; Tokyo, Japan
HITOBUTO YOKAMATA
Savings Account Number 67–800–2656–45–6667
ENDING BALANCE: $236,067.66 (64,918,606.50 Yen)
LAST DEPOSIT: date: 01-15-86 Amount: $56,000 (15,400,000.00 Yen)

Bingo. Whoever this guy was, whatever Saltman and his division or the person from upstairs wanted with him,

Glasgo knew he had hit pay dirt. College professors don't keep almost a quarter of a million dollars in foreign banks.

Glasgo recorded the file, set the International Finances of Hitobuto Yokamata in bold italics, and sent it to Saltman's office. He also sent along a message.

. . . FILE YOU REQUESTED ON THE WAY. CHECK ITALICIZED NOTES. INFORMATION MAY BE HELPFUL TO INVESTIGATION. I'M OFF TO WATCH THE FOOTBALL GAME . . . (GLASGO M.) . . .

NINE

Kaimu, Hawaii, 1986

Retired Full Admiral Joe Tendrey watched the distant aqua-blue sea as it rolled continuously shoreward. Rising, curling, raging across the reef. Yet he couldn't hear its cries even though the reef was only a mile away. His hearing had weakened so that not even the electronic aid tucked behind his ear could pick up the faraway anger.

So he was forced to simply watch and smell the sharp bite of salt that was carried on the air. Hour after hour he would sit at the edge of the huge trimmed lawn and stare at the sea.

The manicured grounds were contrasted with the thick groves of palm trees and vines that surrounded the estate, but the admiral didn't care about the upkeep of the land outside the brick walls of his home, though he owned several of the acres beyond the boundary. He enjoyed it. The jungle sense of it reminded him of the Philippines, of Iwo Jima. Sometimes he would look from his study over the wall and into the thick vegetation and remember.

"Admiral," came the voice from behind him. A sweet voice of comfort and admiration, a young voice filled with eagerness to please. "Admiral," she called again as she walked quickly towards him.

Tendrey winced. What the hell did she want now? he

wondered. He looked back over his shoulder at the sun—1530, he summarized. He had another hour and he was fine where he was. She wasn't going to move him, not today. Not until it was time. It was a beautiful day, blue and bright and warm, and he was fine where he was. Damn it, go away, he thought.

"Admiral." Miss Swanson smiled as she approached, almost blinding him with her spotless white nurse's uniform and her short bleached-blond hair. "You have a phone call from the mainland," she said, pulling out the antenna of the mansion's radiophone.

"Oh," he said, and let a smile form at the edges of his mouth; it caused the soft wrinkles of his face to tighten. He took the handset from her. He flipped the switch on, cleared his throat, and spoke, "Hello."

"Afternoon, Joe," the voice from the mainland said.

"Just a minute," the admiral said as he covered the receiver with his palm. "Thank you, Miss Swanson," he said. "That will be all."

"Can I get you anything else, Admiral? A hat, something to eat, maybe? Here, let me put you under some shade. It's so hot out here," she said, reaching for the brake release on his wheelchair. "You shouldn't be so close to the edge."

"No, no, I'm fine where I am. Just leave me," he said, parrying her attack. "Really I'm fine, thank you."

"I don't think you should be out here too long. It's not good for you," she insisted. "Are you sure I can't get you anything?"

"A glass of ice coffee, please, ice coffee would be nice," he said.

"You know you can't have coffee. How about some tea?"

"Yes, that'll be splendid. Some ice tea," he surrendered.

"Okay," she said with a sparkling smile. "I'll be right back."

As she turned and walked briskly toward the house, Tendrey remembered why he kept her around at all. God, she made his pulse jump. Her breasts were massive for her small

83

frame, such a young firm frame, alive and tan. If he were only fifty years younger.

"Sorry," he said into the phone.

"You got my telegram, I trust?" the man asked.

"Of course," Tendrey said.

"After I sent you the information on Yokamata, I told Saltman to check out the daughter."

"The dancer in New York?"

"Yes. It's nothing really. It's just that she's taken a month's leave from work. The people at her studio said it was spur-of-the-moment, that sort of thing. Probably nothing."

Tendrey could feel the heat of the sun on the top of his head cutting through his thin gray hair as if someone were using a magnifying glass to concentrate it. "But you found out where she went, right?"

"That's why I called. No one at the studio knew nor did her landlady. And San Francisco hasn't been able to find her on the computers, no plane tickets, no travel reservations, nothing. I think she must still be in New York or at least close-by. But I thought you'd want to know."

"You were right to call. I don't want any loose ends," Tendrey said, knowing the owner of the voice would understand. "Keep looking."

"I'll call you as soon as I know anything."

"Good," Tendrey said as he switched off the phone.

"Here you go, Admiral," Miss Swanson said in her sweet voice as she handed him a small glass of iced tea. "And let me put you under the shade." She unlocked the wheelchair's brakes before he could stop her and rolled him near the huge swaying leaves of a ten-foot palm.

He didn't argue with her this time. Didn't say a word. He was thinking again, planning and calculating the next strategy and he was remembering. Remembering Midway, Pearl Harbor, and the war.

TEN

Waikiki, Hawaii, 1986

A droplet of sweat rolled slowly down the center of her stomach, veered to the right at her hip and off her oiled skin. The sun was hot, hot like she had never felt it before, and it bore into her, cooking her where her bikini didn't cover.

Without opening her eyes, Leslie Yokamata reached out with her left hand and found the small plastic spray bottle next to her beach towel. With delicate fingers, she aimed it over her face, pumped the triggerlike handle, and released a cool, fine mist of water and baby oil. It landed in beads on her high cheeks and slender nose and on her forehead where she had pulled her long hair back into a ponytail.

Letting the bottle drop back into the sand, she settled comfortably under the tropical noon sun.

Eric could never enjoy this, she thought. Too much relaxation, too much of nothing to do. Her ex-boyfriend was a workaholic who was never happy unless something at his advertising firm was in the midst of catastrophe and needed his immediate attention. And there was always something in disorder or some client who was ever so important that Eric couldn't make it to her opening night or her finale. Her dancing wasn't important to him. Work was, and only his work.

She was there for him, though, at every formal engagement and dinner party. They were the perfect couple, the successful businessman and his ballet dancer. His clients wives' treated her like a princess; she was a dove in the midst of crows and old owls.

Leslie's roommate, Terry, had a term for her and Eric. Beauty and the beast, she would say, and Leslie would always smile at her joking remarks but she knew Terry's comments were all too true.

Finally their relationship became as empty as his penthouse apartment, which after a time turned into a cold, unwanting cavern. She finally faced the inevitable and told Eric that there was nothing for her. It was all a string of performances, from public appearances at La Caravelle to private ones in his bedroom. He knew it as well as she, but as Leslie stepped out onto Park Avenue from his apartment house for the last time, she felt a release of tension she hadn't realized she carried.

Then came the telegram from her father. A surprise whose timing couldn't have been better. Leslie hadn't seen him in so long. It was perfect. Visiting her father would give her time to get one man out of her life and reintroduce herself to a lost one.

"How about this?" Terry said, holding up a violet-colored string bikini in the small shop just outside Daytona Beach. They had flown down from New York on a whim, one of Terry's whims, which were weekly occurrences.

"I couldn't wear that," Leslie laughed. She was being honest with her roommate, who held the bikini against her. "Really, I couldn't. You don't know my father."

"Believe me, Les, this isn't for wearing in front of your dad. You're going to be in Waikiki for a whole week before you meet him. That's where this comes in," Terry said seriously as she flipped back her long strawberry-red hair over her shoulder. "Come on, you've got to open up. This is your vacation."

"Some vacation," Leslie said solemnly as she looked through the rows of bikinis that hung on plastic hangers, each drooping like shreds of unusable material in a tailor's shop. "I feel like I'm skipping out of town on a midnight train."

"I'm telling you, you need this, you're not skipping out. The reservations are made. I got you the tickets and the hotel room. Les, you're set. When I get back to New York, I'll tell Vincent you had to leave on family business and you couldn't get ahold of him," Terry said as she laid a pair of tan shorts and the swimsuit Leslie wouldn't buy on the front counter of the tiny shop.

The teenager with the pixie-cut blond hair checked the tags and rang up the sale as she kept the beat of the hard-rock music playing over the store's stereo.

"I don't know, Terry. I still feel guilty about just dropping everything and taking off," Leslie said as they stepped from the store and into the sunlight. Leslie lowered her large round sunglasses over her eyes and tucked her long dark hair behind her ears. The breeze off the Atlantic caught her pale cotton dress and ruffled the hem.

Summer must never leave Florida, Leslie thought as they walked down the boardwalk. The sun was arching away from the sea and into a dome of blue.

"You're really nervous about seeing him, aren't you?" Terry asked.

"It shows that much?"

"As if you were facing the plague."

Leslie smiled.

"Why has it been so long, anyway?" Terry asked casually as they moved to one of the cement benches that lined the boardwalk. Terry had a way of asking bluntly what others would avoid.

"I wanted to be a dancer. He thought I should have gotten married and given him grandchildren."

"Different points of view, maybe, but reason enough to cut ties?"

"You've got it wrong. I'm the one who never gets returned letters or phone calls," Leslie said as she watched a volleyball match on the sand between four darkly tanned men.

"What else is bothering you?" Terry asked.

"Nothing."

"Something. Come on, fess up," Terry persisted in a big-sister tone.

"I just don't like the idea of going all the way out there to meet him. We could meet in Hawaii."

"Are you kidding? This place sounds a hell of a lot more exciting than Hawaii."

Leslie shrugged, not enticed by Terry's excitement for the unexplored. "I'm just going to be in the way of his research."

"Research?" Terry asked. The volleyball game was over and most of her concentration was on the tall blond in the red trunks.

"On the war, like always," Leslie said, remembering how his work absorbed him. Then she looked back at her friend. "What time is it?"

"Ten minutes since you asked me last and two hours before your flight," Terry said, exasperated. "Come on, Les, relax."

Leslie nodded. "Thanks again for getting me the reservations."

"Forget it. I'm sorry I had to put it all under my name, but you know how it is with credit cards."

"What, you don't think I look like a Miss Campton?"

Terry laughed. "As much as I look like Miss Yokamata with this hair."

"Excuse me."

The voice woke Leslie suddenly. She sat up and shaded her eyes from the Hawaiian sun. "Yes?"

88

It was Jimmy, the boy from the hotel who always seemed to be near when she needed anything. He smiled; his teeth, covered with braces, sparkled. "Sorry to bother you, Miss Yokamata," he said. "But there's a telegram at the front desk, ma'am."

"Thank you, Jimmy," she said as she stood and pulled the long white coverall over her head. Its hem dropped to the middle of her muscular thighs. Bending down, Leslie quickly tossed her things into the large straw beach-bag.

Jimmy stayed a few paces ahead of her as they walked along the path that led to the lobby of the Hilton Hawaiian Village Hotel. Past the lava-rock waterfall, the path weaved around the pool and cocktail bar, and several male occupants looked up from their colorful drinks to watch her.

Leslie pushed her glasses to the top of her head as she stepped into the open-air lobby. She had sent a letter to her father a week before leaving New York telling him when she would arrive, but she hadn't expected him to write back, though in the back of her mind she hoped he would.

Leslie set her things on the floor next to the desk. "You have a telegram for me, Leslie Yokamata?"

"Yokamata?" The clerk looked at the guest list.

"It'll be under Campton. Room 721," Jimmy said as he leaped onto the brown marble counter, swung his legs over, and dropped on the opposite side. "I'll get it." He reached into the box that held her room key and pulled out the telegram. "Here you go, Miss Yokamata," he said.

"Thank you." She moved to one of the rarely used couches on the far side of the lobby near the fish pond and sat down. A glance at the return address told her it wasn't from her father.

Dear Les,
    Guess who was at the airport to pick me up? Stephen. Was I shocked. I called Vincent the next morn-

ing and told him that you left and would be back in a few weeks. You were right, he was mad. And he got madder when I told him I wouldn't be at rehearsal for a few days either.

Of course, I didn't tell him that I was getting re-acquainted with Stephen, he'd have a cow and I'd be out of a job. So I told him it was something women have trouble with and he didn't want to know anymore.

He did say that someone had been asking for you but didn't say who. Mrs. Beth at the apartment said the same thing. Sounds like Eric wants to kiss and make up. But don't worry, I'll fend him off.

Remember, this is your vacation, so go out and have fun.

Luv,
Ter

Leslie folded the paper and pushed it into her bag. She got up and moved to the desk. Thanking Jimmy again, she picked up her key and headed to her room to change for dinner.

She was glad to hear from Terry, she told herself, trying not to be upset it wasn't from her father. It really didn't matter. She had come too far to go back now. There was nothing to be afraid of; he was her father and she was his only child. Tomorrow she was going to get on that plane and meet him in Truk Lagoon.

And as for Eric, she knew there was no going back to him at all.

ELEVEN

Washington, D.C., 1986

Brian sat uncomfortably in the plastic chair, the morning edition of the *Post* unfolded in front of him. His fingers were black from its ink but his eyes didn't fall on the print. They were roaming, scanning, darting back and forth across the airport lounge and into the crowd that moved in every direction through it. He looked at the people who passed by him, trying to make mental notes of each face. It was impossible. No one seemed to give him a second glance.

He was a businessman waiting for his morning flight back to New York or Chicago. A lobbyist with good news or bad to report to his constituents. A man, like hundreds of other men who were simply waiting for a plane.

"United's Flight Twenty-three to Los Angeles, now boarding at gate thirteen," the female voice said over the loudspeaker above Brian's head.

He ignored it and continued to look past the newspaper. He glanced at his watch. A normal movement for someone in an airport yet he felt suddenly awkward doing it. Ten-thirty A.M. The flight to Boston would be boarding soon at gate eleven.

He looked over at gate thirteen. The crowd was still large as well-wishers said good-bye to family and friends who were heading west. The more experienced travelers were making

91

their move to the head of the lines. The first ones to their seats would guarantee a spot in the overhead storage.

"Commuter Flight Six to Boston's Logan International now boarding gate eleven," a different female voice said. It held a pleasant tone, saying don't rush but hurry and get in line.

Brian folded his paper and tucked it into the side pouch of his flight bag. He stood and stretched and looked around again.

It was then he caught her eyes on him. The tall woman with the dark hair in a loose bun standing at the entrance to the airport bar. He recognized her, but from where? As suddenly as she had appeared, she turned and stepped back into the crowded room.

Had she been looking directly at him or merely surveying the array of people or checking if her husband's plane had arrived. His mind was playing tricks, seeing what it was expecting to see. He hadn't noticed if there was a drink in her hand.

He knew he had seen her before. Where? Think! Where had she been? The front of the airport. She had walked past him as he got out of his cab at the curb. Their eyes had met then too.

But there was somewhere else. He had seen her somewhere else. Needles stabbed the base of his brain as he tried to remember. In the hotel lobby maybe. A different dress, her hair down instead of up. Or had he? He wasn't sure.

This is ridiculous, he thought. He was getting paranoid and for no reason. It was the Chinese woman who said he was being followed and that there were microphones in his room. He'd looked, searching every inch of the hotel room, and had found nothing. There was no reason? No one would be following him. It was crazy.

Brian thought about going into the bar, but a second call for the Boston flight came over the loudspeaker along with another for a flight to Dallas.

Lifting his flight bag, he threaded his arm through the

long strap and pulled it onto his left shoulder. He grabbed his briefcase with the same hand and began to walk slowly toward gate eleven.

Tilting his head slightly, he looked again at gate thirteen. Now only a dozen passengers and a steward remained outside the entrance door. The last call for flight twenty-three sounded through the lounge as he passed gate number thirteen and headed toward the commuter flight.

Now the line at gate eleven began to swell. Brian stood near the rear but not quite in line. He was waiting for the doors to open and the initial rush of passengers to their seats.

Gate thirteen was empty except for the steward, who was looking over a clipboard of papers. Brian saw him look at his watch and then at the large plain-faced clock on the airport wall. He pushed his pencil into his breast pocket, grabbed the door's aluminum handle, and tugged on it to release it from the mechanical latch that held it open.

Quickly, Brian turned and walked toward the doorway. "Wait," he said loud enough for the steward to hear but hoping no one else would. "Sorry, I almost got on the wrong plane," Brian said, forcing a laugh.

The steward stopped him just outside the door. "You have a ticket for Flight Twenty-three, sir?" the young man asked, placing himself in the doorway until he could verify the seating.

"Yes, here." Brian pulled his ticket from his coat pocket and handed it to him. He looked back toward the line at gate eleven. It was rapidly thinning. He glanced back toward the bar, looking for the woman's face. But she was nowhere. Still, he wanted desperately to get inside the door and hear it close behind him.

"Oh, here you are, Mr. Bovan. First class, seat twelve near the window." The steward now put on his professional smile. "I have your name down here." He looked at his clipboard. "Yes, Toni, your hostess, has a package for you. I'll tell her you're aboard, sir."

"A package, yes of course, thank you," Brian pushed the

ticket into his pocket. As he stepped through the door, he looked back into the airport lounge but saw no one watching him.

"Are you sure?"

"Positive. He got on board a United flight to Los Angeles," Karen said, humiliated.

"Didn't you make sure he was going to Boston?"

"I did," Karen assured her boss. "I checked the boarding list and he was on it. But he was also on the one to L.A."

"Los Angeles? What the hell is in Los Angeles?" Troy Merith was still in shock. Easy, this was going to be an easy surveillance job, that's what he had said to himself.

"I checked with the United desk. The flight just stops at L.A.X., then it goes on to Honolulu," Karen said.

"Christ." Merith gripped the phone receiver hard. "Has the plane left?" he asked, knowing there was nothing he could do to stop Brian from reaching Honolulu.

"No, but the doors have been closed. He was the last one aboard."

"There's no way you can get on?"

"No!" Karen said angrily, but Merith knew she was mad with herself.

"Okay, pack it up and come home. I'll have to call Los Angeles and have someone hook up with him there," the CIA man said. There was nothing else to be done. His team hadn't failed, the scope of the job had changed on them. They hadn't been tripped, just outrun. Why was Bovan heading for Hawaii? There was little doubt Admiral Tendrey hadn't told him everything. That bothered him, but there was nothing to be done about it.

"Sorry, Troy," Merith heard her say as the phone went dead. Sorry, Admiral, he would say when he called to tell him that he had lost Bovan. Yet somehow he didn't think the old man would understand as well as he did.

* * *

"We almost shut the door on you, Mr. Bovan," the young slender woman said as she showed him to his seat. She was right off an airline advertisement poster. Clear skin, pixie-short blond hair, perfect teeth. Her face said girl-next-door all over it. "I'm Toni and I'll be your hostess through to Honolulu." She smiled that perfect smile.

"Yes, thank you, I . . . I guess I got in the wrong line," Bovan said. He took off his coat and handed it to her. "The man at the door said you had a package for me?"

"It was dropped off at the front counter by your assistant. He said he had forgotten to give you some papers before you left the office. We'll be taking off in a moment but I'll bring them to you as soon as the captain turns off the seat-belt sign."

"Thank you," Brian said, sitting down.

Toni moved to put away his coat in the curtain-covered closet and disappeared behind the counter of the service station.

With a subtle chime, the FASTEN SEATBELT and NO SMOK-ING signs lit up over Brian's head. Looking around he noticed there were only about a dozen passengers filling the forty-two seats in first class. No one looked at anyone else. That was the promise of first class, he guessed, that one need not be bothered by fellow passengers. You could stretch out your feet and lean back as if you were in your favorite leather chair at home.

The huge Boeing 747 swayed up and down gently as it taxied from the terminal to the runway. A comfortable motion to Brian, a familiar motion. Then the four jet engines began to roar as the pilot was cleared by the tower and the airliner lunged toward the end of the long strip of cement.

It lifted, defying gravity, its long silver wings reaching out to the morning clouds as the plane crossed over urban D.C. and headed out toward the Atlantic. With a mechanical rumble, the claws of the bird retracted into its belly. Then the pilot banked north and Brian could see the brown shimmering waters of the Potomac River.

A few minutes later the seatbelt sign went dark and Toni appeared. "Here you are, Mr. Bovan," Toni said, handing him the small white envelope. "Would you like something to drink?"

"Coffee," he said, trying not to stare at the package. His name was scribbled on the front along with the flight and his seat number. The cover flap wasn't sealed, held only by the brass brad spread through a reinforced hole.

Looking around the first-class compartment, he saw Toni in conversation with another of her passengers. She would not appear suddenly beside him and no one else was close enough to look over his shoulder. He poured the package's contents into his lap.

Three thick stacks of American bills slid out. A bundle of hundred-dollar bills, fifty-dollar bills, and twenty-dollar bills, each paper-clipped together. His heart stopped as he pushed them quickly back into the envelope.

There was also a pair of car keys—their G.M. insignia was shiny and new—and a note typed on a single folded piece of paper. He read:

Dear Cmdr. Bovan,

Do not be offended by the contents of the package. It is merely a loan. You were forced to leave D.C. in such a hurry that I assume the necessities of life, such as money for food and hotel accommodations, were forgotten. If you were to pay for anything with one of your credit cards, it would be easily traced. I warn you not to.

The keys are to a white Chevrolet Camaro parked in the furthest corner on the second level of the east parking structure at Honolulu International. License plate number DML 360.

In the trunk of the car is a suitcase with the appropriate clothes and odds and ends of a vacationer traveling to an exotic island. I hope you like my taste in men's clothes.

Your flight to Truk leaves at 6:20 a.m. tomorrow. Relax and enjoy Honolulu while you are there. It is a beautiful city.

Mimi

Brian returned everything to the envelope and pushed it into his briefcase next to his feet. *Relax and enjoy.* What the hell have I gotten into, he wondered. This was all crazy, she was crazy. He squeezed the bridge of his nose with his index finger and thumb. She was crazy and efficient and wasn't wasting any time getting him to Truk.

"Cornic, it's Troy Merith," the CIA man spoke into the phone. He was tired and he knew what he was in for. Ebony Cornic was a by-the-book man. He didn't like Merith's loose tactics, his use of women on high-priority jobs, his east-coast sector, and, most of all, Merith himself.

"Good morning, Troy," Cornic said.

"I need a man from your sector to pick up a target on a flight bound for Honolulu. United Flight Twenty-three arriving at 12:35 your time. He'll have to—"

"Wait a minute, Merith," Cornic cut in. "Where's the clearance for this. You've given me no authorization. I can't just pull a man from my sector and put him on a plane. Who's this for?"

"A friend, an important navy friend, Cornic. This isn't national security. It's just a surveillance job." Anger was creeping up Merith's neck.

"Just a surveillance job which your people screwed up, Merith. I know, I can tell, you wouldn't have called me otherwise. You had a green target and he smelled your people and lost them. I'll bet you even had a skirt working him, didn't you, and she lost him." Cornic laughed. "You'll never learn, you stupid asshole."

Now the anger took hold. "Cornic, I want a man on that

97

plane and I want him glued to that target until I say. Do you hear me?''

"Your sector doesn't reach out here, Merith. You can't make that kind of an order without authorization."

"You're right, Ebony, I can't. But I hold seniority over you, and when I get there you are going to be sorry you ever signed on to the agency. I'm going to have every file your people have worked on in the last twenty years reopened and checked and double-checked and cross-checked. You and your little brown-nosed peons are going to be up to their elbows in paperwork, you son of a bitch."

There was silence on the phone in Los Angeles.

"You know I can do it, Cornic, and I will. Now, do I get a man?" Merith was shaking mad.

"You got a photo and a file?" Cornic's voice was hoarse.

"It will be over the teletex in ten minutes."

"You make me sick, Merith."

"Thank you very much," Merith said in the happiest voice he could muster from the volcano in his chest.

"Stick it."

"Fuck you." Merith slammed down the phone.

The runway at L.A.X. came up to the 747 with a jolt. It was finally a touchdown, after three attempts by the pilot. The city was having its worst storm in seven years, and unknown to the passengers, the tower had suggested the captain try landing at Burbank Airport or Orange County if he couldn't line up the correct runway this time.

He had, and they taxied to the terminal, locked into the walkway, and shut down the engines. The steel skin of the plane glistened in the rain and floodlights of L.A.X.

Brian watched through his window as a string of metal containers were brought next to the plane. Workmen in bright orange raingear moved quickly to unload and reload the cargo. Luggage for passengers arriving, luggage for the passengers leaving. It went on twenty-four hours a day, seven days a week, nonstop at every airport in the world.

As Toni had suggested, Brian remained on the plane. There was nothing, she said, that was worth seeing in the terminal and they were only scheduled to stay for thirty minutes. He wondered if every suitcase would find its way off the plane in half an hour.

"Excuse me," the small stately-looking man said to Brian as he leaned over the seat next to him. "Can you tell me where 51-H is? Nonsmoking, I hope. My lung, I've only got one. I have to be careful, you know." He tapped his chest.

Brian didn't have a chance to say anything before Toni shot out from the service counter. "Can I help you?" she asked. She angled her body to keep him from entering further into the front of the plane, as if he were a drunk entering a plush New York restaurant. She snatched the ticket from his hand. "Your seat is toward the rear of the plane, Mr. Cranken. No, I'm sorry, it's smoking." Brian heard her say as she escorted him through the royal blue curtains that separated first-class with the rest of the plane.

It took three stewardesses to help Lou Cranken find his seat. He would take smoking, it really didn't matter. What did matter was that 51-H was the last row of the plane and a center seat at that.

To him, the rear section of the craft was the worst place to be. It was at the rear gun of a B-26 that he had seen most of the German countryside.

He took out his small notepad and wrote: *Bovan in first class, seat 12. Wearing light brown suit. Black carry-on, brown briefcase.*

The stately-looking man closed the pad and slipped it into his pocket. Then he leaned his chair back as far as it would go, closed his eyes, and let sleep take him.

TWELVE

Pearl Harbor, Hawaii, 1944

It was a full moon veiled in dark clouds that had promised rain and delivered, leaving the highway black and glossy. Douglas Bovan aimed the Packard roadster more to the center of the narrow road than to the right, where the edge dropped away into the sea below.

He shifted the car back down into first as they came to a tight bend. The road climbed steeply as it turned inland. Mimi sat close to him, her left hand resting on the top of his thigh, her perfume filling the interior of the car. The large beams of the headlights lit the thick jungle ahead as the road weaved along the lower valley paralleling the crest of Diamond Head.

"Jesus, where is this place?" Douglas asked finally. They had driven most of the way in silence and he sensed something was bothering her. Yet, he found it awkward to ask her what.

"It shouldn't be much further," Mimi said softly. "There's a gate before you get onto the grounds." She looked at him. His face was only a dim outline in the dashboard lights. "I'm glad you came tonight," she said.

He smiled at her, "I just hope you're not too embarrassed having only a lonely submariner as an escort."

"Are you kidding?" She leaned over and kissed him on the cheek.

It began to rain again, gently at first, then heavier, cutting the distance the headlights reached in half. The trees and hanging vines seemed to close in as if creating a tunnel over the road. When they rounded the last sharp bend, the high iron gate of the estate stood before them. At the top of its elliptical arch, the two shining brass initials, R.C.

Both of the tall black gates were open but the right side was blocked by a military police jeep. Two MPs checked the guests while a third remained in the vehicle.

Douglas edged the car slowly forward as a white Rolls Royce Silver Wraith drove on. He stopped as they reached the guarded entrance.

"Good evening, sir," the MP said as Douglas rolled down the side window a few inches. The rain had turned into a tropical downpour and in the jeep's headlights, the crashing droplets on the MP's helmet gave him an eerie halo. "Do you have your invitation, sir?"

Mimi leaned across Douglas. "Lai Ming, assistant to Ambassador Lee," she said in a voice loud enough for him to hear above the rain that drummed on the convertible top.

"Yes, ma'am." The MP waved them on without hesitating. "Go ahead, please."

"Every time I'm with you, I'm amazed at all the pull you have," Douglas said. He shifted the car into first and drove forward.

Mimi didn't say anything but looked out the window.

The jungle had disappeared. Now thick manicured lawns, trees, and bushes blanketed the grounds. Statues stood along the gravel driveway indifferent to the weather.

At the top of the mile-long driveway was the estate's white-marbled mansion. From every window in the three-story structure glowed an inviting warmth. In front, six sculptured pillars held a vaulted arch over the double doors that were open wide pouring out the brightest welcome from a crystal chandelier.

101

As Douglas pulled up under a canvas tarp that had been put up for arriving guests, he could see several cars parked around the side of the house. A young native boy, dressed in pleated red pants and a red coat stiff with starch, rushed out and opened the door for Mimi, and another came out of nowhere and welcomed Douglas as he stepped from the Packard. With a wide smile of white teeth, the boy slipped into the driver's seat and pulled it around back.

Mimi straightened her silver-white silk dress as Douglas moved next to her. "Remember, you said you wouldn't mind all this," she whispered to him as she laced her arm through his and they headed up the stairs.

"Just head me towards the bar and I'll be fine," he assured her with a wink.

"Promise me something, Douglas," she said in a soft voice.

"What?"

"That after the party, you'll stay with me tonight. No matter what, you'll stay with me," she said, looking up at him, her almond eyes locked onto his.

"Okay," was all he could say. The directness of her request flattered him, but its intensity, the way she asked, was unsettling. It carried the urgency of a frightened child.

As they walked in through the doorway, the roar of the rain on the tarp gave way to the laughter and conversations of the crowd inside. Few people noticed their entry, but of those who did, their eyes locked onto Mimi.

Most knew of the Chinese ambassador and had heard of his assistant, yet few believed she was as beautiful as the rumors said. But seeing her standing on the entrance stoop several steps above them and wearing a beautiful silk dress that accented her long flowing dark hair, they realized how true the talk had been.

From a balcony that overlooked the hall, another set of eyes looked at the new arrivals. They did not, however, focus on Mimi, but on Douglas. And on every movement the formally dressed submarine commander made as he walked through the crowd.

"You are overeager," Ambassador Lee said as he stepped up beside the naval man on the balcony. He followed his stare down to Mimi and her escort. "The evening is only beginning. Let him enjoy first; Mimi will let us know when the time is right."

The man didn't take his eyes away from Douglas but only nodded in agreement. The ambassador patted him on the back as he stepped back into the hallway and moved to join the party.

The man remained there for a while, half hidden, sipping his whiskey and water, and watching. Then he moved downstairs and joined the party.

Douglas suddenly felt Mimi release his arm and turn. Stretching out her arms, she meet the elderly woman head-on as they rushed at each other. "Auntie Mollie!"

"My word. Look at you," Mollie Cabot said as they hugged. "What happen to the skinny little girl with short hair and dirty hands I left in Peking? Look how beautiful you've become. God, where has all the time gone. How are you, my dear?"

"Wonderful, just wonderful," Mimi said. "And you?"

"Fine."

"Where is Uncle Richard?" Mimi asked, looking around the room.

"Somewhere still being a good ambassador and a terrible host like always. He probably has someone cornered in the study. We'll find him later," she said.

Mimi put her arm around her shoulder. "I have someone I want you to meet." Douglas could see her eyes were sparkling as she looked at him. "This is Lieutenant Commander Douglas Bovan. Commander, Mrs. Cabot, wife of the British ambassador."

"How do you do, Commander," Mrs. Cabot said with the remains of a proper English accent. Her hazel eyes were weighing him. A habit from years of being a professional hostess, Douglas thought. "You are lucky to be with such a charming woman tonight," Mrs. Cabot said.

"That, I am realizing more each minute, Mrs. Cabot," Douglas said, smiling at Mimi.

"My husband and I found her working in the basement of the Peking University and sort of adopted her as our own," Mrs. Cabot said. "That was years ago when my husband was the ambassador to China. It was his first overseas assignment and we were fresh from Dublin. It was exciting, I'll tell you," she said.

"They helped me get the job with Ambassador Lee," Mimi said.

"Oh, we did nothing of the sort. We only introduced you to the proper people and got you away from playing with those skeletons."

Douglas laughed. "With dirty hands, huh?"

"Oh, Commander, let me tell you, she was terrible. Always working on something. Even after we left and she had the job with the government, our friends were constantly reporting to us that she was still spending her off time in the country or at the university," Mrs. Cabot confided.

"We don't have to tell him everything," Mimi said.

Mrs. Cabot laughed. "Tell me, Commander, what type of ship are you assigned to?"

"A submarine, ma'am. The U.S.S. *Seakrill*," Douglas said proudly.

"How exciting," she said as she hooked her arm through his. "Come, I have so many people for you to meet." She turned to Mimi, who followed behind them as they walked through the crowd, and said, "Maybe we could find him an aircraft carrier to command. They are much safer."

Mrs. Cabot led Douglas to several groups in the room. She introduced him to captains, commanders, full admirals, rear admirals, and wives. He met statesmen and ambassadors and dozens of liaisons. To his surprise, even the admirals were pleased to see him. The true fighting men, the men with guts, one had said about the submarine corps.

Mimi tagged along, smiling and shaking hands but mostly watching Douglas. As he talked, he would glance over to her and smile. She wondered if he would be smiling later or even talk to her again when the night was over.

"Commander Mills," Mrs. Cabot said, tapping the back of the officer. He was a big man with broad shoulders and short blond hair that was receding high on his forehead. "I would like you to meet Lieutenant Commander Bovan."

Full Commander Thomas Mills turned around, looked at Douglas, and instantly began to laugh. Douglas also began laughing and then the two men wrapped their arms around each other in a bear hug.

"I'll be a son of a bitch," Douglas said. "How the hell are you, Tom?"

"Goddamn, it's been a long time," Mills said, releasing him. "I've been fine, and you?"

"No complaints," Douglas said.

"Well, I guess you two know each other," Mrs. Cabot said.

"We go back a long ways, Mrs. Cabot," Mills said.

Douglas smiled, then he turned to Mimi. "Tom, this is Lai Ming."

Mills reached out and shook her hand. "How did you get mixed up with this scoundrel?" he asked.

"Just lucky," she said with a smile. "How long have you known each other?"

"Oh, since we were what? Nine years old?" Douglas said.

"Since we were old enough to sneak into the theater and watch Clara Bow movies."

Douglas laughed. "That's right, we did, didn't we?"

"Several times." Mills laughed. "I remember you stealing pies from the market for us to eat during the show."

Douglas began to turn red as the two women laughed. Then Mrs. Cabot saved him. "Let's leave these two to their reunion," she said to Mimi. "We'll go find Richard. I know he will be expecting me to take you right to him. If you gentlemen will excuse us."

105

Mills and Douglas nodded.

"I'll just be a few minutes," Mimi promised. "Commander, it was nice to meet you."

"My pleasure, Miss Ming," Mills said, and Douglas winked at her as she moved away.

"You haven't changed, have you, Doug?" Mills said as he watched Mimi weave her way through the guests. "Still playing the field, and with some Jap."

"She's Chinese," Douglas said flatly.

"Same thing," Mills stopped a butler and lifted a champagne glass. He offered one to Douglas but it was refused. "How's Catherine?"

Douglas looked at his friend. "Fine. She was here over Christmas."

"Nothing resolved?"

"No."

"How's the war treating you, anyway?" Mills changed the subject.

"Just doing the job same as every stupid son of a bitch out here. I thought you were in the Atlantic."

"The Brits are doing a pretty good job now. So a lot of us got shipped over here to paradise," Mills said as he sipped his drink. "It'll be over soon, I figure."

"Yeah," Douglas agreed. "So where are you assigned?"

"Nowhere yet, I just got in yesterday. But I should know soon, or so they say. What sub you on?"

"The *Seakrill*, she's a fleet boat. Has gotten us out of some pretty tight spots and held together. At least so far," Douglas said.

"Commander Bovan," a heavyset man said in a high voice as he moved past a circle of women and toward Douglas and Mills. "Commander?"

Douglas looked up and saw the man was a full captain. "Yes, sir," he said, and as the man approached both Mills's and his postures stiffened.

"None of that here, gentlemen," the captain said, shaking their hands. "I'm Captain Yates. I heard someone

106

mention that you were here tonight, Commander Bovan, and I wanted to come over and thank you."

"Thank me, sir?"

"You picked up a pilot off Dead Man's Atoll in November," Yates said. "He's my son-in-law, and thanks to you and your crew, he's back in the States."

"There's no thanks needed, sir. But I'm sure my crew will be glad to hear that he is doing all right," Douglas said. He felt Mimi thread her arm through his as she stepped up beside him.

"Well, I just wanted to thank you personally. Believe me, my daughter couldn't be happier," Yates said. "Perhaps we can talk again later," he said with a smile, and turned and melted back into the party.

Mimi squeezed Douglas's arm, "That was nice of him," she said.

"Sounds like you're on your way to making admiral, Doug," Mills joked.

"Douglas, I have someone that wants to speak with you," Mimi said softly. "Commander, I hope you don't mind."

"Not at all," Mills said. "I should be mingling anyway. Maybe I'll find my commanding-officer-to-be. But, Doug, when are you sailing again?"

"Late tomorrow, possible the day after. We've still got repairs, why?"

"Maybe we can get together for a drink," Mills said, patting Douglas on the back. "I'll look for you at the docks."

Douglas nodded, then turned and followed Mimi. "Who do you have for me to parade in front of now?"

"Ambassador Lee has something he wants to discuss with you, Douglas," Mimi said.

Douglas suddenly realized she wasn't smiling, and wondered if it was something he had said. She led him out of the main room, through the dining room and study, and into a hallway that went to the rear of the mansion.

As they passed through the house, several people greeted Mimi but she only nodded politely.

"What's the matter?" Douglas asked, but she didn't answer. They entered the estate's library, and as he looked and saw the two men in the room, he understood. "What the . . . ?" he began to say, stopping just inside the door.

Mimi could feel the muscles in his arm tense. They had told her he might be upset but she hadn't expected this.

"A bit surprised, Doug?" Rear Admiral Tendrey said in his slow Southern drawl. He was a tall man with narrow shoulders and narrow hips and thin, almost feminine hands and fingers. His brown hair was razor-cut short and he had cut off his mustache since they had last met.

"Yes, sir," Douglas said, but it was clear he had not intended it to sound respectful.

"No need for formalities here, Doug. This is a social occasion," Tendrey said as he lit a Lucky Strike. "I don't think you've met Ambassador Lee."

Douglas focused on the second man. He was a compact, heavy man with thin jet-black hair, and he looked at Douglas with a wide grin. "How do you do, Commander Bovan. I have been looking forward to meeting you," he said as he lifted himself off the couch.

"Care for a drink?" Tendrey said, walking to the small bar off to the side of the room.

"No, sir," Douglas said. He felt Mimi leave his side, and out of the corner of his eye, he watched her walk to one of the large windows that overlooked the garden. It was still raining.

"Oh, get off the 'sir' crap and unbutton the uniform, Doug. We have real business to discuss here," he said. "You and I may not have seen eye to eye in the past, but we are on the same side."

"Are we, Admiral? Sell any faulty torpedos to the navy lately or are you saving them for the Brits?"

Tendrey looked hard at Douglas. His associations with U.S. contractors who had developed the Americans' defective torpedo exploders had caused him a lot of public embarrassment. But it had cost the U.S. Navy a lot of lives.

The ambassador laughed again. "It seems that I was wrong Admiral. Commander Bovan may be perfect for this."

"For what?" Douglas asked harshly. He had not walked further into the room, and the thought of turning and leaving kept coming to him.

Tendrey looked over at the ambassador and nodded. Lee's smile broadened.

"Well, Doug," Tendrey said. "I've got a proposition for you. Or, I should say, we have one. Interested?"

Douglas looked over at Mimi. She glanced at him, then turned away again. "No," he said.

"You won't hear me out, huh? And I thought you were such a gambler," Tendrey said as he moved around and sat in one of the thick-cut-velvet chairs. Then in a flat, serious voice, "It's worth a quarter of a million dollars to you, Doug."

"I said no, Admiral. I know the kind of friends you keep. Or keep you," Douglas said. He turned and began to walk out the door.

Mimi quickly crossed the room and grab his sleeve. "Please, Douglas, just hear him out. For me."

"For you? You're nothing more than the bait that got me here."

"Please, Douglas. Please."

Douglas looked at her for a moment. Tears formed on the edges of her eyes. He wondered if they were real. "Okay, Admiral," he said, stepping forcibly past her and back into the library. "I'm listening, but that's all I'm doing."

"Wise decision, Doug," Tendrey said. "I would hate to have headquarters find out about your gambling. It's not in your jacket yet, but it could be."

"I said, I'm listening," Douglas repeated.

"It is actually quite simple. The ambassador needs you

to make a delivery and a pickup," Tendrey said with a smile, but his eyes remained hard.

"You need the submarine," Douglas said, looking at Lee. The ambassador nodded. "To bring back two small crates."

"What's in the crates?"

"Fossils, Commander," Lee said flatly. "Fossils of the Peking Man found in the mountains near Choukoutien."

"If you remember, we're at war with the Japanese," Douglas said, his tone hard and direct. He wanted to leave, and leave alone.

"This is not between governments, Commander," Lee said as he stood and walked slowly around the back of the chair Tendrey sat in. "It is the greed of a few men. And greed knows no borders or philosophies. They care nothing about the importance of these national treasures. They are only interested in how much money we are willing to pay. It is their greed that has given us the opportunity to get back the Peking Man. And that, Commander Bovan, is the only thing that matters here."

"Let me get this straight. You need a sub to make the switch. But what's the price?" Douglas asked. He moved around and sat in a chair opposite Tendrey. "What do they want for your precious fossils?"

"Five million in diamonds," Tendrey said.

Unintentionally, Douglas's eyebrows rose. "A lot of money," he said. "What keeps them from blowing me out of the water once they get their money? Honor among thieves?"

"Not quite," Tendrey said. "The crates will be booby-trapped. As will the ones carrying the fossils."

"You want to give me a quarter of a mill for this?" Douglas asked. His face hardened. "What's the rest of it, Admiral?"

"The Japanese freighter you are to rendezvous with will be in enemy waters," Mimi said as she walked over to the bar and poured herself a glass of gin from the opened bottle.

Douglas leaned forward, "Where?"

"Truk," she said without turning around. "Truk Lagoon in the Carolines."

"The Gibralter of the Pacific?" Douglas laughed out loud. "You're all fucking crazy. You want me to take my submarine into Truk for some old bones? Do you realize how many mines and antisubmarine nets there are around Truk?"

"Come on, Doug. You like to gamble. This time it's all or nothing. You make it and no more debts." Tendrey said with a smile.

"A chance to get my ass blown out of the water. How can I pass it up?" Douglas said sarcastically. He stood up. "No thanks."

"Perhaps you don't understand, Commander," Lee said in a monotone. "To what extremes would you go to retrieve your country's Liberty Bell or the Declaration of Independence? Are they just a simple piece of paper or a large casting of metal? Hardly."

Douglas stared at Lee; the ambassador had hit him precisely where he had planned. A philosophical nerve that every human seemed to have intertwined with other undefinable emotions. He made his point clear. "Those are American, not Chinese," Douglas defended.

"But you do understand their importance?"

Douglas nodded.

"It will work," Mimi said. "We've figured it out, Douglas, and it will work. The Japanese have given us a chart that shows an unknown pass in the reef. You'll be able to get into the lagoon undetected."

"You see, Commander," Lee said. "This plan will be carried out. Like you, we have our duties to our government."

"Well then, you'll just have to find another submarine," Douglas said as he turned and looked at Tendrey. "This is one suicide mission you're not going to send eighty men to the bottom on."

"How much is it, Doug? $100,000? I think that's what your gambling partners at the ranch said. It's going to look pretty bad on your records, a debt like that. When the war ends, the navy is going to kick you out of the service so fast you'll think you were shot out of a gun," Tendrey said.

Douglas stopped at the door but didn't turn around.

"Think about it, Commander. We will be in touch with you tomorrow," Lee called out.

"Don't bother," Douglas said as he walked from the room.

"Son of a bitch," Tendrey said, slamming his fist into the arm of the chair.

"He has little choice if he believes you will report him," Lee said, turning back to Tendrey. Then he looked at his assistant. "Well, go with him," he said.

She almost dropped her glass onto the bar as she dashed out the door after him.

Douglas walked down the hallway and out into the main room. The party was beginning to empty, and for the first time he looked at his watch. It was almost midnight. He looked quickly around the room for Mills but didn't see him. Then he saw Yates at the front door.

"Captain," he called out.

Yates turned and smiled.

"Are you heading back to the base, sir?" Douglas asked as he stepped next to him.

"I thought you had come with that young woman?" he said as they walked out of the house.

"I did, sir," Douglas said but added nothing.

"Oh," Yates said, understanding. "I can give you a ride back, Commander," he said, patting Douglas on the back. "It's the least I can do."

Mimi stood on her toes trying to scan the room. She had seen Douglas turn the corner but lost him from there.

"Miss Ming," Mills stepped up next to her. "Are you looking for Doug?"

"Did you see where he went?"

"Well, I saw him for a moment. I think he was heading out the front door," Mills told her.

Mimi didn't waste time thanking him, she walked quickly toward the front door. The crowd at the threshold were saying their last good-byes and thanking their hosts. Mimi had to push her way through. Outside, she saw Douglas climb into an olive-green Chevrolet sedan as it pulled away.

THIRTEEN

Kaimu, Hawaii, 1986

Admiral Tendrey pulled himself out of the rear seat of the blue limousine, refusing any help from either his nurse or chauffeur. "I'll do it, I'll do it," he said, slapping the chauffeur's large hand as he guided Tendrey by the arm and into the wheelchair held by Miss Swanson.

The admiral was mad today. Mad at the world. On such days his employees knew better than to linger near him too long. They each wanted to go about their business on the opposite side of the estate.

He was justified in his anger as he returned from an overnight physical at the naval hospital. The doctors had not given him good news. Among his ailments of age, his sight was deteriorating at rapid rate.

"Quacks!" Tendrey had roared. "Fucking quacks. You call yourselves experts? You're all a bunch of fucking quacks." He had continued to yell as Miss Swanson rolled him down the halls and out of the hospital and into the limousine. Then he sat quietly in the back of the car mumbling to himself as they drove back to the estate.

"Admiral." His male secretary, John Marks, a handsome young man with chiseled features wearing an off-white suit, met him and Miss Swanson in the main entry hall. "I've got two messages from your private line. Neither of them left their names. One left a number and the other said he would call back."

"Push me into my study," he said to his secretary while dismissing Miss Swanson with a wave of his hand.

The nurse hesitated to relinquish the wheelchair to Marks knowing what the doctors had said. The admiral would need her, she thought. But the hard look from the secretary told her to move away. They had business to take care of, important business. Miss Swanson turned and walked briskly toward the kitchen, settling on making sure his lunch would be on time and in perfect order.

"Do the honors," Tendrey said as Marks shut the polished redwood doors of the study and locked the brass bolt.

"You know she'll kill me if she ever finds out," he said as he moved to the high bookshelf, stood on the tips of his feet, and reached the very top shelf. Pushing a copy of Thackeray's *Vanity Fair* out of the way, he found the tiny skeleton key where he had left it. Then he walked over to the small antique chest on the far table.

"Screw Miss Swanson," the admiral said, watching his secretary with anticipation.

"I thought you were," he joked.

Tendrey laughed, and then in a soft voice, a tone darkened by what the doctors had said, "Things were better before. The whole world was better before."

"The good old days, Admiral. The best days," the secretary agreed as he opened the chest and pulled out the half-full bottle of scotch. "Water? On the rocks?"

"Ice, but top off the glass," Tendrey said, rolling around to the back of his desk. "What were those messages you had."

The secretary pulled two scraps of paper from his pocket as he set the scotch in front of the admiral. "The first was at 0600 hours this morning. The caller left this number for you to reach him. I told him it wouldn't be until around noon. The second one was only a little while ago at 1100 hours." He looked at the second paper. "He didn't leave a name or a number but said he would call back." The secretary handed the two pieces of paper to the Admiral.

Tendrey looked at the number that he knew would link him with Washington. "Damn. Is this a three or an eight?"

"An eight, sir."

"Okay, that's all for now. Be sure you put the key back. We wouldn't want Miss Swanson to find out what you've been forcing me to drink," Tendrey said.

The secretary laughed. "No, sir." He returned the bottle to the chest and hid the key. "Anything else?"

"No," Tendrey said as he reached for the phone and dialed. There was the usual clicks of computer links as the line was connected through. Then it rang.

"Red Coats Bar, may I help you," the woman's voice cheered through the receiver.

"Merith," Tendrey said.

Karen looked over at her boss, who was stretched out on the couch of the hotel room, his coat rolled up into an extra pillow under his head. "Troy. It's him," she said, handing Merith the phone.

"Good day, Admiral," he said.

"Not so far. What do you have to report, Troy?"

Merith took a deep breath. "It's not good. We lost Bovan at the Washington airport. He was scheduled for a commuter flight back to Boston and his car is still at the Boston airport. I figured my people were simply going to follow him back to his mother's house. But then, at the last minute, he slipped aboard another plane. From his actions, I'd say someone tipped him he was being tailed. It's the only explanation."

"There was no way he could have simply seen your people?" Tendrey asked, his voice calm.

"No, Admiral."

"What plane did he get on?"

Merith swallowed again. "A connecting flight to Honolulu."

There was silence over the phone that lasted several minutes. Finally Tendrey asked, "What have you done since?"

"I called Los Angeles sector and had them put a man on the plane to follow him. I wasn't sure if you wanted me to fly out there or—"

"No, that won't be necessary," Tendrey said quickly, realizing the CIA man was acting on instinct. He knew Tendrey lived in Hawaii and he had been asked to follow an ex-navy commander who had suddenly boarded a plane heading to the same place. It was instinct, pure and simple gut feelings. Merith couldn't possible know why Bovan was heading to the islands.

But Tendrey did. It was all too clear. The young commander was on his way to the lagoon. "I'll have some of my own people here tag him. Maybe it's better. What time is his flight supposed to arrive?"

"Three forty-five your time," Merith said. "But that's not all, Admiral."

" "What else?"

"During our surveillance of Bovan's hotel in D.C., we picked up on a conversation between him and a messenger. A yeoman from Admiral Thomas Mills's office. He gave some sort of documents to Bovan, which the commander looked over in his room. This Mills is a close family friend of Bovan's and he's the one Bovan went to speak with after being refused to see his navy records," Merith said.

"Does Bovan still have the package?"

"No. He returned it to the messenger after about an hour, Admiral."

"Thank you, Troy," Tendrey said. He was trying to think. First things first. He had to remove the CIA tail from Bovan. Tendrey only planned to use his connections with the agency for surveillance of young Bovan, but now the CIA was becoming involved and that was the last thing he wanted. "Give me the rundown on this man from the Los Angeles sector."

Troy Merith went through the standard procedure of passing a job from one sector to another. He gave the admiral the numbers and the names of the Los Angeles people, the description of the man on the plane, and how he was directed to contact the next sector if a new agent was needed to take over the target.

"Okay, Troy," Tendrey said without anger. "Thank you for your trouble. I'll be in touch."

"Admiral, I'm sorry," Merith said, but the phone line was already dead. There was a pit in his stomach. He had failed, failed miserably, and he knew it.

Tendrey looked at the round-faced ship's clock in its brass case that hung on the wall of his study. It was 1144 hours. Three hours, three fucking hours. He lifted his glass and took a long drink.

He knew who had phoned earlier and not left a name. He never left his name or a number. Tendrey wondered if he would still be in his Pentagon office. He dialed the private line. It was fifteen minutes to five in D.C. No reason his old friend wouldn't be there.

On the sixth ring he answered, "Hello."

"You phoned," Tendrey said, flatly.

"Joe, I figured you'd return my call. Your secretary said you were at the doctor's. I hope everything is in order," said the voice from Washington.

"They don't know their head from their rectums. Why did you call?"

"I've got bad news."

"I've got worse," Tendrey said. "What is it you found out?"

"My friend in San Francisco, Saltman, he phoned me this morning. His people found the Yokamata girl. The computers picked up a credit card charge in Waikiki. It was at some small store, so they weren't able to pinpoint where she is staying, but Saltman said they would work on it.''

Tendrey was stunned. ''How come they didn't find her before now? She had to have reservations on a plane out of New York.''

''He doesn't know. He thinks she may be using another name.''

''Why?'' Tendrey asked. It was inconceivable to the admiral that anyone could get from New York to Hawaii without signing their name to a credit card receipt and therefore be instantly traced on the vast network of the world's financial computers.

''Saltman said it could be the fear of publicity. She is a celebrity of sorts. Maybe she wanted a nice quiet vacation.''

''I would almost find reassurance in that if it wasn't for what I learned two minutes ago,'' Tendrey said. He took a slow drink of scotch. ''Young Bovan is on his way to Honolulu.''

''What? How could you know that?'' There was shock in the voice from Washington.

''He's been under surveillance since the day after his mother's funeral. Sometimes, my friend, the old instincts still work,'' Tendrey said. Those doctors were fools; he was still as sharp as ever.

''I don't believe it.''

''Believe it. His flight arrives this afternoon. I had a hunch he wouldn't just leave the past alone. He is as stubborn as his father,'' Tendrey said, remembering.

''He's going to Truk,'' the voice said in exasperation.

''I know. I was also told he was given a package at his hotel.'' There was a long pause on the other end of the line. ''My guess,'' Tendrey continued, ''is that it was his father's navy files.''

The line from D.C. remained silent.

''They're fuel to the fire now,'' Tendrey said. ''And the girl must be on her way to the lagoon also.''

''Do you think she knows anything?''

119

"It's a possibility," Tendrey admitted. "Her father could have told her everything as far as I know."

"Are you positive she's going?"

"No, but I've never believed in coincidence." The admiral snorted a laugh. "And I don't plan on starting this late in life. They've got to be heading to Truk and I don't think their timing is entirely of their own doing."

"What are you saying?"

"It's the woman," the admiral said softly.

"What woman?"

"The Chinese," Tendrey said.

"Ming? It couldn't be. She's dead."

"Then explain the woman at the funeral who gave him the book. It's the only explanation. Things are falling too perfectly into place for young Bovan. My people told me that when he got on the plane for the islands, it was as if he knew he was being followed. It has to be her. No one else knows. She must be helping him, and that means he is probably already booked on a flight to Truk," Tendrey said, staring across his room. "Get out here. Take the first plane out of D.C. and get to Honolulu."

"You're right. We have to stop him. It's starting to unravel, Joe, after forty years," said the voice from Washington.

"No. We just have to cut off the last loose ends. But get out here, or he will have to be stopped at Truk," Tendrey said, not hearing anything from the other end of the line. Then he heard Washington hang up.

Rising from his desk, the navy man in the Pentagon lifted the crystal decanter and poured himself three fingers of whiskey and split the amount with water. Then he returned to his desk and leaned back in the high leather chair.

Sipping his drink, he wondered if he could get to Honolulu before Brian, and then, what he was going to say to him if he did.

120

FOURTEEN

Honolulu, Hawaii, 1986

The plane banked gently to the left as it prepared to land at its final destination. It dropped down out of the dome of clear blue sky, leveled, and headed toward Honolulu International Airport. Brian was asleep during approach, but the touch of the tires onto the runway and the reversing thrust of the jet engines woke him.

Unlike the 747's landing, his awakening was abrupt and harsh. He was sweating, his forehead wet, his hands cold and shaking. The pilot, without knowing it, had pulled him back to the living.

Within restless sleep, he had found himself entombed in a small steel room, an aft cabin of a sinking ship, its hatchway blocked by twisted broken metal and a rising sea. As the water continued to come in, he was forced to climb to the highest corner of the cabin. He could feel the ship roll to one side as she slipped from the surface.

There was silence in the room, cold unearthly silence, as the water slowly rose until Brian had to wedge his upturned face into a small crevice of the tilting wall and take his last breath. Then the plane's wheels touched down and he awoke.

"Mr. Bovan." Toni appeared on his left with his coat.

121

"We'll be at the gate momentarily. I hope you enjoyed your flight and will be flying with us again."

Brian took a second to answer. "Yes, thank you," he said automatically, the same words a waitress would receive catching a diner rising from his table.

His mind was still clouded with the image, his nerves still tense with the fear that the dream evoked. Letting his head drop back against the set, Brian took several deep breaths to relax. As the plane stopped and the boarding gate was connected, he stood and merged with the crowd of vacationers and honeymooners as they exited through the oval hatchway.

Using the restroom at the front of the plane and remaining there moments before landing, Cranken exited the plane at the same time as his target. It was a simple matter for the CIA man from Los Angeles, that is, if his timing was right and he entered after the stewardess checked the tiny rooms. Otherwise he would have been trapped behind some three hundred passengers moving slowly down the two aisles.

He was either very sure of himself or very foolish, Cranken figured as he stepped behind Brian. His target never once looked around the plane or around the airport as he walked through the open-air terminal.

Cranken paced him, staying twenty feet back and to Brian's right. A man will usually look toward his left first and then to his right, Cranken had discovered after so many years in the agency. Unless he was a Britisher, an Aussie, or someone from Hong Kong. They always look to their right first. A habit acquired from watching for cars as they crossed the street as children, he guessed.

But his target did neither as he walked directly out of the airport's main doors. Cranken reached into his pocket wondering how much cash it was going to take to persuade a Hawaiian taxi driver to follow Bovan's taxi.

* * *

The heat and humidity of beautiful Hawaii hit Brian like a wool blanket as he walked along the sidewalk. He took off his coat and wrapped it through the strap of his shoulder bag.

Then he crossed the thruway at the signal and moved toward the east parking structure unaware of the stately looking man cutting quickly across the street behind him.

It was just where the note promised. The white Camaro sat in the furthest parking space on the second floor. Brian took out the set of keys from his pocket. Moving to the trunk, he slipped the round one into the lock and began to turn it. But he hesitated. Someone was watching him, he could feel it. He spun around.

The man from the plane. The one with the one lung who had come into first class looking for his seat. Their eyes met for only a fraction of a second, then the man made as if he was going to get into the car he was next to. Brian stared at him, somehow hoping he would produce a set of keys from his pocket and get into the vehicle and drive away.

But he didn't. He turned, looked up at Brian again, and then began toward the stairway of the parking structure. Had he forgotten his keys, lost them on the plane or in the airport? The possibilities raced through Brian's head. No, there was no disgust in his face, no anger. Only shock at being discovered.

Brian removed the key from the trunk without opening it and unlatched the driver's door, tossed his flight bag into the back and his briefcase on the passenger's seat, and got in. The eight cylinders started with the first turn of the key.

Cranken didn't panic, he never panicked, but he was surprised. He had been seen, he should have expected it and didn't. He would be reprimanded for that mistake. But now he had to keep walking as if he had forgotten something.

He reached the stairway of the parking structure as the engine of the Camaro started and its tires squealed in reverse. Then Cranken raced down the stairs, dropping two steps at a time.

I might still be able to catch him before he can pay the parking bill, Cranken thought. DML 380, DML 380. He kept repeating the license plate of the late-model white Chevy Camaro, etching it into his brain. When he hit the street, he ran as fast as he could back to the line of taxicabs that waited for hotel-bound passengers arriving in paradise.

Two sets of expressionless eyes watched from inside the dark Cadillac as the CIA man dashed across the street and hopped into the first taxi he could find. They simply watched, uncaring as the taxi edged its way away from the curb and moved into the traffic.

The rear door of the Cadillac swung open and another man slipped into the backseat. Like the other two in the car, he was dressed in light-colored slacks and a colorful Hawaiian-print shirt. "Here," he said, handing a small piece of paper to the man in the front passenger seat. "Phone Marks and give him this number. Tell him we'll take care of the tail."

The man looked at the license number of the white Camaro and nodded. He opened the door and stepped out of the car. When the door slammed, the driver pulled onto the thruway and homed in on the taxi that was still in sight.

It was crazy, all of it, crazy, Brian thought as he drove along Nimitz Highway toward Waikiki. He was being followed. Actually followed, and now there was little doubt to what the Chinese woman had said. But by who and why? Suddenly he wondered if he was only being followed or if they were trying to stop him. If that's what they were doing, he hadn't given them the chance. Without realizing it he had slipped them in Washington and now in Honolulu.

He looked in the rearview mirror. There were dozens of cars behind him, half of which were taxis coming from the airport. The man in the parking structure could be in any one of them. Brian saw the turnoff for Highway 66 and took it. It was a small state roadway that led away from Waikiki.

Now the number of cars running along behind him had dropped considerably. But there were still several taxis. Brian looked ahead. A slow-moving truck, its bed full with boxes of fresh pineapples, was in the right lane just about to pass the turnoff for Pukoloa Street.

The Camaro jumped forward as Brian pushed the accelerator to the floor. He edged past the hood of the truck and cut the wheel hard to the right. The car swerved in front of the truck and across the lane, its rear tires catching the low curb at the edge of the offramp and sending the Camaro skidding sideways.

Keeping his foot on the accelerator, Brian turned the steering wheel into the slide. The Camaro straightened as it headed down the ramp.

"Son of a bitch," Cranken hollered as he saw the Camaro cut past the truck and off the highway.

"Ha, mon, that haole is nuts," the taxicab driver said as he manuvered his cab around the skidding truck.

"Go back, you're going to lose him," Cranken said, looking out the rear window and catching only a last glimpse of Brian's car.

"I can't turn around for another mile or so, mon," the driver said, shaking his head.

"I'll give you another twenty bucks," Cranken said.

"No way, mon. Twenty bucks not going to put in a new street. I'm already on driving probation, mon, too much okolehau, you know."

"Goddamnit!" the CIA man said. "All right then, find

125

me a phone somewhere." He had no choice now, he had to call the local sector and tell them what had happened. They would be able to pick the car up easily enough using their police and local connections. It would only be a matter of time.

The taxi pulled off the main highway and stopped at a gas station. The pay phone was outside and around the back. Cranken found it and dialed the agency's Honolulu number and waited for it to ring.

"Take off," the man in the Hawaiian-print shirt said to the taxicab driver.

"Ha, mon, he told me to wait," the cab driver said looking up, but the face of the man was hidden by the roof of the car.

"I said, take off," the man repeated as he pushed a hundred-dollar bill through the window.

"Okay, mon, okay." The taxi driver said, taking the money. He started the engine of his car and pulled away from the gas station.

Cranken leaned deep into the small phone booth, trying to find as much shade as possible. The late afternoon sun was burning into the back of his neck. Clearance from Los Angeles was taking minutes when it should have been seconds. The relaxed pace of this tropical paradise even reached into its CIA headquarters. Cranken impatiently switched the receiver from his right hand to his left.

"Excuse me," said the voice from behind him.

Cranken had heard that voice a dozen times. A voice that always came to him from behind, from a dark shadow in Nice, a hallway in Moscow, a crowded train in Tokyo. It was the same tone from the same type of man. A deadly man, and he was behind Cranken again. The CIA man smiled as he reached for his small automatic in his waistband.

Cranken had not mistaken the voice, he was right. It was the voice of a killer, a professional. The dark Cadillac pulled

126

out onto the highway, leaving the CIA man's body slumped in the phone booth, its receiver dangling above it.

Brian leaned against the low wall made of thousands of hard volcanic rocks. Below him the blue waters of Hanauma Bay sparkled as a handful of snorkel divers explored the bay's underwater reefs. They were the last, the stragglers trying to stretch out every hour of every vacation day, refusing to yield to the setting sun. The others who had swarmed over Hanauma had gone back to their hotels, giving up Hawaii's sea life for its night life.

It was now past seven o'clock. For more than two hours, Brian had driven around Honolulu. Through its back streets and along the highways. Stopping and backtracking every now and then, trying to see if he was still being followed. He didn't pull over until he was sure he wasn't. But he knew it wouldn't be long before they would spot him again. The man from the plane had seen him drive away and had undoubtedly gotten his license number.

Why was all this happening. The people following him must know he was heading for Truk Lagoon. Why would they want to stop him from going? Or were they simply afraid of what he might find?

He was thinking, desperately trying to analyze the facts and line them up with the possibilities. It was a mental test, like so many he had performed as executive officer on the *John Adams,* each designed to build and refine the abilities of a submarine commander to function under stress. The stress that would accompany the potential fact that the submarine could be the country's last military strike force during a nuclear conflict.

During every evaluation and practice, the commander had to know each detail. For a missile launch, he had to know the surface conditions, weather patterns, his ship's depth, speed, angle. For a torpedo attack, the type of vessel that was in his scope, its speed and course. Dozens of precise facts had to be weighed before any order could be given.

And there was always that unknown factor. The one thing that held success at an arm's length. Was the membrane of the launch tube intact, was there an enemy submarine out there with her forward torpedo tubes in line amidship? "That is something you never know until the smoke clears," MacFife had told him.

Right now the smoke was thick in Brian's mind. Too many things were unclear. If the people after him wanted the diamonds or the fossils or both, killing him would be the simplest and quickest way to keep him from Truk. He had no idea what the present worth was of diamonds valued at five million dollars in 1944. But he was sure the promise of such wealth could make men dangerous.

Yet all Brian wanted were the *Seakrill*'s patrol orders. He had been skeptical about everything Mimi had said. But now it seemed unbelievably true.

Brian looked out at the bay. The water near shore was darkening as the sun began to fall behind the hills, their long shadows stretching towards the horizon. Two bronze-skin teenagers, with beach towels around their necks and masks and fins in their hands, walked up the steep trail from the beach to the parking lot. They gave him a once-over glance as they passed by him and moved to their rented jeep.

For the first time he remembered he was still wearing the same wrinkled brown suit he had worn in D.C. He rubbed his chin and felt the oncoming beard. He was a man in an overcoat in the middle of a desert. Out of place. After getting rid of the Camaro, clothes would be next on his agenda. Then he remembered Mimi's note.

Brian walked back to where he had parked the car at the far end of the lot away from the main highway. Slipping the key into the trunk lock, he opened it and found what Mimi had promised. There was a set of two burgundy suitcases and a matching carry-on shoulder bag. The two cases were full of clothes for different occasions. Mimi had thought of everything, from bathing suits to a black tuxedo. The small carry-on was empty, suggesting Brian get rid of his and put its contents into the new one.

As he removed his things from both his briefcase and his flight bag, he found an envelope in the side pocket of the shoulder bag. Brian opened it and found another note and a Continental airline ticket.

Dear Commander Bovan,

Isn't Hawaii beautiful. I wish I could be there with you but, of course, I cannot.

The ticket is for your flight to Truk Lagoon. Notice the name is not yours. Brian Bovan is scheduled for the flight the following day. This may or may not buy you 24 hours.

I have to stress to you again the importance of remaining unfound in Honolulu.

Mimi

The letter was simple and to the point. Here is the means, the way is for you to find. Brian wondered if she really had any idea how important it was for him to hide. He did, and the first order was to get rid of the car and then to find somewhere to shower, shave, and change.

Looking through one of the suitcases, he pulled out a pair of light brown cotton pants, a white shirt, socks, and a pair of casual shoes. They were deck shoes, the kind wealthy sailors buy for walking around their forever-anchored yachts. Somehow, he knew they would fit.

After putting the new set of clothes into his flight bag, Brian returned the suitcases and shoulder bag to the trunk. Before closing the lid, he took several hundred dollars from the money Mimi had given him and shoved part of it in his wallet and some in his front pocket.

Then he got behind the wheel, pulled out on the highway,

and headed toward Honolulu. As the road began to head down from Diamond Head and into the city, it was as if the island and sky had switched places. The lights from Honolulu shone like a million stars.

It was what the Chinese woman said: Hawaii was beautiful. A sparkling green jewel on a velvet blue blanket. A corner of the world where everything was designed and dedicated to the visitor. Everything convenient, every corner holding a street sign to show an island full of tourists how to get to shopping malls and museums, to the mountains and to the beach. It was all planned and laid out.

It all made it easy for Brian to decide where he was heading. He pulled into the first hotel on Waikiki that had a large parking structure.

Being unfound, as Mimi had put it, was not the same as hiding. What better place for someone to lose himself, Brian had decided, than with thousands of others who were arriving from the mainland with the sole purpose of getting away from it all. He laughed at the irony.

Brian parked on the third floor of the structure of the Pacific Beach Hotel. The lot was crowded but not full. It would do. If the people who had followed him to Hawaii were looking for the car, it would take them days to find it here.

Taking only his old shoulder bag, Brian walked down the stairs and into the spacious main lobby. Passing the two-story aquarium with its huge view windows, he moved to the front desk, his story already in mind.

"May I help you, sir?" the balding Hawaiian asked with a pleasant smile.

"Yes, I need a room for two days. My wife will be coming in then," Brian said.

"You don't have reservations?" the clerk asked with a raised eyebrow. "I don't think we have anything available."

"Are you sure? The trip was last-minute. You know how the import-export business can be. I never know where they are going to send me. Actually, I usually cover our European markets.''

"Oh?''

"This is the first time I've ever been here. Kind of a promotion, I guess. The board has given me the Pacific and the Orient.'' Brian said with a smile. "I'll have to start finding a permanent hotel suite to rent. Better than having an apartment. No worries with a hotel room.''

"What kind of export business?'' the clerk ventured to ask.

"Jewelry, mostly diamonds from Africa, sometimes gems from India. Big market in the Pacific and Orient, they say, just waiting to be tapped. I'll probably be flying out here five or six times a month.''

"That often?'' The clerk looked again at his computerized register. "Maybe I do have something. It is kind of small, but you say your wife is coming in day after tomorrow?''

"Morning flight.'' Brian nodded and smiled. The clerk had taken the bait.

"Well, I'm sure we will be able to move you into one of our suites by the time your wife arrives. You know, we do rent a few selected suites out to steady clients,'' he said, taking out a new register form and setting it in front of Brian.

"Do you? Perhaps I could speak with your manager tomorrow. Maybe I won't have to go running all over the island after all. What was your name again?''

"Daniel, sir.''

"Well, thank you, Daniel. You've been more than helpful,'' Brian said, taking out three hundred dollars from his wallet. "I'll pay for the two nights now, and when my wife arrives we'll see how long she wants to stay. You know how women are, she will probably have the stores in Waikiki bought out in a week.'' Brian laughed.

Daniel forced a polite smile. "Room 535, Mr. Walter,''

he said, looking at the register form Brian had signed. "I'll call a porter for your bags."

"Thank you, but unfortunately that won't be necessary. The airline lost my luggage," Brian said with a shrug as he took the key from Daniel's hand. "It happens so often flying through Heathrow, I've gotten used to it. Now I keep at least one set of clean clothes with me all the time." He patted his shoulder bag and moved to the elevator.

The room was anything but small. It had a living room with a separate bedroom, a large double bed, and a bathroom with both a shower and a tub. Brian made use of the shower.

He stood there, his arms spread out pressed against the ivory white tile, his head down, the hot water shooting out the showerhead at full force and onto the back of his neck.

Something was not right. Over and over his mind went through the details and what he had been told. But something still throbbed in the front of his head. The unknown factor was right there but he couldn't see it. Not yet.

It all banked on what the Chinese woman had said and how much of it was the truth. She had told him the *Seakrill's* secret mission was known only to his father, the Chinese ambassador, and key people needed to make it work. More unknowns.

Stepping out of the shower, Brian grabbed a hotel towel and dried himself off. He had to get to Truk and find his father's submarine. Foreseeably, locating it could take him months. He had read about the famous Gibralter of the Pacific. A hundred and forty miles of coral reefs surrounding a natural harbor the Japanese couldn't have designed better. A lagoon littered with dozens of World War II freighters, all similar to the one in the photograph moored to the *Seakrill*.

That was his edge, the sketch he had outlined from the photograph that showed the nearby beach of one of the islands. It was a starting point anyway, not the best, but at least he wasn't going to search Truk blind.

The red luminous numbers of the small hotel clock next to the bed read 8:30 P.M. He had been in the room for forty minutes. It was time to leave and find someplace else to stay the night. He dressed quickly, not surprised how well his new clothes fit. After hanging his suit in the closet and setting his flight bag on the floor, he went into the bedroom and pulled the covers back and twisted the sheets, trying to give it a slept-in look. Satisfied, he moved to the phone and called the operator.

"Yes, is Daniel still at the front desk?" Brian asked.

"No, sir, he was off at eight o'clock. Perhaps someone else can help you?" the operator said.

"No, that's all right. But I would like to have breakfast brought up to my room tomorrow," he said.

"I'll connect you with room service, sir."

"Thank you." When the man from room service came onto the phone, Brian ordered a large breakfast of bacon, eggs and toast, coffee and orange juice. "Yes, room 535 at nine A.M.," he said. Too bad it would all go to waste, he thought, realizing that he hadn't eaten since the dinner on the plane.

Walking into the bathroom, he took the plastic toothbrush tube from his flight bag and slipped it into his pocket. Then he made one last look around the room. He smiled at his work. The hotel room looked lived in, slept in. As an afterthought, he turned on the light and fan in the bathroom and shut the door. When room service came in the morning, they wouldn't be sure if he was here or not. And maybe, just maybe, he was buying himself more time.

Exiting the elevator and stepping into the main lobby, Brian didn't look at the front desk. Daniel was gone, and to anyone else working the desk, he was just another tourist leaving the hotel for a few hours.

Brian stepped out of the hotel and walked in and out of the shops that were adjacent to the lobby. Using their cluttered, shell-filled windows to look to see if anyone was outside standing in one place too long, he wondered if he was getting paranoid.

Finally, he walked to the third floor of the parking structure and to the Camaro. Quickly he took out the three pieces of luggage from the trunk, tossed the keys inside, and closed the lid. Then he moved down to the walkway that lined the front of the hotel. He set the cases down next to the curb.

"May I help you, sir?" asked a young teenager dressed in the hotel's uniform of white pants and a blue flowered shirt.

"Can you call me a taxi? I'm late for my flight," Brian said, handing the porter a ten-dollar bill.

"Yes, sir," the teenager said. He looked to the far end of the circular driveway, waved his arm, and produced an ear-piercing whistle. Immediately a taxi bolted from the shadows and stopped in front of Brian's bags.

"You go to the airport, mon?" the driver asked as he lifted the cases with huge powerful arms and put them in the back of his cab. "What airline?"

"Ah, TWA," he said.

"Okay," the driver said as he slammed down the trunk lid and they got into the car. They pulled quickly out of the hotel's driveway and onto the busy street.

"Could you find me a pay phone?" Brian asked as he leaned toward the taxi driver. "I forgot I have to make a call."

The man shrugged. "Sure, mon," he said as he pulled into a small shopping center. "There's one over there." He pointed to three booths.

Brian climbed out of the cab and walked toward the phones. It took four calls to four hotels before he was able to find a vacancy in Waikiki. This was the height of the tourist season, what did he expect, a hotel clerk had asked.

"I've had a change of plans. Could you take me to the Royal Hawaiian?" Brian asked as he got in and closed the door of the cab.

"Sure, mon," the driver said.

134

The porter at the huge hotel with its pink decor was a young tanned female with jet-black hair and firm-looking body. She carried Brian's bags effortlessly to the front desk.

The tiny blond girl at the desk smiled as he approached. "Do you have reservations, Mr. huh?" she asked with a New York accent.

"Janson. No, I don't. I phoned a few minutes ago and I was told that you had a cancellation."

"It's not an ocean view," she said with apology.

"That's fine. I'll take it for two days," Brian said as he signed the registration and paid for the room with cash.

She smiled. "Have an enjoyable stay at the Royal, Mr. Janson."

"Thank you," Brian said as he picked up his shoulder bag and followed the porter and his suitcases to the elevators.

The room was probably one of the smallest in the hotel, but it was still large by his submarine standards. And the bed was firm as Brian liked it. He always slept better in a hard bunk.

He was pleased that room service took only twenty minutes with his dinner. Mahi mahi in a sweet coconut sauce tasted better than it sounded. The seahorse salad didn't bring up delectable pictures but it was only shrimp cut and sculptured to look like little horses.

He was tempted to have a bottle of gin brought up with dinner but decided on a half bottle of wine. It was just as well. The hours without sleep from Washington to Hawaii finally caught him as he fell across the bed.

FIFTEEN

CINCPAC, Hawaii, 1944

Douglas leaned against the framework of the torpedo crane and stared at the sleek dark image in the water. Most of the *Seakrill* lay beneath the calm water of the harbor, and with her narrow conning tower she reminded him of a shark, its dorsal fin the only hint at its deadly presence. The picture made him smile and shiver at the same time.

The rain had stopped, coloring the base in a wide brush-stroke of black. Oil puddles reflected the soft shivering light of a full moon as it broke away from the clouds.

Douglas had walked the half mile to the submarine docks from where Captain Yates had dropped him off. He was thinking, walking and thinking about what they had said. About national treasures, the Japs, a quarter of a million dollars, Truk, the Liberty Bell. And about Mimi.

Her face kept coming back to him with tears perched on the edges of those beautiful eyes. "Shit!" he said out loud.

He crossed the unsteady gangplank to the *Seakrill*'s rear deck and then moved up the steel rungs of the conning tower.

"Good evening, Commander," the young voice called down to him from the cigarette deck as he climbed the tower.

Douglas returned the stiff salute of the seaman. "Anything to report tonight, ah?'' he asked, trying to remember the seaman's name.

"Seaman Robert Hathorn, sir. Machinist's mate, second class," he said in a crisp voice that Douglas guessed was being heard across the harbor.

"That's right, Hathorn. Transferred over last week," Douglas remembered.

"Yes, sir."

"So, Hathorn, what do you think of your submarine so far?"

"Well, sir, from the bends in the railing around the tower and sections of deck that are missing, I'd say she's seen some pretty fierce action close-up," the seaman said. A smile crept onto his face. "And to be honest, Skipper, I wouldn't want to be on a sub that hadn't proved herself, sir."

Douglas laughed and patted Hathorn on the shoulder. He turned and began to climb down through the circular hatchway. "Clancy still working on the Fairbanks?" he asked.

"Yes, sir, and he got that bearing on the starboard shaft in place an hour ago, sir," Hathorn said as he watched the top of Douglas's dark blue cap disappear below the steel rim of the hatch.

Even before his eyes adjusted from the outside darkness to the bright lights in the submarine, Douglas moved easily through the mass of equipment that filled the interior of the tower. He had been on the *Seakrill* for two and a half years and he knew every inch of the undersea vessel. It was home.

Climbing down to the control room, he slipped through two hatchways to the forward engine room.

"Any good news to report?" Douglas asked as he entered the narrow cavern dominated by the huge Fairbanks Morse diesel. The heavy air of burning oil and gas choked him.

"Up late tonight, huh, Cap?" Clancy said without lifting his eyes from his work. He pulled harder on the two-inch open-end wrench in his hand until he was satisfied the bolt was tight, then he looked up at Douglas, wiped an oil-stained rag over his brow, and a gave half-hearted salute.

137

This wasn't insubordination. The crampness of a sub lent itself to relaxed formalities. It was accepted, and Douglas especially accepted it from the Irishman. He hated the navy, and he had told him so when Douglas first took command of the *Seakrill*. But the food was passable and it let him do what he loved best, work on engines. He breathed better where the air was mixed with carbon monoxide and full of thundering pistons.

Douglas heard about Clancy completely dismantling one of the *Bluefin*'s diesels out at sea and putting it back together in perfect running order. No, insubordination would never be a rough spot between this engineer and captain.

"You too," Douglas said as he moved around the diesel closer to where Clancy was standing. He could feel the heat of the still engine. "Find the problem?"

"Not yet, Cap. After I got the new head on her, I refitted the water jackets with larger intakes, but she is still heating up like a tea kettle," he said, rubbing the back of his neck and looking down at the mass of iron and rubber, steel and wire.

"Water ports all clear?" Douglas asked.

"Yes, sir," the mechanic answered with a wry smile.

It was a look that made Douglas feel like a fool. The intake ports were undoubtedly the first thing Clancy had checked. It was clear the Irishman didn't think the engine room was the place for the captain.

"Well, Clancy, you're the expert and you know when we're set to sail. So get her running," Douglas said, moving back around the engine.

"Aye, aye, Cap," Clancy said, tossing the heavy two-inch into the tool chest near his feet. The clatter echoed through the submarine.

Douglas headed forward toward the galley through the empty crew's quarters and mess hall. The refitting crew was gone. They had finished their work on the *Seakrill* and had moved on to the next submarine that had returned from patrol. Douglas's own crew was still ashore. It was their last night at the rest camp and tomorrow they would return, ready for patrol.

He looked at his watch. 0100 hours. In a few hours they would fill this deserted hull and it would come alive again, each seaman going over his duties. Checking and rechecking the submarine to make sure she was ready for war.

Pouring himself a cup of coffee from Clancy's warm pot, Douglas sat down at one of the tables. The images were coming back to him. If Tendrey reported the gambling, Douglas's career was over, and if the men at the ranch knew he had turned down the money, they would carry out their threats. An admiral, a fly-boy, or a man on the street, it didn't matter. When you owe money, they said, you pay it back with full interest or you lose a part of your body.

Douglas slouched down and his hand fell back against the chair. The thought of having his finger or an ear cut off with a rusting knife wasn't pleasing. He would pay them back, he thought, some way.

"Commander?" Hathorn stuck his head into the galley. "There's someone on the dock wanting to speak to you, sir. He wouldn't give his name but he's in civilian clothes," the machinist's mate said. "He wanted to come aboard, sir, but . . ."

"You did the right thing," Douglas said as he stood up and laid the coffee cup in the sink. "Tell him I'll be right up."

"Yes, sir," Hathorn said.

Walking quickly, Douglas went to his quarters. Opening the small drawer beside his bunk, he pulled out his .45 automatic pistol. He left its leather holster, and slipped the gun into the waistband in the back of his pants. Then as an afterthought, he took off his dress uniform coat and put on a bulkier jacket which hid the weapon better. He headed toward the conning-tower hatch.

"He's alone, sir," Hathorn whispered to Douglas as he climbed out onto the bridge.

"All right, Robert, watch your post," Douglas said as he

climbed down the ladder and crossed the *Seakrill*'s gangplank to the dock.

"Commander Bovan," the man said as he approached Douglas. He was a stocky man, short and broad, and he wore a fedora tilted high on the back of his head, and like his brown overcoat, it was still wet from being out in the rain.

"That's right," Douglas answered, not meeting the man's outstretched hand. "Kind of late for a visit, isn't it?"

"I guess it is," he said in a monotone, his face expressionless. He drew his wallet from under his coat and flipped it open. "Office of Special Services."

"So what does Dick Tracy want from me?"

"The name is Wagner."

"Okay, what can I do for you, Mr. Wagner?"

"Let's walk, Commander," Wagner said as he turned and moved along the dock. Douglas matched his pace. "We think there is a black market operation being set up."

"Why don't you hang around the mess halls for a few hours, that'll convince you," Douglas said.

"We are not talking about the usual samurai swords and silk, Commander. This has to do with someone high in command at CINCPAC."

"High in command? Then what do you want from me?"

Wagner stopped at the end of the dock and looked across the southeast lock and at the shipyard. Taking a pack of cigarettes from his pocket, he pulled one out with his mouth. Then offered one to Bovan. "We know all about your gambling and the debts in town you've managed to accumulate, Commander," he said with the rolled tobacco-filled paper dangling from his lips. "We've got our sources everywhere, our stoolies, and they tell us you're vulnerable. Very vulnerable."

"You putting me under arrest?"

Wagner smiled. "Not yet."

"Then exactly what do you want?"

"The OSS doesn't know anything about this operation,

just that there is a lot of money involved and the need of a submarine.''

"You're going to have to be more specific," Douglas said.

"There's a certain admiral who's under our surveillance," Wagner said, lighting the cigarette. "But we're never able to do anything about him." Wagner turned toward Douglas and handed him the matches. "We think this admiral will try to contact you."

"You expect me to blow the whistle on a fellow navy man?"

"I expect your alliance to be with the United States government, commander. That's where mine are," Wagner said coldly.

Douglas took a breath through his cigarette. "You got a name yet?"

"Admiral Tendrey, and if I'm not mistaken, he isn't one of your best friends."

"Our paths have crossed, you could say," Douglas admitted. "But you're a little late. He spoke to me tonight."

"Then he told you what he wanted?"

"Yes."

"I want him, Bovan. He is a crooked military man with a lot of friends in powerful places," Wagner said.

"OSS?"

Wagner smiled at the submarine commander. "I didn't think so before, but he manages to outsmart me every time. I can never pin anything directly on him."

"So you're soloing this one. What're you looking for, a pat on the back?" Douglas said.

"Close. My CO wants him more than me, and with your help, maybe I can deliver."

"He said my gambling would go into my jacket if I didn't help him," Douglas said as he took a step closer to the edge of the dock and looked down into the water.

"I don't know if I can stop that," Wagner said, and Douglas understood.

"What did he tell you?" Wagner asked.

"An overview, no details. But believe me, he has the whole thing worked out all right. And we're talking about five million bucks in diamonds."

"Jesus Christ," Wagner said with an outpour of smoke from his lungs. "What in the world is he going after?"

"It's not so much Tendrey as the people he is working for. He's a go-between. From what I can guess, he's being paid just to set everything up, finding the submarine and a willing commander. And like you said, I'm vulnerable."

Wagner let out a silent whistle, "Then I was right about the whole thing. But who is he working for and what is being bought?"

"The Chinese," Douglas said, telling the OSS man what he had been told in the study but being careful not to mention Mimi.

The dark rain clouds had vanished and the two men stood talking under a star-lit night. A light sea breeze coming across the harbor carried their smoke-filled breaths away from them.

"Mother of God," Wagner said, lighting a third cigarette. "Truk Lagoon." He watched as a patrol boat moved out of the shipyard. "We'll need proof."

"I just told you everything," Douglas said. "What more do you need to bring charges against him?"

"I need someone else to confirm your story. Right now it's only your word against his. A lieutenant commander versus a rear admiral who everyone knows hate each other. Proof, Bovan, I need proof."

"What about the ambassador? He'll have to talk," Douglas protested.

"A diplomat. I can't tell my chief that a diplomat from one of our most important allies is backing a black-market scheme," Wagner said, rubbing his face. Douglas could tell he was thinking.

"They've covered their asses," Douglas said after a moment.

"And I know the girl won't talk. She is under diplomatic immunity too," Wagner said as if thinking out loud.

Douglas turned and looked hard into Wagner's eyes.

The OSS man smiled. "You think I didn't know about her? I trust your story was still complete even though you left her out."

"She's not a part of this. You want my help, you leave her alone," Douglas said harshly.

"Listen, I know she is into this thing up to her pretty little rear end. I make no promises," Wagner said. He thrust his bulbous index finger into Douglas's chest. "I'm going to do my best just to keep you and your record clean through this. I told you, Tendrey's arm is long and strong. I've got my orders and they say get this son of a bitch any way I have to and I don't care who has to fall. But I got nothing until they make the next move. You might have already blown the whole thing by exploding and walking out of Cabot's house."

"So we wait until they give us the proof you need," Douglas said. He watched Wagner shift his weight from his right foot to his left.

"Ya, we wait and hope they give us the noose to hang them. But I wouldn't bet on it. Tendrey is no fool," Wagner said, pulling out the cigarette pack again. There was only one Lucky left. He saved it, tucking the pack back into his breast pocket.

"If you don't get your proof or they don't contact me again, what then?"

Wagner looked at the submarine captain and shrugged. "Then Tendrey has outdone me again. And if they don't approach you to carry out the trade for the fossils, then, Bovan, I'll lay odds you're out of time," the OSS man said as he turned and moved back along the dock toward the *Seakrill*.

"What's that supposed to mean?" Douglas asked.

"They're not going to let you live, Commander," Wagner said flatly. "You figure it out. Five million in diamonds and Chinese National treasures. You know too much and too much is at stake.'' Wagner stopped at the gangplank of the submarine. "If they contact you, I'll be in touch,'' he said, and then turned and walked away.

Douglas watched him until he lost the agent's silhouette in the dark shadow of an adjacent warehouse. Then he walked back, crossed the plank, and boarded the *Seakrill*.

Wagner pulled his black Ford sedan into the empty dirt lot, turned off the engine, slouched down in the seat, and waited. Through the front windshield, he watched the small street on the far side of the lot. At three o'clock in the morning, it was void of life.

He tilted the rearview mirror so he could see if anyone tried to approach his car from behind. For thirty minutes there was no one. It was as if the short length of avenue had been quarantined by military order.

Another ten minutes passed when he finally opened the driver's door and stepped from the car. He closed it gently and walked across the dirt lot to the row of shops. He headed toward the one on the end.

The double glass doors were set back a few feet from the sidewalk. The space used daily for small tables filled with shells and natural sponges.

Wagner pulled the single key from his pocket and inserted it into the lock. He turned it, pushed the door open, and stepped in.

The room exploded with an ear-piercing screech. Wagner winced as he shut the door and relocked it. The screeching turned to a clatter of loud whistles and chirps. "Shut up, MacBeth,'' Wagner said as he walked passed the red and blue macaw. With the help of its large hooked beak, the bird was inching its way up the side of its cage for a better look at the intruder. Wagner slapped the cage as he walked by, sending the bird sliding down the thin steel bars.

"I wish you wouldn't do that, Duare,'' said the slender

144

man standing in the doorway at the rear of the shop. He held a machine gun under his left arm pointing at the floor.

Wagner smiled. "I hate that fuckhead bird," he said as he pushed past the man and entered the hallway. "Why don't you feed him some green peppers? That'll shut him up."

"Colonel Gostine is waiting for you in the decoding room," the guard said, ignoring Duare's comment.

"The Peking Man, that's a mighty big prize to go after," the colonel said, closing Bovan's file and setting it on the round table in the middle of the windowless room. Agent Duare, or Wagner as he had told Douglas, had repeated word for word to his commanding officer everything the lieutenant commander had told him. That was Duare's specialty, total memory recall, and it often made him the go-between. Never a note or a piece of paper to fall into the wrong hands.

"What do you think, Major?" Gostine asked Duare.

"In all honesty, sir, if Tendrey gives something to the commander, something that is hard evidence, then there is no question, sir. We'll have him," Duare said with a cocked smile.

Gostine paced the room, his hands together in a pyramid under his chin. The thin-physiqued colonel reminded Duare of an Oklahoma farmer. And he could tell the farmer was worried.

"Peking Man," he mumbled. He looked at Duare sitting at the table. "That's a big, big prize and I know Washington would be very pleased to be able to return them back to the chinks at the end of the war. I hate to pass that up. We lost them, you know," the colonel said.

"Yes, sir," Duare said.

"He didn't tell you how they were going to do it?" the farmer asked.

"Bovan didn't have the details to their plan, but really, sir, I don't think the commander believes it can be done."

"Maybe, but do you think he is the right man? Do you think he'll try?"

Duare looked at his commanding officer, his eyebrows raising, "I couldn't say, sir. I've read his file. There's nothing in there that says he wouldn't carry out a direct order. The navy considers him one of their best sub captains. They say he's seasoned, aggressive, and smart. I imagine he's probably the best submariner in Pearl. But, Colonel, Admiral Tendrey will undoubtedly hear any orders issued to the *Seakrill*."

The colonel was silent for a moment, then made up his mind. "Then tell the commander he is under top-secret orders issued by the OSS," the colonel said. "The importance to the United States in the recovery of those fossils is too great to forgo. And in doing so, we will also build an airtight case around the good admiral."

Duare stared at him in disbelief. "But, sir, the chances of a submarine getting into Truk, let alone getting out, is next to nil," he said, rising to his feet. "It's a suicide mission."

"We're at war, Major, and nobody knows the risks better than a sub commander," Gostine said as if reading from a prepared speech.

"Yes, sir," Duare said weakly.

"That will be all, Major." The farmer saluted.

"Yes, sir," Duare said, dropping his salute and moving to the exit. He stepped into the hallway and closed the door behind him. He leaned back against the wall and suddenly felt ill.

The door from the decoding room, the one that led directly into Gostine's office, opened slowly. The navy man in full dress uniform leaned in. "He'll carry out your orders?"

Gostine laughed. "This is the OSS, Commander, my men never question. He'll tell Bovan what I said and he'll convince him that an order from my department carries the same weight as one from Nimitz," the colonel said reassuringly.

"Admiral Tendrey will be pleased to hear that," the navy man said, lifting his glass in a mock salute.

"I see you found the whiskey," the colonel said.

"And the water."

SIXTEEN

Kaimu, Hawaii, 1986

Tendrey's secretary saw the lights of the limousine as it entered the front gates of the estate. He went out the door and down the steps of the mansion, timing his pace perfectly to meet the car as it stopped.

"Good morning, sir," Marks said as he opened the rear door.

"Morning," said the man in a heavy voice as he stepped onto the gravel driveway. It was the same voice Marks had heard on Tendrey's private line without ever knowing the owner's name. But the navy man fit the mental picture he had developed. He was tall with wide shoulders and a strong face made more solid by the lack of hair on the man's head.

He was a military man, a professional soldier cut from the same mold as Tendrey himself. Marks guessed this man would only be comfortable in a uniform. "The admiral is waiting for you in his study," the secretary said as he followed the man up the stairs and into the house. "Is there anything I can get you, sir?" the secretary asked.

"No, thank you. Just show me the way."

"Right through here." Marks knocked lightly on the double redwood doors. They heard Tendrey's voice on the other side.

After the man entered, Marks closed the doors from the outside.

"You made better time than I would have guessed," Tendrey said, stretching out his hand to his old friend.

"When we spoke, you made it sound like the end of the world was coming."

"It is," Tendrey said flatly.

"No, I've thought this thing through, Joe. We're letting ourself get worked up over nothing," the man said, moving to one of the leather chairs and sitting down.

"Nothing? Are you crazy? Do you know what will happen if Brian gets to Truk?"

"Yes," the navy man from Washington said. "He'll search the lagoon without finding a thing and then he will go back to New Hampshire." He leaned toward the desk. "Don't you think I would have stopped him myself if I thought there was a chance he would find anything?"

"What if he finds the sub?" Tendrey said, tapping his fingers nervously on the desk.

"He won't. Have you forgotten the years the navy searched for the *Seakrill?* Or all the money you and I spent turning up the bottom of that lagoon trying to find her. I'm telling you, Joe, somehow Douglas managed to get the *Seakrill* out before she went down," the man said. This was a familiar argument between them and neither wanted to start it again.

"The professor was on to something," Tendrey said in a low voice.

"Who?"

"Yokamata. He and I had a deal," Tendrey said.

"Jesus Christ, don't tell me you were the one paying him."

"He was going to find his ship and bring up the fossils," Tendrey defended himself.

"Find it?" The navy man ran his hand over his head. "He knew exactly where she went down. It was blown out from underneath him."

Tendrey rolled out from behind the desk. "It doesn't matter."

"He's dead, isn't he?"

"Of course he's dead," Tendrey shot back. "He wasn't telling me everything. It was taking him too long to find the wreck."

"Well, if Yokamata did know anything, you ended our chances of questioning him. Goddamn it, Joe, he probably never knew about the trade until you brought him in," the man said, shaking his head.

Tendrey looked hard at the navy man. "That Jap was the second mate on the *Kuma Maru*. He spoke perfect English, and you want to tell me he had nothing to do with the rendezvous, with *Seakrill*, the diamonds, or the fossils?" Tendrey said, continuing to stare at him.

The man from Washington looked at the retired admiral. "I don't want to see Brian killed."

"He'll find the orders."

"There aren't any orders to find, Joe. The *Seakrill* is gone, sunk in the South China Sea in February of 1944 with all hands aboard. She is not coming back, Admiral. She can't."

Tendrey closed his eyes tight. He rubbed his face with his bony fingers. "We can't let young Bovan get to Truk. It is as simple as that. You have to stop him."

"And if I can't?"

"Then I will have him stopped," Tendrey said. "Otherwise we will both be very sorry."

The navy man stood up and walked to the window. With his right hand he moved the curtains to one side and looked out. He turned back toward Tendrey. "Let him go, Joe. He'll search the lagoon for a few weeks, maybe a month, and then when he doesn't find anything, he'll go home. He may not be satisfied but that will be the end of all this. I'm telling you, there is nothing for him to find."

There was a knock on the door and it opened slowly. Tendrey's butler leaned into the room. "Is there anything

I can get you or your guest, sir?" the butler, not much into his twenties, asked.

"It's too early for anything for me," Tendrey said. "For you?" he looked at the man from Washington.

"Jack Daniel's and water, please, no ice," the navy man said. The butler nodded and closed the door.

Tendrey winced. "Whiskey at two o'clock in the morning?"

"It keeps the blood going," the man said.

"What about Yokamata's daughter? You said she was in Hawaii too. A coincidence? And have you found her? No," Tendrey said, his voice cracking in anger. "What if she is on her way to Truk too?"

"There is no reason she would be. She hasn't spoken to her father in years. Her stage director said she went on vacation."

"I don't find much comfort in what your people find out," Tendrey said as there was another knock on the door. "Come in," he said.

The butler handed the navy man his drink, asked if there was anything else he could do, and then left the room.

Neither man spoke for a time. Then Tendrey wheeled himself away from his desk and moved over to where his friend was standing by the window. He looked out at the raven-black sea in the distance.

"I miss being out there. Sometimes more than I can stand," Tendrey admitted. "Getting old is an awful thing. Your body starts to go long before your mind, and you're left to sit and remember better times."

The navy man looked down at the man he had served with during three wars. "I don't think it's your age, Joe. There's just no war to fight," he said, stepping back from the window.

In the other room a phone rang. After the second ring, it stopped.

The navy man spoke. "There's nothing I could say to

Brian that would keep him from going to Truk. I can't tell him the truth and he already knows the records are all lies."

Tendrey remained silent as he looked out at the sea.

The double doors opened without a sound as Marks stepped in.

Turning his wheelchair around, he looked up, "Well, well," Tendrey said impatiently. He had been expecting the phone call. "What did they say? Have they found him?"

"No," Marks said. "They are still searching for the car. Its license number has been given to their connections in the police department. But they have nothing yet."

"Then why did they call? What did they say?"

The secretary looked away from Tendrey and at the broad-shouldered man standing in the center of the room. "The CIA agent that followed him from Los Angeles is dead," he said nervously.

"What? How the hell did that happen?" Tendrey screamed. "Son of a bitch! I thought you said these people knew what they were doing."

"They do. They said he attacked them. It was an accident," the secretary countered.

"An accident?" said the navy man as he shook his head. He took a sip of his whiskey and water. "This is going to cause us trouble. The CIA doesn't take the death of one of their agents very lightly." He looked hard at the secretary. "I hope these so-called professionals you deal with were smart enough not to leave any traces that could lead them back to us."

"Of course not," the secretary said.

"Oh, of course not," the man mocked. "How foolish for me to even ask. What else have you found out?" he asked, taking control of the conversation.

"The only flights to Truk go out of Honolulu at six-thirty A.M. every morning on Continental. It's an eleven-hour flight with four stops before Truk. Bovan is scheduled on a flight the day after tomorrow," the secretary said.

152

"Then make sure there is someone at the airport to stop him from boarding that plane," Tendrey ordered.

"No," the man said, rubbing the back of his neck. "Get someone there tomorrow. Brian has been careful enough not to use his name in Honolulu; it would be stupid for him to make a reservation he knows can be traced. And what about this car he was able to get so quickly? Did you find out who rented it?"

"It's from an agency near the airport and was picked up two days before Bovan got on the plane in D.C. Paid for in cash with phony information on the rental papers," Marks said.

Tendrey looked at his friend from Washington. "I'm telling you, it is the Chinese woman. She's not dead, this is her work. It has to be."

The navy man didn't say anything.

"That will be all," Tendrey said. "Call me if you find out anything more." When the double doors closed, Tendrey looked back at his friend. "You know I'm right."

"No, I don't, and neither do you. You're guessing. Anybody could be helping him. Or nobody is helping him and somehow he set everything up himself."

"Then explain the notebook. Where the hell did the notebook come from if it wasn't from her?" Tendrey shot.

"I don't know," the navy man said, then he admitted something that had been in the back of his mind. "But I don't think the diamonds or the fossils would bring him all the way out here. He must know about the orders."

"How, how could he know?" Tendrey slammed his fist down on the table. "How could he know if it isn't Ming?"

The navy man could only look at the admiral. He didn't have the answer. "That's what we have to find out. Before we do anything."

"That settles it. He has to be stopped, and so does Yokamata's daughter," Tendrey said.

The navy man didn't argue this time. He watched as his former commander pushed himself toward the double doors.

"The Peking Man and the diamonds don't matter anymore," Tendrey said, looking back at him. "When we were young and greedy, my friend, the thought of them at the bottom of Truk haunted us."

The navy man gave a cocked smile. "They did, didn't they," he agreed. "But, you're right, they really don't matter anymore."

"What are they compared to two brilliant careers?" Tendrey shrugged. He turned and pushed the doors apart. "But if we let young Bovan find those orders, they will destroy us both," he said as he rolled out of the study.

Admiral Thomas Mills sipped the last of his whiskey and water. His mentor was right. He had spent too much of his life calculating, balancing, and weighing facts in order to make correct judgments to stop now. He had to know exactly what Brian knew and how he had found out before he could simply allow him to get to Truk.

The day after Mills had given Brian his father's files, he realized he had only given him more reason to find out the truth about the *Seakrill*. There should have been no reason for him to question those files. Unless someone had told him otherwise.

The image of a young and beautiful Chinese woman entered Mills's mind. Ming was dead, he told himself. Killed with the ambassador and the rest of his party in the plane crash that was supposed to take them all from Honolulu to the States. A sabotaged flight that was listed simply as another act of war by Japanese spies working on the island.

But Mills knew better. The bomb had been for her and the ambassador. She had to have been aboard, he thought, though he remembered it was never confirmed exactly who was on the plane.

Mills set his empty glass on the desk and picked up the phone. He dialed the extension that was marked for Tendrey's secretary. "Will you find out about chartering a Lear to Truk tomorrow. Yes. As early as possible."

SEVENTEEN

Honolulu, Hawaii, 1986

Brian set the phone receiver down in its cradle and walked across the dark hotel room and into the bathroom. Leaning over the sink, he splashed cold water onto his face. He looked in the mirror and rubbed his eyes.

The hotel's operator had woken him at 4:35 A.M., five minutes later than he had requested. But it was the person he had just finished talking to who bothered him.

He had phoned Continental Airlines hoping to change his flight to later in the day when Honolulu International was more crowded. But it was the only flight, the next was tomorrow, and he was already registered for that one.

At six o'clock in the morning he knew the airport would be almost empty. He was going to be spotted, he thought, too easily seen by the man who had followed him across the Pacific to Hawaii. He would be there waiting at the gate. If not him, somebody else would be there to stop him from boarding that plane.

He had to get aboard, somehow he had to get through the entire airport and onto a plane without being seen. Suddenly Brian smiled to himself. Being seen was okay, it was being recognized that was the problem.

He wiped his face off and went back to the phone and

called the Continental desk a second time. Then he returned to the bathroom and started the shower.

It took almost ten minutes for the doorman to call a taxi for Brian. This early in the morning, they were busier picking people up at late-night bars than at hotels. He looked down at his watch as the driver placed his two suitcases and carry-on bag in the trunk. It was now 5:45 A.M. The timing would be just right, Brian figured.

"Here," Brian said, climbing into the rear of the car. He handed the driver a hundred-dollar bill over the top of the front seat as the cab headed toward the airport.

The driver reached back, took it, saw the amount of the currency, and looked at Brian through his rearview mirror. "Thanks, mon. But what's it for?"

"Just don't say anything when we get to the terminal. There will be a porter waiting. Give him my two suitcases. But if anyone asks, you picked me up at the hospital and you don't know anything else."

"At the hospital?" the driver said as he pushed the bill into his shirt pocket. "Okay, mon, if you say so."

The streets and highways of Honolulu were quiet at dawn but far from empty. The city's energy was just starting up again as the day promised new waves of tourists. Storekeepers were washing down their storefronts, their stock refilled during the night. Maintenance workers were finishing raking the beaches and sweeping walkways of their huge hotel complexes, each its own city within the city.

"Those two people. Stop in front of them," Brian directed the driver as he saw the porter and a young woman in an airline uniform standing on the curb.

Brian rolled down the window of the cab as it stopped beside them. "Good morning, I hope you're waiting for me," Brian said, trying to make his voice sound weak and hoarse.

156

"Mr. Brock?" the Hawaiian woman asked as she leaned down toward the window.

"Yes," Brian responded. The cab driver was already out of the car and opening the trunk.

"One second, sir," she said, turning and walking quickly into the terminal. Before the automatic doors had a chance to fully close, she was walking back out pushing a wheelchair. She stopped next to the taxi and locked its wheels.

Opening the door of the car, Brian moved slowly as he climbed out. The woman grabbed his right elbow, gently guiding him to the wheelchair. He forced a groan, trying not to seem in too much pain.

"Thank you so much for doing this." Brian said to her.

"Not at all. The airline is more than happy to help its passengers when we can. I'm just sorry you had to spend your vacation in the hospital," she said as she took his carry-on bag from the driver. "The porter will have the rest of your bags put on your flight."

"Hope you feel better, mon," the taxicab driver said as he smiled and tapped his breast pocket. "I do."

Brian ignored him. He looked up at the young woman. "Thank you," he said again. "The doctors said I was lucky my appendix acted up in Honolulu and not on Kwajalein."

"Oh, you're going to Kwajalein. It is a beautiful island," she said as she pushed Brian into the terminal and down the long empty corridor toward the boarding gates. "My mother's family was from there. Generations ago, of course, but we visited it once when I was a little girl."

Brian wasn't listening to her as she began to describe her childhood trip to the atoll. He was looking ahead of them as they entered the main section of the terminal that fingered out into individual boarding gates. It was crowded with more people than he had expected at such an early hour.

The small coffee shop and the bar to the far side of the gates were almost full of passengers awaiting their boarding calls. The Continental woman pushed him directly to the high check-in counter. "Frank," she said to the heavyset man standing there. "Mr. Brock here is on Flight Four. Have they called for boarding yet?"

"The first call will be in about five minutes," he said, then he looked down at Brian in the wheelchair. "We can put you on the plane right now, sir. Do you have your ticket?"

"Yes," Brian said, handing it to him. He looked back over his shoulder toward the columns of plastic waiting chairs, then across to the other ticket counters. No one looked out of place. He tried to pick who had been planted there to either watch him get on the plane or keep him from it, but he couldn't.

The Hawaiian named Frank was handing him back his ticket. "Hope you feel better, Mr. Brock. Enjoy your flight."

Brian smiled as the woman pushed him toward the gate. A few more feet and he would be aboard. They moved into the enclosed boarding ramp, down its length, and onto the small Boeing 727.

It worked. If there were people trying to stop him from boarding the plane, they had either not recognized him in the wheelchair or had been too afraid to approach him with his airline escort.

Brian began to stand up, but then remembering he was supposed to be in pain, waited for the woman to help him into his seat. He thanked her again.

"It is my pleasure," she assured him. "Here, I'll put this up here." She stretched over him, opening the overhead luggage compartment to put his carry-on inside.

"I'd rather hold on to that," he said quickly. "I have things in it I plan to read."

She handed it back to him. "Have a good flight, Mr. Brock," she said, and turned and left the plane.

* * *

Marks knocked lightly on the door of Admiral Tendrey's bedroom. He listened and then knocked again.

"Come in, come in," the admiral said.

As Marks entered he saw a familiar scene. Tendrey was awake, still in his pajamas and sitting in his wheelchair out on the veranda. The cool tropical air ruffled the thin curtains.

Marks walked up behind him. "Admiral?" he said, stepping around him. He followed his stare toward the sea. A large sloop was rounding the point just beyond the reef, her sails full like bellies of middle-aged men.

"I shouldn't have given up the sea, John," Tendrey confided.

"I never thought you did, Admiral."

Tendrey smiled and put his hand on Marks's wrist. "It's such a beautiful morning, don't ruin it with bad news. What did your people tell you?"

"They said no one fitting his description got on the plane," Marks said.

"Good, good."

"But there was a man that was taken aboard in a wheelchair. They couldn't get close enough to identify him," Tendrey's secretary said, taking the smile from the admiral's face.

"Where's Mills?" Tendrey asked, rolling himself back into the room.

"Having coffee on the patio. He's waiting to have breakfast with you."

"Tell him I'll be down in a few minutes," Tendrey said as he maneuvered himself around his four-poster bed and into the bathroom.

Mills sat cross-legged in the stiff rod-iron chair that wobbled on the red-tiled patio, his fresh-poured coffee in front of him, his third within fifteen minutes. But Mills needed it. He was tired, his eyes red from not being able to sleep

159

in three days. And tonight would be no different. Marks had just told him about the man in the wheelchair heading for Truk Lagoon.

Brian watched each face of each passenger as they walked down the center aisle of the plane. His seat was about a third of the way back from the entrance, giving him a clear view. But of all the faces, none was that of the stately man from the flight from L.A. and then later in the Honolulu parking lot. Nor did any look at him with revealing eyes.

They were simply tourists, each of them in loud Hawaiian-print shirts and shorts, with cameras and wicker bags and suntanned smiles. From their faces, none could have cared less who he was.

"Excuse me," said the young Oriental woman standing over him.

Brian looked up at the face he had inspected coming onto the plane and then let pass as he looked at the next. "Oh," he said, honestly startled. "I'm sorry." He stood partially to let her squeeze past and sit in the window seat next to him.

He watched her out of the corner of his eye as she put her purse and small bag next to her feet. Taking off her light blue coat, she revealed dark tan shoulders holding the thin straps of her pink cotton dress. She began to tuck the coat beside her between her seat and the window.

"Here, let me put that in the overhead for you," Brian offered.

Her almond eyes looked at him as she seemed to hesitate. "Thank you," she said, and with a gentle brush of her hand, she moved her long, unbound hair away from her face and smiled.

As Brian put the coat in the compartment, he looked back toward the entrance as one of the stewards closed the door, turned the large orange handle and sealed it. Brian smiled to himself.

160

The Continental jet rolled back from the terminal building and taxied toward its appointed position. In several areas, the expansion of the airport's concrete was still wet from the evening's brief shower, but the morning sun was already warm and steaming it dry. In the wind that came off the sea, the distant line of tall palm trees waved goodbye to the island's visitors as the 727 lifted off the runway and banked over the white sand.

From her small bag on the floor, the young woman pulled out a stack of brochures held together by a rubber band. She pulled the top one out and opened it.

Brian glanced at the large bold type across the top of the pamphlet. TRUK LAGOON UNDERWATER TOURS. He looked down at the stack on her lap. WAR & PEACE: TRUK LAGOON TOURS.

"You're going prepared," Brian said.

The woman looked up at him, then back at her brochure and at the others piled in her lap. "I guess it does look like a little more than I need, doesn't it?"

He shrugged. "Better than me. I didn't even think to pick any up. I was going to rely on the guide at the hotel."

"You're flying through to Truk?" she asked.

"This isn't a direct flight?"

"Ah, no. We stop on three other islands before reaching Truk," she said.

"Oh." Brian put his hands up. "I didn't make the reservations. You could say it was kind of last-minute."

"Here." She handed him several pamphlets.

"Thank you, Miss . . . ?"

"Yokamata, Leslie Yokamata."

"Brian Brock," he said. Reaching out, his hand met hers; it was soft, dry and delicate with a firm grip.

"Nice to meet you, Mr. Brock," Leslie said.

"It's just Brian, please. Leslie?" he ventured, and she nodded her approval.

He opened the brochure she had given him. It was filled with the typical public-relations words like exciting, beautiful, spectacular, and unforgettable. It described several tour packages that included diving the Imperial fleet, long silent and now coral-encrusted. There was a picture of a bikini-clad snorkel diver sitting in the cockpit of a Japanese Zero and another of a endless white beach.

"Are you on vacation?" Leslie asked.

"No," Brian said without taking his eye off the paper. Then he looked at her. "I mean yes. Kind of yes and no," he said, trying to correct his mistake but knowing he only made it worse. "You?"

"Kind of yes and no too." She smiled. "I'm on vacation but I'm going to visit my father. He's doing research in the lagoon."

"Oh, really," Brian sat up slightly. "Sounds interesting. What kind of research?"

"He is a professor at the University of Hawaii. Teaches World War II history. Kind of ironic, he was in the Japanese navy."

"Not that ironic," Brian said. "A lot of old soldiers are still drawn to those days. They go back and see what it's like forty years later."

"I guess so," she said as if saddened by the thought. "I haven't seen him in a while."

"Too far away?"

Leslie shrugged. "In more ways than one," she said softly.

Brian looked into her eyes but she turned away and looked out the small window. "I didn't mean to pry," he said.

"No, it's nothing, really," she said with a sigh. "I guess you're just sitting in the wrong place at the wrong time."

"I don't think so," he smiled.

She smiled back.

"How long has he been at Truk?"

"He usually visits during the summer months when he's not teaching, but the dean at the university told me he flew over last June. He took a leave of absence without notice," she said.

"Maybe he found something interesting. The wrecks are the reason I'm going there," Brian said.

Leslie turned back to him and smiled. "Really? Then you'll have to meet him. His ship was stationed there during the attack. He was its only survivor."

"Sounds like I'm lucky you sat next to me," Brian said.

"It must be luck. I was supposed to be on yesterday's flight but there was some mix-up at the ticket desk."

"They tell you what the mix-up was?"

"I didn't bother to ask," she said. "I guess I'm so nervous about seeing him that I was thankful for the extra day in Hawaii. Sounds terrible, doesn't it?"

"A little," he said. "What made you decide to visit him now?"

"He sent me a telegram asking me to come. I was kind of reluctant, but a friend of mine insisted. So here I am," Leslie said.

"I'll have to thank that friend of yours," Brian said as he looked into her eyes.

A smile grew on her face as she looked into his dark eyes. They talked during the next hours of the flight as the stewardess brought their coffee and snacks. Leslie talked about New York and Brian listened. When the questions were turned toward him, he avoided direct answers. In the back of his mind, he wondered if she was lying and a part of everything he had been trying to avoid since Washington.

The plane landed on Johnston Island briefly, exchanging passengers and their luggage. Then it flew to Majuro to empty more of its seats, and fifteen minutes later it landed on Kwajalein Island.

"We'll be refueling here," the stewardess said as she walked down the aisle of the plane. "So if anyone likes, they can go into the airport or across the street to some of the small shops. We will be here for about forty-five minutes."

"Let's go," Leslie said, putting her hand on Brian's and standing up.

"Okay," he said, grabbing his shoulder bag. As he stood, the stewardess moved to help him.

"You're feeling better, Mr. Brock?"

"Yes, much better," he said with a smile, hoping Leslie didn't hear her. She was too far away and already on the other side of the emerging crowd. "Thank you," he said with a smile as he stepped past her and followed Leslie out of the plane.

They walked down the ramp and onto the apron of the small airport. From the size of the terminal, Brian guessed it probably never had more than a few jets at any one time. Unlike Honolulu, palm trees and not skyscrapers still dominated the horizon.

Leslie took the lead as she walked through the terminal building and out again on the other side. Like the stewardess had promised, there was a line of three-sided huts filled with wood carvings and shells glued into animal forms for the tourists. Everything from T-shirts with Kwajalein printed across the front to sun-bleached grass skirts hanging on lines across the fronts of the tiny shops.

Brian followed her as she looked over the items on the tables. "A bit different from Madison Avenue," he joked.

"People are nicer here," she said, putting on a necklace of small white shells. "What do you think?"

"You buy," the heavyset lady with the wide grin said as she came out from shadows within the hut. She smiled at Brian. "You buy for your beautiful wife. I'll make you a deal. Ten dollars."

"She's, ah, she's not my wife," Brian said, surprised how fast the woman moved beside him. He looked at Leslie as she tried to suppress a giggle.

"Then all the more reason to buy. She never forget you, you buy her this. Beautiful necklace on beautiful girl," the woman said, putting her arm around Leslie. Now it was her turn to be surprised. "Come, you buy. Seven dollars."

"Okay, okay, seven dollars," Brian conceded.

"No, Brian," Leslie protested.

"I want to."

"Yes, he wants to. Good man, he buy you something," the woman said, putting the money in the deep pocket of her loose dress. "You see anything else?" She lifted a porcupine fish dried in its swelled-up state, its spines lancing out in every direction.

"No, thank you," Leslie said, lacing her arm through Brian's and pulling him down the street. "I didn't think we were going to get out of there."

"Neither did I," Brian said.

"Thanks for the necklace," Leslie said, not taking her arm from his as they continued to walk along the street.

"She wouldn't have let us go if I hadn't," he joked.

Leslie laughed. "Oh, look," she said suddenly as they came to a table stacked with native fruit. "I love papaya. I wonder if he will cut it for us." She moved into the shadows of the hut and after a moment returned cradling two thick slices of yellow-orange fruit, each in a page of newspaper. "Let's go sit over there," she said as she handed Brian his slice.

"Where are you going?" he asked, following her across the street.

A few yards away from the street and hidden by thick low palms, where civilization hadn't yet taken its toll, Leslie found a volcanic outcropping of rock, its surface worn smooth by time and by others finding this place to sit in the shade.

Brian moved beside her. The ground around them was a mixture of decaying leaves and sand. The air was still and quiet as though the traffic and the people nearby had suddenly disappeared.

"It's funny," he said, looking at the dense jungle that surrounded them. "Forty years ago this place was leveled by the Fifth Fleet just two weeks before they hit Truk. For three days straight they bombarded this island."

"You know your history," Leslie said as she took another bite of her papaya.

Brian smiled. "I've been reading up a little."

"You're in the navy, aren't you," she said suddenly as if the thought just occurred to her. "I mean, you were at some time."

"What makes you say that?"

"The look in your eyes." She took a bite of her papaya. "My father has the same far-off glare. It is almost as if he is only comfortable when he is near the ocean or in a place like this." She smiled.

"Maybe I've been reading too much," Brian said as he stood up and ate the last of his fruit. "We better get back to the plane before it leaves without us."

"My father is going to like you," Leslie said as she brushed herself off. "You talk about the things he talks about and in the same way. If I didn't know you were too young, I'd say you had been here forty years ago," Leslie said as they walked out of the shade and towards the airport.

The 727 climbed into a sky once dominated by U.S. Navy Hellcat fighters. It soared through a quiet layer of stratus clouds once black from antiaircraft fire, then turned and headed toward Ponape and finally onto Truk. The route that once took the American forces over three years and thousands of lives to complete would be finished by the Continental jetliner in less than eleven hours.

EIGHTEEN

Honolulu, Hawaii, 1986

"This who you're looking for?"

"No."

"You sure? He fits your description."

"Thanks, Sergeant, but it's not him," Merith said.

The Hawaiian police sergeant shrugged. "If you say so."

"This guy's too old," Merith confirmed as he looked at a gapping slash that started under the left ear and then down across the jugular and through the larynx. The neck and shoulders were covered in dark dry blood.

The sergeant nodded to the young man in the white coat holding the sheet off the body. "Okay, Doc, put him back in the freezer," the sergeant said as he and Merith stepped away.

"What happened to the guy?" Merith asked, trying to sound casual.

"Typical thing. A bunch of punks try to take some vacationer for his wallet. The guy's whole life savings is in it and he's not willing to give it up. So he ends up here. Happens all the time. People think this is paradise." The sergeant shook his head. "It's New York with sun, palm trees, and blue water."

Merith turned. "I'll remember that, Sergeant. And thanks again for your time," he said.

167

Fuck, Merith thought as he stepped out of the refrigerated air of the morgue and into the hot tropical day. He saw the brown Dodge that Honolulu sector had given him waiting against the curb. He headed for it.

"Well?" Karen asked as Merith opened the passenger's door.

"Ya, it was Cranken. Whoever took him out wasn't after his wallet," Merith said, drumming his fingers on the dash board.

"What now?"

"Get me to the airport. I'm going to make a little house call on someone," he said, staring out the windshield, trying to put the puzzle together.

It took the Bell 222 Twin Executive helicopter only a short time to fly from Honolulu International Airport to the big island of Hawaii. The pilot knew where Merith wanted to go. He had never landed there but he had flown the admiral's guests to Hilo plenty of times.

Merith watched out the window of the jet chopper as it sped along the coast of the island. The back of his mind was wondering how much crap he was going to take for renting an executive helicopter instead of waiting for a smaller one to become available. There was going to be a lot of paperwork and it was all crap, all fucked, and a man from another sector he had assigned to a simple surveillance job was now lying in the morgue. That's what the front of his mind was working on, why? Son of a bitch, he thought. Why?

"They tell you where I should land?" the pilot asked.

"Anywhere, just set it down anywhere." Merith inspected the isolated estate from above. The red-tiled roof of the house came into view below them. It was larger than Merith had imagined.

The helicopter touched the trimmed green lawn gently, and before its blades slowed, Merith was out the door.

"Mr. Merith, how do you do?" Marks said, meeting the

CIA man at the edge of the lawn, his charm turned on to the fullest. "John Marks, Admiral Tendrey's personal secretary. I hope your flight was comfortable. We use that charter now and then." Mark extended his hand but Merith didn't meet it.

"Where is he?"

"The admiral asked me to show you to the veranda. He'll be down in a moment."

"Then show me," Merith said.

"Right this way." Marks was working to keep his smile.

They walked across the gravel driveway and passed a marble fountain, its water jetting high into the breeze, the spray falling cool against Merith's face. To the other side, the chauffeur was washing a blue limousine in the shade.

The veranda overlooked more trimmed lawns and the cliffs where the sea broke over the reefs.

A young Hawaiian girl with short black hair was clearing the glass patio table of lunch dishes when Merith and Marks came around the corner of the house. Marks looked at her, his eyes hard, then he turned to Merith and smiled. "Please, have a seat, Mr. Merith. She'll be finished in a second. I'll tell the admiral you're here. Can I have the butler get you anything?"

"Nothing," Merith said, and as Marks walked into the house, Merith looked back at the girl and the silver tray she was piling plates on. Two cups, one for coffee, one with a tea bag hanging from it. Two food dishes, two sets of silverware. And a tumbler of a small amount of gold liquid in the bottom. Who's the guest? Merith wondered.

"Ah, Mr. Merith." The admiral smiled as Marks pushed his wheelchair out of the double glass doors. "Your phone call was a surprise. You've given me little time to prepare myself, but I'm sure that was your intent."

"Not at all, Admiral, and I apologize for the way I dropped in. But I have my reasons."

"Of course, the agent killed in Honolulu." The admiral waved his hand slightly and Marks let go of the wheelchair

169

and walked into the house. "But you said the police reported it as a mugging."

"That's what their report says."

"You don't believe it."

"He was too good for some street punk to open his throat," Merith said, looking down at the admiral.

"No one is immortal, Mr. Merith."

"My superiors had me set up surveillance on Brian Bovan as a favor to you, Admiral. Why?"

"You read his file. He's a security risk. An ex-commander of a nuclear submarine has a lot of knowledge, Mr. Merith, a lot of important knowledge," Tendrey said as he wheeled himself to the edge of the patio. He looked out at the sea. "I'm sure you understand the concern."

"Oh, I understand the concern, Admiral. I just don't understand your place in it."

Tendrey spun around and looked hard at Merith. "I have my reasons. My own reasons."

Merith stared back into his watery red eyes. "Where is Bovan now?"

"At last report, he's on Maui taking in the sun," the admiral said.

"Being watched by your people?"

"Exactly."

"Where on Maui?"

"As I said over the phone, that is no longer your concern, Mr. Merith. I'm sure you will receive new orders this afternoon instructing you to return to Washington." Tendrey turned in his wheelchair. "Thank you for your help, but I won't be needing it any longer," he said, making the same gesture of dismissal he had given his secretary.

As if on cue, Marks stepped out of the house to show Merith back to his awaiting helicopter. Merith looked at the back of Tendrey's hand. "You're right, Admiral, no one is immortal," he said, and then followed Marks around the side of the house.

Tendrey didn't move, the comment wasn't made. In the

170

admiral's mind, the man from the CIA had never come because such insubordination in front of a commanding officer would never be tolerated.

Merith followed Marks along the narrow walkway until they came to a side door. "Do you mind if I use the bathroom," Merith asked, forcing a smile. "It's a long way back to Honolulu."

Marks looked at him. "Through here," he said, opening the door and leading him through the brightly lit stone kitchen with its copper pans and bowls hung in perfect order along the walls.

The secretary pointed to the double doors that led into the rest of the house. "Down the hall, third door to the right," he said.

Merith nodded as he stepped through the door. Once out of the kitchen, he looked back and saw Marks hadn't followed him.

From a different door, a butler stepped out with a small silver tray in his hand. On the tray was a tumbler of gold liquid and ice. Merith smiled at him as the butler passed, then he followed him silently a few paces behind. The butler walked down the maze of hallways oblivious to Merith.

Coming to a set of double redwood doors, the butler opened them with one hand, and as he stepped through, Merith moved close behind him and looked in.

The large man with the strong face and bald head standing near the far wall with an open book in his hand looked up and saw Merith. Their eyes met for an instant before the doors closed.

Merith crossed the rear driveway toward the helicopter in a quick pace. His mind was reeling so much so he didn't see the small suitcase lying near the rear bumper of the limousine until he stumbled over it.

"Sorry," he said to the chauffeur, who gave him a dirty

look as he picked up the case, brushed it off, and stacked it on top of the other matching suitcases in the trunk.

Merith looked at the suitcases, at the chauffeur, to the house, then again at the suitcases. He turned and ran to the helicopter.

"Can you hide this thing behind the hills? I want to see where that limo goes," Merith said as the helicopter lifted off the lawn of Tendrey's estate. "But make like you're heading for Honolulu first and then loop back."

"Whatever you say. It's your bill," the pilot said. "They'll have to go north along the state highway. The only other highway goes back through the national park."

"Can you follow them without being spotted?"

The pilot grinned. "Cake, man, a piece of cake. We'll drop behind the trees and when they leave, we'll pop out. Just like 'Nam."

Ya, Merith thought, just like 'Nam. He remembered the Vietnam war and how he had fought in it from alleys and backrooms in China. He watched as the red-tiled roof of Tendrey's mansion fell behind the tops of the green palm trees.

"He saw me!"

"Goddamnit, how?" Tendrey said, looking at Mills.

"He was in the house," Mills said. He felt himself wet under the arms. He didn't like the CIA; they thought of themselves apart from every other arm of the government and they never seemed to take orders. This Merith was a prime example.

"How the hell did he get into the house?"

"What are we going to do now?" Mills was pacing the veranda.

"You get to your plane. I'll take care of Mr. Merith," Tendrey said.

172

"What are you going to do, kill another CIA agent?" Mills asked as he turned and walked briskly into the house.

"John!" Tendrey yelled at the top of his lungs. It made him cough in spasms but he didn't care. How did Merith get into the house? "John!"

The vet pilot was right. He set his chopper down in a field hidden from the road, and when the limousine passed, they popped out, arched high above and behind it, and let it lead them to its destination.

"They're going to Hilo, man. To the airport," the pilot said after twenty minutes. The sleek Bell helicopter felt uncomfortable pacing the slow-moving car below. It was designed to speed executives from boardroom to boardroom.

Merith said nothing; he simply watched the car go along the uncrowded highway, through the series of turnoffs and toward the airport.

"I told you, man." The pilot smiled.

"You got binoculars in this thing?"

"Behind the seat."

Merith grabbed the Zeiss binoculars from the small elastic pocket on the seat back. "Get us closer," he said as he raised the glasses to his face.

"I've gotta get clearance from the tower."

"Then do it," Merith said without taking his eyes off the limousine.

Tendrey's car wound its way past the visitor's parking and through two airport gates. It stopped at a third with a guard and then proceeded undetained. Turning left, the car moved to the airfield apron.

Then it stopped next to a small Lear jet, the white skin on the narrow body and its hawk-sharp wings glistening in the sun. The rear of the limousine opened and Merith saw the man step out.

He had no doubt who Tendrey's guest was. Admiral Thomas Mills. Merith had seen his photograph in the files he had looked over after the yeoman had come to Bovan's hotel suite with the package. And now here he was in Hawaii. No coincidence, Merith thought.

"Get me closer. I've got to see the numbers on that plane."

"Hey, the tower said I could land, but not here. This ain't the heliport, man. It's on the other side of the runways," the pilot protested.

Merith reached into his breast pocket and pulled out his wallet. He snapped it open and pushed his CIA identification in front of the vet's eyes. "Get me closer, just till I get the numbers."

"Shit. This is going to mean my license," the pilot said as he dropped lower. "You're going to be paying the fines for this."

Through the binoculars, Merith picked up the first letter and four of the numbers from the fuselage of the Lear. It was enough. "Okay, let's get out of here," Merith said, hoping they hadn't gotten too close and were spotted. "Land it so I can get to a phone."

"You need a phone? There's one in the back between the rear seats," the pilot said. "Remember, this is an executive chopper."

Merith unclipped his seatbelt and pulled the headphones off his head. Crouched over, he moved to the rear section of the helicopter.

"Where to?"

"Honolulu," Merith hollered back to the vet. He felt the pilot lift the helicopter higher into the sky and increase its speed. The vibrations and noise Merith had felt before suddenly disappeared as the chopper reached its designed speed and altitude.

Merith picked up the black telephone and dialed the Honolulu sector's special number. Then he had to wait for the operator to connect him. She gave him the wrong office twice until finally Karen picked up the line.

"They've got me in this stupid little room, Troy, you

174

won't believe it. It's hotter than hell in here," she complained.

"Okay, okay, I'll take care of it," he promised, trying to calm her. She wasn't used to the heat and it was getting to her. "Listen, find out the flight plan for a Lear Jet, number N1414 something something. I didn't get the last numbers. But it took off from Hilo airport not more than ten minutes ago. It must be a charter out of Honolulu."

"Got it."

"And run Bovan's name through the computers again," Merith told her, and then, as an afterthought, "Karen, run Admiral Thomas Mills through too, but keep it quiet."

The helicopter was only fifteen minutes out of Honolulu International when Karen called on the executive phone.

"The computer came up with Bovan's name on a Continental Airline's flight leaving tomorrow morning," Karen said. "But I wouldn't trust him to make it."

"Going where?" Merith was anxious.

"It's goes to the Caroline Islands with several stops in between."

"And what about that Lear and Mills?"

"Nothing on Mills at all. What made you ask?" Karen said.

"Did you get the flight plan for that plane?" Merith was trying to think.

"You were right. It was a charter out of Honolulu. Registration number N141467. Stopped at Hilo to pick up its passenger and then was to continue to its destination."

"Where?"

"Truk Lagoon, Caroline Islands," Karen said.

"That Continental flight, does it land in Truk?"

There was silence for a second and Merith could almost see Karen push her hair out of her eyes as she went over her notes. "Ya, it's the last stop."

Merith leaned back against the seat of the helicopter. He could feel it slowing as they approached Honolulu. He pressed the phone tight against his face. "Get me on that flight," he said in a low voice. "Don't say anything to anyone. Do it from a phone outside the building."

"What about me?"

"I'll meet you at the hotel," he said, then he hung up the phone.

Merith watched the skyscrapers of Honolulu creep up the side window of the chopper as it landed in the large white circle of the heliport.

"We're home," the pilot said as he shut down the engine. But Merith didn't hear him.

What the hell was going on? Merith wondered. Mills was heading to Truk, and he was sure Bovan was either there or also on his way.

NINETEEN

Honolulu, Hawaii, 1944

The cylindrical length of steel dangled at a sharp angle over the deck of the *Seakrill*. A crewman, with a foot on each side of the oval opening, reached up and guided the nose of the torpedo carefully into the forward torpedo room below.

"Number twenty-four, Skipper," Michael said, standing next to Douglas on the bridge. He looked down at his clipboard and checked off the torpedo. "That's the last fish."

"What else do we need?" Douglas asked.

"Frank is at the supply house trying to get some green food coloring. Says he's going to make a cake on St. Patrick's Day," Michael said, shaking his head.

Douglas laughed.

"Otherwise we're all stocked with food and water. Batteries are up to full charge and we're in line to top off the diesel tanks at noon. The *Scamp* is refueling now and the *Sunfish* is next at the dock," Michael said. "Then we're set, Skipper."

"When can I tell Whither we're ready for sea?"

"Once Clancy gives the okay on that forward engine."

"How's he doing?" Douglas asked.

"He said she'll be ready."

"Good." Douglas turned and climbed down through the hatch and into his submarine. He wondered if he should have had the repair crew stay aboard an extra day and double-check the diesel. No, he trusted Clancy's work and his word. If the mechanic wasn't a hundred percent sure, he'd say so.

Unlike the sleeping hull of the night before, the *Seakrill* rumbled with the sounds of life. In every compartment, seamen moved in and out securing stores and double-checking the equipment. It was music, this clatter of movement, of each man doing his task of preparation. But there was little talk, some joking and thin smiles all that hid what was on each crewman's mind.

Tonight began another patrol and the ship was filled with unspoken tension. The kind of fear that pulled nerves taut like violin strings. Fear of not knowing what was going to happen tomorrow or the next day or the next week. Each wondering if they would die in this steel coffin they called home, their bodies turning cold with the chill of the sea as it rushed in through a shattered hull. But they didn't talk about it. That was bad luck.

Douglas knew each of his crew was wondering what sector the *Seakrill* would patrol. If they would follow the *Scorpion* to the bottom of the Yellow Sea, or the *SS-238* or the *Capelin*. But then, it didn't really matter; they were leaving Pearl and again going to war. The same danger was at every compass point over the horizon.

Douglas sensed the heaviness of the air as he moved through the control room. It would linger like an oily fog until their first confrontation with the enemy. Then it would dissipate little by little until they saw the mouth of Pearl Harbor again. He knew because it was that way with him. He nodded to the officers in the control room as he passed through and headed toward the radio room.

"Everything check out, Danny?" Douglas said as he leaned into the doorway of the tiny room.

The young radioman with only patches of soft blond hair on his face snapped to attention. "Yes, sir. All set, Skipper," Danny said.

Douglas looked at the young seaman. He was fresh out of New London's sub school and this was his first patrol in the Pacific. "Why don't you see what kind of music you can find on that thing and pipe it through the ship," Douglas said.

"Aye, aye, sir. I could use a little of that," the seaman said, trying to hide his nervous voice.

"Believe me, we all could," Douglas said. He stepped back into the corridor and moved forward toward his quarters.

"Skipper!" Michael yelled from above as Douglas walked back through the control room.

"Yes." Douglas saw his face through the conning tower's hatch.

"Messenger on the docks for you."

Douglas climbed the ladder two rungs at a time. When he got to the bridge he heard the forward diesel start up. He turned to his exec. "Sounds like Clancy got her together after all."

Michael smiled. "Never had a doubt," he said. "He's been working on it all night with the mechanic from the repair crew."

"Good," Douglas said, climbing down the tower. He crossed over to the dock to where the messenger stood a few yards away, leaning on his jeep. He stiffened and saluted as the submarine commander approached.

"Admiral Tendrey requests your presence at his office, sir. He asked me to drive you there, Commander," the messenger said.

Bingo. The proof Wagner wanted is now being served, Douglas thought. "Thank you," he said, returning the salute. "I'll be ready in a minute."

"What's up?" Michael asked as he followed Douglas into his cabin.

"Tendrey wants to see me up at headquarters. I'll pick up our orders when I'm there."

"Tendrey? What the hell does he want from you?" Michael asked.

Douglas looked into his six-by-six-inch mirror and tied a loose knot in his black tie. "Won't know until he tells me," he said flatly.

"This stinks. His name has been coming up in too many places lately," Michael said, sitting down on Douglas's bunk and leaning back against the bulkhead.

"What do you mean?"

"He was the one who assigned that new machinist's mate to us."

"Hathorn?" Douglas asked in disbelief.

"Ya."

Douglas shook his head, "I didn't see that in his papers."

"It wasn't there. I talked to Flatwood, the exec on the *Tang*. Hathorn was originally assigned to her. He told me Tendrey had personally requested the transfer. I just wonder why Stein went along with it?" Michael said, putting his hands behind his head.

Douglas knew. Their squadron commander, Captain Linus Stein, was an old buddy of Tendrey's. The two of them served on K-boats together after the first war. They were tight; and it would only take Tendrey to ask, and Stein would sign the papers without question. Then Tendrey would have his venomous eyes aboard the *Seakrill*.

"Flatwood say anything else?" Douglas asked.

"No. He said the kid performed without a hitch during their four-day testing. Now he is in the same position we're in, going out on patrol with an untested seaman," Michael said.

"If he did okay on the *Tang*, he'll be all right with us." Douglas lifted his cap off the hook on the back of the door. He stepped from his cabin and headed toward the tower. Michael followed. "Just keep an eye on him," he said over his shoulder.

"You going to say anything to him?"

Douglas shrugged. "What's to say?"

Michael had no answer.

"If you have the chance to top off the tanks before I get back, do it. I'd like to tell Whithers we're ready for sea."

"Aye, Skipper."

Douglas paced back and forth in the small office, waiting for Rear Admiral Tendrey. The absence of pictures on the walls and the few books on the shelves showed this wasn't going to be the admirals' permanent niche. Douglas could guess why: it was an old office in an old building, hot and humid, and the air was stagnant because the fan in the corner didn't work. He could imagine Tendrey's rage when he found out where the administration had placed him.

The office's only door squeaked open and Tendrey stepped in.

"Sorry to keep you waiting, Doug," he said pleasantly, almost sincerely, in his Southern drawl. His khaki uniform was dark with sweat.

"You wanted to see me? About last night, I gather," Douglas said directly.

"Precisely," the admiral said as he moved behind his small steel desk. He opened the top drawer and pulled out a letter-sized envelope. From the bottom drawer, he took out a larger manila envelope. "Here you go." Tendrey handed Douglas the smaller one.

"What's this?"

"Those are the orders you'll need to supplement your combat orders from command. I was, of course, able to convince them to assign the *Seakrill* reconnaissance patrol off Truk. But I know you will have to show your exec some kind of orders telling you to enter the lagoon and to rendezvous with the Jap freighter. Those are the orders. They look official," Tendrey said with a cocked smile.

Douglas couldn't believe what he had in his hand. Forged naval documents from a rear admiral. A man he hated. He could never have dreamt it would be this easy.

Douglas smiled. "You sound as if I've agreed to your plan."

"Like I said last night, you have little choice, Doug. That is, if you want to keep your jacket clean," Tendrey said. He reached down and grabbed the second envelope. "These are the charts to get into Truk. They show where the freighter will be anchored and how to identify her. They came from the ambassador's staff, so they're not the easiest things to read, but I trust you'll manage."

He tossed the package to Douglas. Then he sat down behind the desk and folded his arms over his chest. "The orders from Whithers has the *Seakrill* setting sail at midnight tonight. At 2345 hours a naval truck with three men will come to the docks and deliver the diamonds. They will be packed in a single footlocker. Inside the locker will be the explosives and detonator. One of the men will give you the instructions to activate it and the instructions to defuse it." The admiral smiled. "The explosives are your ticket out of the lagoon."

"You really think this is going to work?" Douglas asked, staring hard at the admiral.

Tendrey leaned back in his chair. "I figure you've got a thirty-percent chance of coming back from this."

"It doesn't matter to you either way, does it?"

"No, not really. I've done my part," Tendrey said.

Douglas opened his leather briefcase and dropped the two envelopes into it. Two solid packages of proof that would set Tendrey behind bars for the rest of his life. He saluted the admiral and turned to leave.

"Oh, Commander," the Southerner said as Douglas moved toward the door. "You'll have to be in and out of Truk by the sixteenth. Stein will brief you on that."

Douglas nodded as he left the hot office. He stepped out onto the grass-lined walk that led to the curb where the driver had dropped him off. He was gone.

CINCPAC headquarters was a quarter of a mile away up the street. Loosening his necktie, Douglas started toward the command buildings. The Hawaiian sun was already beating down on the black pavement and the wind off the coral blue sea was just enough to move the palm leaves gently overhead. But he felt neither the sun nor the breeze; his mind was on last night and what she had said to him: "No matter what, you'll stay with me."

The "no matter what" was too much. She had baited him, tricked him, and pulled him directly into the sharks' mouth. But now everything had shifted and it was Tendrey who would find himself with nowhere to turn. A down-the-throat shot, Douglas thought.

The sharp metallic beep of the jeep's horn startled him as the vehicle pulled up along side of the curb. "Offer you a ride, Commander?" the driver yelled.

Douglas saw the shoulder marks of a lieutenant junior grade, and when he looked to thank him, he saw it was Wagner.

The OSS man didn't smile at Douglas when he recognized him. He shifted the jeep into gear and pulled quickly out into the street. "I got bad news for you, Bovan," the agent said.

Douglas smiled. "And I've got great news for you. Here," he said, opening the flap of his briefcase. "I just walked out of Tendrey's office and you won't believe what he handed me."

"Direct orders to infiltrate the Japanese base at Truk lagoon. All signed and sealed and forged by him," the agent called Wagner said.

"How did you know?"

Now Wagner smiled. "You're kidding, right?"

"Oh, ya, it's your job."

"It sure is, and it is also my job to tell you to hang onto those orders," Wagner said. "You'll be needing them."

"What do you mean? I thought all I had to do was to turn them over to you and you'd hang Tendrey. Last night you told me you needed proof. Well, here it is. Shit, it is

183

practically a signed affidavit of guilt, what more do you want?'' Douglas said.

Wagner braked for two WACs crossing the street. Then he accelerated, shifted, and accelerated again. He was driving to nowhere. Driving around the base in order to talk and not to be overheard.

''It's not what I want, Commander, believe me. But the OSS wants you to carry out the admiral's plans. Completely,'' Wagner said.

''You're crazy.''

''I won't argue that. But as it was explained to me, the importance of retrieving the Peking Man fossils is too great to pass up,'' Wagner said. ''Look, we have the signed orders from Tendrey. He is ours, Commander. The rope is secure around his neck. Whether we pull the noose tight now or when you return, it doesn't matter. But if we do it now, there will be no chance of getting those fossils. I don't know if you realize it, Bovan, but those fossils are important. Maybe not militarily, but diplomatically.''

''As important as the Liberty Bell,'' Douglas said, staring out the windshield of the jeep.

''What?''

''Nothing. I understand their importance to the Chinese.''

''Then you understand you are now working under orders of the OSS,'' Wagner said, his voice stern as if the words should have evoked something deep in Douglas.

''Officially?''

''No,'' the agent said. ''Tendrey would hear about anything official. I've told you what my CO said to me.''

They drove a few blocks in silence until Douglas finally said, ''Tendrey had a crewman transfered to my sub last week. It wasn't on his papers but my exec found out.''

''I'd guess he has a definite reason for being there, Commander,'' Wagner said. He looked over at Douglas. ''What time are you to set sail?''

''Midnight.''

184

"I'll be there before you shove off. What do you need, an ensign, a petty officer?" Wagner asked.

"You're not kidding, are you?" Douglas said, figuring that the agent could probably arrange any transfer orders he needed and with any rank he wanted. He shook his head. "My boat has a complete crew."

"How about a naval observer then, assigned directly by Washington. The old boys at the State Department want to know exactly how their Silent Service is operating," he said as he pulled the jeep to the curb.

Douglas suddenly realized they were in front of CINC-PAC headquarters. He turned to the agent, "Thanks for the ride, Lieutenant."

"My pleasure, Skipper. I'll see you before midnight, sir," Wagner saluted.

Douglas watched as the OSS man pulled away from the curb. It was undoubtedly a good idea to have the agent aboard, he thought as he entered the offices of SUBPAC. He was the expert in this type of thing, and like he said, Tendrey's man was on a mission. Pawn for pawn, Douglas thought, but he didn't like the gameboard being his submarine.

"Flintlock, Commander, Operation Flintlock is a total success," Captain Linus Stein said, slapping his hands together and rubbing them palm against palm as though he were trying to start a fire. "The Japs didn't know what hit them. The first reports came in this morning."

Stein was a short square man, carrying twenty pounds excess at the beltline. A gray-haired veteran excited by the battle reports. He moved around his desk with the spring in his walk of a new father. He pulled out his ever-present checkered handkerchief, blew his nose, and then pushed the crumbled cloth back into his pocket. "Kwajalein is on its knees, it will be flattened by dusk," he smiled.

"That's good news, sir," Douglas said, stiff at attention before his squadron commander.

"It's great news, Douglas, but I have better," Stein said. "Operation Hailstone has been moved up eight weeks. They hit on the sixteenth."

"Truk, sir?" Douglas was shocked. He'd been told officially about a large assault being planned for April, and then through scuttlebutt, he'd heard that it was going to be against Truk. But he didn't expect the fleet to move ahead so quickly in its attack on the Gibraltar of the Pacific.

"Exactly. COMSUBPAC is already issuing orders to the submarines in the area to support the fleet operations. As soon as the Marshalls are secured, Mitcher's task force is heading directly toward the atoll," the squadron commander said. Then in a lower tone, "I know you've been having trouble with your engines, Doug, but we need the *Seakrill* at Truk before the operations begin. Whither's staff asked me to issue you your new patrol orders.

"The *Searaven* and the *Darter* are going to be on lifeguard duty just to the north and south of Truk. They want you to position the *Seakrill* east of the lagoon. Our fly-boys are going to run into a lot of Zeros coming off those islands, and the last thing I want is to lose a pilot from drowning," Stein said.

"It's going to be tight, sir," Douglas said. His mind was figuring at least twelve days to travel the four thousand miles to Truk. Tendrey couldn't have planned the events better, but then he was on the admiral's staff and undoubtedly had a tap on every information source, official and otherwise. It was suddenly clear why the Chinese ambassador had picked Tendrey to find a submarine for his mission.

"I know, that's why the orders are specific. You are not to engage with any enemy vessels with antisubmarine capabilities. Don't get me wrong, Doug, if it's easy prey, take it, but Operation Hailstone outweighs everything on this patrol. If our boys can take Truk, then the rest of the Pacific islands are only a matter of time, Doug, only a matter of

186

time," Stein said. He was smiling. "Here." He picked up the *Seakrill*'s patrol-orders package from the desktop and handed it to Douglas. "Good luck, Commander."

"Thank you, sir. You can be sure we'll be in place by the sixteenth," Douglas said. He tucked the package under his arm, saluted, turned briskly around, and headed out of the SUBPAC office.

As he walked through the outer offices, Douglas stopped and set his briefcase on the edge of one of the secretary's desks. He opened it and shoved his patrol orders inside.

"Oh, Commander Bovan," a slender brown-haired secretary called to him from down the hallway.

Douglas turned and watched her approach. "Yes?"

The woman walked up next to him. "Margaret O'Tullie was looking for you a few minutes ago. I think she's outside," the woman said, keeping her face down, too shy to look directly at the tall lieutenant commander with the dark eyes.

"Thank you," Douglas said, lifting his briefcase off her desk. What the hell did O'Tullie want? he wondered, walking directly out the door.

The yellow Packard rested at the curbside. Margaret sat alone in its passenger seat, looking out at the harbor. A flowered pink scarf surrounded the top of her head and thick dark sunglass hid her eyes. Her thin right arm dangled lazily over the edge of the door.

"Oh," she said, startled when Douglas touched her shoulder gently.

"Looking for me?"

The surprise left her face and she frowned. "She's at my house crying her head off, Doug," Margaret said directly.

"She has reason to," he said, leaning against the long swooping fender, his briefcase in front of him.

"Listen, I don't know what went on between you two last night, but you have to go talk to her," Margaret said. She reached out and put her hand on Douglas's arm.

187

"Please, Doug, go talk to her. That's all I'm asking. She knows you're leaving tonight."

Douglas looked at Nimitz's secretary and smiled. That, he knew, was an understatement and he wondered if Margaret realized it. No, she didn't know anything. There was a kinship between her and the Chinese assistant to the ambassador, at least that's what Margaret thought. She saw herself in Mimi. Two women far from home with the heavy burden of being the right hand to important men of war. But that's where it ended.

"Please, Doug."

Douglas looked at his watch. 1130 hours. Michael could handle the boat to the fueling dock. At 1600 hours he had planned for a quick shakedown cruise off Maui, but that was four and a half hours away. "Okay," he said, walking around the long hood of the automobile.

"Oh, great, Doug. You can drop me off at my office," she said. "I told her you would come. She'll be so happy."

I doubt it, Douglas thought as he slid into the driver's seat. There were a lot of things he wanted to discuss with Lai Ming. One of them was his new machinist's mate.

TWENTY

Moen Island, Truk Lagoon, 1986

Brian lifted his two suitcases off the long wooden table where the airport crew had deposited them with the other passengers'. He walked back to where Leslie stood encircled by her own six pieces of luggage. She was scanning the terminal building, standing on the tips of her toes trying to see beyond the shifting waves of people walking about. Her hands were clenched nervously in front of her.

"See him?" Brian asked as he set his bags near her.

"No."

"Did he know you were coming in today?"

"I sent him a telegram yesterday. It's not like him to be late," Leslie said, looking at Brian and giving him a half smile.

"Miss Yokamata?" asked the tall lean police officer as he approached them. The second officer beside him was shorter, stout with a thick muscular neck. Both, Brian noted, looked to be natives to the lagoon.

"Yes," Leslie said.

"Would you come with us, please?" The tall one gestured toward the far side of the terminal that was lined with small offices. "Zeen will see to your luggage," he said politely.

"Why?" Leslie said as she stepped closer to Brian and

slipped her arm through his. She clutched the sleeve of his bone-white coat.

"Is there a problem, officer?" Brian asked.

"Please?" he said again. Brian recognized the look in his face. There was a problem, but this wasn't the place to disclose it.

Leslie didn't let go of Brian as they followed the policeman into the small sterile office. A single gray steel desk filled one side of the room, its top empty. Two folding chairs were set in front of it and a padded swivel chair behind. A box air-conditioner in the window hummed noisily in the corner. Pinned to the wall behind the desk was a chart of the lagoon.

"The sergeant will be with you in a moment," he said, stepping back out of the room and shutting the door.

Leslie turned and looked up at Brian. She was frightened, terrified, and imagining the worst. She put her hand into his and held it with all her strength.

As the office door opened, the same policeman who had escorted them stepped in followed by an older man. He wore a similar light brown uniform as the other officers, but it was wrinkled, as if he had slept in it and had been awoken prematurely. The soft loose skin associated with age along the back of his jaw was badly pockmarked from a childhood disease, and the several days' worth of beard didn't hide it.

As he moved around the desk, there was no question of his authority. Under his poorly kept uniform, there was a strong powerful man, and Brian could feel it as soon as he spoke.

"Miss Yokamata," he said in a deep monotone voice as he sat down. "I'm sorry to have to tell you, but your father was in an accident while diving one of the deep wrecks."

"Where is he?" Leslie asked, her eyes widening in panic.

"He's dead."

"Oh, God, no," Leslie said in a soft, childlike voice. Her legs buckled and Brian moved her into one of the chairs.

"It happened last week. We sent a telegram to your New

190

York address, but then yours came yesterday saying you were arriving on today's flight," the sergeant said. "We figure he was doing research and became disoriented and couldn't find the line that led up to his decompression tanks," the sergeant said. "It happens a lot."

"He was diving alone?" Brian asked.

The sergeant looked up at Brian. "Are you traveling with Miss Yokamata, Mr. . . ?"

"Yes, he is," Leslie said as if defying the police officer.

"It's Brock, Sergeant . . . ?" Brian looked for the name tag on his shirt but there wasn't one.

"Sergeant Wuun," the man behind the desk said. "The professor always dove alone, Mr. Brock. We found his body washed up on Tsis."

Brian glanced up at the chart. "Pretty deep water around that island."

Wuun turned in his chair and looked up at the wall chart. He looked back at Leslie. "Your father rented a house on the north end of the island, Miss Yokamata. Officer Magun will take you there. We have the accident report," Wuun said as he opened the top drawer of the desk and pulled out a manila folder.

Leslie's head snapped up. "I don't want to see any reports."

"I'm sure it can wait until tomorrow, can't it, Sergeant?" Brian said as he looked down at Leslie. Then he looked at Wuun.

"There's no hurry." Wuun nodded. He stood up and moved around to the opposite side of the desk and leaned against it. He folded his arms over his chest. "Until tomorrow then."

Leslie stood slowly and moved toward the door.

"Anytime you want to come by the station," Wuun said. He looked at Brian. "Too bad about old Hitobuto. He was a good friend."

Brian nodded as he looked into Wuun's eyes. They were empty of the sadness the man spoke of. As they stepped out of the office and followed Officer Magun, Brian put his arm around Leslie's waist.

Wuun watched them walk down the center of the terminal, then he moved to the office next door. This office was the same as the other but smaller. It had the same type of desk but with only one chair. A similar wall chart hung behind it. The top of the desk was cluttered with papers and books, a phone, and other officeware.

Sitting on the corner of the desk, Wuun pulled the phone next to him and dialed. After getting through to the operator, it took another minute before he heard the phone at the other end of the line ring.

"Admiral Tendrey, please," Wuun said, then he waited another two minutes.

"Tendrey here."

"It's Ty."

"What do you have?"

"Bovan is here with the girl," Wuun said flatly.

"Christ," the admiral said through clenched teeth. "Then you know our arrangement. They are not to get near the *Kuma Maru* or near any other wreck unless you are sure of what it is. Do whatever you have to do, but stop them. Do you understand?"

"Yes, Admiral," Wuun said.

"What about Yokamata's house?"

"It's been cleared out of all the professor's charts and books, and they've been destroyed like you said."

"Good, Ty. And what about Admiral Mills? Has he arrived?"

"No."

"Have him phone me when he does and keep me informed on what they do," the admiral ordered as if he were talking to a crew member of his ship. "Ty, I don't care what Mills tells you. You take orders from me. Understand?"

"Completely, Admiral."

* * *

192

"My truck is just outside," Magun said as he grabbed two of the suitcases. Brian took his and two of Leslie's and Zeen picked up the rest.

"Are you okay?" Brian asked as they walked out of the terminal and into the heat of Truk's afternoon. Her face was pale, her eyes far away.

She nodded slightly, her right hand on her neck, her left hand holding his tight.

After they filled the back of the dark brown Land Rover with their suitcases, Brian and Leslie climbed into the back seat while Magun and Zeen sat up front.

"It is only a few minutes from here," Magun said as he pulled out onto the smooth asphalt road. "But it is away from everything. He liked it that way."

"How well did you know the professor?" Brian asked.

"Barely. He stayed mostly to himself. But I met him fishing on the reef a few times."

Against his shoulder, Brian could feel Leslie shaking as she cried quietly. She moved closer, turned her head, and pushed her cheek against his chest.

The asphalt street changed to dirt road, and after two miles, Magun slowed the Land Rover and turned off the road and down a sandy trail. It wound around a thick stretch of mangrove and coconut trees, then widened out and became beach. He went left and drove around a large chunk of coral rock long ago cast up onto the beach by a tropical storm.

Further down, on the other side of the finger of land that stuck out into the lagoon, the white stone-roofed house stood almost hidden in the mango grove. Only the one side and its raised porch could be seen from the lagoon.

"Here we are," Magun said, stopping next to the steps of the porch.

Leslie climbed out and moved up the stairs of the porch.

"The key's under the mat," Magun called to her as he lifted the suitcases from the back of the Rover. "This place was built for one of the army engineers," he said to Brian. "Not many American-styled houses in these islands.

The small stucco house with its framed doors and glass-paned windows did seem out of place. The rest of the island's inhabitants lived in structures made of palm wood and leaves and pieces of sheet metal.

"She gonna be okay?" Magun said, tilting his head toward Leslie as he held out the last of the luggage with his brittle-looking arm.

"I hope so," Brian said honestly. "She hadn't seen him in several years."

Magun slammed the tailgate closed. "The bends are a terrible way to go," he said, shaking his head. "When I heard his daughter was coming, I had my wife buy some things for the icebox. Not a lot, but you two won't starve."

"Thanks, Officer Magun," Brian said as he shook Magun's hand.

"Call me Fumio," the officer said with a smile.

Brian smiled back and then looked at the other officer. But there was no warmth in the younger man's face. He was staring at Brian with stone-cold eyes.

Fumio noticed it. "Get in the truck, Zeen," Fumio said, and the young officer moved around the Land Rover. "Don't mind him. He's not part of our welcoming committee." Fumio forced a laugh. "If there's anything else I can do, just ask."

"One thing," Brian said, leaning on the open car door. "Where can I get a dive boat?"

"The professor had a skiff in the harbor. He had that, the house, and the jeep all rented till the end of the year," Magun said. "I guess it's yours to use. Can't see any problem with that. Just go to the pier and ask for George. He'll show you which is the professor's boat and get you anything else you need."

"Thanks again," Brian said as he shut the Rover's door. He watched as they drove back down the beach, turned, and disappeared into the mangos.

Walking up the weathered steps of the porch, Brian stopped by the rail and looked out at the lagoon. The water was a cool aqua-blue in the shallows but darker on the other side of the reef. Beyond the walls of staghorn and stony corals that held back the sea's power and kept the inner lagoon calm, it was deeper. Much deeper.

He brushed his hands off the dried peels of paint that came off the rail. Turning, he walked into the house.

"Leslie," he called, but there was no answer. Moving first through the kitchen, then down the hallway, he looked into the single bedroom. Her suitcases were tossed on the bed, unopen. He continued to the end of the hall and opened another door.

What must have once been a spare bedroom, the professor had converted into a workroom. Against one wall was a workbench, a vice, and power tools. Lining the other side were scuba tanks and diving equipment. An underwater welding torch was next to the bench.

Brian walked into the study. The room was so cluttered, he had to step around the piles of books and cardboard boxes. One wall was covered floor to ceiling with more books. The other walls were shelves filled with World War II artifacts, pressure wheels, levers from ships' helms, fine china dishes, bottles still sealed, an array of bosun's lamps, a sextant looking in perfect order, and other unidentifiable brass objects yet to be cleaned. There were more stacked in boxes in the corner.

The only wall not lined with shelves or books was a sliding glass door that opened out onto the porch and looked out over the lagoon.

In the center, two large desks were pushed back to back. Leslie sat quietly in the swivel chair behind one of them, her knees up to her chest, clutching a small picture frame in her arms. She stared out the sliding glass door at the lagoon.

"Leslie, you okay?" Brian asked.

She turned slowly and looked up at him. She handed him

the picture. "It was the only one in the whole house," she said softly.

Brian turned it over. It was a black-and-white photograph of Leslie and her father at her college graduation. In the photo, a younger Leslie had her arms wrapped around her father. His face was small and round and creased with age. An unyielding sort of man, Brian guessed as he looked at the professor staring directly into the camera without a smile. No, there was a smile just forming at the edges of his mouth.

"I keep thinking that I should have come straight to Truk and not stayed in Hawaii for that week. Maybe he'd still be alive."

"He was diving alone in deep water; there wouldn't have been anything you could have done if you were here," Brian said as he moved a few things on the cluttered desk and cleared a place to stand up the frame. Then he moved closer to the sliding glass door and looked out.

"I don't know why I waited for him to ask me to come. I should've done it on my own," she said, resting her chin on one knee.

"Last week my mom died," he said, staring down the long stretch of white beach against the lagoon. "I was able to spend a few days with her, but even that wasn't enough. When someone you're close to suddenly dies, you realize how distant you are and you think of all the things you should have done."

Standing, Leslie moved past Brian, slid open the door, and walked out onto the porch. He followed her. "My mother and brother died in a car crash when I was seven," she said, pushing her hair back over her shoulder. "I remember thinking that one day they would come back and everything would be just as it was." She looked at him. "But they never did."

Brian said nothing.

"You're welcome to—" she began to say, then stopped

196

and looked at him. "Please stay. I don't want to be here alone. Do you mind?"

"To tell you the truth, I didn't have any hotel reservation anyway." He smiled, then pushed himself away from the rail. "Magun said his wife put some food in the icebox. I'll see what I can come up with for dinner."

"You cook?" Leslie asked, a little smile on the edge of her lips.

"Out of necessity," he said, walking back into the house.

The afternoon sun was falling fast to the horizon. Fine-webbed fingers of cirrus clouds became gold as they curled upward in the distance.

Leslie shut the glass door behind her as she went back into the study, and moved to the bedroom to unpack.

"Here, try this," Brian said with a steaming chunk of white fish on the end of his fork. He had spent half an hour finding all the right pans and ingredients to make the fish. Most he'd had to fake by using some spice that smelled close to what he wanted. He leaned into the bedroom, "Leslie?"

She was asleep. Wearing only a thin cotton T-shirt and blue nylon shorts, she lay stretched out on the bed between her opened suitcases. The dress she had worn on the plane was hung over the chair.

Brian stepped back out of the room and closed the door. He ate the cooling piece of fish and returned to the kitchen. Putting Leslie's dinner in the icebox, he picked up his plate and a bottle of soda pop he found and moved into the study to finish his dinner.

He balanced the plate on the book-covered desk, took a drink of his soda, and walked over to the bookshelf. He glanced over the titles on the dusty backstrips. From the array of American classics, he guessed most came with the house when Yokamata rented it.

Closer to the desk there were books on World War II and some more specifically about the Pacific war. Several were in Japanese but most were in English. Eating his dinner, he continued to look through the study.

Finally he sat down in the swivel chair. There was something wrong here, something missing. He opened the large lower drawer of the desk designed to hold files. It was empty.

"Find anything interesting?" Leslie said as she stepped into the room.

Brian looked up as he shut the drawer. "Not a thing," he said. "And that bothers me."

"What do you mean?" she yawned.

"Your father was doing research here since June, right?"

"Ya." She walked around the desk and picked up a small brass wheel that looked like it had been taken from one of the wrecks and was now being used as a paperweight.

"Then where are his charts and notes? The books on the war are only general ones." He handed one to her. "None of them are specifically on Truk. Look—" Brian opened the file drawer. "Empty. It doesn't make sense. The professor has enough equipment in the back room to outfit a full research team. Magun told me he even has a boat in the harbor."

"Maybe they're on the boat."

"Could be, but he wouldn't keep them all there. They'd be damaged too easily." Brian shook his head.

"Maybe he hid them around here somewhere."

"Hid them from who?" Brian asked, raising his eyebrow.

Leslie looked at him. "What are you getting at?"

"I don't know," Brian said as he stood up from the desk and moved toward the door. "But it looks like someone did some housecleaning before you arrived."

"What would anyone want with his notes?" she asked, setting the brass wheel and the book on the desk.

Brian didn't say anything. He shrugged, stood up, and moved toward the door.

"Where are you going?" she asked as she followed him into the hallway.

"I thought I'd check out the diving equipment and see what's working and what isn't. Your dinner is in the kitchen. I'll heat it up."

"I can do it. You cooked, the least I could do is reheat," she said, following him into the workroom. "You don't think it was an accident, do you?"

"I'm not saying that at all," Brian said. He turned and looked into her eyes. Beautiful almond eyes that were suddenly filled with apprehension and fear. He smiled at her, hoping to dilute what he had said. "Of course it was an accident. I'm just curious where his stuff is."

Suddenly he realized that he was scaring her for no reason. "Come on, you can give me a hand," he said. It was crazy, he was crazy. But in the back of his mind he couldn't help to think that somehow the professor was tied to what had been happening to him the past week. Somehow tied to the U.S.S. *Seakrill*.

TWENTY-ONE

Moen Island, Truk Lagoon, 1986

Leslie was quiet. She had been all morning, and Brian understood. Yesterday was more a strain on her than she would admit and she had turned inward to deal with it.

She had been silent the night before while they inspected the professor's workshop and diving equipment. But that was his fault. Brian had brought up the foolish questions about the missing research notes. Now he was sorry he had said anything about it.

At midnight, she had gone to bed, and he took up residence on the rattan lounger on the patio with its stiff pad. The tropical evening was warm and scented and almost silent, save the ever-present sounds of the surf. A sound that soothed him.

Yet he still lay awake listening through the open window to distinct sounds of Leslie tossing and turning on the steel spring bed. During the night, they both slept but a little.

Now, the midmorning sun beat down on the backs of their necks as they drove toward the town. Brian had found the keys to the old gray Willys jeep with its missing right fender parked around the side of the house. Although slow to start because of a low battery, the little engine had finally kicked over, coughing a cloud of smoke and rattling free chips of rust from the undercarriage. They brushed the fallen leaves off the seats, climbed, and were on their way.

"It's beautiful today," Leslie finally said as they headed along the narrow brown road lined by the lush green jungle.

Brian smiled at her. "You hungry?"

"A little."

"I thought we'd see what kind of local dish we can find near the harbor," Brian said, glancing over at her. Her long hair bellowed full over her shoulders. She wore a simple white blouse buttoned low but not too low and lime-green shorts tailored to be loose around her muscular legs. She's a dancer, Brian remembered, taking a second glance at her legs.

Brian wore what he found in his supplied suitcases, khaki-colored slacks, a light tan shirt, dark brown matching belt, and matching deck shoes. Ming's taste was perfect, all picked out of the spring edition of *Vogue* magazine.

"I don't care to go to the police station."

"It can wait," Brian said.

"You think I should go now, don't you?"

"I think you should get it over with," Brian said flatly. "But it can wait."

More and more open thatched houses, each built on stilts a few feet off the sand, showed along the side of the road, indicating they were closing on the town. Brian slowed as the jeep rolled onto the two-lane asphalt street.

The town was small, smaller than Brian had imagined it would be. He knew the dozens of shipwrecks made Truk one of the world's most famous scuba-diving havens and he expected to see side-by-side diving shops, hotels, and expensive restaurants all feeding off the hordes of broad-smiling tourists.

Instead Uola Road, as the area near Truk Harbor was called, was a series of small one- and two-story buildings painted with shades of white and brown. Most of the second-story windows had small balconies overhanging the street and reaching out to the calm bay.

Brian pulled over to the curb in front of the Blue Waters hotel. The two-story white-walled building sat on the edge of the street directly opposite the pier. Painted on the wall next to the open front door was the word *Vacancy;* next to that, hanging from a nail, was a small wooden sign that said simply, *Yes.*

They climbed out of the jeep and walked into the hotel. Brian hadn't realized how warm and bright it was outside until he felt the cool air of the dimly lit lobby. Leslie lifted her dark sunglasses and rested them on her head.

A robust woman with thick curly hair and a wide smile looked up from her magazine. "You need a room?"

"No, is the restaurant open?" Brian asked as they crossed the lobby and looked into the large room lined with tables, only half of which were set for dining.

"Sure, sure, go in. Boggy!" she called over their heads and a young boy dressed in tattered cut-off Levis and a starched white shirt appeared at the entrance, menus in hand.

"Two?" he said, his eyes locking onto Leslie.

Leslie smiled and nodded.

The boy's smile widened and from his grin Brian could tell he was the large woman's son.

"Let me seat you outside, it's always much nicer outside," Boggy said as he led them around the tables, through the narrow opening, and out onto the wood-plank veranda. "Is this okay?" he asked as he pulled the chair out for Leslie.

"Fine, thank you," Brian said, noting the native boy's English. It was unbroken, a generation better than his mother's.

Boggy opened a menu for Leslie, but simply handed the other to Brian. "Anything to drink, coffee?"

"Do you have orange juice?" Leslie asked.

"It's not fresh but okay. We have papaya."

"That sounds good," Leslie said, and Boggy nodded, happy that she had taken his suggestion.

202

"I'll have coffee," Brian said, wondering if he had broken the boy's concentration away from Leslie enough for him to hear his order.

Brian leaned back in his chair and looked out at the harbor. It was scattered with boats bobbing in the slow-rolling swells that had managed to ease past the distant reefs. On a large ketch anchored near shore, a bikini-clad girl climbed the mast, carefully walked to the end of the spreader, and dove into the lagoon. It was a beautiful sight. The dive itself was awkward, but the whole act radiated with playful foolishness.

Although there was some dockage near the south entrance, the main structure that caught his eye was Baker Pier. The three-hundred-foot length of splintering dark timber on unsure legs bisected the harbor.

Both expensive teak-decked yachts and shabby native fishing boats parried for a set of cleats along the pier to tie onto. The fishing boats rocked gently from the commotion of their crews emptying the morning catch of shark and stingray, indifferent to the people along the dock inspecting their quarry in the midmorning.

"Doesn't seem possible that this place was the target of an entire fleet," Brian said as he looked at Leslie. "They called it the Gibraltar of the Pacific, an impregnable base."

Leslie followed his gaze out to sea. The tears began to fill her eyes. She picked up the paper napkin from the table and wiped them.

"I'm sorry." Brian leaned forward and reached across the table and took her hand.

She held it tight. "Don't be." She smiled. "We have to go to the police station right after breakfast and get this over with," she said with a breath of strength, and then looked into his dark eyes. "Will you go with me?"

"Of course."

Leslie pulled her hand away and sat straight in her chair. "I don't know why I'm so upset." She brushed her blouse with nervous intent.

"He was your father, that's reason enough," Brian said.

She stopped and looked at him. Looked at his dark eyes as they scanned the lagoon, his tight square jaw, his strong hands. And the scar on his forearms. "What's that from?" she asked.

Brian rubbed his hand over it. He hesitated. "It was a tattoo but I had it removed.

"Why?" She was intrigued.

"It didn't fit any more," he said, shifting uncomfortably in his chair.

Leslie wanted to ask him what it had been, but thought better of it. Boggy appeared with their juice and coffee. The young boy took two orders for the house specialty, a tropical omelet with coconut, papaya, and pineapple, and a few minutes later he brought it out. Then after they had finished, he cleared the empty plates. "My sister is the cook," he said, taking the last plate from in front of Brian.

"Well, tell her she is an exceptional cook," Leslie said. "And you're an exceptional waiter."

"Thank you, thank you." He kept smiling ear-to-ear as he disappeared through the door.

Then Boggy's mother came out and pulled a chair up next to their table. "Everything okay?"

"Fine," Brian said, finishing his coffee.

"I'm very sorry about your father," she said. Shaking her head and looking down at her callused bare feet. "Good man, he was. Very polite."

"How did you know the professor was my father."

A smile crept onto the woman's face. She spread her arms out. "These islands not very big, but I have sharp eyes and big ears," she said, touching the corner of her eye and then the lobe of her ear. "He also come here a lot. Sometimes his friends stay in the hotel." She pointed over her head. Brian looked up at the yellow curtains flapping out the open balconies.

Boggy came back with the check, but his mother put her

hand on it and shook her head. "No," she said to the young boy.

"Please, let me," Brian began to insist.

"No." She continued to shake her head from side to side. Then she looked hard at Brian as if he were one of her sons. "The professor brought many people here that spent their money. You don't have to."

"Thank you," Leslie said.

"Anytime you two come, you leave money in the truck." She motioned to the Willys. "and if you need anything, you ask for me, Rota."

"Thank you, Rota," Leslie said as they stood to leave.

"Officer Magun told me to ask for someone named George. Where can I find him?" Brian asked.

Rota laughed. "George you find in only two places, on top of the pier fishing or under the pier drunk."

"You up to this?" Brian asked as he climbed in behind the wheel.

"Like you said, I have to get it over with."

Brian tried twice to find first gear of the old jeep, grinding the teeth until finally they clunked in and he pulled away from the curb.

From behind the yellow curtains of the hotel's largest room, Admiral Mills watched them head down the street. He took out the white terry-cloth towel and soaked it for the third time in the carved wooden bowl. All the ice Boggy had brought up from the kitchen, not an hour before, was gone. But the water was still cool and the drenched towel felt good on the back of his neck.

Mills opened the side pocket of his flight bag and pulled out a pair of black Nikon binoculars. He walked back out onto the balcony and tried to find the gray jeep driving toward the north side of the lagoon.

* * *

"Here's the file," Fumio said, setting the manila folder on the front counter of the police station. He pushed it in front of Brian and then lifted the open cardboard box and set it in front of Leslie. "And here are his personal belongings."

Leslie reached for the folder, turned it toward her, and stared at her father's name typed on the tab. She slipped her manicured nail under the flap and began to open it.

Fumio quickly put his hands on the folder, holding it closed. "Brian, why don't you take a look at this?" he said, and then looked at Leslie. "Please, Miss Yokamata."

Leslie looked at Brian, tears at the edge of her eyes.

"We had to take photographs of the body," Fumio said gently.

Leslie shuddered, and she pulled her hand away from the folder as if it was suddenly red hot.

"Why don't you go outside? I'll look through this stuff," Brian said. He put his hand on her back.

Without a word, Leslie stood and walked out of the police station. The steel door with the wire-embedded glass window closed slowly on its hydraulic hinges.

After the door closed, Brian opened the folder. Fumio had been right not to let her see this. The black-and-white photo showed a grossly deformed figure of a man twisted from a painful death. His skin was bleach-white and looked to have the texture of wet paste.

Bits of his flesh had been ripped away by scavengers of the reef. Blue damsels or butterfly fish or any of the hundreds of other species of fish had taken their share. No food source would be untouched—it couldn't be, if the creatures of the lagoon were to insure their own survival. The sea is a vicious and beautiful place, Brian thought.

"We found his body washed up on the south side of Tsis. His boat was anchored on a wreck that's in about two hundred and seventy feet of water. We figured he was dead before he reached the surface," Fumio said.

"How long was he missing before you went looking for him?" Brian asked.

"About three days. It wasn't unlike him to disappear for a time. You know, take some supplies and equipment and head over to one of the uninhabited islands to do his research."

Brian read over the report.

Hitobuto Yokamata   Japanese
Citizen of the U.S.   Age. mid 60s
Cause of death: Diving accident; air embolism
Buried in Moen Cemetery

He closed the folder and handed it back to Fumio. He opened the box and took out the professor's dive mask, a fin, and his wetsuit jacket folded on the bottom. In an envelope, the police had put the professor's simple gold wedding ring and his diving watch.

"That's everything," Fumio said.

"What about on his boat?"

"We left it as we found it. Moored it in the harbor."

"What about the house. Anybody go through his things there?" Brian asked.

"No." Fumio shook his head. "When the postmaster received the telegram from his daughter, he gave it to me. I had planned to ship all his belongings to the university, but when I read the telegram, I figured it'd be best to wait. To tell you the truth, I knew he was a widower, but he never mentioned anything about a daughter. I didn't think he had anybody."

Brian remembered what Leslie had said about her relationship with the professor. "All that stuff at his house. He was shipping it out."

Fumio nodded.

"I thought artifacts couldn't be taken out of Truk."

"Not by the tourists. But he was doing research. He had

the permits to excavate a number of wrecks and anything American."

Brian's eyes widen. "What do you mean, American?"

"There've been several American planes found on the bottom of the lagoon. Anything in them was his to bring up. I guess Americans aren't as superstitious as the Japanese."

"I wouldn't be so sure," Brian said, dropping the diving gear back into the box. He slipped the professor's watch and ring into his shirt pocket. "Thanks, Fumio."

"Sure," the officer said as he moved around the counter and held the heavy door open for Brian.

Brian stopped. "How do I get to the Moen Cemetery?"

Leslie knelt with her head bowed in the long soft grass before the weathered plank of driftwood that stood at the top of the slope of Truk's cemetery. Japanese kanji writing was burned into the wood and Brian guessed it was the professor's name.

Leslie was silent. She held the watch and wedding ring in her hands.

Finally she stood up and wiped her eyes. She moved to the plank of wood and ran her finger over it gently. Then she turned and walked back to the jeep.

Brian waited for a moment, letting her walk alone. He looked back at the freshly turned dirt of the grave. It was dry, black dirt brought up to support life on this island by an ancient volcano, long since dead and silent.

Truk Lagoon had finally claimed a soul that had eluded her for more than forty years. Brian wondered if she had claimed his father, or if he had gotten his submarine out beyond its reefs.

TWENTY-TWO

Honolulu, Hawaii, 1944

Mimi knew it was her car pulling into the driveway by the distinctive squeak of the Packard's brakes. She tossed the copy of the *Saturday Evening Post* onto the couch and stood up. Margaret would be upset when she walked in and saw her like this.

Moving to the oval mirror on the wall, Mimi looked at herself and wiped her eyes; they were puffy and red. It was past two o'clock and she was still in her loose white cotton nightdress. Breakfast and lunch had been a cup of coffee and a single piece of toast and she hadn't made much effort to do anything else.

Last night she had come directly to Margaret's after the party, woke her up, and cried on her shoulder for the next two hours without telling her why. It was easy enough for the naval secretary to guess it had something to do with Douglas, but Mimi wouldn't tell her exactly what.

She couldn't tell her friend that it was her fault. That she should have told him why she had been instructed to go to the bar and meet him, and why she had asked him to the party. Now she wondered if it would have been better to have told him everything from the beginning.

God, she thought. This was supposed to be an official mission. What had happen? How could she have let herself

209

become involved with one of the main objectives of the operation? How could she fall in love with him, so fast, so easily?

The knock at the door was light, but she heard it against the background of the silent house.

"Why is he on my submarine?" Douglas asked, stepping past her as she opened the door.

"Douglas," she said, wrapping her arms around him.

He pushed her away and closed the door. "Who is he, Mimi, and why did Tendrey get him transferred onto the *Seakrill?*"

She stepped back, the surprise of his appearance gone. He was here to question her. "I don't know what you're talking about. Who is on your submarine?"

Douglas looked hard at her, wondering if she was lying, wondering if he could tell. "There's a new machinist's mate aboard and my exec tells me he was transferred over on Tendrey's request. I want to know why."

"I don't know anything about it, Douglas, honest. You have to believe me."

"Like I was supposed to believe you last night and the other day?" Douglas laughed. "You have to be kidding. Lady, the last thing in the world I would do is believe you."

Mimi couldn't stop the tears once they began to flow. She fell onto the couch, her face in her hands.

Douglas let out his breath in a slow whistle. "Come here," he said, sitting next to her. He lifted her head gently with his hands. "Stop," he said softly. "You really don't know."

"No."

"Okay, I believe you," he said. "I can't figure out why Tendrey would want this guy on my boat."

"I don't know. Honest, I don't. Oh God, Douglas," she said, wrapping her arms around his neck and pulling him to her. She kissed him, holding her lips against his. Then she turned her face ever so slightly, keeping her face pressed against his. "I'm glad you said no. They can find another submarine. Someone else can go into Truk."

Douglas leaned back. "You don't understand. It's not whether it's the *Seakrill* or another boat. Truk is suicide. There's no way into that base without being spotted and blown out of the water. We're going to be sitting ducks if a Jap patrol catches us sneaking into one of the passes."

"But the chart was supplied by a local fisherman and the hole in the reef isn't known by the Japanese. He said a submarine would be able to slip through undetected," Mimi said.

"Since when can a fisherman determine the size of a U.S. submarine?" Douglas said skeptically. "And one of Tendrey's boys are suddenly moved to my boat. It smells, the whole thing smells."

Mimi looked away from him. She fiddled with the edge of her nightdress. "We have to find some way to make the trade, somehow," she said softly. Her eyes rose to his. "I made a promise I would get the Peking Man back. Doctor Hoffmann worked for ten years to find those fossils. They were his life's work and then I lost them. They were my responsibility."

"I'm sure he doesn't hold that against you. No one could have known when the war was going to break out."

Mimi frowned. "He died from jaundice the day after it happened. I was the one that had to tell him and I'll never forget the look in his eyes. I felt like I had killed him myself."

Douglas stood up and moved to the window that overlooked the backyard. It was a sea of roses, red and pink and white. Another contradiction to his assessment of Margaret O'Tullie. "I picked up the orders from Tendrey this morning right before I picked up my official orders from the squadron commander," he said. "I'm going into Truk."

"But I thought you told him no. You just said it would be suicide," Mimi said. Her eyes darted across his face. "Why did you change your mind?"

Douglas moved back to the couch knowing he couldn't

211

tell her about the OSS plan. He told her half the truth. "If they're that important, then I'll get them out. But you have to make me a promise."

"What?"

"That once you leave for the States tomorrow, you won't come back to Honolulu. Not until you hear from me. Promise me, Mimi. You'll stay away until I say it's okay for you to come back," Douglas said, placing both hands on her shoulders.

"I don't understand."

"Just promise me you'll wait on the mainland and won't say a word about my coming here. Not to anyone, especially to Tendrey or your ambassador."

She looked into his dark eyes, trying to see what he would not say. "Okay," she said. "I promise. But tell me why."

"No," Douglas said sternly.

"What about the man that was assigned to your submarine?"

Douglas rubbed his chin. "I will take care of him once we are out to sea."

"I'm afraid, Douglas," she said, and Douglas could see her body begin to shake.

He moved close and put his arms around her, calming her. "There is nothing to be afraid of. We'll be in and out of the lagoon before anyone knows. Then it's just going to be another patrol."

She leaned against him, and when she stopped shaking, she looked up into his eyes. Then slowly she pushed him back onto the couch. Moving forward, she covered his mouth with hers. With one free hand, she loosened his tie and then unbuttoned his shirt and peeled it away. She ran her nails across the soft hairs of his chest, feeling his breath deepening as she reached for his belt and unbuckled it.

His hands moved slowly along the sides of her legs and up under the thin cotton nightdress. He found her naked and warm and wanting. With his left hand he pulled the material over her head.

212

He let it fall to the floor as he kissed the hollow of her throat, then lifted her high over his body so his mouth could reach her breasts. They were firm and fit into the cup of his hands, his palms recognizing her growing hardness there. His lips encircled a nipple of one and then the other as he tasted her, the saltiness of her skin.

He could hear the speed of her breath and it increased his own.

With one hand she reached back, ran her hand slowly down along his thigh, finding him, his warmth radiating. She grasped tight, controlling him as she moved her legs to each side of his body. Then she leaned back as he arched up, and she enveloped him slowly, fully. And with a gasp, she brought her lips to his again.

Seaman Reilly looked at the shiny yellow Packard with envy. ''Fucking Jap,'' he said to himself in a low voice. He didn't care that Admiral Tendrey had told him Lai Ming was the assistant to the Chinese ambassador. Chinese or Japanese, they were all the same. And the thought suggested by the admiral that the commander inside might be fucking the yellow bitch disgusted him.

Reilly watched the house from across the street, crouched uncomfortably on the bench seat of his father's Ford pickup truck. He figured Tendrey asked him to keep an eye on this commander because he knew Honolulu, knew every back street and dirt path on the island. He had, in fact, grown up here, riding with his father on every milk delivery from their small farm.

Reilly knew Honolulu all right, and now he was thinking of the quickest route back to the base. Tendrey would be interested about the commander's extended ride in a jeep driven by an old-looking lieutenant junior grade.

* * *

Douglas traced the smooth line of her backbone with his index finger stopping at her neck. He kissed her there, causing her to giggle. It made him laugh.

"Oh, you're laughing at me," Mimi said, her smile turning to a pout. She rolled away from him on the double bed, stripping him of the sheets. The material clung to her body, except for a part of her stomach and one leg.

He sat up and looked down at her. Her long hair unraveled over the pillow like strands of silk. "Ya, I'm laughing," Douglas said, slipping his arm around her waist and pulling her back next to him. He uncovered her breast and kissed her there, then leaned forward and kissed her neck.

"I don't want you to go, Douglas," Mimi said as she snuggled against him, her left arm across his chest, their legs intertwined.

"I have to," he said, wanting to tell her about Wagner and the OSS. "You made a promise to your Doctor Hoffmann. If I can get into Truk, I'll get those fossils out."

She looked up at him, studying his face. He wasn't telling her something, she sensed it. She held him tight.

Douglas kissed the top of her head, smelling the natural fragrance of her body. It stirred him deep inside. "What are you thinking?" he asked her.

"There was a Zen poem my mother used to tell me when I was a little girl," she turned to him. " 'The white crane on the highest branch, spreads his wings wide. Below, the mountain is still. Both wait for sunset.' "

"I'm afraid I don't understand," Douglas said honestly."

"Some things are inevitable. Whether you stand to the side and watch or you try with all your heart to change them, they are unyielding," she said, sitting up on her elbows.

"What are you saying?"

She looked at the sunlight coming through the lace curtains. "I was eleven when we dug up the first skull from Dragon's Tooth Hill. My whole life has been spent studying the Peking Man. What he ate, what he drank, if he was advanced enough to use fire and make tools. We think he was a cannibal but we're not sure.''

''These fossils are important to you, aren't they?'' Douglas said as he watched her speak.

''The fossils are a part of my country's history. They are a part of everyone's history, if the world wasn't too busy killing each other to recognize it,'' she said. ''But now, you're important to me, Douglas.'' Tears were running down her face.

He kissed her, wiping away the salty droplets. She rolled over and ran her arms around his waist. Pulling him, she guided his body over hers, welcoming him. She arched her back as he moved between her long legs and they joined again.

Through the delicate curtains that hung across the open window, the tropical scent drifted in from the early afternoon. The sun followed the breeze inside, lighting the white sheets of the bed as they made love. Warming them as they laughed and talked and made love over and over.

''I . . . I'm falling in love with you, Douglas,'' Mimi whispered in his ear. She was afraid to say it to him but needed to. At the same time, she found herself more frightened now that she had.

Douglas rose up on his elbow, smiled down at her and into her eyes. Then he lowered himself and kissed her right cheek, then the left and the tip of her nose and her forehead and chin, gently kissing every part of her beautiful face. ''When I get back, we'll start this again,'' he said.

''Could things have been different?'' she asked him as he rolled to one side of her.

''What do you mean?''

''I mean, would we still have been together like this if things were different?'' She turned on her side, perched her head on her right hand, and looked at him.

''If there were no fossils and no Tendrey to be bothered with? Like if we had just simply met in the bar?''

Mimi nodded, her eyes locked onto his.

"Probably," he said.

"But would it have been different?"

"Yes, I wouldn't have become so involved," he said.

She smiled to herself as he leaned over her and took his watch from the nightstand.

"Jesus, it's after three o'clock. Come on, you have to drive me back to the docks. We're going on a shakedown run at four," he said, lifting himself out of bed.

Panic suddenly shot through her. "I'm not going to see you again," she said, realizing the time Douglas was to leave on patrol was closing.

"Not for two months. You stay in touch with O'Tullie and I'll have her tell you when you can come back to Honolulu. Remember, you promised me. You won't come back until you hear from me first," Douglas said as he fastened his pants and began to button his shirt.

Mimi slid off the bed and moved toward him. Douglas had to catch his breath as she pressed her naked body against him. On her tiptoes, she kissed him again. Then she began to help him dress before she put on a simple red sundress and high-heel shoes.

"Don't you wear anything under that?" Douglas asked her, but she only smiled, answering that she wanted him to remember she was ready to make love to him the second he returned.

Neither of them noticed the Ford truck whose engine started the same time Mimi turned over the Packard's straight-eight. Nor did they see it pull away from the curb and follow them down the street and onto the main highway.

The Packard glided up to the submarine dock accompanied by the usual stares from hard-stomached crewmen and dock workers. But to Douglas, the Detroit convertible couldn't compare to the beauty of the three-hundred-foot warship from Portsmouth Naval Yard.

The *Seakrill* lay beside the main dock, her skin covered in

216

new coats of dull black paint. Gone were the abrasions of depth charges and machine-gun fire. The rear platform rail lost to a destroyer's near hit was replaced yesterday but hadn't had a chance to be painted. It was still undercoat red, a reminder of a close call.

Only a few men were in sight. A gun crew was checking one of the 40mm Bofors guns on the cigarette deck while others were lowering the last stores through the forward hatch to men below. She was ready, Douglas could sense it in the way she sat in the water. Her diesel tanks were topped, her batteries at full charge.

Douglas climbed out of the car and then reached back for his coat and briefcase behind the seat. Mimi put her hand on his. "Tell me that you'll be back. Make me believe it," she said.

"You won't be able to keep me away," he said. "And I'll bring you back that box of old bones."

She kissed his hand and then pulled him down to her and kissed his mouth. "Don't worry," he said as she released him. "I'll be back." He lifted the bulging briefcase and his coat, but he didn't notice his small black notebook fall from its inside pocket and drop behind the seat. He stepped away from the car as Mimi shifted it into first gear and pulled slowly away.

"How are we doing, Michael?" Douglas asked his exec as he climbed up the conning tower. He knew the answer. The dock lines were already singled up, two of the usual three mooring lines gone, the submarine being held by only one line to each cleat. She was ready for immediate castoff.

Michael looked over his clipboard and then down at the crew finishing with the 40mm gun. His grin widened. "Give the command, Skipper. We're sea-ready."

"You have the bridge. Let's take her out and shake her down a bit," Douglas said.

"Aye, aye, Skipper," Michael said. He gave the orders to take away the gangplank and to cast off the dock lines. A man at each cleat caught the line being thrown to him by a corresponding dock-line handler. "Aft engines astern slow," Michael ordered.

Douglas looked back one last time toward the dock but the Packard was gone. He felt a hole in his stomach as he watched the oil-tainted water of Pearl sweep up along the black hull of his submarine. Leaning down, he handed his briefcase and coat to a man in the conning tower. "Put these in my cabin," he said to the seaman.

The *Seakrill* glided through the calm harbor, around Hospital Point, and toward the channel that led out to open sea. There was the usual group of patients on the point taking in the last rays of the afternoon and watching the ships cruise passed. The bright colors of plumeria, orchids, and hibiscus flowers along the shore seemed to defy the ugliness of war that had come to Pearl only a few short years before.

As the submarine cleared the first set of black and red channel buoys, two lookouts perched themselves on the small platforms on the periscope shears. Their eyes were locked into their binoculars as they scanned the sky. Two more lookouts stood on the more comfortable cigarette deck watching the sea and the horizon astern.

Passing the entrance buoys, the vintage minesweeper that guarded the harbor maneuvered out of their way. Several crewmen waved to the submarine. They assumed she was heading out on patrol.

With the palm of his hand, Michael switched on the press-to-talk button on the waterproof bridge speaker. "Conn, rig for diving," he ordered.

"Aye, aye, Bridge," came the response from the conning tower. And a moment later, "Bridge. Rigged for dive."

Douglas stood between Michael and Quartermaster Dustin Blare. He turned to his exec. "Head out past Barbers Point and take her up to full surface speed on all four."

"Aye, aye, Skipper," Michael said. He leaned toward the bridge speaker. "Answer bells on four engines. All ahead full."

Douglas wanted to get out beyond the harbor defense

218

zone before they dove. Beside the problems with the Fairbanks, the *Seakrill* had had extensive repairs done to her hull and he wanted no doubts about her ability to handle depth. From his crew or himself.

Several minutes passed as the submarine pushed effortlessly through the slow-rolling swells. Heading directly into the wind, the sea spray covered the bridge with a light mist. Douglas expected Clancy to relay that the Fairbanks was overheating but the message never came.

"Okay, Michael, I'll take her from here," Douglas said to his exec.

"You have the conn," Michael replied.

"Let's take her down. Lookouts below, clear the bridge!" Douglas ordered, and instantly the men on the periscope shears dropped through the circular hatchway. The other two lookouts followed directly behind them as if the first were connected to the others. Blare disappeared and then Michael.

Douglas heard the distinct thud of the induction valve being close by the hydraulic system. The valve was the throat of the four diesels giving the Fairbanks their air. Now the submarine's propellers would spin under the power of electric motors, as the control room shifted to the batteries.

Reaching for the button on the Klaxton, he pressed it twice, sending the high-pitched alarm throughout the ship. Instantly he pushed the button on the bridge speaker. "Dive! Dive!" he ordered. Looking quickly at the bow, Douglas saw the sea devour the bow planes as the *Seakrill* began to head toward her domain. He turned and climbed down through the hatchway. Once inside, Douglas pulled on the wire lanyard to hold the hatch closed as Michael reached up past him and spun the hand wheel. The mechanism released the steel levers dogging it tight.

From the control room came the familiar noises of the diving submarine. Venting air whistled like a soft breeze in a cave, the popping and gurgling of rushing water as the sea swept across the deck, into the hollow deck of the bridge.

"Pressure in the boat; green board, sir," came the report that the *Seakrill* was sound, all hatches sealed, the hull airtight.

On Douglas's order, the periscope rose smoothly out of its greased port. He caught the two handles that lay ninety degrees to the eyepiece, spread them, and fixed his right eye against the scope. "Ahead fifteen hundred a side," Douglas ordered without looking up from the scope. Moving slowly, he rotated the periscope, searching the complete horizon above.

"Make your depth five zero feet," Douglas ordered. He looked at Michael, who stood on the opposite side of the periscope. "Ready to test her?"

Michael nodded. "Better do it now then surrounded by depth charges. She'll hold," he promised.

"I hope so," Douglas said. "Take her down. Left rudder ten degrees. Rig for depth charges!" he shouted. Immediately, the Klaxon horn blared again as the nose of the submarine began to dip. Michael hit the switch to lower the periscope as Douglas slapped the handles into their up position.

Below the conning tower, within the three-hundred-and-eleven-foot length of tempered hull, eighty-five men jumped to their stations. Throughout the *Seakrill,* bulkhead hatches slammed shut. Fire and repair crews prepared for the worst.

"Seven five feet, sir."

The *Seakrill* continued to dive deeper into the cold and silent sea off the Hawaiin chain.

"One hundred and twenty feet, sir," the helmsman reported.

The new air-conditioning unit clicked on as the temperature of the submarine began to rise in the small space of the conning tower. The air was still sweet, fresh from just being pumped in from the surface, but that wouldn't last and the sharp bitter smell of men would soon become apparent.

"Rudder amidship. Straighten us out, Bill," Douglas spoke to the helmsman.

"Aye, aye, rudder amidship, Skipper." Bill made the adjustment.

"One hundred and sixty feet."

There was silence as the *Seakrill* continued to dive. Only the constant electronic sweep of sonar and the hum of the cool air coming from the vents could be heard. Even the ship's motion was negligible.

At two hundred feet, Douglas smiled at his exec. "Not a sound," he said.

"Not even a whimper. They did a good job," Michael agreed.

"Let's see what three hundred sounds like," he said.

The first moan from the intense pressure surrounding the submarine's hull came at the two-hundred-and-thirty-five-foot mark. It sounded like a large man's stomach turning from too many spicy foods.

The sounds increased as the *Seakrill* pierced the two-hundred-and-eighty-foot depth of the dark ocean. The weight of the sea was trying to find a way into the steel eggshell of a ship.

"Speed through the water?" Douglas asked.

First Class Electrician's Mate David Casey looked at his set of voltmeters, ampere meters, and the motor shaft-revolution indicators. "Seven knots, Skipper," he answered.

"Level off at three hundred feet," Douglas ordered as the men in the conning tower watched the needle sweep around the depth gauge.

The helmsman made the correct adjustments. "Three hundred feet, sir."

The interior of the submarine echoed from the strain of tons of water pressing down on her. The hull groaned as it fought the sea in an effort to remain solid.

"Good enough." Douglas nodded to his officers. "Michael, you have the con. Take us back to Pearl." He said as he climbed down the ladder that entered the control room.

"Yes, sir, Skipper," Michael said, and turning to the others, "Secure from battle stations. Take her up to four five feet."

"Aye, aye," came the reply from the control room.

Like a sleek shark, the deadly United States submarine lifted her nose and headed toward the surface. It took only a few minutes for the *Seakrill* to reach periscope depth. After scanning the circle of the horizon and finding it clear, Michael gave the final order to surface.

Douglas felt the ship climb and then level off on the surface as he sat in his cabin. Then the distinct rumble of the Fairbanks came as the induction valve was opened.

It was almost 1800 hours by his wristwatch. They would be at the dock by 2000, Douglas figured. There were no last-minutes needs; the submarine was completely stocked and supplied for the fifty-day patrol.

He wondered if Stein would be at the docks to see them off. It was the usual procedure for the squadron commander to wish his submarines well as they left for patrol. But the *Seakrill* was leaving at an unusual time. COMSUBPAC was cutting it close trying to get Douglas's submarine to Truk before Operation Hailstone got underway.

He also wondered what time Wagner was going to show up, and if the truck carrying five million dollars worth of diamonds would arrive precisely at 2345 hours. It would be there, Douglas knew. He had little doubt Tendrey would see to that.

TWENTY-THREE

Moen Island, Truk Lagoon, 1986

"Excuse me," Brian said, crouching down next to the man sleeping in the bottom of a small abandoned rowboat, beached and half filled with sand. He wore dirty white pants, each leg torn short at different points below the knees, and a shirt that at one time could have been a pale yellow, but now was colored with motor oil, dirt, and dried spots of fish blood from successful mornings on the pier. It was unbuttoned and revealed his mountainous stomach.

With his head perched on the small vessel's rowing thwart and one arm over his face, he basked comfortably in the noon sun.

"Excuse me," Brian said again, but the man didn't stir.

"Are you sure?" Leslie said, standing behind Brian and looking over his shoulder.

Brian turned. "Fumio said to ask for George and Rota said he'd be by the pier."

"Rota knows nothing."

Brian and Leslie both looked at the man but still he hadn't moved. Yet the voice had come from him, or at least from his direction.

"You awake?" Brian ventured.

George let his arm slide off his face and drop into the bottom of the boat. He yawned, his mouth stretching open to an incredible size revealing only half a dozen teeth, all crooked and stained. Slowly, he pushed up into a sitting position.

He ran his stubby fingers through his thin jet-black, stood up, and walked a few unsteadily steps to the water. Reaching down, he splashed a handful into his face. Then he returned and sat down on the port quarter of his bed. "Yes," he said, grinning at them. "I am awake."

"It's always very bad for everyone," George said, absorbing the shock of the wave with his legs as the eighteen-foot Skipjack skiff crashed through, sending a cool spray over the bow.

Brian's knees also gave, taking the jolt of the fiberglass vessel. Using the first rule of boating, one hand for the boat, one hand for yourself, he held onto the cold stainless-steel rail next to the helm.

"After someone dies from scuba diving, nobody wants to come to the lagoon. They think the wrecks are too dangerous, that you will get trapped below or blown up from the ammunition still in the holds," George said, pressing his lips together, then popping them open, mimicking an explosion. He laughed. "All the divers go to Tahiti or Fiji with their big hotels and little reefs."

With the gesture of outspread arms, he said seriously, "Truk is the most beautiful lagoon in the world, and even though the war was terrible, it made these waters more wonderful."

Brian looked at George with a half smile.

"You will see. You dive once on our wrecks and you will agree. There is no place in the world like my home."

"I already think that," Brian said.

"No." George smiled. "You think the lagoon is a nice place to visit, but soon it will take hold of you here." He tapped Brian in the center of his chest. "You will see," he grinned with his crooked teeth.

224

Brian looked back at where Leslie was sitting against the transom, her back on the rear rail. The wind and the speed of the Skipjack lifted her hair behind her neck full like a spinnaker running before the wind.

"Why do you want to come out here?" George said, absorbing another wave.

"I just want to take a look," Brian said.

"She doesn't," George said, tilting his head toward Leslie.

Brian nodded and moved to her, his feet sure on an unsteady deck. "It's beautiful out here," he said.

She smiled, and she stood up, mistakenly letting go of the rail. The boat lurched and Leslie lost her footing. She felt herself falling, then her body stopped its downward motion and suddenly she realized Brian held her. He pulled her to him, his arms tight around her waist.

"Careful," he said. "We wouldn't want lose you in the middle of the lagoon."

"No," she said, somewhat embarrassed. She looked up at him, staring into his dark eyes. They caught her for the first time off guard. She was suddenly flustered and had to step back away. "What island is that?" She pointed over to the left.

Brian didn't know. "George," he yelled over the wind. "What island is that."

"Fefan, it is one of the biggest. Many of the original buildings from the Japanese base are still there."

The island rose steeply out of the blue water, yet it reached only nine hundred feet into the sky, falling short of touching the cotton-ball clouds that were sprinkled above. Its slopes were dominated by the green carpet of jungle.

Brian stared at Fefan's shoreline trying to see the rusting turrets and pillboxes of the Japanese. George had said the old installations were there, but in his mind, Brian saw them new with infantry ducking into their doorways, manning the antiaircraft guns and using their rifles to fend off the Hellcats attacking like a mass of hornets buzzing over their nest. He saw the bombs dropping, heard their stabilizing fins roar in the wind, and felt the air jolt from their explosions.

Red hot flames billowed under thick greasy black smoke that blinded the soldiers and burned in their lungs. But still they fought as the blue wings of the U.S. planes blocked out the morning sun as they came, hour after hour. Until Truk was a blaze of steel and jungle and flesh.

"How long until we get there?" Leslie said, smiling up at Brian."

"What?" She brought him back to the present. "A few minutes. That's Tsis there." He pointed to the island off their starboard bow. There was no war here now. Only the wind and the sun and the sea.

Like all the islands of Truk, Tsis was an emerald-green gem in the middle of a sapphire sea. It was on the smaller side, long and narrow with a hill only seventy feet above the sea.

But its pure white beach was identical to all of the beaches of the lagoon, caught between the sea and the thick tropical jungle pressing at its opposite edge.

George maneuvered the skiff to the southwest side of the isle, slipping gingerly through unseen shallows until he closed in and nudged the bow onto the rough coral sand.

Brian jumped over, carrying a line fastened to the bow cleat. He ran up and tied it to the thick trunk of a low arching palm tree. With all his strength, George tossed the small anchor over the stern, then pulled its line tight. It would keep the boat perpendicular to the shore.

Leslie slid over the gunwale and stepped into the crystal-clear water. The air was warm and the breeze filled with the sweet scents of orchids. Carrying her sandals in her hand, Leslie walked up the beach. George followed her.

"Where is the wreck from here?" Brian asked as the three of them stood in the direct heat to the afternoon sun.

"About two hundred meters straight out." He pointed. "We crossed over her when we came in."

"You look down that way and we'll cover the beach this way," Brian said.

George nodded and turned in the direction he was supposed to search. Brian and Leslie started out. Then George called to them.

"What am I looking for?" he asked.

Brian was surprised, but then realized he didn't know exactly what they were looking for either. "Anything the professor might have been diving with. Especially a clipboard or something he took notes on."

George nodded again and headed off.

Brian began walking along the beach a few feet above the small breaking waves. He could see where the tides and storm waves had tossed driftwood and shredded parts of plants high up on the island.

Leslie walked a few feet behind him, looking off unconcerned at the distant reefs.

There was something bothering her and Brian could feel it, but he pushed it behind the other things that filled his thoughts. There had to be something out here to give a clue to what the professor was doing. He had searched the skiff and found nothing. Not one thing that would prove that both he and Leslie's father were looking for the same wreck. Maybe it was too much of a long shot.

"Why are we here?" Leslie asked, suddenly walking at his elbow, her hand over her brow to block out the sun as she looked at him.

"Because I thought maybe we could find out why your father was diving off this wreck," Brian said awkwardly.

"I don't want to know," she said, stopping. With her right hand she pushed her hair out of her face.

Brian looked away, not wanting to meet those eyes. "I've got to know what he was doing," he said flatly.

"Why?"

He let out a sigh. "I came out here looking for a wreck. A particular wreck," he said. "I think your father might've known where it was."

227

"Then you came to Truk looking for him. Why didn't you tell me?" Anger was creeping into her. "Why did you have to lie to me?"

"No." He put his hand on her shoulders. "I didn't know about him. Not until we talked on the plane. Honest. I didn't lie to you." Then he shrugged. "Well . . ." He hesitated.

"What?"

'I did lie about one thing. May name is not Brock, it's Bovan."

"Great," Leslie said with a sarcastic laugh. She sat down in the hot sand.

Brian sat next to her. "Okay. You want the truth?" Brian said, leaning back.

Leslie looked at him, her head cocked to one side. "It would be nice for a change."

"Two weeks ago I was a commander of a nuclear submarine and up for promotion," he began and he told her everything. From the records that had been given to him by Admiral Mills to the man that he thought had followed him at Honolulu Airport. He told her what Mimi had said, what was written in his father's notebook, about the Peking Man, and the diamonds.

"And you didn't think twice? You just took the airline ticket and got on the plane?" Leslie questioned.

"I thought twice. I thought about the dates in the book and I thought about what his records said." Brian stood up. "The marines losing those fossils forty-five years ago doesn't mean a whole hell of a lot now, but back then it was an embarrassment. Those men were taken as prisoners without firing a single shot," Brian spoke as he paced back and forth in front of her.

"There were people who would have done anything to get the Peking Man back. And I think there are people who still would."

"You think there was a cover-up?" she asked quietly.

"If there was, it was a major cover-up. Everything

228

that Mimi said sounds farfetched, but that guy in Honolulu was following me," he said, sitting back down next to her.

She listened to him, watching his eyes as he continued to talk about his father, about the orders that might still be aboard the *Seakrill*. Then he spoke about what he had heard growing up around his father's friends and shipmates.

"They always told me he was the best submariner. A pure captain all the way through," he said, finally looking at her. The scar on his forearm burned as he realized he had been scratching it.

"What makes you think my father knew?" Leslie asked in a soft voice.

Brian shrugged. "If he was doing research, he must have known every wreck in this lagoon. He was here during the attack, so maybe he remembered where the *Kuma Maru* was moored."

"He talked about the war a lot, but I never paid much attention. Now I'm sorry I didn't," she said.

"It doesn't matter," Brian said, standing. He smiled as he took her hand and gently helped her up.

"Could those orders really still be there?" she asked as they headed back toward the boat.

"It would depend on where the sub took the hit. If the crew had time to secure the hatches. But I doubt it. I'm chasing ghosts."

"No." She stepped in front of him. "We'll look. We have the boat and you said we had enough gear. All we have to do is find it. I mean, if we dive together, it won't be that dangerous, right? I could learn."

"Leslie, I can't ask you—"

She put her finger to his lips. "You don't have to ask," she said softly, and moved against his chest, leaned up, and kissed him on the mouth. "I want to help."

* * *

229

George was already there waiting for them when they walked up. He was stretched out over the foredeck of the skiff, sleeping.

"Let's go," Brian said, slapping George on the shoulder. The native looked up. "You find anything?"

"No," Leslie said.

"Me neither." He hopped off the bow. "I don't know why you look. Anything floating that the professor lost would be in New Guinea by now."

Brian looked over his shoulder as he moved to untie the line from the palm tree. "What do you mean?"

"Things over the wreck would go straight out the south pass. The current goes that way. It's a very strong current when the tide shifts."

Brian stopped. "What about all this driftwood?"

"That's from closer in. The wreck is two hundred meters out," George reminded him.

Brian looked at Leslie, who was listening intently. "What about a body? The police said they found it here on the beach."

"Maybe he swam to the beach," George said.

Brian though about the police photo. "No, he didn't swim."

George rubbed his chin, thinking. Then he began to shake his head. "The police said they found him here?"

"They said he was diving this wreck." Brian moved closer. George was still shaking his head in thought. "What's the matter?"

"Today the fuel tank was almost full," George said.

"So."

"I fill the professor's tanks every night after he uses the boat. Every night. But after police towed it back, I never touched it until today."

"I don't get it."

George moved to the rear of the Skipjack and leaned into the stern. He slid the oval-shaped red fuel tank closer and unscrewed the top. "You see," he said, leaning out of the way so Brian could look in. "It is half empty. We have to switch to the spare to go back to Moen."

"But this morning it was full." Brian began to understand. "And the police said they towed the boat back from where they found the body."

George nodded, proud of himself for making the connection.

"If he was here, it should've been almost empty this morning," Brian said.

"What are you saying?" Leslie grabbed Brian's arm.

Brian looked at her. "That wherever your father was diving, it only took a little bit of fuel to get there."

"He must have been diving closer to Moen," George said.

"You're sure no one else could have used the boat and filled the tank?" Brian questioned.

"No one. He only trusted me. I was the only one with keys."

"But the police said they found his body here," Leslie argued.

Brian looked hard at her. "Ya, that's what they said."

TWENTY-FOUR

Honolulu, Hawaii, 1944

Wagner wrapped the German-made Walther P-38 in a small towel and then set it next to his duffel bag. He folded the rest of the clothes he thought he would need and placed them on the bed next to the bag. He had never been on a submarine before but he had been on several warships. The difference, he figured, was simply that this one could return to the surface after going under.

His second-story apartment became suddenly quiet as the Zenith phonograph finished the record. Now only the sounds of the early evening traffic came through the open window on the breeze.

He stopped his packing, walked to the dresser, and pulled out another record from the stack. He placed it on the platter and set the needle gently in place. The small speaker crackled at first and then released the vibrant orchestra performance of Beethoven's opera, *Fidelio.*

Closing his eyes, he smiled as he moved his right hand with the music. He laughed at himself and returned to the business at hand.

He inspected the neat piles of clothes laid out across his bed. Pants, shorts, shirts, underwear, jacket, hat. Moving into the bathroom, he cleaned out the drawer next to the sink. Straight razor, shaving soap, toothbrush, and a comb.

There was nothing else he could think of. Taking a small knife from his nightstand drawer, he rolled it and the bathroom utensils in a face towel and set it next to his clothes.

Last, he pulled out the single sheet of paper from the envelope that rested on the top of his dresser. It was his orders. Typed on CINCPAC letterhead, it was perfect, right down to Nimitz's signature. It explained briefly the need of Washington to know firsthand how well the Submarine Corp was operating and how well its men worked under the intense pressure of their patrols.

Bovan's executive officer wouldn't question the orders. No one would.

Wagner refolded the letter and placed it in its envelope and that envelope into another. Then he wrapped oilskin around it and tossed it on the bed. He was set, or at least his tools were all gathered.

But something bothered him. A throbbing in the back of his mind warned him this mission wasn't right. A word or a phrase had been said that was causing an unbalance. It was screaming at him to to rethink, to replan, to be careful.

He had approached Gostine with his idea of going aboard the *Seakrill* to make sure Tendrey's so-called operation went as planned. The OSS colonel was at first furious with the suggestion. He didn't want one of his men so cut off from contact with his office. But then after he told him about the crewman that was transferred by Tendrey, he agreed.

"Perhaps you are right, Major," Gostine said. "I don't like the idea of this machinist's mate suddenly being transferred in secrecy. Watch him."

As he kept going over the conversation in his head, Wagner walked into the bathroom and turned on the water. He splashed it up into his face. There was something there. Something in what Gostine had said.

He grabbed a towel and dried his face. He looked into the mirror. "Machinist's mate," he said. "Fuck. Gostine called him a machinist's mate." But Wagner remembered he had referred to the guy only as a crewman. He always remembered and now he was somehow sorry it was so clear. Gostine was in with Tendrey. There was no other way around it.

The Zenith crackled and the performance of the opera suddenly became louder and louder. Wagner dropped his towel and looked into the room. The old record player was always doing funny things as if the machine had its own personality.

As he leaned through the door, he felt the thin wire noose drop over his face and across his chin. He didn't have time to react. The tension on it was immediate, it jerked against his throat with a viselike grip, snapping his head forward.

Wagner struggled, trying to turn and grab his attacker. But he couldn't. He reached back to scratch at the eyes but his hands found nothing. Dropping low, he went for the groin but again there was no one to grab. He tried to slam himself back against the wall but he was held where he was.

The wire slipped tighter around his throat. He reached for it, trying to force his finger inside, but it was already digging deep into his flesh.

Balckness finally followed the intense pain. Death was quick for the OSS officer named both Wagner and Duare. It was a combination of lack of oxygen and blood to the brain as the wire cut into the carotid artery and crushed his throat.

The body dropped heavily to the floor. After a moment, the small elderly man with thick sun-dried skin stepped down off the sofa that rested against the wall next to the bathroom door. Releasing his grip on the wire, the slip-knot loosened at the opposite end of the five-foot pole. He had seen the devise used in capturing gazelle in Africa and was amazed at the leverage it gave its user against his prey.

Satisfied, he pulled the noose from around the corpse's head. The job was simple, silent and effective and worth half the money he had been paid. As he walked from the room, he removed the needle of the old Zenith. Personally, he preferred Mozart over Beethoven.

Douglas leaned against the cold rail of the cigarette deck as he watched the small crowd of well-wishers and family on the dock. He looked at his watch, it was almost 2330 hours. In a half an hour the lines would be cast and the *Seakrill* would be at war again.

"Skippper," Michael called as he crossed the gangplank and walked toward him. From the deck he jumped up and pulled himself over the rail. "A messenger just gave me this," he said, handing him a folded piece of paper.

Pushing his hat back on his head, he angled himself to catch the light from the dock. His name was penciled on the front. He opened the handwritten note.

Sorry I won't be able to make it aboard, Commander, but I have been given new orders.
Good luck with yours. I'm sure you will be able to carry them out to the fullest. I will see you upon your return to Pearl.

Wagner

A knot suddenly formed in Douglas's stomach. This wasn't like Wagner. Even though he had only known the OSS agent briefly. This wasn't like a man who was so sure of himself.

"Who gave you this?" he asked.

"Some messenger on the dock," Michael said.

"What did he look like? Young, old, tall, short, what?" Douglas asked, grabbing his exec's shoulder.

Michael raised his hands, his palms outstretched. "I don't know. Young, I guess. I didn't get a good look at him."

Douglas saw the shock in his officer's eyes and realized what he was doing. He looked back at the note. It was handwritten, but that didn't mean a thing. He had never seen Wagner's writing.

"What is it, Doug?" Michael asked.

"Nothing, nothing," he said, and as he looked back toward the dock, he saw the navy truck pull up near the gangplank. Two men and the driver stepped out and walked around back.

Without saying anything more, Douglas shoved the paper in his jacket pocket and climbed down from the deck. He moved to the dock where the truck had stopped.

"Good evening, sir," the ensign said as he and the two men came to full attention.

Douglas returned the salute. They were young, all three boys right out of boot camp. The ensign fresh out of officer's school.

"I have orders to turn this crate over to you, sir," said the ensign as he walked around to the rear of the truck and opened its tailgate. "And to brief you with several instructions, Commander," he said and then added, "In private, sir."

"Here, Charlie, grab that end," the second sailor said to the driver, and the two men lifted the dark green footlocker-sized crate from the truck.

"Set it down," Douglas ordered.

The two men looked at each other and then did as they were told.

"My orders are to be sure this is placed aboard your vessel, Commander," the ensign said.

"I'm not questioning your orders, mister. But I don't allow unauthorized personnel aboard my boat. With you I'm forced to make an exception, but only with you," Douglas said flatly. Then he turned toward the small gathering of crewmen and their friends standing a few yards away. "Epstein, Shear," he called to two of his crew. "Take this crate below and put it in my cabin," he ordered.

"Aye, aye, Skipper," they said, lifting the crate and moving to the forward hatch.

"After you," Douglas said to the ensign as he motioned toward the gangplank of the *Seakrill*. The two officers followed the seamen as they maneuvered the crate through the tight opening of the forward hatch and carried it into Douglas's quarters.

"Where do you want it, sir?" asked Epstein, a stout man with thick red hair.

"Just put it in the center of the floor for now," Douglas said. "Go on and get back up topside with your girls. We'll be shoving off soon."

"Yes, sir," they said excitedly, and left Douglas and the ensign alone.

"How much do you know about this?" Douglas asked, looking down at the crate.

"I know only that there is enough explosives lining that box to rip a man-sized hole through this hull. Why the navy would want to bring this kind of thing aboard a submarine is beyond me, sir," the ensign said. "My orders are simply to explain how the detonation mechanisms works, how to set it and how to disarm it."

Douglas nodded. "Okay, explain."

The ensign knelt down beside the crate and unlatched the two flip locks that held the lid. He opened it.

Packed along the inside walls of the box were several brownish claylike squares. They were connected by three color-coded wires, all leading into a brass clock that rested in the left corner. A loose flap of black cloth covered the box's true contents.

"These are it," the ensign said, pointing to the brown cubes. "Plastic explosives guaranteed to open up anything within fifty feet. The army has been developing it over the past two years. Extremely stable and extremely effective. You could leave these suckers in the water for a year and nothing would happen."

"It wouldn't hurt it?" Douglas was amazed. He had heard of the explosives but he had never seen it before.

"Plastic isn't bothered by anything. It will last forever.

237

Now the clock is wired so you can set it to go off anywhere from a minute to twelve hours. It has to be disarmed through this little hatch.'' The ensign closed the lid of the box and showed Douglas the small door that opened directly over the clock. ''But I also hooked up this.'' He pointed to a simple spring plunger. ''It's right out of the head. It flushes the bowl,'' he said with a laugh. ''When I was told to set up something with these kind of explosives, I figured you wanted it as reliable near the water as possible.''

''How do I set it?'' Douglas asked.

''The hands work like a combination lock. To set it, un-screw this ring and remove the glass.'' The ensign demon-strated how to open the clock face. 'Then turn the hands counterclockwise to how long you want the timer to go for. It detonates at twelve o'clock. Set it at eleven fifty-nine and that gives you a minute, at two o'clock gives you ten hours and so on. To disarm it, turn the hands counterclockwise until you reach twelve o'clock again. Simple as that,'' he said, closing the lid and standing up.

''Simple as that,'' Douglas said. The only hard part was delivering it, he thought.

Douglas followed the ensign out of the forward hatch. As they reached the dock, the young officer turned and saluted him. ''Good luck, Commander. I don't know where you're headed but I have a feeling you're going to need it.''

Douglas returned his salute without a word. Then he watched as the ensign and the two other men climbed into their truck and drive off.

''What was that all about?'' Michael asked as he stepped up next to Douglas.

''Are we ready to shove off?'' he said, turning back to-ward the *Seakrill*.

''Yes, sir,'' Michael said, understanding he was asking the wrong questions at the wrong time. ''Just give the or-der, Skipper.''

''What time is it?''

''Five minutes till midnight.''

Douglas sighed. "You think Stein is going to see us off?"

"It's late, but I've never known him not to be dockside when one of the boats leaves for patrol," Michael said.

"Okay, we'll wait."

"Doesn't look like we're going to have to. Here come his car."

Turning Douglas saw the headlights of the olive-green Ford come around the warehouse and stop. Captain Linus Stein stepped briskly out of the car and walked toward the edge of the dock. "Line them up on deck, Michael. Let's give our squadron commander what he deserves," Douglas said as he moved to meet Stein.

"Thank you for coming, sir," Douglas said, bowing to the usual formalities of going on patrol.

"Are you kidding, Commander? I haven't missed a single time one of my subs has left on patrol. You and your crew mean a lot to me, not just as seamen but as men. The least I can do is to show my gratitude and respect to your boys," Stein said.

"Well, thank you, sir."

"You have a long journey ahead of you, Doug. And I know the orders you're under doesn't make it any easier. But you have to get to Truk as soon as possible," Stein said as if he felt there was a need to remind him.

On the deck of the *Seakrill,* her crew lined up at attention. Douglas heard his exec give the orders to single up on the dock lines. 'You can count on us, Captain," Douglas said, shaking his hand and then giving him a final salute.

"I know I can, Doug." Stein smiled.

Douglas was the last across the gangplank. He climbed the steel ladder to the bridge. "Okay, Michael. Take her out," he said.

On order, the aft diesels kicked to life and the lines were unwrapped from their iron cleats. The linemen stowed them below the deck and returned to their places. Then, slowly at first, the *Seakrill* slid away from her home base and backed into the black water of the bay as Michael continued to relay orders to the helm.

On the dock, hands waved in the air along with cries of good luck and well wishes. Stein stiffened and saluted the crew and ship. He was sending another eighty-five men to war. God, he prayed silently, let them come home.

From within a dark shadow near one of the warehouses, a slim figure watched the submarine leave. She desperately wanted to walk out onto the dock and wish them well but she couldn't. A tear rolled down Mimi's cheek as the man on the bridge became only a silhouette against the evening sky that was bright over Pearl Harbor.

They were fourteen hours out when Douglas finally decided to confront his new machinist's mate. He had sent Michael to bring him back to his quarters. His exec was as anxious as he to find out if Hathorn had something to say in his own defense.

"Skipper," Michael said, stepping into Douglas's small cabin. Hathorn followed him in.

"Ah, Hathorn," Douglas said, looking up from the small square of wood that was hinged to the bulkhead and became his desk.

"Yes, sir." Hathorn was at full attention.

"It has come to my attention that your transfer from the *Tang* to *Seakrill* was requested by Admiral Tendrey. I'd like to know why," Douglas said, coming right to the point.

Hathorn's eyes shot from Douglas to Michael and then back to Douglas. "I'm not exactly sure what you mean, sir," the machinist's mate said.

The room was quickly becoming unbearably hot. "Tendrey had you transferred to my boat. I want to know why, mister, and I want to know now."

Again Hathorn's eyes moved nervously about. "But I . . . I thought you knew why, Skipper?"

Douglas didn't look at Michael, but out of the corner of his eyes he saw his exec glance toward him.

"What did Tendrey tell you?" Douglas asked, wondering if he should tell Michael to leave.

"That I was to explain my credentials to you on the third day of our patrol, sir."

"What credentials?" Douglas asked.

Hathorn looked at the first officer. "Sorry, sir, but the admiral was explicit that we were to be alone when I spoke with you."

"Well, mister, you are now on my ship and only my orders carry any weight here. Now, answer the question." Douglas pressed. He could see the sweat forming on Hathorn's brow.

"Two reasons, Skipper. Before the war I was a student of anthropology at Berkeley. My specialty was with *Homo erectus javensis*. In identification and classification," Hathorn said, his voice changing from nervousness to matter-of-fact.

"Homo what?" Michael said.

"*Homo erectus javensis,* sir. Java Man, who lived about a half a million years ago," Hathorn said. He looked back to Douglas. "We think he is closely related to the Peking Man. Of course, Hoffmann's theories of *Sinathropus pekinensis* being three million years old are probably way out of line, but the fossils are an important find." He looked at Michael. "They could be the missing link to our own evolution, sir. The doctor's studies were incomplete and most of the records were lost. But once we get the fossils from the Japs, sir, we can pick up where Hoffmann left off."

Michael didn't say anything. What Hathorn was talking about lost him. The boy's brains were waterlogged, he figured.

But Douglas knew, he knew exactly. "Then you're to verify the bones."

"Yes, sir, I'll be able to tell you on the spot if they are the real thing," Hathorn said proudly.

Douglas took a deep breath. "And the second reason, Mr. Hathorn?"

"When I was part of an excavation team for the university, I was in charge of the explosives," he said.

Douglas nodded. "Thank you, Hathorn. I understand. You may return to your station."

"Yes, sir," Hathorn said, and slipped passed Michael's shoulder and out of the cabin.

"Well?" Douglas said finally after a moment of silence. "Aren't you going to ask me what the hell that was about?"

"Okay," his exec said, nodding his head. "What the hell what that all about?"

Douglas reached down beside his bunk and lifted his briefcase onto the desk. He pulled out the wrappings of oilcloth, stripped the envelope of its waterproof protection, and handed it to Michael. "Read it," he said.

Michael pulled out and opened the letter from Admiral Tendrey explaining their mission.

From his expressions, Douglas knew his exec understood what the *Seakrill* had been ordered to do. He wished he could tell him about the OSS, but there was no need. In Michael's mind the orders, even from Tendrey, were real.

"This is crazy," he said in a slow voice.

"Those were my very words," Douglas said, clearing the desk and stowing it against the wall. "But the orders are clear. I have charts of Truk never seen before. The Chinese ambassador supplied them."

"Are they accurate?"

Douglas shrugged. "We don't know until we try to get through the reef. And if we do, we've got to be back out before our fly-boys start bombing the lagoon. It's going to be tight even at full speed."

"You make it sound as if it were life or death if we don't," Michael said, handing him back the letter.

He folded it carefully and replaced it in the oilskin. "Let's just say, it's important to me, real important," he said, and the image of Tendrey in front of a navy investigations panal came into his head.

"The Japs give us the Peking Man. What do we give them?" Michael asked.

Douglas reached under his bunk and pulled out the heavy crate. He opened it and flipped over the black cloth. The diamonds sparked in the twin bulbs of the cabin.

"Oh, shit," Michael said in astonishment as he knelt down. "These are real?"

"Five million dollars' worth," Douglas said.

Michael leaned back against the bulkhead. "It's going to be a bitch to get into Truk even with those charts."

Douglas closed the crate and slid it back under his bunk. "Yup. And then we have to tie up to a freighter, make the trade, and get out as fast as we can."

"What happens if a Jap patrol catches us inside the lagoon?"

Douglas smiled. "We've got twenty-four tin fish to make a little chop suey with," he said. "We'll have two dozen of their ships on the bottom before our fly-boys are even in sight."

Tell me, Doug." Michael looked straight at him. "Do you think caveman bones are worth the lives of eighty-five good men?"

Douglas stood up, took his hat off the hook behind the door, and centered it on his head. "This is not an easy mission, Mr. Albert. Nor is it one we like. But it's a mission nevertheless and we're to carry it out to the letter."

"Yes, sir."

Douglas stepped out of his quarters, but stopped in the doorway. He looked at his exec and smiled. "We'll be in and out of that lagoon without those the bastards ever seeing us. Then we'll slip them a fish or two so they'll know."

"I hope you're right, Skipper," Michael said, following him toward the control room. "I hope to God you're right."

Douglas hoped the same thing, but said nothing.

TWENTY-FIVE

Moen Island, Truk Lagoon, 1986

Zeen ran both hands quickly along the suitcase, one on the inside, one on the outside. He felt only lining between his fingers. This was the last of Leslie's luggage and he was satisfied she had nothing hidden.

He pushed the suitcase off the bed, letting its delicate contents scatter over the floor. He went into the study and to Brian's suitcases. He popped them open and rifled through each, tossing the clothes to the side as he came to them.

Nothing. Now he began to get nervous. They wouldn't be happy unless he found something. They would say he didn't look hard enough or would assume he missed something in plain sight. He kept looking. Behind every book and in every box, he searched, but still, nothing.

He moved to the desk and pulled every drawer out. They were still empty like he had left them the last time he had been in the professor's house.

He hated this sneaking around and crawling through the jungle. He would have preferred to simply step up to the front door and demand to search the house. What could Bovan and the girl do? He was the police.

Walking out of the study, he moved down the hall and back toward the kitchen. He had already gone over the kitchen. There was nothing to be found here, he thought. It was that simple. They were wrong. The professor's house held no more secrets.

If there were charts, Brian had them with him. And the only way to get those would be a face-to-face confrontation. Zeen smiled at that thought. He turned to leave, but as he was about to step out of the house and back into the jungle, he stopped.

He looked down the hall. There was one place he hadn't looked.

The tiny bathroom was lit by a naked bulb in the center of the ceiling. Zeen lifted the toilet's tank lid but found only the normal assembly. He looked under the sink and the counter and around the large four-legged bathtub.

He grabbed Leslie's cosmetic case from the countertop. Finding the latches locked, Zeen pulled his small boot knife from its ankle sheath. The aluminum latches gave easily to his prying. But the police officer found only the woman's makeup.

Frustrated, he threw the case to the floor and slammed his first into the wall.

As if on cue, the medicine-cabinet door swung slowly open, revealing Brian's toothbrush, shaver, clippers, and their assorted plastic travel cases.

"I need a chart of the lagoon," Brian said as he leaned on the counter. It was hot inside the old Quonset hut that housed the Truk Trading Company. The steel corrugated building with its dull white and rusting finish retained heat better than an oven.

The big, thick-armed native in his pure white shirt didn't seem to notice the heat. "Which one?"

"One of the entire lagoon."

The man pulled out a rickety footstool. It barely held his bulk as he reached the overhead storage. He slid the tightly rolled chart out and dropped it on the counter. "What

245

else?'' he asked, moving to the antique brass cash register, its engravings shining bright in the sun that came through the open double door.

Brian shook his head. "Nothing . . ."

"Wait," Leslie said as she stepped up next to Brian, her arms full of cans and groceries. They suddenly slipped and fell across the counter with a clatter. The pineapple she had gotten from the table outside rolled to the edge but Brian stopped it from falling.

"Oh," she said, opening the small weaved basket that held the half-dozen eggs. Her eyes sparkled. "All safe."

The man behind the register smiled.

"What's all this?" Brian corralled the rolling cans.

"Dinner," Leslie said. "It's my turn."

"This it?" the man asked again.

"Add a six-pack of beer," Brian said.

"No beer on these islands, man. No alcohol sold in a public place," he said. Then he smiled. "But if you really want, I'll see what I can find."

"Maybe later," Brian said.

The big man shrugged and loaded everything in a cardboard box. It was partly torn, but it held as Brian carried it out to the Willys. He set it in the back under George, who was already spread across the rear of the jeep, his feet hanging over one fender. A white hat that hadn't been there before rested low on his head.

"Where did you get the hat?" Leslie asked as she jumped into the passenger seat.

"Rota," George said without moving. "I think she wants to marry me." He laughed. "I have to be careful not to take too much from that woman." He laughed again.

Brian laughed too as he started the jeep and backed away from the trading company. He pulled onto the street, slowed for a young boy walking from the pier carrying his afternoon's catch of small black groupers.

The sun was falling fast to the sea. Night was minutes away, but the warmth of the day was holding and would to the next dawn. That's the way it was at Truk. One beautiful day evolving into another beautiful day. Even during the hurricane season when the waters within the reef turned into white-foamed chop like the tongue of a rabid animal lashing out at the islands, it was beautiful.

The wind was strong off the lagoon by the time they pulled up next to the house. The Willys' tires pushed a mound of sand before them as Brian applied the squeaking brakes.

George rolled lazily out of the jeep and headed toward the porch. Brian handed the chart to Leslie, then grabbed the cardboard box and followed her up the patio steps.

"Do you have enough food?" Brian asked, tilting his head toward Geroge.

"Don't worry, I planned on him staying."

George was ten paces ahead of them but he stopped at the door. He looked back at Brian. "You two had company," he said flatly.

"Oh, no." Leslie was through the door first.

"Son of a bitch," Brian said as he entered.

The intruder had left nothing untouched. Every closet and drawer in the house had been opened, their contents tossed out.

"Why would anyone do this?" Leslie said, bending down to pick up the pots off the kitchen floor. George helped her.

Brian set the grocery box down, sidestepped them, and rushed deeper into the house.

"Brian," Leslie called out after him.

He ran into the study. The intruder had taken every drawer of the desk and tossed them to the floor. Brian reached under the main frame of the desk and felt the smooth hard cover of his father's notebook. He pulled it out. Then another thought shot through him and he moved to the bathroom.

Leslie walked into her bedroom. "My clothes. Damn it," she said. Picking up her suitcase, she began to refold her blouses and skirts and set them in it.

Brian stepped into the room and sat quietly down on the

247

edge of the bed. Leslie saw him holding his toothbrush container, a section in each hand. "What is it?" she asked as she looked at Brian's drawn face.

"I hid a drawing in this," Brian said, disgusted. "It showed the shoreline where the *Seakrill* might have gone down."

"That's what they wanted." She was beginning to cry. "They came here and tore up my father's house to find a stupid drawing."

Brian nodded.

"They killed my father and they did this. Why?" Tears were streaking down her soft cheeks. She collapsed next to Brian. Wrapping her arms around him, she pressed her head into his chest. "Why are they doing this?"

"Mimi is right, somebody doesn't want me to find the submarine."

George leaned in the doorway. Brian looked up at him. "I'll begin in the kitchen," the native said.

Leslie wiped her cheeks with the back of her hand. "I should help him."

"Here," Brian said, looking at the small dark line of mascara. With the tip of his finger, he gently wiped the corner of her eye. "It'll be all right," he said.

She looked at him, into his dark eyes, and was suddenly drawn to him. She leaned forward and they kissed.

He felt her lips, soft and open. His body warmed and he could feel her arms wrap around his neck. His heart quickened a beat with every second they held each other. He leaned back onto the bed and she followed him willingly.

She could feel his muscular chest expand with each breath and it pressed against her breasts. She didn't want to let him go, afraid it would all end as quickly as it began.

She moaned slightly as his hand moved from her hip under her thin cotton blouse and up along the parallel muscles of her back.

There was a sudden and loud crash in the kitchen. It jolted through them like an electric shock. Brian automati-

248

cally moved her off him and sat up. Then he realized it was George putting away the pots and pans.

Leslie ran her hand up his back and to his shoulders. She could feel his body tense, like a cat with its hair up.

"You have to go home," Brian said, leaning back down next to her.

"What?" Leslie sat up. "What you mean, go home?"

"If your father was murdered and it was the same guys who did this, they're not going to be gentlemen when it comes to you. And I don't want you hurt."

Leslie stood up.

"I'll find who did it, I promise."

"Then what? Are you going to call me in New York and say everything is peachy keen?" She was shaking her finger at him. "Listen to me, Commander, I'm not leaving until I know who killed my father and they pay for it. I'm not afraid to stay until I do."

Brian shrugged. "I'm glad you're not afraid," he said as he lifted himself from the bed and stepped through the door. "Because I am."

George was in the study. The room was still a mess but he had cleared off the desktops and stretched the chart over them. It fit perfectly, and for the first time, Brian noticed several tiny pinholes at each corner where the professor had laid out his own charts.

George looked up as Brian entered. "Did they take anything important?"

"No," Brian lied. He leaned over the chart. "How much fuel did you get this morning?"

"About three gallons."

"How far could the professor go on that?"

George scratched his nose. "A few miles, maybe to here." He pointed to a spot a few inches away from Moen.

Brian found a pencil next to the desk leg where it had rolled after being dumped on the floor. "Okay." He marked under George's fingernail. Then he took a piece of wrapping string from the boxes against the wall. "That's about six miles," Brian said as he pinned one end of the string in the center of Truk Harbor and stretched it out to the pencil mark.

Keeping the string taut and placing the pencil at the distant of the mark, Brian traced a light circle with a six-mile radius.

"You've done this before," George said, watching him intently.

"Once."

The circle filled up a larger part of the lagoon than Brian liked to think about. It completely contained Moen, Dublon, and Param islands, part of Fefan, and hundreds of outcroppings of reef. But the worst was Dublon. The waters around the onetime Japanese base were littered with wrecks, both identified and unidentified. So many, in fact, the United States Defense Mapping Agency had a note on the side of the chart that said the waters off Dublon Island were a danger to navigation.

"That's a big area," George said, tapping the circle.

"How many sunken ships are there?"

"Many, too many to pick which the professor went to."

"We'll dive each one," Leslie said as she walked into the study and stepped up to the desk. She held three glasses of iced tea. She handed one to Brian but George shook his head.

The native pushed his white hat off his forehead. "It will take months," he said.

"Not if we can figure out which are the most likely to be the one we want. Most of the wrecks' names are known, right? And how deep they rest?" Brian said.

George nodded.

"When you serviced the boat, how much equipment did the professor take with him?"

George thought for a second. "A set of twin tanks and two single ones, each with regulators."

"Figure he dove with the double tanks, and the other two were for decompression."

"Yes, he said they were for that," George remembered.

Leslie walked to one of the chairs that was clear of artifacts or boxes. She sat down, her long legs crossed beneath her.

"So he dove once a day. That means she was deep, probably a hundred and fifty feet or more."

"Why not dive more than once?" Leslie asked.

"Too many deep dives will curl you like a pretzel," George said.

Brian shot George a hard fast look. He didn't want Leslie thinking about the details of her father's death. "You can get the bends from repetitive dives just the same as coming up too fast," he said in a matter-of-fact tone. "You have to give your body time to release the nitrogen."

Leslie nodded and took a drink of her tea. Brian noticed her hand shaking slightly.

"It'll still take a long time," George said. "A lot of ships are in deep water."

"Officer Magun told us my father had the house and the boat until the end of the year. That's enough time," Leslie said. "And we have enough equipment in the extra room."

Brian smiled. "Well, George, you going to help us?"

George looked at Brian for a moment and then over at Leslie. "I don't know, I have a lot to do at the pier."

"I'll pay you what the professor did."

"He paid me only to keep the boat in shape, not to dive the wrecks. The few times we dove, it was for lobster on the outer reef. Never deep."

"There's nothing different in diving deeper. You just have to be more careful coming up."

"That doesn't make me worry less," George said.

"It'll be okay," Brian assured him.

"I know most of the wrecks near Dublon, but towards the north lagoon, not so good. I have friends that will be able to help us. They are fishermen and they know where the fish are and the fish know the wrecks better than anyone," George said with a big smile.

"Then it's settled." Leslie stood up. "You two pick where we start tomorrow and I'll get dinner." As she walked past Brian, she touched him lightly on the back, but when he turned, she didn't look at him and he wondered if he had imagined it.

The two men decided on concentrating their first dives on the wrecks in water between 120 and 170 feet and away from Dublon. If those didn't pay off, they would move to the shallower ones.

Then they would search off Dublon beginning with the deeper depths again.

George would ask his friends about the ships off the small islands of Falo and Osakura. He would also ask them if they had noticed the professor's skiff in any particular area in the last few weeks.

"Can we get more acetylene and oxygen at the trading company?" Brian asked him.

"Yes," George said. Then he leaned forward and looked Brian straight in the eye. "If the professor's death was not an accident, I can understand why we must find where he was diving to prove it. But why do you need the cutting torch?"

Brian didn't say anything.

"You are looking for the diamonds." George smiled widely with his crooked teeth.

"Is that what the professor was looking for?"

"He never said it, but I knew. Too bad it killed him." George shook his head, his smile gone, and Brian knew he meant it. "We will have to be careful, I don't want to follow his footsteps too closely."

"How do you know about the diamonds?"

"A couple of years after the Japanese surrendered and the Americans cleared the lagoon of the mines and fixed the airfield, some other men came." George paused and Brian wondered if he was trying to remember or if it was for the effect of his story. "They were military men too, but none of them wore uniforms. Many of the islanders helped them search the lagoon. I helped.''

''What make you think they were in the military?'' Brian asked.

George laughed. He pointed one finger to the corner of his eye. ''I have lived many years in the company of military, and most of that time in fear. I can see it in the way a man stands.'' He smiled. ''You can't tell, my friend, because you stand that way.''

''You're grabbing at thin air,'' Brian said as he shifted in his chair.

George laughed again. A deep chuckle that caused his whole body to shake. He was pleased with himself and he slapped Brian on the back. ''Don't worry. Remember, your navy gave me back my lagoon,'' he said, then he turned serious. ''But that doesn't matter. There are no diamonds, there never were in the lagoon.''

Brian locked his fingers behind his head and leaned back. ''How do you know they didn't find them?''

George gave him a half-cocked smile.

''Oh, yeah,'' Brian remembered what Rota had said. ''It's a small island.''

''If they found them, it would have gotten around. If they didn't and the diamonds were truly in the lagoon, those men would still be here. They were very professional men and very persistent.''

''But you'll humor me and help us look?''

''You are paying me to dive and keep the boat running,'' he said. ''The humor I will throw in for free.''

''Dinner!'' Leslie's voice carried in through the window that opened over the porch. The sweet smell of pineapple and brown sugar met them as they stepped out of the house and onto the patio.

Leslie had lit and hung four large bosun's lamps on the overhang above the table. Their light cast eerie flickering shadows on the planks of the porch and out a few feet onto the beach as they swung in the warm evening breeze.

253

The rusting circular patio table was covered with a white cloth and three place settings of fine white china, each plate decorated with delicate hand-painted patterns showing the steep mountains of Japan. They were arranged in perfect dining order with stemmed crystal wineglasses on the correct side above contemporary mismatched silverware.

"Here it is," Leslie said as she backed out of the kitchen door. She turned, the platter in front of her steaming with sliced ham and pineapple. "What's the matter?" she asked from the doorway. Both men stood behind their chairs staring at the plates. Brian looked at her, then at George; the native's face was pale.

George lifted one of the dishes and inspected it. "Tonight we dine with ghosts," he said in a low tone that sent a shiver through Leslie.

She looked at Brian, her eyes wide. "I found them in a box in the kitchen. I didn't think . . ."

"It's okay." Brian moved to her and took the platter. It matched the settings. "Come on, sit down. Let's eat." He moved to the table and took his seat.

Leslie walked quickly back into the kitchen.

George was hesitant until Brian pushed his chair out. "I'm not a superstitious man," the native said. "But this will bring bad luck."

"No, it won't," Brian shot at him. He didn't like the idea of eating off the plates brought up from the lagoon either, but he didn't know why.

"I don't mind, but I wonder if they will," George said, nodding toward the sea.

"Shut up and enjoy the dinner," Brian said.

Leslie brought out a bottle of white wine she had found. Where did you get this?" George asked as he inspected the bottle.

"Behind the door in the kitchen."

"The professor must have brought it," George said as he opened it and poured himself a full glass first.

As with the wine, most of the ham went to George. The

meat, imported from the States, was an expensive commodity, and although there were plenty of pigs on the islands, their meat didn't have the tenderness of farm-fed pork. George was indulging himself.

No one said very much as they sat and ate, though George commented on Leslie's cooking several times between bites. Brian went to the kitchen for another bottle of wine.

"You are lucky that Rota doesn't know you can cook so well. She would have you in the kitchen of the Blue Waters," George said, wiping his face.

Leslie smiled. "Thank you, George," she said, glad the plates had been forgotten.

"What time will you be at the boat?" Brian asked the native as he filled his glass.

"Early. I will take the boat and meet you at the end of the pier. We will need the rest of the professor's equipment if we are both going to dive."

Brian stood up. "Let's get the extra tanks out of the back room," Brian said as he picked his empty plate from the table.

"I'll get those." Leslie took the plate from Brian's hands. George smiled at her.

As the two men walked into the house and toward the extra bedroom, George slapped Brian hard on the back. "Leslie is acting like Rota," he said with a wide grin. "She wants do to everything for you. Be careful, she has that look in her eyes."

"You're crazy," Brian said, but a similar thought had crossed his mind too.

"You will see," George assured him with a now serious voice. "Women know how to plan their every move. She will trap you, you will see. I'm lucky Rota is a widow and has forgotten those things or I would be washing dishes at the Blue Waters."

As they entered the room, the light from the hall fell on the canary-yellow scuba tanks stacked one on top of the other against the far wall. The cylinders reminded Brian of miniature torpedos.

He felt the light switch behind the door and flipped it on.

"The professor had an air compressor here," George said as he pointed to a corner, empty except for the dust and the steel trash can next to it. "It is in Guam being repaired. In the morning, we'll have to wait until Kulado's dive shop opens to fill all of these."

Brian grabbed the valve of the double tanks and pulled it off the top of the pile. He leaned it against the doorway, then pulled the next one out and set it against the first.

George found a mask under the scattered boxes. It was the one he had used before while diving with the professor. The intruder had gone through this room too. The mask's glass was broken. "I would like to find out who did this," he said, placing the mask on the workbench.

"Me too," Brian said as he attached a diving regulator and pressure gauge to one of the tanks. It was empty like the other one. "You're right, they'll have to be filled in the morning."

"Try this one," George said as he reached for the valve of a single tank that lay under the bench. Brian had not noticed it, and as George pulled it out, the top of the tank caught the bottom edge of the bench.

Suddenly something snapped and George found himself toppling backward, slamming against the hard floor. With his legs straight out in front of him, he looked up at Brian, somewhat dazed.

"You all right?"

George shook his head to clear it. Without a word, he opened his hand. The tank valve was between his fingers with the top dome of the steel tank still attached. Brian took it from him slowly. The dome wasn't steel but dried clay painted yellow to match the other scuba tanks.

Both men looked back at the remaining section. The real top of the tank had been cut off and replaced with the phony.

256

The light from the ceiling showed the edge of a rolled tube of paper deep inside it.

On their hands and knees, they moved toward the bench. Brian reached in and pulled the tightly rolled chart. With it came a spiral-bound notebook.

"He knew," George said. "He knew someone would search the house."

Brian unrolled a few inches of the chart. It was heavily marked in pencil. "He sure did." He smiled. In his chest, his heart pounded against his ribs. He felt like a boy finding a treasure map in the attic. He looked at George.

The native's eyes were wide, his mouth opened like a starving man looking at a lamb.

Brian picked up the notebook and opened it and flipped through the pages. "This won't be very helpful," he said, handing it to George as he stood up. He took the chart into the other room.

"What's wrong?" George looked through the notebook's wrinkled pages as he followed him. He saw the entries were all written in Japanese. "I can get Yoko to read this," George said.

"No," Brian shot at him. "If you tell anyone, whoever ripped through here today will be back." Brian moved to the table and quickly stretched the chart out over the one they had bought.

Leslie came into the room. She had changed into a cool white cotton dress with shoestring straps over her slender shoulders.

"Look," George said excitedly. "We found the professor's chart."

"Where?"

Brian pushed the last pin into the corner to hold it down. "He hid it in the workroom."

The chart was of the eastern side of the lagoon. A dozen points were marked in heavy pencil near the east end of Moen. There were more near Falo, Herit, Bush, and Small islands.

257

"These must be the names of the wrecks," Brian said tapping the Japanese kanji characters next to each point. "We'll dive each one."

"The *Sakusa Maru,* the *Fujiware.*" Leslie ran her finger over the chart. She stopped at each point and read the lost ship's name. "The *Yamaguro.*"

Brian looked at her. "You can read this?"

Leslie smiled. "Of course."

Brain took the professor's notebook from George. "Can you read all of this?"

Leslie opened it. She didn't realize what it was until she began to read. Tears filled the corner of her eyes. "Entered the bridge of the *Gosei Maru.* She rests on her port side in shallow water and in silence. Against the bulkhead, buried half in silt is the skull of her captain. Matsuda-san never left the ship. My old friend still commands with honor."

Leslie dropped the book on the table and swallowed hard. Brian reached over and took her hand.

"I'm okay," she said. Then she leaned over the chart. She ran her finger along each point, reading the names to herself. Finally, she put her finger on the pencil mark next to the small island of Bush. "The *Kuma Maru,*" she said, and she felt Brian gently squeeze her hand.

TWENTY-SIX

Moen Island, Truk Lagoon, 1986

The breeze of the night before was gone, and like the scent of the mangroves, the heat of the early morning sun hung heavy in the air. Brian was already sweating as he put the last set of scuba tanks into the rear of the Willys. He went back to the house for the gear bag.

After Leslie had found the location of the wreck on the chart, the three of them had moved out to the patio. Only one bosun's lamp remained lit and Leslie moved her chair close under it. Settling in, she began to read aloud from her father's notebook, and at first no one objected, though the professor's words carried a cryptic breath.

The professor had dived a number of wrecks and in his notes had made specific references to each. He wrote about the ships with familiarity and knowledge and he mentioned the men he had served with. And how he had watched their ships burn with billowing clouds of black smoke before finally surrendering to the sea.

Brian had sat on the steps of the porch, looking out at the lagoon and listening to her. It was a quarter moon and the slice of sea it illuminated reflected up onto the porch and filled the shadows the bosun's lamp didn't reach.

After a while, George became restless and couldn't sit

still. Brian noticed him lean his head back against the rail to get comfortable enough to fall asleep, but he couldn't.

"I will be at the pier in the morning," he said suddenly, standing and stepping around Brian and down to the beach.

"Aren't you going to stay?" Leslie asked.

His head turned toward her. Though she could not see the expression of his face because of the darkness, it could be heard in his voice. "I do not want to know their names," he said slowly.

"You want a ride back to town?" Brian asked. He understood George a little better now.

"No, I want to walk along the beach to clear my head. I will be at the end of the pier in the morning."

Brian watched him until he was only a white hat drifting over the sand. Then he was gone.

"I'm going to bed," Leslie said after a few minutes. "Good night."

"Night."

What had happened between them earlier was gone. She was trapped in her father's words. Brian understood. He had become involved with his own father's notes only days before. But he felt a little empty now that she had gone into the house.

He moved to the lounge and stretched himself out on the stiff pad and listened to her climb into the spring bed. When he finally fell asleep, her light was still on.

In the morning her door was closed when he walked by and entered the kitchen to start a pot of coffee. He decided to let her sleep until after he had packed the jeep. He had no thoughts of leaving her behind. He had meant what he said last night, he wanted her to leave the lagoon, but only for her own safety.

Brian set the canvas gear bag behind the passenger seat. That was everything, masks, fins, weight belts, lights, tanks, and the empty acetylene and oxygen tanks for the torch. George said the trading company would exchange the tanks for full ones. But not until the afternoon.

260

Brian went back one more time to the workroom. The phony tank top and valve was still on the bench top. He took it and then leaned down and pulled out the bottom half of the professor's hiding place.

The thought of being boarded while in the middle of the lagoon, even for a friendly visit, wasn't pleasing to him. Once they found the wreck, losing the chart wouldn't matter, but he didn't want to let go of the professor's notebook.

As he pulled the phony tank bottom out from under the workbench and stood it up, he heard something slide to the bottom and hit with a clang. Brian laid the tank down and lifted the bottom end.

The handgun slid out and bounced heavily on the wooden floor. Brian picked it up. He was familiar with this type of gun, a Colt .45 caliber automatic, U.S. military issue. He pulled back the slide and a round jumped out as another replaced it in the chamber. He popped out the clip, counted the rounds, then added the one that had be ejected. It was full. He slapped the clip into the handle and reloaded the .45.

This was an added bonus from the professor. He took a torn rag from the bench and wrapped it around the gun. Then he walked into the study and took his father's black notebook from his suitcase and wrapped that too in the rag.

He walked out onto the porch and down to the beach. Moving to the rear of the house, he felt along the wall until he found a loose plank along the bottom. With his fingers, Brian managed to pry it open enough to set the gun and book behind it. Then he pushed the plank back. He kicked the sand where he had knelt, spreading it around until he was satisfied it covered his footprints.

Walking back into the house, he moved to Leslie's bedroom. The door was still closed. He turned the knob and pushed it open slowly. "Leslie, let's go," he said. The bed was empty. He stepped in and looked around. "Leslie?" She was gone.

He moved to the kitchen. "Leslie?" The pot was still on the stove, only his cup on the table.

He stepped quickly out the kitchen door. "Leslie!" he called from the edge of the porch. He ran out to the water and looked up and down the deserted beach. "Les!" he yelled. He went to the side of the house. "Les!" he called into the mangrove.

"Here," her voice carried to him as she stepped out of the thick jungle. She had her father's notebook in her hand.

"Where the hell were you?"

"I went for a walk," she said innocently.

"Tell me the next time you decide to for a walk, and go along the beach, not through the trees," he said in a stern voice.

"Sorry," she said.

"Sorry?"

"I didn't go far," she said with a shrug.

He looked at her and sighed. "No, I'm sorry. I was worried."

She smiled and stepped closer to him. She leaned forward and kissed him on the cheek. "Thanks, but you don't have to worry."

"Just don't do it again, okay?" Brian said as they walked toward the house.

She hadn't seen or heard the man following her through the mangrove. He had been watching the house since late last night and had listened to her as she read from the book to Bovan and the native. But the words meant nothing to him.

And when the girl left the house while Brian was still asleep on the porch, he had followed her. He was expecting something, but she did only what she said. She walked through the jungle. She had become disoriented twice, but stopped and listened until she heard the surf and used that to keep her bearings.

Why the hell is Bovan sleeping outside? the man wondered. This girl is beautiful. In the thickness of the tropical jungle, he had been able to get very close to her as she walked in her peach-colored shorts and loose white blouse with its open macrame woven neckline. He could just imagine her breasts beneath the thin material of the blouse.

But now Troy Merith pushed those thoughts from his mind and got back to his job. He looked past the two of them as they walked into the house, and saw the jeep was full of diving equipment. That he had expected. He had already rented a small boat and it was waiting for him at the pier.

The CIA man moved deeper into the jungle and walked quickly to where the dirt road cut through the grove. Near its edge, where he had hid his motor scooter, he would be able to watch Bovan and the girl leave.

"We've got to get going before George changes his mind about diving," Brian said as he downed the last of his coffee. It was cold and bitter.

She nodded. "Look what I found," she said, following him out of the house. She opened the notebook to the last pages.

"What?" He dropped down the porch stairs.

Leslie followed him as he read. "Kuma's forward and stern holds secure. The amidships hold must have been opened by the torpedo. Should be able to get through the hull there."

Brian stopped in mid-stride. "Through her hull?"

The dry braid of rope pulled taut in George's hand as he knelt over the skiff's bow. The line stuck out at a low angle, entering the water twenty feet beyond and then disappearing into the depths. George waved his hand over his head and heard Brian switch off the engine. He pulled in a few more feet of anchor line in and then tied it off.

"Do you think we're above her?" Brian asked.

George shrugged. "The anchor hooked on something. Not sand. But it's deep water, could be anything on the bottom of this lagoon."

The waves were gentle in the midmorning and the wind could hardly be felt. The skiff rolled lightly.

Leslie pulled herself onto the upper deck and sat with her legs swinging freely over the companionway. Lifting her blouse from the bottom, she pulled it over her head revealing her purple string bikini top. She folded the blouse and set it beside her.

George was watching with a smile, and when she looked at him, he grinned wide with his crooked teeth. "It is a beautiful day," he said. Leslie smiled back with a nod.

Brian was checking the tanks. He looked up at George and followed his gaze to Leslie. Brian felt a surge in his chest as she turned and looked at him, her eyes smiling.

"Can I help with anything?" she asked.

"No," Brian said. "George, hand me that regulator." He took it from the native, and attached the first stage to the single decompression tank. Then, using the professor's hemp rope that was marked with plastic yellow tags every ten feet, Brian lowered the four sets of tanks over the side and into the aqua-blue water. A heavy iron weight at the rope's end held the line vertical in the water. The first two tanks hung at twenty feet and the second at ten.

Brian figured they would use their own reserve air for the short deompression stop at thirty feet. This was only going to be a scouting dive.

"You ready?" Brian asked as he checked over George's equipment. He flipped the black Dacor underwater lamp switch on and off twice making sure it was working. The heavy lights hung from their weight belts on a three-foot leash. Brian checked his own, its beam bright even in the sunlight.

The native looked reluctant as he leaned over the rail and stared at the water. "How deep is it?"

"The chart says about a hundred and sixty feet," Brian said. "You ready?" George nodded, but Brian looked into his eyes, trying to see if he was telling the truth. There couldn't be any hesitation while diving, especially diving so deep.

"Okay," Brian said, believing him. He lifted his set of double tanks to the rail, balancing them as he slid one arm through the straps, and when he searched for the other, Leslie appeared beside him. She pulled the second shoulder strap out and helped him push the end through the buckle.

"Be careful," she said. Suddenly, she didn't like the thought of what the two men were doing.

"We'll be up in an hour and ten minutes," he assured her.

"You have enough air?" she asked.

George looked nervously from Leslie to Brian. "Good question, do we have enough air?"

"Plenty. We'll follow the decompression line down to the wreck," he said, picking up a bundle of white nylon line. "I'll tie this off at the weight and we'll use it to find our way back."

George nodded, but silently he wondered what he had got himself into. He stepped closer to the side of the skiff.

"Please be careful," Leslie said. She looked into Brian's dark eyes. Though the day was warm and windless, a chill crawled up her back.

"An hour and ten minutes," Brian reassured her again. Then he stepped past George and through the opening in the rail. In one motion, he jumped off the skiff.

The clear water enveloped him with an explosion of silver sparkling bubbles. The sea was cool and crisp compared to the hot air above. Brian let himself drift a little ways from the boat.

A moment later, George crashed through the surface. He kicked frantically to keep his head above the water.

Brian looked up. "You all right?" he called.

The native lifted his mask from his face and let the water out. Once it was cleared, George felt better. He gave Brian the thumbs-up sign and put the regulator in his mouth.

Brian gripped his own regulator mouthpiece between his teeth and let himself sink a few feet below the surface. He could hear his breath as it was amplified in the rubber diaphragm of the regulator.

His bubbles flowed out the exhaust port and around his head. George followed him down as he kicked toward the hemp rope. Brian grabbed it with his right hand and headed down into the blue-green darkness below.

Through the pair of a polarized lenses of the Nikon binoculars, Merith watched Brian and then the native enter the water. When he was sure they had begun their descent, he turned his attention to Leslie.

From behind a large palm tree on the tiny sand mound called Bush Island, Merith focused in close on the skiff. He had followed them at a distance in his small rented outboard which was how hidden on the opposite side of the island. Struggling through the thick mangrove trees, he was in time to see them anchor and prepare to dive.

Now he watched as Leslie brought a beach towel from the cabin and moved to the bow of the skiff. Holding it by one end, she tossed the towel into the air and let it settle out on the sloping foredeck. Then she peeled off her shorts to reveal the bottom half of her purple bikini with only its thin strings holding the sharp vee that cut tight between her legs.

Merith swallowed hard as she bent over to straighten the towel and then sat down and began to apply suntan lotion on her slender legs and arms. Through the binoculars, he could see the shimmer of the tropical sun on her skin.

"The waves are beautiful from here," the voice suddenly beside him said.

Merith spun around, his right hand instantly drawing his

revolver from the side of his trousers, his thumb automatically cocking back the hammer.

But the elderly Oriental woman with long braided gray hair simply smiled at him without so much as a blink of her eye. "Out that way is the northeast pass." She turned and pointed beyond the skiff. "They have the best shape out there."

"Well, if the dragon lady has come out of her lair," Merith said; shock was still reverberating within him and it made his voice loud.

"Don't be so melodramatic, Troy," she said.

The CIA man continued to hold his revolver on her, its hammer still cocked. "What's your business here, Mimi?"

"You could be a little nicer. We haven't seen each other since Manila," Mimi said with a wry smile.

"We were on different sides there."

"That's what makes the world so wonderful, Troy. It's always changing," she said, and then waved her hand. "Put the gun away."

Merith hesitated, then slipped the revolver back into his trousers. He was still apprehensive.

"Okay, so why are you here?"

"You'll excuse me if I sit?" she asked as she moved to a fallen palm tree, its trunk half buried in the sand. She brushed it off with the tips of her fingers and sat down. "An old woman's legs are not much for hiking through jungles."

"You are evading my question, Mimi. You haven't changed one bit."

"I'm here to see you don't interfere." She looked directly at him. "Not yet."

Merith studied her for a moment. There was no threat in her voice, no violence. It was a statement of fact and Merith could not help but believe her. "My business here is official. I hope we won't have a problem of overlap with our operations."

"Official, Mr. Merith? You gave up the international side for domestic years ago. So you can hardly be on official business with your sector on the other side of the world. Or am I mistaken and you've been transferred from D.C. to Truk?''

Merith stood there feeling his mouth drop open. How could she know? He was a top agent, holding the utmost security. His name and position were known only to high-ranking Pentagon officials.

He had crossed paths with this woman may times over the years and he knew she was good. So good in fact he had never determined exactly which government she worked for, or if she contracted herself out. It really didn't matter. They had never been in direct conflict on an operation. She had the qualities of a top agent and he respected that. But this information, how could she?

''I have many friends, Troy,'' she said as if reading his thoughts. ''Just like you. Friends I am in debt to and are in debt to me.'' She smiled up at him. ''We both know what kind of favors one can win in our business.''

''We may be in the same business,'' Merith said. ''But are we really on the same side this time?''

Mimi laughed lightly, then she looked at him seriously. ''Commander Bovan is not a security risk.''

Merith moved and sat down next to the woman. He looked out at the skiff. ''You don't know that.''

''But I do,'' she said firmly. ''There is much at risk here, but not in what you think.''

''That'll take a lot of convincing, Mimi.''

She nodded understandingly.

Merith raised the binoculars to his eyes and looked at Leslie's oil-drenched body in the sun. Then he looked at the waves coming over the distant reef by the northeast passage. Mimi was right; their shapes were perfect in high-arching crests and beautiful on this side of the lagoon.

At ten feet, Brian checked the decompression tanks hanging on the line. He took a breath from each. It was a precautionary measure where not enough could be taken.

He did the same at the twenty-foot stop and found the tanks as he expected. Their life-giving air would be waiting for them on the ascent.

The two men kicked gently through the water as they sank deeper. The sun followed them, cut by the ocean into distinct rays that danced about.

Brian let the rope pass through his hand, the plastic tags with their red letters scratching at his palm. Below seventy-five feet, they were no longer yellow but gray as the ocean absorbed the wavelengths of light that the human eye recognized.

At a hundred feet, the sharp colors of their tanks, masks, fins, and gloves were dulled. Everything became shades of gray and black under the green haze of the sea.

The two men drifted in a boundless void. Below them was a still darkness that gave no indication of the bottom, and above, in the direction their bubbles raced, was only diffused soft light.

Brian was comfortable here. He dove often as a boy, even though the water of the sound was cold and visibility was usually less than a few feet. He looked at George, and putting his index finger to his thumb, he gave him the okay sign.

George looked at him and nodded. Then as the native looked back toward the bottom, he began pointing excitedly.

The eerie outline appeared below them. It was huge, dark, and foreboding, and seemed suspended from their line. Brian felt a twist of excitement in his stomach as he flipped on the Dacor lamp.

It was as if they had descended upon a forgotten cathedral, its steeples adorned with lace and velvet. Brian's light caught the silver cloud of sardines schooling thick above the wreck. As if giving benediction, they circled the cross of the ship's forward mast.

The two men continued down the decompression line to where it stopped at the iron weight. It hung twenty feet above the foredeck of the freighter. They descended further until they found footing on the highest point of the deck. It was the port side where the rail still guarded the edge. The ship listed forty-five degrees to starboard.

George swung his light into the opening of the forward hold. A lone, three-man tank appeared ready for unloading onto a base that no longer existed, to fight a war fast becoming only words on the pages of history books. In the light beam, they could see the weapon cloaked thick with encrusting orange and purple sponges. Lumpy sea squirts had made the barrel their home.

Brian tied the nylon line to the rail and let it trail behind them as they swam along the deck and toward the bridge. Every edge and surface of the wreck was softened by the years of silt that had come to rest here and by the generations of algae and deep-water corals. The dive lights washed across each, revealing their beautiful colors naturally hidden at 160 feet.

Brian could feel his heartbeat race as they moved to the hatchway of the bridge. The door was rusted open and Brian pulled himself through. A sharp clang rang out as he hit one side of the hatch with his tank. He turned and continued in.

The native didn't hesitate. He followed right behind Brian as they swam into the superstructure. Their wedges of light swept from side to side as they picked out their passage through the chaos of twisted and fallen steel.

Two short posts stood alone in the center of the bridge and Brian guessed they had once held a chart table. He could almost hear the commands of new orders and the concurring course changes.

George moved in front and drifted closer to the floor. The fine silt billowed up under him. He saw something sticking up from the mud, and as he pulled at it, the bridge erupted in a black cloud that cut the beams of their lights to a few inches.

Brian reached out for George, found his forearm, took hold, and pulled him to the side. But the newly suspended silt seemed to follow them like the odor of a cigar. Brian's light picked up another hatchway and they headed for it.

Moving into the narrow hall, George still clung to the instrument he had released from its forty-year tomb. It was the bridge compass; its white face and black letters written in English spun gently inside its oil-filled case. To their surprise, the north mark spun around freely and still aimed north.

George set the compass on the floor of the passageway and gave Brian the okay sign. Brian nodded. He turned and proceeded deeper into the ship.

The narrow passage with its slanting walls stretched another twenty feet before it ended at a stairwell that turned back and took them down into the main hull of the freighter. Tiny opal sweepers sparkled as they darted away from the approaching lights.

This was their home, their domain, and the tiny fish thrived on the crustacea that lived on and around the algae that gripped the bulkheads of the silent freighter. But then larger fish, like snappers, found the wrecks where these small fish lived and the cycle of prey and predator continued. And bigger fish found the snappers and even bigger fish found those and the cycle flourished on the bottom of Truk where, the day before U.S. Hellcats and Avengers struck, there was only a flat sandy bottom.

The water was cool and still at this depth and it was comforting. Too comforting, as it could lull a diver into forgetting his limits of air and time. Brian checked his watch. They had been down fifteen minutes. He checked his air supply and then George's.

Brian knew that a man's breathing rate increased under stress or when he was forced into an unfamiliar environment. And none was more unfamiliar than diving a deepwater wreck.

George was a textbook example. He had consumed almost half his air while Brian still had three fourths the amount he had begun with. Their dive would have to be shortened by several minutes, Brian calculated.

They continued deeper into the hull. Through one open door, Brian saw a large tilted steel cabinet balancing delicately on one leg. Thick wires protruded from its top, and on its front panel frequency dials were frozen. There was little doubt that the last call from this radio room was a plea for help.

Brian didn't know the layout of the freighter, but he had a sense of ships and their design. When his light landed on the heavy steel hatch door with its half-dozen doglegged latches, he knew the engine room would be on the other side.

What he hadn't expected was the stainless-steel chain that held the door open against the bulkhead. Brian inspected the doorframe and found fresh scrape marks. George tapped him on the shoulder, and when he turned, the native lifted one of the latches from the floor. It had been cut in two by an underwater torch.

This was the professor's work and both men knew it. For the first time, George's nervousness disappeared and was replace by excitement. He eagerly followed Brian into the engine room.

They swam down through the maze of catwalks hanging above the huge engines that had once rumbled with life bringing the *Kuma Maru* to its final port.

Brian pulled himself over the twisted pipes and lines that encaged the engines and toward the forward wall. Using his light, he searched for one more doorway.

He hoped some things were international, and like American ship builders, the Japanese had the need for repair crews to move from hold to hold through smaller hatchways.

In the far corner, he found exactly what he expected. But the small maintenance hatch that connected the amidships hold with the engine room hung closed in the slanted wreck.

George pointed to the four-foot iron crowbar leaning against the wall, its paint still bright and new. Brian saw it along with the marks where the algae had been scraped clean from around the latches. Each handle lay in line with the doorframe, indicating they were unlocked.

The professor had been here too, but no further. Brian tried lifting the door but the sea had frozen the hinges. It was solid against the bulkhead.

George tapped Brian on the wrist indicating for him to check the time.

Brian looked. Twenty-five minutes in the wreck. He was pushing the limits, but he had to see what was on the other side of the door.

Brian reached for the crowbar and shoved its sharpened end under the lip of the door. He pulled at it. George looked into his facemask and shook his head. Brian ignored him and continued to pull up on the bar. The strain was making him lightheaded as the muscles in his neck knotted.

George grabbed hold of the bar and both men, with their finned feet wedged against the wall, pulled up with all their strength.

The hatch refused them at first. Then it began to give, half an inch by half an inch. They slipped the bar in deeper for better leverage and pulled again. The hatch gave more, yawning open ever so slowly. Again they moved the bar and pried the hatch a few more inches.

Brian motioned George to hold it and the native understood, but when he saw Brian kneel down and begin into the small fissure, he shook his head frantically and tried to call out through his mouthpiece.

But Brian had no intentions of going in. He only wanted to make sure it was the amidships hold on the other side of this bulkhead.

The bright beam of the Dacor cut into the huge cavern

that had not seen light for over four decades. It skimmed across the steel ribs of the starboard side of the ship, rusted red but void of the film of silt that covered every other square inch of the sunken freighter.

Then he saw the torn and twisted steel that had allowed the sea in. Brian moved his light along the jagged edges where the Avengers' torpedo had ripped open the *Kuma Maru* like a fist through paper.

His beam picked up something on the other side of the pierced hull, but as he swept the light over the structure, he heard the screech of metal as the tip of the crowbar slipped and he felt the heavy steel hatch begin to fall.

George gripped the bar with all his strength, but it was giving and he was weakening fast.

Brian quickly pulled himself from the hatchway as the crowbar gave the door crashed down. Moving his hand just in time, the door landed on the underwater light, crushing it like an eggshell.

George looked down at Brian and then shook his head. Brian gave the native the okay sign and then moved and tied the nylon rope to the hatch's handle. He motioned George to follow as he pulled himself along the rope and out of the engine room.

It would take them forty minutes to reach the surface. Tomorrow, Brian thought, they would be back with the cutting torch and he would see what was in the hold of the *Kuma Maru.*

TWENTY-SEVEN

Truk Lagoon, 1944

Second Officer Hitobuto Yokamata looked over his log-book. In the light of the candle that burned with greasy black smoke, he double-checked each cargo entry of the *Kuma Maru*. They delivered everything to Dublon that had been requested. Everything but that stupid tank, he thought.

It still sat in the forward hold waiting repairs. The colonel in charge of the island's armaments wouldn't allow it unloaded unless it was in fighting condition. Foolish man, Yokamata thought. the shore mechanics could have the tank working in a day, but the colonel blamed the damage on the freighter's crew and wouldn't accept it. Yokamata had argued the point with him but to no avail.

Now in the morning Yokamata had to find a mechanic from some other command to repair the tank before he could have it lifted off the freighter. And he wanted it off as soon as possible so they could begin their journey back to Japan.

He had watched Admiral Koga's fleet of carriers and de-stroyers leave the safety of Truck and head out to sea early yesterday morning. It was a bad omen strengthened by the merchant fleet's orders to unload their cargo and leave the lagoon as soon as possible.

''Yokamata-san,'' the voice came from the other side of the door.

"Yes," Yokamata answered, jumping to his feet. The deep voice of Captain Shimito was unique to no one else. Yokamata immediately opened the door of his cabin and stood at attention.

"Good evening, Yokamata-san," Shimito said with an unfamiliar smile. He was a big man with a large round belly and a naked head and had been nicknamed Little Buddha by his crew.

Yokamata had heard the men say it under their breaths on occasion but he had never taken it up with Shimito. Not that he liked his captain or wanted to save him from the humiliation. He didn't. But the ship's crew were good men and he didn't want to bring on Shimito's anger.

"You are still working," Shimito said as he saw the log-book open on the small table.

"Yes, sir," Yokamata was still at attention, his muscular chest firm under his sleeveless undershirt. "We have only the tank in the forward hold to unload, sir."

Shimito stood smiling at Yokamata for a long moment. "After you get the front armor replaced," Shimito said with a wise nod. "I saw the damage from the crane."

"Yes, sir."

"Come, my second officer," Shimito said as he stepped out of Yokamata's cabin. "We have something to talk about."

Yokamata took his uniform shirt from his bunk and followed the large man out of the cabin.

"I am not worried about the tank, Yokamata-san," his captain said as they moved along the dark passage. "I like this lagoon, it is a paradise and there are no torpedos here to rip open my ship."

"The orders . . ."

"The orders are only made to rush us back to Sasebo. I am in no hurry to leave. One or two days more will not matter," Shimto said.

Yokamata said nothing. He preferred the open sea rather

276

than resting at anchor, an easy target for American bombers.

"I thought the fleet left the lagoon because of the American plane," Yokamata said.

Shimito laughed harshly; it echoed through the quiet ship. "A thousand planes would not chase Admiral Koga away."

At first, Yokamata felt foolish at what he had suggested. A thousand planes wouldn't send the admiral away. He would stay and fight to the last man. But the single American plane that had flown high of Truk a week ago was not a bomber, it was reconnaissance.

Koga wasn't running in the face of an attack. He was avoiding it. After so many recent Japanese losses, he could do nothing else. He had to move his weakening fleet to Palau and order the remaining merchant ships home. Yokamata realized what Shimito did not. An attack was imminent.

"How long did you live in America, Yokamata-san?" Shimito asked over his shoulder as they continued down the narrow passage toward the stairway that led to the bridge.

"Twelve years," Yokamata said reluctantly.

"Ah!" Shimito looked back and smiled. "Then you know how the Americans think?"

"That is something difficult to determine with any man, sir," Yokamata said.

"Yes, yes, but you can judge better than I," Shimito said as he stepped through the hatchway and onto the bridge of the *Kuma Maru*.

The two men standing midnight watch on the dark bridge saluted the captain and second officer as they walked through.

Shimito opened the door to his cabin and stepped in, but he didn't move to his desk as Yokamata expected. The captain went to the cupboard over his bed and took out a gray ceramic bottle of sake and two palm-sized drinking cups.

He smiled again at his second officer and Yokamata saw

in the lamp light his red eyes. As he suspected, the captain had already indulged in the strong rice wine.

"Come." Shimito waved his thick hand.

Again the men on the bridge saluted their commanding officers as they passed.

"The Americans are strange people, Yokamata-san, very strange people." Shimito stepped outside the superstructure and walked along the upper deck through the darkness of the moonless night.

Neither man needed the railings to guide them. They had walked a thousand miles on the *Kuma Maru* and instinct told them where to step.

"They think the whole world needs them," Shimito said as they descended a set of stairs and entered another hatchway that led into the bowels of the freighter. They walked down a series of catwalks and into the engine room.

This was always the quietest place on the ship when they were at anchor. Or perhaps it just seems so since it is so noisy when we are under way, Yokamata thought.

The three sailors working on the generator and covered with thick brown grease to their shoulders stood and saluted. Shimito nodded and asked them how it was coming.

"It will be finished by morning, sir," the dirtiest promised.

The generator was completely dismantled and spread over the steel floor, but Yokamata knew the man would keep his word.

Shimito nodded again. He reached into the small wooden bucket that held the mechanic's tools and took out a claw hammer. Then he continued through the ship toward the amidships hold. They slipped through the small workmen's hatchway in the bulkhead.

On the other side, Shimito lifted the kerosene lamp hanging on the wall. He lit it, and walking within its flickering pool of light, they moved deeper into the large empty hold. It was cold and damp and the lamp's beveled glass cast strange shadows into the far corners of the ship.

"Are the Americans trustworthy, Yokamata-san?" Shimito asked, and Yokamata wasn't sure if he was joking or much drunker than he seemed.

Shimito stopped and lifted the light to his second officer's face. "Well?" he asked.

"I would not trust one with a pistol to my head, Captain, if that is what you are asking."

"No, it's not."

"I am sorry, sir, I do not understand what you want to know."

Shimito continued along the narrow lengths of planks that ran down the center of the hold in silence as if he was contemplating how to re-ask his question. Then he stopped and turned and, lifting the light, leaned close to Yokamata. "Will an American keep his word?"

Yokamata looked into the dark eyes of his captain with their hints of red in the corners. It was an impossible question, a foolish question really, but the young second officer knew Shimito was no fool.

"How can one man say what another will do, sir? Each sees differently, thinks differently."

Shimito nodded solemnly. Yokamato wasn't giving him the answer he wanted.

Yokamata said, "They do not know honor like us. They have respect but not the honor that has kept Japan alive for so many centuries."

Shimito looked at his second officer and smiled. "No honor," he mumbled to himself and nodded again. "That is it," he said as he turned and continued along the boards. "They have no honor."

They came to the rear of the hold and to a green tarp hiding something beneath it. Shimito handed the lamp to Yokamata.

"Without honor, how can I trust an American to keep his word?" Shimito said as he pulled at the stiff heavy canvas. It slid off, revealing a large wooden crate.

Yokamata took a step closer. He had never seen this crate

before. It had no markings or tags on the lid to tell its destination.

"This crate isn't in the log," Yokamata said, moving to it.

Shimito laughed. "I hope not," he said. "What about the Americans keeping their word?"

"Some of them will, others won't," Yokamata said as he inspected the crate.

Shimito hooked the claw of the hammer under one corner of the lid. Leaning his body back, the first nails gave with the cry of a wounded alley cat. The captain moved the hammer to the center edge of the lid and pulled again and then he slid it along until all the nails gave and the lid was off.

Moving closer and holding the lamp high, Yokamata looked into the crate. He saw the two footlockers lying on their sides. His eyes lifted slowly up to Shimito.

"They are American," Shimito said.

"What is inside?"

Shimito smiled widely. "Chinese wealth," he said as he reached in and grabbed the rope handle at one end of the first locker. He pointed and Yokamata grabbed the opposite end. The two men lifted it out and onto the cold floor of the hold.

Yokamata saw the red insignia of the U.S. Marines painted on the lid.

"Open it," Shimito said.

Yokamata knelt down and unbuckled the two latches and opened the lid. In the light, he saw the newspaper-wrapped objects filling the bottom of the locker. The paper was old and brittle and tore easily as he unraveled it. To his amazement, it revealed a long thin bone. The dark brown fossil looked like the upper arm bone of a human. Yokamata looked up at his captain, who sat on the edge of the large crate, smiling.

Yokamata's eyes widened. "The Peking Man fossils?"

Shimito laughed again. "They educated you well in America, Yokamata-san. Here," Shimito pulled the sake bottle from his coat pocket, and the two cups. He handed one to Yokamata. Twisting the cap from the thin ceramic neck, he poured the clear liquid into the cups.

"I took this from the case that was going to the colonel who left us that tank. We will drink to him."

Yokamata felt the rough surface of the bone in his hand. He was suddenly unsure of Shimito. He nodded and they swallowed the wine together. It stung Yokamata's throat. He rarely drank.

"Before the war, I had a hobby in Kochi." Shimito smiled, filling Yokamata's small cup again and then his own. "I was an artist."

"An honorable hobby, Shimito-san. As honorable as being a ship's captain," Yokamata said. With the burning of the sake in his stomach and the unexplained American footlocker in front of him, he was becoming uncomfortable.

"I carved jade. Few of my pieces are in Kyoto and owned by some of the most beautiful women in all Japan, Yokamata-san," Shimito said, gulping down his sake and refilled his cup without offering to fill Yokamata's.

"Once," he said wiping his forearm over his wet fleshy lips, "Three geisha came to my house. One was a maiko and ending her apprenticeship to become a full-fledged geisha. Her onesan wanted to purchase a delicate peachblossom carving I had done. I told her there was no money that could buy it. It was from the finest piece of jade I had ever found," Shimito said, then he became quiet as he looked into the lamp. The corners of his mouth curled slightly as he smiled. "But the maiko went home with my carving, Yokamata-san, and she paid no money."

Shimito reached into the open footlocker and pulled out the odd-shaped clavicle bone. "Do you know the worth of this, Yokamata-san?"

Yokamato shook his head. He honestly didn't know.

"It is worthless. Why should anyone care about dead men's bones? Not even men, monkeys," he laughed. Then he leaned forward and spoke softly, almost in a whisper.

"Unless they are bones of your family, of your ancestors. Then suddenly they become priceless and you will do anything to bring them to rest."

Yokamata looked down at the bone in his hand. "The Chinese?"

Shimito nodded. "They are sending a submarine to take these off our ship."

"You're giving them back?"

"For a price," Shimito said as he set the sake bottle down and leaned forward, his hands on his knees. "When I was an artist, I learned to choose a good piece of jade that would not crack under my fingers. I had to be able to see the impurities in the stone."

Yokamata stared at him.

"These bones will be traded for 400 million yen, Yokamata-san. 400 million yen in diamonds from Hong Kong."

"Why tell me?" Yokamata stood up.

"You speak English," Shimito said with a shrug.

"Not since I returned to Japan," Yokamata said, defending himself.

The captain ran the palm of his hand over the crown of his head. "Nevertheless, I need you to help make the trade. It will be an American submarine that will rendezvous with us in a few days."

Yokamata looked down the footlocker. "You are trading with the Americans?" He couldn't believe what was said. "This is . . . this is treason!"

Shimito shook his head gently from side to side. "This is business, nothing more."

"No!" Yokamata dropped the fossil from his hand.

Shimito stood. "We will pay you," he said, his voice calm, but Yokamata could see the anger growing in his face. "I need you to translate."

"No! I won't," Yokamata said firmly. "This has to be reported."

Reaching for the claw hammer, Shimito moved closer to

Yokamata. "No, my second officer, there will be no report."

Yokamata stepped back away from the large man and out of the flickering pool of light, and for the first time, he sensed someone else was in the ship's hold with them.

TWENTY-EIGHT

Mid-Pacific, 1944

"Skipper, we've got a problem," Mouse said as he leaned in through the hatch into the mess hall.

Douglas looked up over his coffee, about to take his first sip. "What is it?" he asked, setting the cup down.

"I'm not sure, sir. I just came on duty. Clancy just sent me up to get you."

Douglas moved around from behind the table and followed the crewman toward the engine room. Mouse was a small man with rail-thin arms and legs. One look at the features of his face and you knew where he picked up his nickname. But that was only part of it. He seemed to live in the darkest bowels of the engine room, appearing only for breakfast lunch and dinner.

"What you got?" Douglas asked as he looked over Clancy's shoulder.

"Bad news. She's starting to heat up again," Clancy said, leaning back away from the Fairbanks diesel. He wiped his hands on a rag. "As soon as she starts to rev up, she turns red as a torch. The water isn't passing through the block, but for the life of me, Skipper, I don't know why."

"If you found the problem, could you fix it?"

"It would be wiser to wait until we were alongside a

tender," the Irishman said. "If I could start taking her apart now, it would mean less time we would have to be tied up."

Douglas leaned closer to Clancy and said in a low voice, "We're running on a schedule, Clancy. So I'm going to need everything you can give me from the other three engines."

"You tell me how much speed you need, Skipper, and I'll find it for you."

Standing up, Douglas patted the mechanic on the back. Then he headed toward the bridge. It was almost dawn, and he liked to be topside when the sun came up and the next shift came on duty.

"Morning, Skipper," one of the crew said as he passed Douglas in the control room. He nodded.

"You have the con, Mr. Albert," came a voice from the conning tower as Douglas climbed up the ladder. The shifts were changing and Michael had just taken command of the ship.

"Good morning," Douglas said as he passed through the hatch on the floor of the bridge.

One at a time, the new lookouts switched places with the old, and two pairs of tired eyes were ready for sleep.

"That forward engine is down again," Douglas said as he moved to the forward rail of the tower and next to Michael.

"I just got the report," Michael said. "It's going to cut it close getting to Truk before Wednesday."

"We'll run on the surface as long as we can to make up time. I figure we'll make the lagoon by sundown on Tuesday. And if the chart is correct and we can get through the reef, we'll be all right."

"If it's not?"

"If it's not, we'll find another way in," Douglas said. Michael nodded.

Douglas looked out at the horizon where the sun was just starting to rise, its gold color blending with the fading purple night sky.

The morning was becoming the typical mid-Pacific day, a cloudless sky painted blue over head. The wind was coming directly from behind them, creating a light surface chop on the southwesterly rolling swells. It also brought the *Seakrill*'s own choking diesel exhaust across the bridge. Until it shifted or the submarine changed course, it would make this watch unbearably long.

It was afternoon and Douglas was on the bridge when the radarman's voice came over the speaker. "Bogey coming in from the south. Range seven miles."

Instantly Douglas lifted his binoculars to his eyes and looked in that direction. Thick cumulus clouds now dominated the southern horizon.

"Call out when you see him," Douglas hollered to the lookouts perched above him. Trained eyes scanned the sky, but the plane was undoubtedly still inside the clouds.

Then a flicker of reflection from the sun off the fuselage. "Coming in from four o'clock, Captain, bearing directly on us," one of the lookouts called out. "It looks like a lone Val."

"Clear the bridge," Douglas ordered.

"Give me a shot at him first, Skipper," said Parker, a muscular young boy, new to the *Seakrill* and not many months off an Iowa farm. He was a lookout on the cigarette deck.

Douglas looked at him and saw his smile, then he looked back at the Val. The sub had been spotted and their location and direction would be broadcasted to a destroyer if the pilot was given the chance. But first the Jap would try for the kill himself. It would be better than to report a simple sighting.

"Okay, man the aft Oerlikon," Douglas yelled down to him. Then he turned and focused on the direction of the plane. It was a dark spot quickly taking form as it came toward them. "Lookouts below," Douglas called out, sending the two men on the periscope shears through the hatch.

The Japanese Val was a dive bomber, and Douglas didn't want to find out if this lone pilot had his bay loaded.

Pressed into the shoulder braces of the machine gun, Parker swung it around toward the approaching plane. He aligned himself with the sights, his hand firm on the trigger.

Douglas hit the Klaxon and then the bridge speaker button. "Take her to twenty-seven feet. Right full rudder. Prepare to dive," he ordered. He stepped closed to the hatchway and hollered down. "Michael, check with the radio room and see if you can pick up any transmissions." The hydraulic door of the induction valve slammed closed and the submarine shifted to its electric motors for power.

"Aye, aye, Skipper," he called back.

Twenty-seven feet would submerge most of the hull of the *Seakrill* while keeping the conning tower and the cigarette deck above water. He and Parker would end up wet from ocean spray, but there would be less of a target for the Jap to aim at.

Looking again through the binoculars, Douglas saw the Val had cut his distance from the submarine in half in surprising time.

"You got one pass and then we're going under, Parker," Douglas said as he watched the plane bank and begin its swoop towards them.

Parker didn't bother to answer. The 20mm machine gun suddenly came alive with a ferocious bark and jackhammer force. The gun spit its bullets into the air. Cooper shells discharged from the feed plate, bounced off the platform, and into the sea.

Undeterred, the Val came in low, its own set of three 7.7mm machine guns blazing back at the dark enemy submarine. The water portside exploded in three lines of white eruptions as the bullets raked across the sea and then into the *Seakrill*'s rear deck.

The pilot had hoped to at least damage the periscopes or

287

radio equipment before the submarine dove. He had not expected the American submarine to stay on the surface and fire back at him. He heard the American slugs enter the body of his plane.

Pulling back on his control stick, the pilot took the Val into a climb. Two thousand feet above the blue Pacific, he banked, pivoting on his wing, turned back toward earth and began his dive toward the enemy ship. He reached down with his left hand and opened the Val's bomb-bay doors.

"Stay with him, Parker," Douglas yelled as he climbed down to the forward platform and the other 20mm gun. Pulling the cock handle back, Douglas spun the gun around and aimed at the diving plane. Even before he looked through the sights, Douglas pulled the trigger.

The Val's pilot had little chance of surviving the attack of both 20mm guns locked on to his dropping plane. His windshield shattered as the bullets came through, their force exploding into his head and upper body. His hand released the controls and clutched his face as the pain swept him an instant before death.

Without releasing its bombs, the Japanese plane passed just feet above the number-one and -two periscopes and crashed into the unforgiving sea. Its wings were torn from its sides as it hit, and in seconds, the Val's tail rose a last time into the air and then the plane and its pilot slipped under the rolling swells.

"Not bad shooting, Skipper," Parker said as he walked to the forward platform and next to Douglas.

"Ya, not bad," Douglas said. "But next time, Parker, I think we'll go under."

The crewman shrugged, reached into his breast pocket, and pulled out a crumpled carton of Lucky cigarettes. He took out one for himself and offered the last to Douglas. He lit them both with his lighter.

"He didn't have a chance to broadcast, Captain," Michael said as he looked over the rail of the bridge. "Should I secure from general quarters?"

Douglas nodded. "Bring us back to course and to full speed."

"We could take on the whole Japanese Air Force, Skipper," Parker said with a grin.

Douglas smiled at the young crewman as he climbed back up to the bridge. Beneath his feet, he felt the ship raise and return to its southwest heading. "Keep your eyes open, gentlemen," he said to the lookouts as he moved to the hatchway. "Where there is one Val there is undoubtedly more."

Michael met him at the bottom of the ladder as he climbed down into the conning tower. "The plane had about an eight-hundred-fifty-mile range," he said. "I just looked it up."

Douglas moved to the chart table and leaned over it. There was a circle around their present location and a note to mark the encounter with the enemy plane.

"Either he came off a carrier or one of these." Douglas pointed to the Marshall Islands.

"I thought we controlled those islands," Michael said.

"They could be anywhere. There's a thousand mounds of sand out there big enough to hold a small squadron."

"My guess is he came off one of Koga's carriers here." Michael pointed to the small odd-shaped atoll and tiny islands west of their position. It was Truk.

TWENTY-NINE

Moen Island, Truk Lagoon, 1986

George leaped from the bow of the skiff to the pier and quickly tied the line to the tarnished cleat. Brian shut off the engine, but the boat still drifted hard into the old tires that hung off the pier and into the water.

"I'll go check with Ramon about the acetylene tank," George said, his voice still high with excitement.

"George!" Brian jumped from the boat. He moved quickly to him, grabbed his arm, and pulled him close. In a low voice, he said, "Take a deep breath and settle down." Brian walked him back to the rear or the skiff. "Remember, someone killed the professor because of diving the *Kuma Maru*. They're not going to have second thoughts about doing the same to us."

George's eyes widened and his brows lifted. "You are right," he said. He had convinced himself the diamonds were on the other side to the bulkhead door.

"Today is like any other. Find out about the torch. If anyone asks, the jeep's frame is cracked and you're going to weld it for the professor's daughter. Nothing more."

"Yes." George smiled. "Ramon will believe that."

"Okay." Brian slapped George on the back. "We'll meet you up at the end of the dock," he said. Brian knew Ramon would believe it. So would most everyone else, everyone who thought Yokamata's death was an accident. But there was someone on the island that knew otherwise and there was no fooling him.

Brian watched George walk the length of the pier and head toward the Quonset hut of the Truk Trading Co. A handful of men, dressed in stained pants and unbuttoned shirts, sat near the entrance talking. They all nodded at George as he passed them.

It was quiet around the harbor. With dusk less than an hour away, the usual activity of Moen was already winding down. A group of three small boys fishing off the end of the pier were huddled in excitement, two crouched over on their knees, grabbed for the third's catch as he brought it out of the water.

Brian could hear the dinner music coming across the harbor from the Blue Waters hotel. Rota would be work in the kitchen with her daughter now, Brian guessed, and Boggy would be setting the tables with expectations of large tips from the tourists who came to eat and drink at the hotel.

Then tomorrow the tourists would swarm out over the lagoon in rented boats or over the island on motor scooters to explore the remnants of history left by the forces of Imperial Japan. They would not be disappointed. Many of the armaments were still scattered through the jungle and mangroves, quiet and rusting in the sun and now conquered only by spiderwebs.

"Leslie," Brian called to her as he hopped back into the skiff, stepped over the scattered diving equipment, and went below.

"Coming," she said over her shoulder as she heard him step down the companionway. She slid the charts from the table and rolled them tight. Dropping them into the phony diving tank, she began to set the dome top in place. Brian stopped her.

"The notebook too," he said.

"I was going to read it on the way back."

"You can read it at the house."

291

She stared at him and he realized he held her wrist. He let go.

"George thinks whoever ripped through the house was after the diamonds."

Leslie brushed her hair from her eyes. "Maybe they're the ones who killed my father."

Brian leaned back against the stainless-steel table of the small galley. "We don't have any proof of that. But since they took that sketch, I'm sure they don't want us finding the *Seakrill*."

Leslie's eyes moved quickly over Brian's face. "Maybe George is right and they just want the diamonds and they don't know about the submarine."

Brian shook his head slowly. "Why kill the professor if he knew where they were? Why not wait until he brought them up?"

"He could have brought them up."

"Then why the visit to the house?"

Leslie took a deep breath. "They'll find out we were there today."

"Rota said news travels fast around the lagoon. George said it too."

"You're scaring me, Brian," Leslie said, looking up at him. A chill crawled slowly up her back, and almost instinctively she stepped next to him and wrapped her arms around his waist.

He held her, her softness against his chest. He looked into her eyes and said not what he wanted to but what he had to: "I want you so scared you'll get on the plane in the morning."

"I'm not."

"Yes, you are," he said, taking the notebook from the table and sliding it into the phony tank. "Les, this is not a time for heroines." He set the lid in place.

"Or heros," she said. "We both have too much at stake. I wouldn't ask you to back away, don't ask me."

Brian looked around the skiff's cabin trying to avoid her

eyes. She was right. Nothing could make him turn away now. For some reason, he felt too close, as if touching the *Kuma Maru* had taken him back forty years and closer to the truth about his father.

If there was the chance he could find the sub and the orders inside her, nothing was going to keep him from it.

He took her hand in his and pulled her back to him. "I don't have much choice, do I?"

Leslie smiled as she wrapped her arm around his neck. "No," she said as she stood on the tips of her toes and kissed him. "No choice at all."

"Nothing, just their equipment," Wuun said into the phone. He was standing next to the window, bending the dusty slats of the horizonal blinds with one finger and looking out at the harbor. From his office he could see the full length of the dock.

"How? How in the hell could Bovan find it so soon?" the voice screamed through the line.

Wuun released the blind and it snapped back in place.

"I don't know, Admiral. The guy must have had another copy of that sketch."

After a moment of silence, Admiral Tendrey spoke more calmly through the phone. It was as if he had conceded to his decision. "Is he with you?"

"Yes."

"Let me talk to him," Tendrey said.

Wuun looked down at the man sitting quietly in the chair in front of his desk. He handed Admiral Mills the phone.

Mills cleared his throat. "Hello, Joe," he said in a defeated voice.

"There's nothing else to be done, Tom. We're in a corner. He'll find it, sure as hell, he'll find it if he hasn't already."

"I know. But maybe it won't matter. It's been so long, Joe. They couldn't still be there. Not in the saltwater,"

293

Mills could hear the pleading in his own voice. He looked at Wuun, who had moved back to the window and was staring out.

"Do you want to take that chance?"

Mills paused. He thought hard on what he was going to say. He had held Brian in his arms when he was six months old, taught him how to throw a football and how to stain and varnish the wood on the family's small sailboat. He had helped Brian along his career in the navy, giving him guidance when he needed.

But now Brian threatened Mills's own naval career, a career that spanned almost two thirds of his life. A perfect military record decorated along the way with countless medals and commendations. A textbook career and an honored name he had worked so hard to gain. Mills took a deep breath and said, "No. No, I don't want to take that chance."

"Let me talk to Wuun," Tendrey said without hesitation.

Mills looked at the islands' police sergeant. "Here," was all he said.

"Yes, Admiral," Wuun said, turning his back to the man in his office.

"Just like we talked about, Ty. Do what you have to. I don't care if you make it look like an accident or not. I'll leave that up to you," Tendrey said in a calm but stern voice.

"Yes, sir."

"And, Ty."

"Yes, Admiral?"

"Don't let anyone stop you from carrying this out. Do you understand?"

Wuun turned slightly and looked over his shoulder at Mills. "Yes, Admiral, completely."

* * *

"Ramon said we can pick it up tomorrow morning," George said as he climbed into the rear of the Willys jeep.

"Good enough," Brian said, shifting into gear. As he began to pull out on to the street, he saw Boggy running toward them waving his hands.

The boy stepped around the jeep to the passenger side where Leslie was sitting. "My mother asked if you'll come to the hotel for dinner. She has three giant lobsters for you," Boggy said, holding his hands far apart to express their size. He had been talking without taking his eyes off Leslie.

"Tell her thank you, Boggy, but we have to get back to the house," Brian said.

"Why?" Leslie leaned toward Brian, putting her hand on his arm. "It'll be a celebration."

"That's what I don't want," Brian said.

"Rota makes the best lobster in the Carolines," George said as he sat up.

But it was Leslie's dark eyes that won Brian over. "Okay. But no a word about anything."

"Not a word," Leslie promised.

Brian looked at George.

"If I say one thing you can cut out my tongue," George said with his crooked-toothed smile. "But after the lobster."

Brian couldn't help but smile. "I'll hold you to that," he said.

"Come on, Boggy," Leslie said as she moved closer to Brian, giving room for the young boy on the seat next to her. Boggy beamed as he jumped into the jeep.

Brian drove the twenty yards down the street and parked in the same place they had the day before. Boggy ran ahead to tell his mother they were coming and Leslie laced her arm through Brian's as they entered the Blue Waters's restaurant. George trailed behind.

"On the veranda, on the veranda," Rota said as she came out of the kitchen, rubbing a dish towel between her hands. "Boggy set a table outside just for you two." She reached out, squeezed Leslie's free hand, and smiled.

295

"What about me?" George protested.

Rota turned and said in a stern voice, "Shhh. You eat in the kitchen with me."

"I'm sure all four of us can eat together," Leslie said to be polite, but her eyes conveyed she hoped it would be only Brian and her. Rota understood.

"Good," George said as he moved to one of the chairs that surrounded the perfectly set table tucked in the far corner of the veranda.

"No, Shimbo," Rota said using George's native name. "We'll eat together in the kitchen. I saved you an extra lobster tail, but only if you eat with me."

George shook his head as he backed away from the table. Stepping past Brian, he said in a low voice, "She thinks she can sway me to marry her because she is such a good cook." He shook his head again.

Brian smiled. "We'll talk about tomorrow at the house," he said. Then George and Rota disappeared back into restaurant.

"This is beautiful," Leslie said as she sat down and leaned back in the tall wicker chair. She looked out at the golden dish of the sun poised just above the horizon. The silhouette of a visiting yawl anchored in the middle of the harbor seemed etched within it.

Brian moved to the chair next to her, but before he sat down he looked over at the Willys. He could see their diving equipment stacked in a pile behind the rear seat. The phony tank was safe beneath it all. Brian had made a point of putting it there. He settled down in his chair.

He turned to Leslie and found her staring at him. Her almond eyes held him until he had to force himself to look away and out at the sunset. He let his left hand play mindlessly with his fork on the tabletop.

After a few minutes, she reached up and rested her hand on his forearm. "What are you thinking?" she asked gently.

He looked at her and shrugged. "I was thinking it was

too bad man ever found this lagoon. That we ever found any of these islands.''

Leslie said nothing for a while. From the time spent with her father she knew that look Brian had in his eyes. Sailor's eyes, she called it. She thought herself foolish at times; there was no secret bond between men and the sea. Not really. Her father had talked about the sea as if he had some kind of heritage with it that a woman could never understand.

But Leslie did understand, whether it was true or imaginary, there was something that held a man who was a sailor. She thought of it like an old coat or hat that he once wore and then would search for because a new one never felt as comfortable.

Boggy came with a bottle wrapped in a napkin. ''Rota says this is okay to give you. It was the professor's and no one ever bothered him when he drank it here,'' he said in a gentle voice. He showed the label to Brian. It was French wine, a rarity on the island. He poured for them, lit the single squatting candle in the center of the table, and left with a wide smile.

''He likes you,'' Brian said.

''He's cute.'' She smiled and lifted her glass. ''To success in finding your—''

''Past,'' Brian filled in.

She nodded and they tapped their glasses and sat back in their chairs and drank.

Brian looked back out at the lagoon. ''When George was holding the hatch open and I looked in,'' Brian said without turning, ''there was . . . It looked like . . .'' He hesitated, looked over his glass, and into her eyes. She was waiting for him to finish.

''What?''

''It's stupid.''

''What's stupid?''

Brian leaned forward and rested his elbows on the table. He looked directly at her. ''I though I saw something inside

297

the ship. Something that looked . . . looked familiar but then it didn't,"he said.

"You don't have any idea what it was?" Leslie moved her chair closer to his. Her knee brushed against his, but Brian didn't feel it. His mind was a hundred and sixty feet below the lagoon.

"I feel like I should but I don't," Brian said.

"Tomorrow you'll find out," she said soothingly and he smiled at her. She was right. He would find out what it was soon enough.

Boggy returned with a fresh broad-leafed salad with native fruits and shreds of coconut and they ate quietly, deep in their separate thoughts.

The night tried to cling to the heat of the day but slowly it relented with the easterly breeze. In the distance, the side-stays of anchored sailboats chattered against their masts like broken metronomes trying to keep time with the soft music of the hotel's bar. Inside the restaurant it was mostly tourists who ate and drank at cloth-covered tables and spoke about their adventures of the day.

Suddenly the crisp smell of the sea was overpowered by the seasoned aroma of the lobster as Boggy and Rota brought it out to their table. "This is the Blue Water specialty," Rota professed, and it was understandable why. Both plates held giant lobster tails resting on cleaned palm fronds, steamed rice with salted fish and breadfruit and yams.

It was a magnificent meal, and when they were finished it left both Leslie and Brian too full to move from their table. Boggy cleared the dishes and brought hot coffee and let them sit in the darkened part of the veranda alone. He wanted to stay and talk with Leslie, to talk about anything in order to be near the beautiful lady. But his mother had been firm in telling him to leave them alone.

Brian looked out at the water and listened to the waves rush up the coral sand beach. "It's a big lagoon," he said as he turned and looked at Leslie.

"You'll find it," she said softly.

"I don't know how." He turned back to the lagoon and shook his head. "How the hell am I going to find her out there?" Brian said.

Leslie brought the cup of coffee to the edge of her lips. "What would you have done?"

"What?"

"If you were the captain and your sub was tied to a ship that was under attack. What would you have done?"

Brian leaned back in his chair. What would he have done? He hadn't thought of that. Every time he looked out at the lagoon, he tried to picture what the attack on Truk was like, his mind creating the images of warplanes dropping out of the sky every thirty seconds. But he hadn't tried to imagine what his father had gone through. That was only a photograph, and his mind seemed to refuse the reality of it.

"My stomach is full and I am happy," George said as he stepped up to their table. Rota was beside him, her shoulder under his heady arm. "This woman is the best cook on all the islands," he said with a broad smile.

Rota giggled like a schoolgirl. "He is always so happy after he eats," she said, and Brian could see in his eyes that George had been supplied with an excess of wine.

"George, do you want some coffee?" Leslie asked. She too could see the red in his eyes.

"No, no. It will ruin the lobster," he said.

On the way back to the house, George slept over the uncomfortable pile of diving equipment in the rear of the jeep and his snoring must have been a mysterious sound to the animals ducking away from the jeep's headlights in the jungle.

To Brian's surprise, he was wide awake by the time they had reached the house and unpacked.

"It will be safer to cut the door off at the hinges," Brian said as he leaned over the desk and looked at the sketch George had made on a piece of paper.

"But it will be quicker to prop it up,' George said.

They were in the professor's study going over the steps of tomorrow's dive. Leslie sat in one of the swivel chairs, listening. "What if it fell while you were inside?" she said.

"She's right. It's worth the extra time it takes to cut it off. Then we both can go in to search the hold."

George nodded. His thoughts of diamonds had made him forget about the dangers of diving the wreck.

"We'll use a lift bag for the acetylene tank," Brian said.

"And another to lift the crate," George said.

Brian looked up at George and then moved around the desk. "Yes," he said. "We might as well take an extra and another scuba tank to fill them."

"Tomorrow, we'll be rich men." George smiled.

"I want to dive early. Real early in case we have to make a second dive tomorrow night."

George nodded, but the expression in his face showed the idea of diving at night didn't sit well with him. "I will have to wake Ramon in the morning to fill the scuba tanks and get the torch. He will not like it, but . . . ." George shrugged.

"That's it then," Brian said, trying to think of anything forgotten. He couldn't.

"I'll be on the pier," George said as he moved for the door.

"You can sleep here tonight, George, on the patio lounge," Leslie said.

Brian looked at her. Where was he supposed to sleep? he wondered.

"I told Rota I would come by," he said with a sheepish grin. He looked at Brian. "She is a good woman. A good cook and a good woman." He moved to the door.

"Let me drive you into town," Brian offered, but as he suspected, George shook his head.

"I will see you two in the morning," he said as he left.

THIRTY

Moen Island, Truk Lagoon, 1986

Leslie moved silently from the bedroom to the patio. The moon was bright again and the breeze warm. She walked up behind Brian as he leaned back in the chair, balanced on its two rear legs, his feet on the rail. She put her hands on his shoulders and squeezed the muscles in his neck hard, then those along his shoulders and the tops of his arms.

"This is supposed to be your vacation. I should be giving you the massage," he said, looking up at her.

"Okay," she said with a quick smile.

Brian laughed as he stood. "Well, I didn't have to ask you twice. Sit down."

Brian began at her shoulders, rubbing the tight firm muscles of a dancer. Her skin was soft under his fingers, and as he moved his hand forward to her collarbone, he could feel her breath was deep and slow. He wanted her, needed her. It was all he could do to keep from reaching further forward.

She let her head fall back, her eyes closed and her mouth open, and Brian leaned down and kissed her. She wrapped her arms around the back of his neck and held him there.

Then she released him. "Let's go for a swim."

"Now?"

"Why not?" she said, letting the robe fall from her. She

301

wore a black one-piece strapless bathing suit. It cut high along her slender legs and low down her back. Brian was still in his swimming trunks.

Leslie helped him pull his shirt over his head and they walked down to the water, her hand fitting naturally into his.

The lagoon was bathwater warm compared to the cool night air. They walked in up to their knees, the water swirling around them as it rushed up the shore. Brian pulled her to him and kissed her. He could feel the passion within him growing steadily.

Leslie responded to him by pressing herself tight against his chest, her arms locked about his waist. She kissed him deeply on the mouth, promising, then suddenly she pushed away, turned, and dove into the water.

"Come on," she called.

Brian dove after her as she headed out deeper into the lagoon. The water felt good, as if it were cleansing her, releasing her, healing her. She wanted Brian badly, she had since the first time she'd laid eyes on him. But too much had happened in the last two days for her to let her feelings surface. Until now. Now the water and the moment made her forget.

In two powerful strokes, Brian had caught up with her. With his outstretched hand, he grabbed her ankle and pulled her back to him.

They were in deeper water now. Brian could barely touch the coral sand bottom and Leslie could not. She wrapped herself around Brian, her legs twisting around his. They laughed like two children who had sneaked away from their camp.

She gazed into his eyes and looked at his dark hair slicked back by the water and shining in the moonlight, and she felt a hunger for him. Her laughter subsided into a contented smile.

"I see evil thoughts behind that smile."

"You can not," she giggled, embarrassed she had been so easily read.

He was thinking his own. With one arm around her waist, Brian brought his other hand to her face. He kissed her ever so gently.

She responded, kissing him with parted lips, and he felt her tongue tease his and then she pressed herself hard against his chest. Brian felt the quickening of his heart.

Feeling her pull herself higher on him, he glided his hand from the outside of her knee to the inside of her thigh. Suddenly she released him and pushed away.

She dropped under the dark night water and disappeared. Brian spun to the left, then to the right, looking for her. She popped up to his right, giggled playfully, and swam back to him.

Again she wrapped herself around him, but now there was no bathing suit separating their skin. Her breasts were soft against him, soft in the palm of his hand as they kissed.

Pulling at his trunks, she slipped them from Brian's waist and let him kick them free from his legs. She pressed her heels into the back of his legs and drew him to her. She arched and Brian's hands grasped her, his fingers in line with the ripples of her rib cage. He pulled her, her inner warmth absorbing him, slow at first then deeper and complete.

She cried gently and he gasped as their movements churned the water around them. Her head fell to his shoulder as her body began to shake and she buried her fingers into the muscles of his back, but their rhythm didn't stop. She looked back at him, her eyes more eager than before.

Her mouth found his again, found his cheeks, nose, ears. Then she felt his breath deepen suddenly and his whole body tense. His moan came from the back of his throat as she felt him shiver, release, and ripple within her.

He sighed and his head fell back into the water. Then he looked at her and they smiled and kissed.

"Let's go in," he said, his voice heavy.

She said nothing but swam beside him until they were in shallow water and stepped from the sea. They walked back to the house, his arm over her shoulder, hers around his waist.

They made love again. This time with the bed turned down and the window open to the breeze and the sound of the waves rushing in. He glided over her body with tiny kisses from the nape of her neck to her toes. The touch of his lips jolted her like sparks on her skin.

Then, rolling and catching her breath, Leslie pulled him to her. She was like a slender and powerful animal, a gazelle or a cheetah, hungry again like she had never been before, as if they had not yet made love, though they had just moments ago.

Brian yielded to her, let her take him this time, absorb him. She kissed his chest, his throat, his chin, and then covered his mouth with hers and they loved again in the tropical night until they lay stretched out beside each other in comfortable silence.

Their passion had not gone unnoticed. The open window had let the breeze in and the sounds of their surrendering out. But now the man kneeling at the edge of the mangrove heard nothing, and with the stillness he moved closer.

He wore only the Trukese wrap, a tight-fitting length of cloth tied high on his waist, down across his front and snug between his buttock. It was the traditional dress of the men of Truk, the dress of a once mighty warrior people. Now as the man moved along the side of the house toward the patio stairs, his heritage was coming back to him and the fierceness could be seen in his olive eyes.

He stepped gently on the edge of the wooden stairs and moved to the kitchen door. It was locked. He moved to the sliding glass door, slipped the narrow tip of his machete into the doorjamb, and cracked open the latch.

Leslie opened her eyes. The room was cool and dark and silent and she could just make out the paint peeling on the ceiling. It reminded her of wind waves on the lagoon. She felt Brian's left arm weave under her head and around her shoulder. His left hand rested on her breast. With her cheek against the side of his chest, she could feel his deep, gentle breathing and it made her smile.

She didn't want to move, afraid of disturbing him, but she needed to get up and couldn't wait until he woke. She lifted his arm up, and turning slowly, she slid out from under it, off the bed and ungracefully onto the floor. She walked on her toes out of the room.

"Hurry back," Brian said in a deep half-sleeping voice as he rolled over to one side.

"Go back to sleep," she whispered as she closed the door. Through the louvered windows of the bathroom, she could see the purple-blue of the night sky. It was still early morning and she was glad of that. It meant a few more hours beside Brian, and maybe, she thought with a grin, he would make love to her again.

As Leslie walked back to the bedroom, she didn't hear the man behind her with the machete. He held it tight in one hand and raised it high over his head. And as she moved from the hallway, he brought it down.

"Leslie!" Brian yelled as he stepped from the bedroom.

She saw his eyes on something behind her. Instinctively she dropped but it was not soon enough. The tip of the assailant's blade ripped into her shoulder.

Brian rushed him, hitting like a defensive tackle, and they both fell to the floor.

Brian grabbed at the machete as they wrestled in the hallway. In the darkness he could tell the man was much smaller than him, but he had amazing strength.

The man pulled away from Brian's grip and slipped from beneath him. They rolled over and the man moved on top of Brian. He lifted the giant knife above his head.

Brian moved as the blade came down hard into the wooden floor. With all his strength, Brian lifted the man up and pushed him over his head. Brian got to his feet and launched himself at the attacker.

Leslie clutched her arm, blood pouring out between her fingers, and the pain making her body shake in convulsions. Sliding up the wall, she stood and moved after them.

The two men were again struggling on the study floor, and again the man had gotten on top of Brian, their arms twisting around each other, four hands battling for the handle of the machete. The man brought Brian's hand to his mouth and bit down hard. Brian screamed as the man snapped the machete free.

With a free hand, Brian hit him in the throat sending him backward, choking. Brian scrambled to his feet and moved between the intruder and Leslie.

Regaining his senses, the man smiled and began to wheel the blade back and forth in front of his body so fast it blurred. "You die now, Commander," he said in a heavily accented voice, and then the blade stopped high over his head and he screamed a primordial cry of his ancestors' as he rushed them.

The bullet shattered the sliding glass door like thunder as it went through and hit the man in the side. It jolted him, stopping him where he stood. With one hand he felt the warmth of his blood dripping down his ribs.

He lifted the machete again, screamed again, and stepped forward. The second shot caught him in the neck and he toppled to the floor.

Brian grabbed Leslie and pushed her back into the hallway and into the bathroom. Moving her hand, he looked at the wound. It was a three-inch-long gash, deep into the muscle but Brian could see it didn't reach the bone.

"Stay here," he whispered.

She swallowed hard and nodded.

Brian moved quickly in to the study. He took the machete from where it dropped and went through the kitchen and out the patio door.

It was still dark, and the jungle around the house was only a montage of shadows and silhouettes, and as he moved

306

with his back to the side of the house, he felt naked as he had never felt before.

Finding the loose board on the side of the house, he pulled out the .45 automatic and unwrapped it and his father's notebook from the cloth.

Around him, the breeze brushed leaves against leaves and tree against tree and the waves hit the beach with an amplified roar. Brian could hear nothing but the tropical sounds that had played this symphony since the beginning of time.

But he stood and listened and watched, the gun aimed into the darkness. Who was it? Who had fired the shots and saved their lives? The night revealed nothing and finally he went back to Leslie.

She was still huddled on the floor, her arm painted red with blood. She had gotten a towel but it too was soaked red.

"Come on, we've got to get to the hospital," Brian said as he tucked the gun in his swimming shorts and helped her to her feet.

Quickly, he leaned in the workroom and dropped his father's notebook into the phony scuba tank and replaced the lid.

"Who was he?" Leslie asked, her voice weak and her eyes filled with tears.

Brian lifted her into the jeep. "Get in," was all he said. He had recognized the dead man's voice and had made out his face in the dim light of the study. But now all he wanted to do was put space between them and the house.

There were eyes in the jungle and he could feel them watching as he slid behind the wheel and start the engine. He looked over the hood as the jeep's headlights swung around, lighting up mangroves, but he saw nothing. Then he headed down the beach and toward the road.

* * *

Merith popped open the cylinder of his revolver and reloaded the two spent rounds. Then he looked over at the Chinese woman. She had settled back down into the vee of the mangrove tree to sleep again. Without opening her eyes she said, "It is like I told you."

"It was lucky we were here."

"Luck?" she smiled. "Is for old women playing cards."

Rota came from her room behind the check-in counter at the sharp sound of the buzzer. "What! What!"

The heavy woman's waist was covered loosely with a cotton night wrap, her breasts bare. Her eyes were half asleep until she saw the blood. "My God. Come, come." She took Leslie into the kitchen. "What happen?" the big woman asked as she turned on the lights.

For the first time Brian saw Leslie's face clearly and the trails of tears running down her cheeks. She had remained silent all the way into town and he hadn't realized the amount of pain she was in.

"Someone tried to kill us," Leslie said, her lower lip shaking. Fear was catching up with her and she began to cry out loud.

Brian put his arm around her as Rota opened the kitchen's first-aid kit and took out some gauze. "You have to go to the hospital."

"There was no one there," Brian said.

"No. Not on Truk, on Guam. This is deep. It has to be cleaned so it doesn't get infected. The mail plane comes early. You can go with them."

Brian agreed.

Leslie watched as Rota lit the stove and put on some water. "It is easy to get infected," she was mumbling, and shaking her head. She took a small bottle half filled with an orange powder and poured a little into the pot.

Boggy came in. "What's the matter?" He was still waking, rubbing his face.

"Nothing. Go back to bed." But his eyes widened when he saw the blood.

"What happen?"

"I said go!" Rota dipped the rolled gauze into the hot water. "This is going to sting," she said. She held the soaked roll above the cut and squeezed it. The hot orangish water ran down Leslie's arm and into the open cut. More blood rushed down her outstretched arm and onto the floor. Leslie screamed and buried her head into Brian's shoulder. Brian held her.

Boggy receded into the doorway to watch. He didn't want to see the blood or to see Leslie cry, but he couldn't pull himself further away.

It was then Brian heard the front door. He looked up and saw Boggy turn to see who it was. The boy made no move as the man's silhouette stepped up behind him.

Slowly Brian drew his .45 automatic from the back of his waistband. Rota saw him pull the gun and hide it behind Leslie's back. Her eyes locked on it for a second, then she looked up at Magun as he stepped into the kitchen.

"I heard someone scream . . ." He saw the blood and moved toward them. "Jesus, God, what happen?"

Brian tucked the gun back into his trunks. "Someone broke into the house and tried to kill us," he said flatly, watching for Magun's response.

Magun looked up from Leslie. His olive eyes showed shock and disbelief. "Who?"

"He's at the house."

"Still?"

"He's dead." Brian said.

"Hold this," Rota said to Leslie as she continued to dress her wound. The large woman didn't look up as she worked. She would have no part of men's doings. But Leslie was not a Trukese woman.

"Brian, who was he?" she asked. Things were happening too fast.

Brian looked down at Leslie then back at Magun. "It was your partner, Zeen."

"You killed him?"

Brian shook his head. "Someone else shot him through the window."

"Take care of Miss Yokamata, Rota. We'll be back." Magun looked seriously at Brian. "Show me."

The police truck pulled out onto the sand and headed slowly toward the professor's house. Both men rode in silence. Brian stared into the predawn darkness, and as they approached the house his eyes searched the mangroves.

As they reached the porch stairs, the sky was turning a deep violet. The sun would be above the sea soon and another day in paradise would begin.

Inside it was still pitch-black. Magun turned on the light in the kitchen. He looked over his shoulder at Brian, who motioned him forward.

The body lay on its side in the center of the study where it had fallen, but now a large puddle of dark blood encircled it. Magun bent down and rolled him over.

Brian heard the Trukese police officer take a deep breath as he moved away from the body. Magun sat down in one of the chairs. He was shaken.

"You want something to drink?"

Magun shook his head.

"Any guesses on why he tried to kill us?"

"No," Magun rubbed his face. He had known Zeen since they were children. What would he say to his family? "I have to call the sergeant before he leaves the island," he said as he began push himself from the chair.

"Not yet."

"What?"

"Give me a couple of hours," Brian said. "Until I can get Leslie on the plane to Guam."

"I have to report this," Magun stood up.

Brian grabbed him by the upper arm. "This wasn't a burglary." Brian picked up the machete off the table where

310

he had left it. "He was after us, Fumio. He called me Commander. No one here knows I was in the navy."

"What are you talking about?"

"I resigned from the navy only a week ago. Tell me how the hell he knew it if he wasn't working for someone."

"Who?" Magun said, looking down at the body.

"The same people who killed the professor?"

"That was an accident."

"No, I don't think so. But either way, I have to get Leslie out of Truk."

Magun looked back at the body. "The sergeant will be going to Tol for most of the day. I'll give you until he gets back."

The two men wrapped Zeen's body in a bedsheet and carried it out to the police truck. Brian watched as Magun laid it gently in the back.

The edge of the sun had just broken away from the sea's surface as they pulled from the house and headed back to town. Magun would put the body in the hospital, he said. There was a small operating room that was air-conditioned.

Brian thought about Leslie. About the gash in her arm and the pain in her eyes, about the love they had made hours before. She would be okay in Guam. He knew people at the navy base. They would take care of her until he got there tomorrow or the next day.

Magun saw it first lying right above the water's edge but he thought nothing of it. The white brimmed hat was half buried in the sand. Then Brian saw it and his stomach turned.

"Stop!"

Magun applied the brakes. "What's the matter?"

Brian climbed from the truck and picked up the hat. Slowly he looked up and down the undisturbed beach.

"It's George's. He was wearing it last night when he left," Brian said. He turned and began walking up the beach. Magun followed slowly behind him in the truck.

Brian hadn't gone far when he found turned-up sand

311

where men had struggled, and the dried tarlike patch of blood in the center. His eyes caught the two parallel furrows that ran up into the jungle. He followed them.

Magun stopped the truck and ran after Brian, who had already disappeared into the foliage. He pushed through the thick heavy leaves of the small palm trees and found Brian kneeling beside George's body.

"Jesus," was all Magun could say.

Brian turned George's head from one side to the other. The slashes into his neck severing the carotid artery were deep and precise, but they had come after a hard battle. The dozens of cuts from the machete across George's arms and chest spoke for themselves.

THIRTY-ONE

South Pacific Sea, Truk Lagoon, 1944

Douglas pulled his face away from the periscope and looked at Michael with a nod. "This is it." He turned toward the helmsman. "Take us to course 186. Fifteen hundred a side."

"Aye. Course 186. Fifteen hundred a side," Billy responded.

"Time?" Douglas asked, his face back against the periscope.

"2200 hours," Michael said. "We're cutting this close."

"But we're here. I'm not turning back now, not with a chance of getting inside," Douglas said.

Tension was always high in a submarine on patrol, but to look at Douglas's face one could not tell what had been eating at him for the last week. His eyes were calm and sturdy; only Michael knew Douglas was at his boiling point. Going into Truk only hours before the U.S. Navy's planned raid was a risk neither of them wanted to take, but they both knew the stakes.

Douglas scanned the dark silhouettes of the twin peaks of Haru Shima Island. In the distance, he could see Natsu Shima quiet and still. Douglas knew Natsu held the command post and the submarine base.

As the *Seakrill* glided effortlessly south through the dark waters outside the reef, he watched for the flashing beacon of the lighthouse on the west point of Haru Shima. The island seemed so peaceful, so gentle in the darkness of the tropical night. It was hard to believe that these islands held more than 7500 enemy soldiers.

After several minutes he saw it. The dim light came into view, a solitary eye opening and closing in a slow rhythmic manner. "There's the lighthouse," Douglas said. "Mark."

"274," Michael said, recording the bearing.

In the back of his mind Douglas hadn't expected to find it. He would never understand why the Japanese would keep lit such a perfect signal for their enemy. But then again, there was nothing for them to fear here. This was their territory.

Douglas remembered the ambassador's instructions and allowed the *Seakrill* to continue south. He looked now for two small lights hanging off the side of the Japanese freighter, the *Kuma Maru,* which they were to rendezvous with. One light would be toward the bow, the other toward the stern.

"The plan was to position the submarine so that the lighthouse would line up behind the freighter and in between the two small lights. That would guide the *Seakrill* to the unknown opening within the reef.

Douglas had little trust for either the Chinese ambassador, Tendrey, or the captain of the *Kuma Maru.* "Anything on the sonar?"

"I'm still getting a solid wall to our starboard, Skipper," Tony, the sonarman, said.

"Keep picking at it," Douglas said, not looking away from the periscope.

Finally they came into view. Two twinkling lights just above the horizon. At first Douglas couldn't make out the outline of the *Kuma Maru* as she sat in the foreground of the dark shadow of Haru Shima. Then he saw her. She was a cargo vessel at least four hundred feet long and anchored parallel to the reef. Her size and length would easily hide the *Seakrill* from the lookout posts and shore guns. Ambassador Lee and his Japanese colleagues had planned well, Douglas thought.

"Got her," Douglas said almost in a whisper. "Slow to one-quarter speed."

"Aye, one-quarter speed."

The submarine traveled another minute until the lighthouse was directly behind the freighter. "Mark!" he gave Michael the order, and his first mate read the compass heading.

"Bearing 284."

Douglas leaned away from the periscope. "Care to look?" he said, and Michael moved into the eyepiece. He had read the plan in Douglas's cabin.

He looked up at his skipper, his mouth holding a wry smile. He didn't like the idea of trusting the Japs. But going into Truk, the Gilbralter of the Pacific, was different. No other American submarine had ever attempted it, though there had been plenty of times it was talked about over drinks.

Douglas smiled as he turned to the helmsman. "All stop."

"All stop."

"Left full rudder, astern one thousand a side," Douglas said, and he felt the *Seakrill* respond. "Tony, what do you got?"

Tony listened to the electronic ping in his headphones. He adjusted his sonar sweep and listened again. "Reef ahead of us, Skipper, as solid as Fort Knox."

"Maybe they expect us to fly over it," Michael said.

Douglas missed the humor at the moment. He looked back into the periscope. Maybe the freighter wasn't exactly in the right spot. They'd have to search the reef for the opening and that would take time, time they didn't have.

"Skipper!" Tony's voice perked up. "I got twin screws bearing down on us. Heading 358, speed twelve knots."

Douglas spun the periscope around. Instantly he found the owner of the twin screws filling his view. A destroyer with the sea foaming at its bow. "Take her down fast, Billy! Right full rudder. Dive! Dive! Rig for silent running."

The blasts of the horn echoed through the *Seakrill* as she pitched left, coming about and pulling away from the reef ledge. Her nose dropped drastically as she dove deeper into the tropical waters of the Pacific.

As was the natural geography of a lagoon, the outside ledge fell almost vertically to 3000 feet. It gave the submarine plenty of room to maneuver once they pulled away from the reef. They dove concerned only with what was above.

"Her sonar isn't on, Skipper," Tony whispered.

Douglas nodded.

"She must be heading for the southeast pass," Michael said. "We could follow her in when they move the nets." Shadowing a surface vessel into an enemy port was a tricky maneuver and it had already crossed Douglas's mind.

"And if she's leaving for patrol we'll be out of luck, and time."

For a few minutes there was only silence, then the high-pitched whine of the ship's engines could be heard echoing through the *Seakrill*. Douglas felt himself holding his breath. Michael leaned uncomfortably against the chart table.

Suddenly there was another sound, a steel-against-steel ringing that vibrated through the hull. At first Douglas thought the destroyer's sonar had come on, but as he looked at Tony, he saw confusion in the young man's face. "That's from inside the sub," he choked.

Douglas dropped from the conning tower into the control room without touching a single rung of the ladder. When his feet hit the floor, he didn't have to guess where the sound was coming from. Every crewman's head was turned toward the hatchway that led toward the engine room. Douglas bolted through the submarine, Michael right on his heels.

The ringing stopped as he moved through the forward

316

engine room and into aft. Against the stern bulkhead Clancy had his hand clamped around Hathorn's neck. In his other was a small hammer.

Hathorn's eyes were wide with terror, his face white. He pulled at Clancy's hand as he grasped for air, but the old mechanic's hold was firm.

"What the hell?" Douglas tried to keep his voice down. The destroyer was still above them.

Clancy whispered. "This son of a bitch was beating on the side of the piping."

"Let him go."

Hathorn fell to the floor as Clancy pulled his hand away. "I . . ." He took several deep breaths. "I . . . I didn't hear the order, Captain." He took a few more breaths and began to calm, but he didn't try to stand. "I was working behind the intake."

Douglas looked at Clancy.

"He was," the mechanic admitted. "But I don't know how he could have missed hearing your orders."

Douglas starred at Hathorn for a moment, then he leaned down and with powerful arms lifted him to his feet. He pushed him toward Michael. "Stick him in his bunk and put someone there to watch him until I say otherwise," Douglas said, his eyes not leaving Hathorn's. Then he turned and headed back through the hatchway.

A hundred and fifty feet above them, the two diesels vibrated in the hull of the destroyer as it thundered by. Throughout the sub, the crew listened silently, every man's eyes looking upward trying to see beyond the pipes and wires and the sub's bulkheads, through the water and into the mind of the Japanese captain who was commanding the destroyer. Each wondered if he knew they were there.

Finally the sounds of the enemy began to subside.

"Continuing on her original course, sir," Tony reported as Douglas climbed back into the conning tower.

"Secure from silent running. Head us back toward the

reef and bring her to periscope depth. Let's find that hole this time," he said.

As the *Seakrill* climbed from the depths, she turned and pointed her bow back toward Truk Lagoon. Douglas was beginning to understand how it got the title of Gibralter of the Pacific. He looked at his watch. It was 0100. Sunrise in five hours.

The periscope slid up and Douglas slapped down the grips. He walked it once around making sure the horizon was clear, then he looked back toward the lighthouse on Haru Shima. They were three miles off the reef now and the beacon was too dim to see.

"Heading 312, full speed," Billy reported.

Without taking his eyes from the scope, Douglas knew Michael was beside him again. "Who's with Hathorn?"

"Richardson. He's off duty for the next seven hours."

"Good," Douglas said. He stood up and gave the periscope to his second-in-command. "See if you can find that lighthouse."

For several minutes Michael had no luck, then, "Got it! Mark!"

"284. Bring her on course," Douglas ordered and Billy turned the wheel and the *Seakrill* responded. "That's back in line with the freighter. Can you see it?"

"No . . . wait. There she is. The lighthouse is directly behind her."

Douglas turned to Tony but the sonarman was intent on his dials. "I think I have a hole, Skipper. It's at seventy-five feet. Three degrees starboard."

"Take her down to seven five feet. Right rudder three degrees." Michael stepped away from the scope. "Periscope down."

Tony spun two dials and then slowly turned the third as he tired to home in the area of change in the reef. "Another hundred yards."

"Slow to one-quarter speed."

In the quiet sea, the three-hundred-foot submarine glided

318

toward the ageless reef of Truk Lagoon. A tiger shark cruising the coral heads for prey felt the presence of the huge intruder along the lateral nerve of his body. He turned and darted back down into the darkness and safety of the sea.

"I'm not getting a return reading, Skipper."

"So is it an opening?"

Tony looked up. "Maybe, or the reef isn't reflecting a clear sonar signal. It's big enough to enter but I can't tell how far it goes in."

Douglas looked at Michael.

"It's a big reef, Doug. It could bottle neck or just make a bend and we'd be stuck. This whole thing could be a trap."

That, Douglas was more than aware of, and he didn't want to hear it. He knew the danger, knew the chances they were taking for a crate of Chinese bones. But they were overwhelming proof he would show at Tendrey's court-martial. And he knew the promise he had made to Mimi.

"Skipper!" Tony's voice had that high ring of terror again. "She's coming back, sir, the destroyer. Her sonar is on."

"What's her range?"

"Five thousand yards. Speed nine knots."

Douglas looked back at Michael. "Well?"

His first mate shrugged. "You're the captain."

Douglas smiled. "All right, Billy, nice and easy. Ahead one thousand a side. Tony, give me your readings. If the cavern ends, I want to know before we run into it."

"Aye, Skipper."

The *Seakrill* moved ahead with her twin props spinning by silent electric motors. Slowly she entered the gashlike opening in the reef. It was only twice the width of the sub's beam, and its walls rose steeply upward arching like a vault painted more brilliant by sealife than Michelanglo had done in the Sistine Chapel.

"We've got ten feet on each side," Tony reported.

"What about the destroyer?" Michael asked.

Tony adjusted a dial. "I can't pick her up from in here, sir."

"Then he can't locate us," Michael said, and Douglas nodded.

"The roof is sloping down, Skipper."

"How much?"

"Twenty feet."

"Take her down to nine five feet. Hold her steady."

The air in the conning tower was becoming unbearably thick and each man felt it as his shirt began to stick to his back. They were six hundred feet into the reef when Tony spoke again.

"There's a wall ahead, sir, and the floor is beginning to rise," the sonarman said.

"A dead end?" Michael looked at Tony but he didn't look away from his dials.

"All stop," Douglas ordered.

"Aye, all stop," the helmsman said.

"Well, is it a dead end?"

Tony continued to adjust his dials and knobs as if he hadn't heard Douglas at all. "Can we go on another fifty feet, Skipper? I could get a better reading. I think it might just be a bend to port."

Michael shook his head. "You got three hundred feet of ship here, mister. And there's no hinge in the middle."

"Ahead, dead slow," Douglas ordered. He turned to Michael. "We're already here. If it's a dead end, what's another fifty feet."

"It's a bend, sir." Tony's voice was high again.

"All stop." Douglas looked at him. "How much room do we have."

"Yards."

Douglas rubbed his chin and wiped the drying sweat from his forehead. He looked at his watch. Almost 0200. Time was racing away from them.

"If we get around this, you can't be sure it doesn't bend

again," Michael said, his eyes darting over Douglas's face. "We could really get stuck."

"Ahead dead slow. Left full rudder," Douglas said flatly, not taking his eyes away from Michael.

"We're not going to be able to back out," Michael said.

"Then pray it goes through."

The *Seakrill* remained almost motionless. The tide was outgoing and it held her there, then finally she began to move forward.

"Another two degrees to port," Tony said as if he had taken the helm.

Douglas didn't argue, he simply relayed the message to the helmsman.

"It opens through, but I don't think—" Tony didn't have time to finish his sentence when the bow rammed the giant outcropping of coral with a crashing jolt that echoed through the hull and sent everyone lurching forward. Some to the floor.

"All stop," Douglas yelled, and the *Seakrill* drifted back away from the coral.

Michael grabbed the microphone from over his head. "Forward torpedo room, damage report?"

"All tight here, Lieutenant, but our ears are ringing," the crewman reported.

"Well," Michael said.

"It goes through, Skipper. I'm almost positive," Tony said.

"Almost?"

"I'm getting an earful of traffic. It's the Japs on the other side."

"Okay." Douglas nodded. He turned to the helmsman. "Again, Billy, put her nose into the reef and give it hard left rudder."

"Aye," Billy said, easing the controls to set the twenty-four hundred tons of steel into motion. The crew barely felt it.

Tony counted off the feet until impact. "Fifteen, ten, seven, four, now."

Again the *Seakrill*'s knife-shaped bow hit hard into the reef and the shudder ran through the ship.

"Reverse port, quarter speed, starboard up to twelve hundred."

The helmsman didn't repeat Douglas's order, he just carried them out.

Douglas imagined the nose of the submarine pushing against the living rock as the bow began to rise and they moved forward by only a few feet. The sounds of the calcareous coral shattering came through the hull like fingernails on a chalkboard.

"Bring it up to fifteen hundred on the starboard side."

The *Seakrill* began to tilt toward the left as her bow rose higher and the stern dropped.

"There goes the paint," Billy said under his breath as he held tight onto the wheel. It vibrated through his wrists and into his shoulders. Now everyone was holding on to something to keep from falling and sliding to the rear of the sub. An unattended coffee cup bounced off the table and crashed to the floor.

A voice came over the speaker. It was Clancy. "We're heating the motors real fast with no water flow, Skipper."

"It's going to get worse. Holler when the bearings start to go," Douglas said, holding onto the periscope shears with one hand.

"She's your ship," he said, he voice unmistakably harsh. It was Douglas's command, but they were his motors.

"Billy, shift to series and give her two thousand on starboard," Douglas ordered. The batteries of the U.S. sub were normally connected in parallel, but by switching to series, Douglas knew they would get twice the voltage by halving the current.

"Series, aye, two thousand starboard!"

"Skipper." Tony's voice was high again and it put a knot in Douglas's stomach. "The bow is breaking the surface."

"We're going over the top," Michael said. He was holding onto the chart table with both hands.

Thunder railed through the sub as the bow suddenly dropped back into the sea and the *Seakrill* crashed into the side of the reef. Tony heard the four-ton outcropping of coral that had held them break away, slide along the hull, and sink to the bottom.

The sub lurched forward as she leveled. "All stop."

"Aye, all stop," Billy said as he wiped his palms on his pants.

Michael grabbed the microphone and asked for damage reports. There were none.

"What's our depth?"

"Sixty feet," Billy answered.

"It's clear above us, Skipper," Tony reported. "The cavern bends to the right but there's plenty of room before she opens into the lagoon."

Douglas turned to Michael. "Let's get inside and get this over with." He looked at Billy. "Ahead two thousand a side."

"Five degrees to the starboard," Tony guided.

"Right rudder five degrees."

Michael moved close to Douglas and said in a low voice, "How do you plan on getting out of here when we're finished?"

"Not that way, that's for damn sure," Douglas said, thankful they had gotten in through the reef, and, at the same time, unthankful. "Keep your ears open, Tony. I don't want any surprises."

"Aye, Skipper," Tony said as the *Seakrill* inched her nose out of the coral-reef opening and into the clear waters of the lagoon.

THIRTY-TWO

Moen Island, Truk Lagoon, 1986

Brian held the door to the hospital as Leslie stepped out. Her arm was bandaged now with clean white gauze and held in a sling made of a colorful blue handkerchief. The gash had taken twenty-two stitches put in by the Jesuit priest from the high school on the other side of the island. He had been a doctor, he said, before he found the healing powers of Jesus.

They walked the half a dozen stairs to the curbside without a word between them. The dawn was blue and orange and already becoming hot. Brian still heard Rota's screams echoing in his brain. The big woman had shuddered uncontrollably as he drove her and Leslie and Boggy to the hospital.

Magun had put George's body in a separate room from Zeen's, and there Rota had screamed so horribly Brian felt it rip at his insides. When she knelt at the end of the small bed where George was covered by a white sheet and clutched Boggy as he cried, Brian had to turn and leave the room.

Leslie was in the doorway, tears rolling down her face, her arm forgotten for the moment. Then Magun came back with the priest and they took Leslie to a small ten-by-ten-foot room the priest affectionately called the operating room. He poured a solution of warm water and dusty yellow powder through the cut much as Rota had, and when it was numb he sewed the skin together, saying there would be a scar, but only small one if the doctors on Guam got to it soon enough.

Brian stepped around the jeep and helped Leslie in. "You okay?" he asked.

"Yes." Her voice was soft, childlike, and she didn't look at him.

Brian climbed in behind the wheel. "We've only got twenty minutes to get you to the airport," he said, trying to find first gear. After a grinding attempt, he succeeded and they pulled away from the curb.

"I'm not going," she said.

They had argued about it as the priest stitched the gash in her arm. He had agreed with Brian. "It's going to be a nasty scar if the doctors don't look at it," the priest said. "And you have to be careful with infection, my child. This is the tropics."

But now she wasn't arguing. Her voice was low and firm and Brian knew she had made up her mind.

"Les, please. You saw what happened to George. I want you off this goddamn island."

"But Zeen is dead."

"But who shot him?"

Leslie didn't say anything for a moment as the jeep continued down the hill toward the airport. "You might as well head back to the house. I'm not getting on that plane."

Suddenly Brian slammed on the brakes and stopped the jeep in the center of the road. "Les, I have to know you're safe."

She looked into his eyes, "Where else could I be as safe as when I'm with you?"

"Guam."

"I'm not going."

Brian took a deep breath. He looked over the hood of the jeep. "I care too much for you to let anything else happen. We were lucky last night."

325

"And I'm not leaving you." She put her hand on his shoulder. "Besides, who's going to help you anchor the boat?"

Brian popped the clutch and the jeep lurched forward. He turned left at the Y in the road and headed back toward the professor's house.

"Two men dead."

"Shit!" The voice on the other line was hard and cold.

Mills rubbed his face with the wet cloth. The water coming out of the cold side of the faucet was warm. The Blue Waters hotel had never put insultation around their pipes. He had heard everything from the heavy young girl who brought his coffee and breakfast danish into this room. She was taking Boggy's place, and her mother was in the kitchen for Rota.

Mills called Hawaii as soon as the door shut behind her.

"Where's Bovan?"

"Jesus, Joe, how the hell should I know? I've been cramped up in this goddamn room for two days. I can't even go downstairs to have a decent meal without being afraid he'll see me!" The heat and the isolation was getting to Thomas Mills and he wished he had a bottle of Jack Daniel's.

There was a pause on the other end.

"They got a doctor from the other side of the island. Someone was hurt bad but I don't know who it was."

"If it was Bovan he'll still try to find the sub," Tendrey said. "Have you heard from Ty yet?"

"No. He left for some other island and won't be back until the afternoon."

"I can't believe that. If his man is dead, he should be there."

"Maybe he ran scared," Mills said, and the sarcasm was clear in his voice.

Another pause. "Go to the house and wait for Bovan.

326

Whether he finds something or not, he'll have to go back there."

"And what do you want me to do if he comes back empty-handed?"

"Kill him," Tendrey said without so much as a breath. "Because he'll keep diving Truk until he does, and neither of us can afford that."

This time it was Mills who dropped the receivers into its cradle and let the phone line die.

The numbness in Leslie's arm was wearing off as she held onto the skiff's wheel with her other hand. There was wind chop across the lagoon and the small vessel rose off one wave and collided with the next. It amplified the throbbing in her arm.

Brian sat in the stern, checking the scuba gear and the acetylene tank and the smaller oxygen tank for the underwater torch. He had found the two cylinders leaning outside the door of the trading company, with a piece of paper with George's name.

As Leslie cut around the shallow outcroppings of coral off Hermit Island, Brian stepped up beside her. "I'll take it," he said, putting his hand on the wheel.

She looked down at the crystal-blue water racing by beneath them and the white foam of water coming from under the hull. Her arm was throbbing now into her shoulder and at her temples. She closed her eyes and hoped the wind would draw the pain out. She felt Brian's hand touch the center of her back.

"You all right?"

She forced a smile. "Yes."

Brian headed passed Hermit Island and turned north toward Bush. As the navy had trained him, had bored into him as he moved toward his goal of submarine commander, his mind was racing ahead setting a strategy, planning his moves. He would search the perimeter of the wreck for signs of the submarine. If the *Seakrill* had taken a hit from the Hellcats, she wouldn't be far off. Leslie's question was right on the mark. What would he have done if he had been in command forty years ago? He would have taken her to the bottom.

But first, he knew, he had to get into the hold of the *Kuma Maru*. Something gnawed at the back of his brain, an image he had seen for a fraction of a second as George held open the hatch and he waved his flashlight into the darkness.

"Aren't we almost there?" Leslie put the flat of her hand over her eyes and looked toward Bush.

Brian slowed the boat as they passed the small island. He kept heading north for several hundred more yards. Then he looked back toward Hermit and then turned and tried to see Small Island another mile north of them.

"Here, take the wheel and head out a little more," he said as he moved to the bow and pulled the anchor free from the twist of rope.

"How do you know where it's at?"

"When we came out before, I lined up the three islands with three parts on the skiff. We line them up again and we should be right over the wreck," he said. Leslie watched as he took his bearings again. "Okay," he yelled, and threw the anchor twenty feet off the bow and let the line pay out like a retreating snake.

"Now back her up slowly." After a moment he tied off the line. "Kill the engine," he said, and as the engine stopped, the lagoon suddenly seemed unnaturally quiet.

"All you can hear are the waves," Leslie said in a soft voice as she looked at the surf coming over the outer reef. "Like it should be in paradise." She turned to him. "But it hasn't been paradise, has it?"

Brian moved to her, careful of her arm, and kissed her. "When we get back, I'll take you to this restaurant in Washington I know. It's wonderfully crowded and noisy."

She smiled.

He grabbed the torch, wrapped its hoses and nozzle

328

around the valves, and tied it a few feet above the iron weight of the decompression line. Then he lowered the weight and the tanks into the water. After they sank ten feet, he tied a single scuba tank to the line and set that over the side. As the line slid through his palms, Leslie stood behind him making sure it wouldn't tangle.

When there was forty feet left, Brian tied a fresh tank to the line and dropped it into the water.

"You didn't put on this many tanks last time," Leslie said as Brian tied on yet another tank at the twenty-foot mark.

"I'm going to stay down longer."

"How much longer?" Her voice was suddenly high and her eyes wide.

"An hour. It will give me plenty of time to get into the hold and time to search around."

"But what about decompressing?"

"That'll take another two hours," he said calmly.

Three hours! Leslie felt a chill crawl over her like a spider. "No. You can't stay in the water for that long."

He slid his weight-belt strap through its buckle and looked up. "I'll be okay, Les. And if I find anything, I'll come right up. I promise."

"Please, Brian."

"I have to, Leslie, I may not have another chance at this wreck."

Tears began to swell in her eyes.

He moved to the cabin and reached in. "Here," he said, taking out the .45 automatic pistol. He set it on the towel that was lying on the companionway. "Don't let anyone come aboard. No matter who it is. Do you understand?"

She nodded.

Brian lifted the set of twin scuba tanks onto his back, struggling with the shoulder straps. Leslie stood there, her eyes darting over his face. She realized he was having trouble and moved to help him.

"I don't like this," she said, standing close to him in the gently rocking boat.

He touched her chin and tilted her face up to his. He kissed her. "You think I'm going to let anything happen to me knowing you're up here waiting?"

She looked up into his dark eyes and a smile came to the edge of her lips. He was right, she would wait for him. Whether it was in this damn little boat or on a cold street corner in New York, it didn't matter. She had fallen in love with him and the thought of losing him frightened her.

He kissed her again. "Remember, Les. No one comes aboard," Brian said, and he moved to the edge of the skiff. He grabbed the large rubber-coated liftbag from the deck and pushed it into the nylon mesh bag on his belt. He took a large step over the side and jumped into the water.

After hitting the water, he surfaced and looked up at her through his mask. She was leaning over the edge of the skiff, her long dark hair loose and hanging in the wind. It was the image he remembered as he lifted one hand, waved, and then descended.

God, please don't let anything happen, she thought as she watched the eruption of bubbles as they reached the surface and then disperse, creating a calm circular print on the water.

The water seemed colder than before, and somehow darker, though Brian could see the fingers of the sun reaching past him and into the deep.

He sank effortlessly along the decompression line and beyond the sets of tanks. As he drifted down, he double-checked his Dacor Flashlight and the extra one tied to his belt. Both lights were strong.

In the darkness of a hundred and ten feet, Brian could only gauge his descent by the line racing through his hand. He stared at the void below him until finally the edges of the four-hundred-foot shadow started to come into view.

The iron weight hung directly over a small toppled lifeboat on the starboard side of the quarterdeck. Still in its davits, the boat seemed to be patiently awaiting launch.

Pulling the liftbag from the small mesh bag on his weight belt, Brian attached it to the two tanks of the torch. Then he unclipped the single scuba tank that hung on the line and brought it close. Opening its valve, he filled the liftbag to the size of a small watermelon. It was enough to give the torch buoyancy.

He followed the white nylon rope still tied to the entrance into the *Kuma Maru*. There was no looking from side to side into the cabins and the yesterdays of the ship this time. He was in a hurry, and the sealife and the artifacts disturbed as he pulled the cumbersome tanks and hoses behind him down the corridors went unnoticed.

Entering the engine room, he dropped to the forward bulkhead where the maintenance hatch awaited him. He released the air from the liftbag by tilting its open bottom upward. The bubble escaped, slipping away like mercury in the Dacor's light.

Unraveling the torch hoses, Brian opened its valves and the gas mixture bubbled from the nozzle. Using the professor's magnesium striker, he ignited the torch. Instantly the flame brightened the corner of the sleeping ship as it had never been before. Brian looked away, blinded momentarily.

He moved to the hatch and positioned himself over the first hinge. Drawing the torch over the thick heavy steel, the encrusted algae immediately burned away, revealing the black oxidized metal.

Patience was unavoidable now. Brian could not hurry the torch nor could he stop the surrounding water from stealing the heat and multiplying the time it took to cut the metal. The thunder of popping and crackling torch echoed in the room. Then slowly, the steel of the hinge began to drop away like wax under the flame.

After cutting through the first, Brian began on the second hinge. He glanced at his watch. Twelve minutes it had taken him. He hope the next would be quicker. It was, two inches of it was already cracked open, possibly from George's and his efforts the day before.

He moved back as the torch made the final cut through the hinge. But as he extinguished the flame and let the nozzle settle on the floor of the engine room, the hatch remained in place.

The light of the Dacor showed both frame leaves of the hinges cut clean, but still the hatch held, too stubborn to reveal the secrets it guarded.

Brian lifted the crowbar from where George had dropped it and pressed the claw behind the top hinge. It took more effort than expected, but the hatch gave and fell to the floor with a dull thump.

Brian felt his breathing become rapid as he approached the dark oval hatchway. The Dacor illuminated the first few feet of the hold's lifeless bulkhead. Brian kicked gently and drifted in, his scuba tanks scraping the edge of the hatchway.

It was as if the *Kuma Maru* had gone down yesterday. Her steel ribs and skin were dark red with rust, but there was not the accumulation of silt or debris.

Brian swam further into the tilted hull, his light sweeping back and forth in front of him until he came upon the twisted metal in the side of the freighter. It was the unhealed scar of her fatal wound.

The *Avenger's* torpedo had ripped into the thick hull, shredding it and curling it inward like the petals of a huge grotesque flower.

But as Brian moved closer and directed his light from the edges of the hole to the center, his eyes widened, his breathing stopped, and his body began to shake uncontrollably at what he saw.

THIRTY-THREE

Truk Lagoon, 1944

The *Seakrill* lay motionless in the predawn darkness with only five feet of her conning tower out of the water. Douglas cracked the hatch and stepped slowly out on to the bridge. From below, Michael handed him a small flashlight.

The jagged figure of Haru Shima was ink black against a night sky of bright stars. A warm gentle breeze brushed Douglas's face as he brought the binoculars to his eyes. Around them the water was still and quiet and empty. There were no patrol boats waiting.

The *Kuma Maru* lay at anchor no more than fifty yards off the starboard bow. She too was quiet and still. Douglas covered the flashlight with his hand and turned it on. He cracked open his fingers and released a sliver of light. In the enemy stronghold, the smallest amount seemed like a sunrise to him. They had to have seen it, he thought, but still the freighter remained dark except for the two small lights that hung over her hull and had guided them here.

After a minute, Doulgas released another sliver for a second longer this time. Then, one at a time, the two lights on the ship went dead and from the bridge a light flashed twice and then three more times.

Douglas took his hand from the flashlight and clicked quickly on and off. He handed it to Michael, who stood in the hatchway, his head just above the rim. "Ahead a thousand a side," Douglas whispered to Michael, who relayed it to Billy. "And get Hathorn up here."

"Aye, Skipper," Michael said.

The *Seakrill* crept slowly forward in the dead-calm water of the lagoon. "Left full rudder," Douglas ordered, and he could feel the sub come about. Her nose glided just below the surface near the stern of the Japanese freighter as she came alongside. He looked up at the looming ship now beside them.

At first the freighter seemed deserted, then Douglas made out the silhouettes of heads and shoulders of several men looking over the railing.

"All stop. Blow tanks." The *Seakrill* foamed at the edges as she rose from the water, revealing her true length. Hathorn climbed up the ladder and stepped onto the bridge next to Douglas.

From the sub's forward and aft hatches, two crewmen came up onto the deck. Reilly was on the bow. "Holy Jesus," he said as his eyes caught the distinct white flag with its red rising sun in the center dangling high above him from the ship's superstructure. He caught the line tossed down to him, tied it to the number-one cleat, and then, as ordered, returned below.

Douglas waited until both men had cleared the deck, then he and Hathorn climbed down the rear of the tower. As they did, Michael slid out on his hands and knees into the bridge. He stayed low and out of sight behind the waist-high steel wall. In his right hand, he clutched the Thompson machine gun.

From the deck of the Japanese freighter above, a rope ladder was dropper, unreeling against the hull. Douglas looked back at the empty decks of the *Seakrill*. He knew Michael was there and that Reilly was just below the forward hatch with five men behind him, each with a machine gun in hand. The aft hatch held the same and the bridge had crewmen ready to man the 20mm guns.

But still, as he put one hand on the swaying ladder, he

felt a football-sized pit in his stomach. "Don't say a thing unless I say so, understand?" Douglas said in a stern voice.

"Yes, sir," Hathorn said. The machinist's mate was only a dark shadow against the darker shadow of the freighter.

They climbed the ladder side by side, and as they reached the rail four pairs of hands grabbed them by the shoulders and they were lifted to the deck.

Instantly, they were pulled away from the edge and out of sight of the *Seakrill*. A big man as tall as Douglas but carrying another fifty pounds pressed him back against the bulkhead with one hand on his throat and another filled with a pistol aimed at his temple. Douglas grabbed the man's hand as he gasped for breath and felt a forearm as big as his leg. He tried to pry off the grip but he couldn't. The round-faced Japanese crewman stared straight down the length of his arm with narrow eyes.

The big man barked an order, and in the darkness Douglas felt several hands move quickly along his legs, waist and his chest. They found the .45 automatic tucked in his trousers. It disappeared.

The man released his throat and Douglas dropped to the deck grasping for air. The gun barrel was now pushed into the back of his neck. He saw Hathorn getting the same reception. After a few deep breaths, Douglas looked up to see two other men standing in front of him. It was another big man, not in height but in width. And a smaller man who stood to the side and behind the other.

The big man with the gun lifted Douglas to his feet. He turned, grabbed Hathorn, and pushed him next to Douglas.

The wide man took a step forward and smiled with crooked teeth. *"Ohayo gozaimasu,"* he said in a deep raspy voice.

Now as he stood up, Douglas realized the man couldn't have been over five foot five, but as he looked into his deep set olive eyes, he knew instantly he was the captain of the freighter.

"Captain Shimito greets you, Commander," the smaller man standing to the side said.

"You speak English?" Hathorn was clearly surprised.

"Shut up," Douglas said, not taking his eyes off the smaller man.

The man nodded mechanically. "I grew up in Los Angeles, California."

The captain snapped at the smaller man, "Yokamata-san. Tell him I want to finish this business quickly. The less time these Americans dogs are on my ship the better."

Yokamata looked at Douglas and said, "You understand my captain is eager to take care of our business."

"Sooner the better," Douglas agreed. It was then, as his eyes had become adjusted to the darkness, that he saw the line of Japanese crewmen armed with rifles crouched behind the bulkheads ready to fire on the *Seakrill*.

"No different preparation than I'm sure you have on your submarine, Commander," Yokamata said.

"No," Douglas conceded. "Not much different."

The captain spoke again in sharp harsh tones, and Douglas sensed he was irritated by not understanding the conversation.

Yokamata nodded repeatedly and then looked back at Douglas. "This way, Commander. Patience is not my captain's best virtue," he said, and as they turned to follow the captain, Douglas saw the small man's hands were tied behind his back.

They stepped into the first cabin, closed the door, and turned on the light. It was the map room, and on the floor in the center were two U.S. Marine footlockers. As the captain bent down and opened one of the lids, Douglas looked at the small man.

He was staring at the back of his captain with more hate than Douglas had ever seen in a man's eyes. Yet he hadn't heard it in his voice. He wondered why Yokamata had been tied.

The captain spoke and Douglas and Hathorn moved beside him. Tucked tight in and around the wrapped packages were over a dozen sticks of dynamite, each wired to one another and then up to the lid. Douglas looked at the array of wires and connections and hoped Hathorn could diffuse them. The thought of taking these two bombs aboard the *Seakrill* suddenly made him sick.

As if reading his thoughts, Hathorn looked back at him and nodded reassuringly. Then he pulled one of the packages from inside the first box and handed it to Douglas. The paper was covered with Chinese writing as had been expected. Ripping through the paper, Douglas tried to remember what Mimi had told him. The bones had to be smooth and heavier than non-fossilized bone. Minerals over time, she had said, fill in the pores making them more dense and stronger.

Hathorn ran his fingers slowly over the frontal lobe of one of the skulls, through the eyesocket and over the upper jaw. He inspected it carefully, holding it only inches away from his eyes.

Using his fingernail, he scraped a clod of dirt from behind the first and second molars and into his palm. "Final test." He smiled at Douglas, and then spit into his hand and mixed the saliva with the dirt. He showed Douglas the red paste. "Hematite, an iron ore," Hathorn said. "Dragon's Tooth Hill was saturated with it." He smiled broadly. "Commander Bovan, meet the Peking Man." Hathorn held up the skull.

"You are satisfied, Commander?" Yokamata asked.

Douglas nodded. "Who's going to inspect your package?"

"My captain."

Douglas looked at the man next to him and at his huge round belly. "He's going to have a hell of a time getting down that ladder."

Yokamata shook his head. "You will bring the diamonds aboard for him to inspect."

"You expect me to turn the diamonds over and then trust you to give me the fossils?" Douglas stood. "Tell your captain he can fuck himself."

Yokamata's thin lips turned into a smile. He spoke to the

captain, and even without understanding the language, Douglas could tell Yokamata had repeated word for word what he had said.

The round-bellied man's eyes widened then narrowed. He blurred out an order in sharp grunts and the big man with the gun grabbed Douglas again, pushing the barrel up under his neck. Douglas stared into his unblinking eyes.

The captain moved close, bringing his face an inch away from Douglas's. For the first time, Douglas smelled the unmistakable sour odor of alcohol. "Tell this dog that he will bring the diamonds aboard or he will die right here," he said to Yokamata, and the first officer translated.

"Remind him that the sun is going to be up soon and then we're both going to have a lot of trouble breathing down our necks," Douglas said. "And tell him that my first officer has orders to sink this freighter first if I don't return."

Yokamata translated as the captain stared at Douglas. Then a slow smile came to his face and his white teeth glittered in his dark face. He laughed out loud. "Okay," he said to Yokamata. "Then you will go with this dog to his submarine and his crewman will remain here. Tanaka-san, release him and free Yokamata-san."

The big man released Douglas and moved to Yokamata. Pulling a small square-tipped knife from his belt, he grabbed Yokamata by the shoulders, turned him, and cut the twine that bound his hands.

"You must have pushed his patience pretty far," Douglas said as Yokamata rubbed his wrists, trying to bring blood back to his hands.

Yokamata looked up. "Your man will stay here," he said.

"Skipper?" Hathorn's voice raised in panic.

"Let him return to the sub, I'll stay."

"Don't worry, Commander. A soon as the diamonds are aboard, your crewman will be released. The last thing Shimito wants is to explain how an American submariner came onto his ship."

"But, Skipper!" Hathorn grabbed at Douglas.

"It'll be all right," he promised.

They stepped out of the cabin and moved down the hallway. "So you left the States to joint he Imperial Navy and you end up hogtied. Wise decision."

"I refused to help him trade contraband with the enemy." Yokamata cocked his head toward his captain. "This is treason, what you're doing."

"I have orders," Douglas defended.

"Unquestionable orders, I'm sure," he said as he stopped at the rail of freighter.

"You're helping him now?"

"He threatened to have my sisters in Osaka killed if I didn't," Yokamata said flatly. "I am not foolish enough to think he wouldn't do it," he said. "Or that he won't kill me after this is finished. We all have our fates to meet, Commander. Today I will meet mine. Perhaps you will meet yours."

Douglas studied the man's face as he swung his leg over the rail, found a loop in the rope ladder, and began down. Yokamata pulled himself over the rail and followed.

The deck of the *Seakrill* was as steady as if she were an extension of the freighter. They walked quickly toward the forward hatch. Douglas tapped on it twice, and when it opened Yokamata saw the figure of a man and a machine gun. Then he saw the other behind him and then still another.

"No different preparation," Douglas said to him. "Reilly, pass up the crate." There was a scurry of whispers and then the seaman moved his body and the narrow box slid out through the hatch and onto the deck. Douglas pushed it in front of Yokamata and opened the lid.

Even in the darkness of the moonless night, the diamonds seemed to sparkle with their own radiance. Yokamata had never seen such beauty.

"Give me your pistol," Douglas whispered to Reilly as he watched Yokamata out of the corner of his eye. The Japanese was intent on the diamonds and didn't see Douglas slip the automatic into his coat pocket.

339

Yokamata pulled a white handkerchief from his breast pocket and laid it out on the deck. He scooped a handful of diamonds from the crate and deposited them on the cloth. Then he pulled in the corners and tied them in a knot. "For inspection, Commander," he said, and Douglas nodded.

Moving close to the side of the freighter, Yokamata tossed the bundle up to the rail. A hand reached out and snagged it from the air.

"Skipper." It was Michael's voice coming from the bridge above them. "Look at the time. We can't stop the sunrise and our boys are going to be right under her."

Douglas pulled back the sleeve of his jacket and looked at his watch. 0545. The freighter and the *Seakrill* were both now being lit by a royal-blue sky, and the first slivers of sunlight were reflecting off the cargo booms. "Secure the bridge and the aft hatch and prepare to dive on my orders," Douglas whispered.

"Aye, Skipper," Michael said, his voice solemn. He knew they had only minutes.

Yokamata looked at him.

"The sun is going to be up in a few minutes and I don't care to see it today," Douglas said.

In the *Kuma Maru*'s map room, Captain Shimito eyed each diamond through his small magnifying glass. It was old and scratched and didn't make his inspection easier. He had never really seen a diamond, though he had read about how to estimate quality.

But he had also heard about the advances of making replica diamonds and the precision of phony gems. He wondered if the Americans had been able to create worthless pieces of glass he couldn't detect. No, he decided, even if they had, this submarine commander would not risk so much on only imitations.

"These are real," he announced to the big man leaning over his shoulder. "Bring the crates," he said as he moved around the table, out of the cabin and to the rail. He looked

340

down at Yokamata standing on the submarine deck and waved.

Douglas saw him. He shut the crate lid quickly and unclipped the small hatch and opened the clock face. He turned the hands counterclockwise and set it.

Yokamata leaned over his shoulder. "How much time have you given us, Commander?" he asked calmly.

"Thirty minutes. Just enough time for us to get out of the lagoon and not enough time to have second thoughts about telling us how to disarm the fossil crates."

"That's fair," he said as Douglas resealed the small hatch with the clips.

Douglas heard the diesel engine within the freighter throttle up as the crane turned and reached out over the deck of the submarine. The two footlockers, wrapped in a cargo net, hung in the warming tropical air high above them. The top edge of the sun was just above the distant line of the sea. The day was beginning.

Douglas turned and looked quickly up and down the reef. Another sound registered in his brain. A droning that he expected to be a patrol boat bearing down on them.

But there was nothing on the water. Only the persisting sound that seemed to grow with the rising sun. Yokamata heard it too and followed Douglas's gaze.

The black spots flying in formation appeared high above the horizon. "Oh, Jesus," Douglas said under his breath.

Shimito and his crew were also staring into the sky as the U.S. Hellcat fighters began to splinter away from their tightly held packs and drop down toward the lagoon.

Suddenly, a dozen Japanese Zekes and Tojos roared over the freighter and lifted into the morning sky to intercept the American forces.

With amazing speed, a handful of Hellcat fighters wooped past the Zekes, came down across the water, and began their attack. Two navy fighters roared only a dozen feet above the freighter's crane, on their way toward Take Jima's airstrip. Clearing the skys for the bombers was their primary task.

Douglas and Yokamata instinctively dropped to their knees and the warplanes passed over head. Then suddenly, the wooden deck next to Douglas's face exploded as the Japanese crewmen fired down at him. Douglas rolled over, drew the .45, and fired two quick rounds.

Yokamata scrambled to his feet and dove at Douglas, grabbing for the gun. With his other hand he smashed the submarine commander twice in the stomach before Douglas could stop him. They rolled across the deck, each struggling to control the hand with the gun.

Reilly popped open the forward hatch and, like a man in a pillbox, released a barrage from his tommy gun into the rail of the freighter. A Japanese crewman defiantly stood and fired down at him. Six of Reilly's rounds opened up his chest and the man crumbled backward.

Douglas rolled onto his knees and twisted his free hand from Yokamata's grip. He planted his elbow in the small man's face, then slammed the butt of the gun into the side of his head. It stunned Yokamata.

More rounds ripped into the deck around them as Reilly was taking a fresh machine gun from below. Douglas grabbed Yokamata by the collar and pulled him behind the conning tower. He slammed the Japanese officer into the steel and pushed the automatic into his right eye.

"You knew," Yokamata said, gasping.

Douglas's chest heaved up and down. All he could do was nod.

"Now your own planes will sink you."

"Not if I can help it," he said. He looked quickly around the side of the tower. A bullet ricocheted off the hull.

Above them, seventy-two blue Hellcat fighters and more than forty Japanese planes met in the clear sky above Truk Lagoon. For the first twenty minutes, a plane would fall in a fireball every thirty seconds in one of the war's most vicious air battles.

Reilly turned his machine gun on the freighter each time he saw movement. Another man stepped to the rail and Reilly wheeled around, firing before his mind recognized Hathorn. It was too late. The machinist's mate's riddled body fell between the hulls of the freighter and submarine.

Reilly screamed but he never heard his own voice. A Japanese bullet ripped through the side of his head.

"Reilly!" Douglas called.

"Skipper!" It was Michael on the bridge.

"Take her down! Now!" Douglas ordered.

There was no hesitation in Michael's response. "Aye, Skipper."

Douglas looked at the small man on the other side of the gun. Yokamata was still breathing heavily. Douglas knew it wasn't fear, he could see it in the eye not covered by the barrel. This man had accepted his death.

Douglas slowly pulled the gun away. "Meet your new fate, buddy," Douglas said as he grabbed him by his uniform collar. Yokamata's eyes widened as he felt Douglas yank him off his feet. Then the American commander threw the small man off the deck of the *Seakrill* and into the lagoon.

Under him, Douglas felt the *Seakrill* shudder as her valves opened and the sea rushed into her ballast tanks. He looked quickly around the side of the tower and saw Reilly's body half out the forward hatchway, its lid pressed down around him. The hatch moved like a choking clam as the men below tried to pull in or throw out the body.

Scrambling on his hands and knees, Douglas moved to the hatch. "Push," he screamed as he grabbed Reilly's arms and pulled. The body seemed to rise on its own as his men lifted it from below.

Reilly's legs cleared the opening and the lid slammed closed as the bow tilted downward and the sea rushed up her deck.

Douglas saw the locking wheel spin and secure. Then it was underwater and he felt the sea, white with foam, swirl

343

around him. He released Reilly's body as the *Seakrill* sank from beneath him.

Douglas pushed off the deck and leaped for the rope ladder dangling from the freighter. He grabbed it with one hand and pulled himself up out of the water. There were no bullets ripping into his body as he had expected. The crew had forgotten him as they turned their guns into the air.

He climbed halfway up the hull when the stern line holding the aft cleat of the sub snapped.

Finally, as if the last thirty seconds had taken a lifetime, the twin periscopes of the *Seakrill* disappeared beneath the surface of the lagoon. He smiled as he hung from the ladder. His submarine had made it.

But the smile faded as he saw the vee of gray birds coming in low across the northeast passage.

The pilot of the lead TBF Avenger torpedo-bomber saw his four-hundred-foot target sitting perfect before him. The freighter would be this veteran's fifteenth victim in the last six months and the first of the day. It was an easy mark.

Dropping low, the pilot set his hand on the release lever of the twenty-one-inch torpedo that lay tucked under his fuselage. At fifty feet above the water and doing two hundred miles an hour, he dropped it at a hundred yards off the freighter.

He never felt or heard the impotent rifle fire coming from the deck of the enemy ship, but as he pulled back on the Avenger's control stick and rose safely into the sky, he looked out the side of his canopy.

The white line of the torpedo streaking through the water was distinct and straight. A heartbeat later, with a flash of gold flame and black smoke, it hit its mark. The blast opened the *Kuma Maru* and sent her to the bottom in less than two minutes.

THIRTY-FOUR

Truk Lagoon, 1986

Brian didn't feel himself sinking until his knees bumped against the bulkhead. Even then he was unable to take his eyes away from where the pool of his flashlight illuminated the long familiar pipelike structures that pierced through the torpedo hole and reached high into the freighter's hold.

Pushing away from the rusting steel under him, he forced himself to move closer, to be sure nitrogen narcosis had not set in making him hallucinate. He swam around to the opposite side of the opening.

Then he felt the blood drain from face and a cold uncontrollable shiver ran through his body as if the temperature of the tropical water had suddenly dropped to freezing.

Now he knew why the *Seakrill* had never been found in the lagoon. His light traced the two periscopes down to the top of the conning tower and part of the cigarette deck that filled the gaping hole in the side of the *Kuma Maru*.

They had done exactly what he expected. The sub had gone straight to the bottom during the air attack. But twisted fate or simple bad luck and an airman's torpedo had brought the freighter directly on top of them.

Brian moved forward along the starboard side where the saltwater had not fully stripped the *Seakrill* of her numbers. The 3 and the 1 were still visible.

345

Brian kicked once and glided over the top of the cigarette deck. In the center of its torn and twisted handrail, the 20mm gun still stood secure on the platform, awaiting the crewmen to unbolt its barrel and swing it into action.

The light moved further up the tower and Brian followed, hand over hand, toward the bridge. Reaching out, he touched the top of the discolored and etched steel and pulled himself over.

The small deck area of the bridge was clear except for a small broken piece of the lookout platform. Brian managed to dislodge it and move it to the side.

He pointed the light toward the conning-tower hatch at the rear of the bridge. Again Brian felt his heart pounding in his throat as he saw the hatch was still closed, its locking wheel jammed by a small two-foot piece of tubing that had fallen across it.

The *Seakrill,* like so many other submarines, had held her crew like a mother unwilling to lose them. She had become their tomb. And then the sub herself had been encased below the steel blanket of the Japanese freighter. Her hull must have been crushed under the weight, Brian thought.

The Dacor lit the darkness above him and around the main hold of the *Kuma Maru.* If they had gotten the hatch open, the first man out would have carried a knife, cutting any obstacles from around the hatch to give the rest of the men a clear path to the surface.

But there was no such path here. He would have escaped the sub only to find himself trapped within another tomb. Perhaps it was better, Brian thought, that they had not gotten out of their ship.

Brian turned and looked into the darkness where the forward section of the sub disappeared below the torpedo hole and under the freighter. For a brief second he imagined the waves of the Pacific crashing over her bow and deck as his father ordered her to dive.

He shook the thoughts from his brain. She would never again break the surface and open her hatches to the sun and air. The lagoon would absorb her, heal over her as it was doing with the dozens of other war wounds resting on the bottom. Steel hulls slowly turning into homes for Truk's sealife. The cargo and ammunition ships that once carried the supplies of the mighty Imperial Navy would be conquered again by corals and algae until they could not be distinguished from the lagoon's true reefs.

The sea would hold her secrets forever. Brian had come as far as he could. He pushed off from the bridge and glided through the still water toward the freighter's maintenance hatch.

Midway, he stopped and, with the stroke of one hand, turned and looked back at the conning tower of the *Seakrill*.

She was one of the most successful submarines out of Honolulu, with over twenty kills to her credit. The *Seakrill's* crew should have been decorated but instead they rested in oblivion, their sub, like their war records, hidden from view. Both labeled traitor.

"Those orders may still be aboard," Mimi's words came forward from the back of his mind. Maybe, he thought, just maybe they still were.

With two strong kicks, Brian swam back to the bridge. They'll forgive me, he decided as he reached down and moved the piece of tubing from the hatch. Bracing his legs against the steel of the bridge, he grabbed hold of the wheel and began to turn it. It resisted at first, but then it gave and spun freely as if the crew were still pushing frantically from below.

The mechanism connected to the locking wheel withdrew the dog latches that had held the seal for forty-two years, and as Brian began to pull at the hatch, it blew open in his face.

The mushroom of bubbles exploded into him, ripping the regulator from his mouth and pulling the mask from his head. Instinctively, he grabbed for the mask first before it could sink out of reach.

The bubbles lifted him off the bridge and suddenly he

found himself slammed into the freighter's hull above. He pushed himself out of the onslaught of the bubbles as they continued to rise out of the sub, echoing like the intestinal belching of an obese man.

Brian reached back over his head and found the regulator hose on the tank's manifold and traced it to the mouthpiece. He took several long slow breaths as he let himself sink below the edge of the bridge.

He settled on the submarine's deck between the conning tower and where it disappeared through the torpedo hole. Brian pulled the mask back over his face, tilted his head, and cleared the water from it. In the blackness, he flipped the switch of the Dacor back and forth. Nothing; the bulb had been shattered.

He unclipped his backup light from his belt and turned it on. Its beam cut into the now cloudy water. Like smoke out of a chimney, thick debris rose with the bubbles out of the hatchway, hit the bulkhead of the hold, and then sank back down.

Brian watched in amazement as a dozen lifejackets popped out of the hatch in rapid succession and raced upward. They clustered like bats in the shimmering pool of air that was still swelling, locked in the uppermost corner of the sealed hold.

Then something cut across his light beam, arched to the left, sank a few more feet, banked right, then left again, and dropped in front of him. Brian reached out and grabbed for the tube-shaped object.

Holding the light under his right arm, Brian unrolled the paper. It was one of the sub's charts of Midway Island. He could still see penciled-in course headings crisscrossing it. This had come from the control room. The hatch between it and the conning tower must be open, he figured.

Brian ripped at one edge of the chart. It took only a small effort, but the paper tore cleanly, not dissolving in his fingers as he would have expected after forty years in saltwater.

He looked back up at the tower. Only a few bubbles were still finding their way out of the conning tower now and into the corner of the hold.

He looked at the chart. This hadn't been in water for forty years, nor had the lifejackets or anything else that had been torn from the interior of the sub. They had been encased in an airtight vault until the moment he opened it.

He let the paper slip from his hand. If this was preserved, so would all the other papers aboard, he thought. But he wondered how much of the sub had been sealed off. Looking at the length of deck between the front of the conning tower and mangled hull of the freighter, Brian tried to guess where the officers' quarters would be.

It was then, as he moved his light across the rotting planks, that he saw the crate wedged against a port cleat and stanchion.

He grabbed its rope handle and dragged it to the center of the deck. The water had eaten away most of the olive-colored paint and all of the emblem from the lid. But the footlocker was unmistakable.

He ran his hand along the front edge of the lid and found the rusting padlock. It would be easy to pry open with his knife, but not now. It had waited over forty years to be found again; a few hours wouldn't matter.

He looked back at the tower. The bubbles had stopped and the water was clearing. He looked at his watch. Twenty-five minutes on the bottom. Thirty-five left to the hour he had planned, but that didn't matter now. Nothing did except getting inside the *Seakrill*.

Brian pushed himself off the deck and toward the bridge. They'll forgive me, he thought again as he swam over the rail and aimed his light into the black hole of the hatchway.

Swimming down into the opening, Brian forgot the diameter of the hatch was only that of a man's shoulders. His scuba tanks banged into the rim. Unbuckling the waist and shoulder straps, he pulled the tanks off. Holding the manifold by one hand, he pushed the twin tanks through the hatch as he swam into the opening and forty years back in time.

The conning tower was cramped and so dark it seemed to absorb his light as the beam found every corner filled with some type of equipment. He put his hand on the smooth cold steel of the periscope. How many times had this been raised from its well to break the surface and take a bearing? he wondered.

As a lieutenant, Brian had trained on a Gato-class submarine such as the *Seakrill*, but that had been the *Carp* and she was a postwar sub, commissioned in 1945. Her armaments were different, her conning tower slightly changed.

A brown piece of cloth hung suspended near the second periscope, hooked on its training handles. Brian recognized the khaki-colored shirt of a submariner. He turned his light to the diamond-plate floor of the tower and moved it along until he found the hatchway that led deeper into the *Seakrill*.

As he expected, the hatch was still open, chained back against the bulkhead. He took a deep breath and swallowed hard when he saw the round object wedged behind the lid.

It was a skull, blackish in color and covered by a crop of thin white hair. He would find no sun-bleached bones here. Though decay would take its toll on the bodies, decomposition would be incomplete. The thought sickened him but he was already inside. They'll forgive me. The image of the crewmen watching made him take a quick look around. He felt foolish but he looked a second time. Then, he swam down through the second hatch pushing his tanks ahead of him.

The control room was much larger than the tower, larger than Brian had remembered from the *Carp*. The room was filled with unrolled charts, some floating, some settled on the floor. He pushed them aside as they clung to him, wrapping around his legs like jellyfish.

A white porcelain cup sat balanced at the edge of the charting table. Brian pushed it to the center. He moved to the diving station and turned the trim wheel. It spun freely.

Severed lines, he guessed. But severed where. How far forward had the *Seakrill* kept her dignity?

A pile of dark bones lay like a child's game of pickup sticks under the trim-pump controls. Some were held together by stiff cartilage. When the sea poured in from the conning tower, it had swept them up, disrupting their resting place and depositing them in the eddy under the control area.

Brian looked away and moved forward, finding the oval hatch that led to the officers' quarters. It was unlatched and opened easily, as if its hinges had been greased the day before. Brian swam through, and as he entered the hallway, he felt his head break the surface of the water.

A pocket of air had been trapped during the onrush of water and held by the bulkhead. Brian stood up awkwardly, his fins bending under his feet and keeping him from gaining his balance. The light cut through a foglike mist that rested on the water and filled the air.

Continuing to breathe from his tank, he pulled the mask from his face. Instantly his eyes began to burn and tear. The air, now condensed into the upper half of the hull, was filled with the sulfuric acid given off by the sub's shattered batteries.

The acid explained the color of the skeletons' hair. He dropped down into the water, replaced the mask over his face, and cleared it. He surfaced again and, weaving his left arm through one of the tank's shoulder straps, lifted them to his back. Then he moved further into the submarine.

Coming to a doorway, he flashed his light inside knowing it was the first officer's cabin. A jolt shot through his body, and for an instance, his mind said *turn and run.* But he simply looked away for a brief second until he could slow his breath.

Then he looked back at the body with the drawn blackish skin and the bleached white hair resting on the upper bunk and undisturbed by the water that had not reached it. The acidic air locked inside the submarine had literally melted the skin of the officer's bones like plastic left too long in the sun.

Clothed in the once-white full dress uniform, Brian recognized the insignias of the *Seakrill*'s first officer. The details he studied about his father's crew flooded unwilling back into his mind. Michael Albert was twenty-three years old, single and the only son of a newspaperman from Detroit.

How long had the air lasted, Brian wondered. Hours? Days? A week until the air turned thick and heavy with the taste of battery acid. Which of them had screamed for mercy, and who, like Albert, had come to his quarters, quietly changed into his best uniform, and patiently waited the end?

Brian pulled himself to the next doorway, to the captain's cabin. The door was closed. He tried the knob and found it unlocked.

Two deep breaths and he pushed it open. The dark water swirled around the door's edge, sucking out the floating debris. His father's thick jacket drifted out, the material, like Albert's skin, discolored. Brian moved the light quickly around the room above the water level and then dropped his head below and searched for what he didn't want to find.

The room was empty and his heart started again. He moved to the cabinet against the bulkhead and rifled through it, finding bits and pieces of a man he'd never known, a hair brush, a navy-issued straight razor, three packs of Lucky Strike cigarettes pushed into the corner.

Brian put his head below the surface and moved to the set of small drawers near the desk. There were shirts and pants but nothing more.

He unlatched the fold-down desk. The small area behind it was filled with only books, pencils, and fountain pens. The leather book covers were stained but otherwise unbothered.

He shined the underwater light along the floor, under the desk and the bed and into the unreachable corners. A shoe was wedged under the chair; otherwise there was nothing.

Where else would he have put it? Time was fast becoming an enemy. Brian looked at the pressure gauge of the regulator and then his watch. Fifteen hundred pounds of air and twenty-five minutes left. Just enough to make it out of the wreck and begin up.

He turned to search elsewhere. Maybe in Albert's cabin, he hoped. While moving about his father's quarters, the swirling water had closed the cabin door.

And there his light caught the briefcase hanging by its handle on a hook. Brian smiled under his regulator as he reached up and took it off the door.

The embossed lettering on the cover flap was faded but he could make out the name:

Lt.Cmdr. DOUGLAS BOVAN
U.S.S. SEAKRILL
SS-321

The colored tanning came off sticky in his hand but the leather was still strong and complete. Nervously, he fumbled for the brass turn lock, released it, and opened the cover flap. He pulled the oilcloth-wrapped papers from it and unpeeled the first layer. There were two, and under the second he read the first sentence on the pristine white paper of the orders.

The U.S.S. Seakrill and her crew are to proceed directly to Truk Lagoon in the south quadrant of sector 17.

Brian resealed the oilcloth and silently prayed that it would hold against the sea for a few more hours. He closed the cover flap of the briefcase and moved out of the captain's quarters. Aiming his light into his father's cabin, he stopped and looked one last time, then closed the door.

Moving back toward the hatchway, he stared into the face of the first officer. There was nothing to say, nothing to promise. Brian would get the orders to the right people and maybe, only maybe, someone in Washington would care enough to clear the names of the men of the *Seakrill*.

There was no expression in the bone face, but somehow, Brian felt Albert had been waiting for him and now, finally, his watch was over.

Brian dropped below the water level and swam back into the control room and up through the conning tower and into the main hold of the freighter.

Swimming back to the machinist's hatch, Brian tucked the briefcase under the edge of the acetylene tank. He cut an unused length of rope from the line he and George had set and untied the liftbag from the torch. Then he swam back into the hold and to the footlocker.

Tying the line around it like a ribbon of a Christmas present, Brian secured the liftbag to the loop in the center knot. He spared just enough air from his regulator to fill the bag and lift the footlocker off the submarine's deck.

He grabbed the briefcase with his free hand as he pulled the now-buoyant crate with the other. Struggling through the slanted corridors of the ship, twice he considered leaving the crate, but finally he managed through the superstructure and to the decompression line.

Clipping the briefcase handle to the brass hook that had held his extra flashlight, he switched from his twin tanks to the fresh single tank still dangling from the line.

Brian checked the rope around the footlocker. He opened the mouth of the bag and shoved his regulator into it. He pressed the purge valve and a blast of air rushed inside, expanding the bag to its fullest. Filled, it pulled away from him and raced toward the surface, dragging its precious cargo behind.

Brian tilted his head up and watched it disappear into the brighter waters above him. He knew it would surface close to the skiff and Leslie would see it.

Taking hold of the decompression line and looking at his depth gauge, he began his slow ascent to the first stop at forty feet. As he kicked upward, he looked back at the huge dark shadow of the *Kuma Maru* and thought of the secret she had hid so well.

The sea had been kept at bay by the submarine's thick pressure hull, and only now could she touch the crew and take them back to her womb. "Sailors, rest your oar," he said through his regulator and into the sea.

THIRTY-FIVE

Truk Lagoon, 1986

Leslie had sat on the gunwale with her legs to her chest, her chin on the cleavage of her knees, for the last forty-five minutes. First she had tried pacing the skiff's small deck, but now she only stared at the spot where Brian had disappeared under the surface.

Time was incredibly slow here, she though as she glanced at her Rolex. The breeze caught her hair and blew it into her face. She moved it unconsciously with a sweep of her hand, her eyes not leaving the imaginary hole Brian had climbed into.

The wind had picked up considerably in the last half hour. It came from the east, pushing large white-crested waves, like the snow-covered ridges of the Rockies, before it. They pounded the eastern reef wall of Truk undauntedly, sending only a remnent of themselves into the lagoon.

Leslie stretched out her legs; the blood had left them and they tingled with a million needles pricking her skin. A hundred yards away, Bush Island's palm trees swayed in unchoreographed rhythm.

Leslie stood and retrieved her green cotton blouse from inside the cabin. Even under the clear sky and hot sun, the wind racing off the water was cool. As she stepped back out of deck, she heard the liftbag break the surface with a *whoosh*.

The air that had filled only half the yellow bag at a hundred and sixty feet now hissed from the release valve in the side panel.

The bag settled, bobbing in the chop a few yards from the skiff and looking like the head of a miscolored octopus. Leslie watched it for a few seconds half expecting, half hoping Brian would surface next to it. But he didn't, and the liftbag and its load were drifting steadily away.

She pulled her blouse back off, stepped over the stern and onto the swimboard, and dove into the water. The current was more swift than she expected and she found herself swimming as fast as he could to catch up with the bag. As she reached for one of the lines dropping down to its cargo, she saw the footlocker dangling precariously in the clear water. Grabbing the bag by the center knot, she began to sidestroke back to the skiff.

The waves and the current both seemed set on keeping her from the boat. The harder she swam, the further it seemed. Twice she thought about letting the liftbag go, but she couldn't. She didn't know how long it would stay afloat.

She continued to kick and pull with her one free arm until, at last, she reached up and grabbed hold of the swimboard. Then, suddenly, another hand reached down and grabbed her wrist. She screamed.

"For a while, I didn't think you were going to make it, Miss Yokamata," Wuun said as he lifted her out of the water and onto the swimboard in one smooth motion. "Let's see what you've salvaged from my lagoon."

Wuun was dressed as before, his wrinkled shirt out of his pants. But now he wore a thick black leather belt that supported a holster and revolver. He released her, bent over, and reached below the liftbag, grabbing ahold of the crate.

He slid it onto the swimboard and then lifted it to the stern rail and let it balance there. "The commander has found a prize," he said, running his hands slowly along the badly eaten wood. The film of green and orange algae that covered part of the crate was smooth under his fingers. "Yes, a very, very big prize."

"What do you want?" Leslie asked. She saw his police boat tied to the bow of the professor's. She looked at where Brian had put the .45 automatic. It was gone and suddenly she was terrified.

He looked up at her with a half smile. "Ever since I was a boy," he said as he ran his hand over the crate again almost as if caressing it, "I knew the diamonds were here. But no one believed me." He laughed. Then he drew a small double-bladed knife from his belt and dug it under the lip of the crate lid.

"Don't." Leslie grabbed as his wrist but Wuun pulled away, slapping her across the face with the back of his hand.

Leslie stumbled and fell to the deck. She reached up and felt the swelling of her cheek and the shattered front tooth. Her almond eyes moved slowly up to Wuun's. Then, with the speed of a cat, she jumped to her feet and went at him.

Wuun leaned back as she swung wildly at him. He laughed and it fired her attack. But he fended her off.

Leslie dug her fingernails into his outstretched arm, causing him to pull back; when he did, she lunged at him and racked at his face, her nails tearing several layers of skin and drawing three parallel lines of blood.

She stepped back, shocked at what she had just done. Wuun too was shocked. He reached up and lightly touched his cheek. The scratches stung in the salt air. He looked at her and his eyes seemed to draw deeper into his head. "You like to scratch?" He lifted the knife in front of him and pointed it at her. "Okay, Jap, we'll play your game."

He grabbed her at the elbow and pulled her to him and pressed the knife to her throat. "I will give you something to remember," he said. He turned and jabbed the knife into the lid of the crate. Then he smiled, and with one hand ripped her bathing suit from her slender body.

Leslie screamed and swung again at him, but now he had her, and on the small skiff there was no place to run. He

358

forced her to the hot fiberglass deck and it burned the skin on her back and buttock.

Wuun sat on her, his full weight crushing her stomach. He pinned her arms under his knees as he pulled his shirt over his head and then began to unbuckle his pants.

Merith dropped the binoculars from his eyes. "Jesus Christ, we've got to get out there. He's raping her." He jumped to his feet and turned to Mimi.

She lowered her set of binoculars slowly. "He won't kill her. Not yet," she said flatly.

"You don't know that," Merith said, his voice high. He looked back at the skiff across the choppy water. "Come on." He turned and headed toward their boat beached on the other side of Bush Island.

Mimi made no effort to rise from the fallen tree trunk that she rested against. She simply closed her eyes and laid her head back.

Merith stepped in front of her. "What the hell's the matter with you?"

Mimi opened her eyes and looked up at him with no expression.

"He's going to kill her if we don't get out here," he said. "They brought up one of the crates, what more do you want?"

"There's one more thing missing," she said.

"The crate is enough to clear Bovan's name."

She was silent.

Merith turned again to the skiff but could see nothing; he could only imagine. "I'm going out there, give me the keys to the boat," he said.

"No," she said, emotionless.

He spun on his heels and looked hard at her. "I said I'd go along with your scheme to see what Brian finds. But I didn't agree to standing by and letting that girl get raped. Now give me the keys." He thrust his hand out at her.

Mimi looked up at him, her narrow eyes unblinking. There was a scream and a cry from across the water, and Merith turned toward the skiff. He saw Wuun's head come up above the rail and disappear again.

Then from behind him, Merith heard the slight but distinct mechanical click of the hammer on a revolver being pulled back. He turned and met the polished nickel-plated barrel of the .357 magnum.

Mimi held it in her frail right hand. It'll shatter her elbow when it goes off, Merith thought, but only after the first round cuts through me.

"I've waited a long time to see this through, Troy. A very long time. I can't expect you to understand." She motioned toward the skiff. "I don't like sitting here any more than you. But we have our orders, more or less. We wait until Brian comes up."

Merith's jaw shot forward. "You uncaring bitch," he hissed. He turned and sat down in the sand. Mimi lowered the hammer and set the gun beside her.

During his first stop Brian recalculated his decompression time. He was on the wreck for thirty-five minutes and should have calculated it as forty minutes, but he figure it as only thirty and in doing so cut forty minutes off his time.

Now at twenty feet, Brian unclipped the fresh tank and tied his empty one to the line. Eleven more minutes here and then twenty-five at ten feet.

Boredom would have normally sunk in after dangling from the line but his mind was too busy racing over what was in the leather briefcase drifting above him, secured to a small piece of rope tied to his wrist.

Leslie and he would have to take the boat straight to the cove in front of the house. There would be too many eyes at the harbor.

In the morning, they would book themselves on the flight to Hawaii, then onto Washington.. He knew that what was in the briefcase would clear his father if the right people saw it. He would take it to Admiral Mills's office and demand a full investigation.

The crate would have to wait, though. They'd leave it here in Magun's care and he would somehow contact Mimi in Honolulu.

Brian rechecked the line and the time on his watch, then he leaned back and looked up at the skiff.

Panic hit him first, then anger. There were two hulls silhouetted against the sparkling waves above him. The professor's wide skiff and a sleeker one drifting off the bow.

He had told her no one was to come aboard. But maybe it was Magun. Maybe the Trukese police office had seen the skiff and come out.

Brian couldn't surface, not yet. Cutting the time short would be pushing the limits and increasing his chances of embolizing. He could only hope it was Magun.

As he hung there feeling helpless, he wondered why he even trusted Magun. Where was Mimi right now? Maybe that was her boat. What if the guy in Hawaii had found him? If it was, there would be no escape now, he thought as he watched his bubbles rise up and crash into the bottom of the professor's skiff.

Wuun stood and moved to the rail. He saw Brian's bubbles at the waterline. From their size, he could tell he was right below them.

"Come on," he said to Leslie. She slid away from him and into a corner of the deck, her eyes low, like a small child cowering from an irate parent. She pulled on her blouse and clutched the remains of her bathing suit in one hand. Rubbing her face with the back of her hand, she felt the sting where he had bitten through her lip.

Wuun moved to the bow and grabbed the line tied to his boat. He unleashed it and walked it to the stern of the skiff.

Leslie's eyes fell on the knife still stuck into the lid of the crate. She looked quickly at Wuun as he secured the line to a cleat, his back to her.

She moved quickly, her breath held deep in her chest. But before she reached it, lightning exploded in her brain. Wuun caught her with his fist just below her left ear and she crumbled to the deck.

"Now get up," he said, his voice sharp like needles.

She looked at him, but couldn't look into his eyes. She drew her legs into her chest, wishing for a small dark hole to hide in.

Wuun grabbed her wrist and lifted her to her feet. "Get in the boat."

"Leave me," she said softly, "please, just leave me."

"Get in the boat, Jap. You're not gonna want to stay here." He smiled, and pushed her toward the opposite rail where the police boat was tied.

Weakly, she climbed over the rail. Wuun lifted the crate and slid it across and let it fall to the deck of his boat. He climbed in and pulled Leslie to the opposite rail.

Using only a small piece of line, he tied her right wrist to a steel stanchion. Then he pulled the red five-gallon can of gasoline stored under the gunwale of the police boat and climbed back into the skiff. Starting at the bow, he poured the fuel over the boat's entire length.

Smelling the gas, Leslie stood up. "What are doing?" Her eyes were wide.

"A boating fire, they happen all the time," he said. "It will only be one more hull on the bottom of the lagoon."

"No!" Leslie screamed. She pulled at the line that held her wrist, but the knot was secure. Wuun had grown up on boats and he'd tied her like cargo he didn't want to lose.

He ignored her screaming as he completed his task, soaking every inch of the skiff. He put the empty gas can back on the police boat and inspected his work. Satisfied, he stepped over the parallel rails and into the police boat.

He looked back at the water and saw a large cluster of bubbles erupt along the hull. The commander had moved to his ten-feet mark, Wuun knew, and he was locked there for several minutes.

Wuun moved to the center console and started the black Mercury outboard. He released the lines and the sea chop began to separate the two crafts. From his pocket, Wuun took out the blue-tipped matches. He struck one on the matchbox and tossed it into the skiff.

Instantly, the gasoline ignited and the flamed grew. The sea breeze fueled it further and it raced across the deck, down into the cabin, and over the foredeck. By the time Wuun moved behind the center console, put the Mercury in reverse, and began to back away, the skiff was engulfed, the black smoke rising into the blue dome of the tropical sky.

Brian heard the whine pierce through the water as the engine of the sleek boat started. He looked up and then at his watch. Fifteen more minutes of decompression. It didn't matter, he had to surface. If Magun was in the boat, he wouldn't leave. They had to have seen his bubbles.

Brian had begun to untie himself from the decompression line when he heard the engine whine deepen. He looked up and saw the three-bladed brass propeller spin and pull the boat away from the skiff.

It backed off until Brian could no longer see its silhouette, though he could still hear the engine as it increased, and he invisioned its bow lifting out of the water as it sped away.

As Brian finished untying himself from the decompression line, it suddenly went slack in his hand. He pulled on it and the ten feet that trailed up to the surface snaked down to him. He found the end black, its nylon fibers melted through.

His heart stopped as he looked up at the skiff only ten feet above him. then, as if in slow motion, he saw the hull expand, contract and expand again.

The shock wave of the explosion hit him like a sledgeham-

363

mer in the chest. The glass of his face mask shattered and he felt himself pulled up through the water and then forced downward as the professor's skiff splintered across the lagoon, spewing gasoline-fed flamed over the water.

Brian fought to stay conscious though his ears rang and he was breathing rapidly. He tried to turn and kick toward the surface but he couldn't. Something held him.

The decompression line was wrapped around his legs and fins. He began to untangle himself when he realized the briefcase had come loose from his wrist.

He automatically gazed upward, but instead of the briefcase, he saw the outline of the transom and engine compartment of the skiff bearing down on him. It had been ripped apart by the explosion and its weight was taking it down fast.

Brian kicked furiously to move out of the way but the line still held his legs. The transom slammed hard into him. Consciousness left just as the pain came. The swimboard pinned him to the stern as it spiraled downward toward the bottom.

THIRTY-SIX

Truk Lagoon, 1986

Death is a terrible place, a painful and cold place, he thought. The brightness of the fireworks is blinding and the accompanying thunder deafening.

"Evasive action, Mr. Bovan," Captain MacFife's voice came through the darkness.

"Aye, Skipper," Brian heard himself say. But the voice came as though it was from someone else.

"Depth charges!" Another voice screamed, and then suddenly there was more thunder. Brian felt his body jerk with the charges as they exploded in his mind.

A man screamed suddenly. "No, no," he yelled in broken English, and Brian realized it was George.

"Take her down! Hellcats coming over the horizon! Dive, dive!" a strange husky voice ordered. It was the voice of his father, the one he had imagined as a kid.

The roar of the torpedo-bomber flew from one ear to the other and Brian's body felt the concussion of its torpedo. Then suddenly, there was a woman's scream. Leslie! He woke.

The cool of the deep water brough this senses back quickly. He shook his head and discovered the thunder was a growing bump above his right ear. His eyes burned in the seawater and his left arm was numb.

Immediately he brought the pressure gauge close to his face. The blurred number showed his air supply at a thousand pounds. He had been unconscious for only a few minutes. He looked at the depth gauge. Its needle rested somewhere between sixty and seventy feet. He had no idea how deep the transom had taken him.

Leslie! He looked up but he was in a green-hazed fog; without his face mask nothing was clear. He pulled the remaining rope from around his legs and began to kick upward.

The ascent seemed to take forever. But it was more from the lack of wanting to reach the surface than from the distance. His body told him to give in and let the sea have him. Ironic, he thought; he would die in the same waters that took his father. It could be some sort of broad scheme to balance the world. Who am I to change such a plan? Let go, just let go and sleep.

But his mind kept his legs in motion and he rose steadily toward the surface of the lagoon.

Leslie is dead. No, don't think that. He forced the thoughts out of his head. The other boat, there was a fire, and she escaped to the other boat before the skiff blew.

At twenty feet Brian heard the outboard engine above him. He leaned back and tried to make out the boat's shape. His skull exploded with pain and he began to feel faint. He quickly looked back down at his fins until his brain settled.

As he listened to the changing tones of the engine he could tell that it was circling his bubbles. Then the tone changed again as the engine slowed, and then suddenly the only thing that broke the silent sea was the roar of his bubbles escaping his regulator.

At ten feet, Brian tried to look up again but faintness came back. His decompression was throw off completely and he didn't have the mind to refigure the depths and times to start again. But it wouldn't matter if he could. Only one thing filled his thoughts, and he had to see her face again.

Finally, he felt the warmth of the sun as he broke the surface. The bright day forced him to squint as he pulled the remains of his mask from his face and spit the regulator from his mouth.

The shadow of the small boat came over him from behind. He spun around in the water and saw the two silhouettes leaning over the side.

"Are you all right?" It was a woman's voice, a familiar voice, but it wasn't Leslie.

"Grab him," Mimi said as Merith reached down to help her.

Brian held on the side of the boat as Mimi released the straps of the scuba tanks and Merith pulled them from his back. Then he was lying inside, his shoulders pressed awkwardly into the narrow bow. He felt Mimi lift his head and set it back on something soft.

"Can you hear me?" she asked, looking at the side of his head. Blood was trickling from his right ear.

"Where's Leslie?" Brian asked as he rubbed his eyes; there was a slight ringing and a distinct pounding within the walls of his skull.

"Wuun has her," Merith said as he stepped over the center seat and moved to the stern. He turned the ignition key, pressed the starter, and the outboard came to life.

As Brian lifted himself up, he felt every joint in his legs and arms burn as it they were on fire. Decompression sickness. "We've got to find her!"

"We are," Merith said. "Just sit back."

"What happened?"

Mimi ran her small hand gently across his forehead. "He took her and the crate and then set the professor's boat on fire. The gas tank must have exploded."

Brian rubbed his eyes. "That son of a bitch. He must have been the one who killed her father."

"How do you feel?" Mimi asked him, her eyes concerned.

"Like I was just shot from a torpedo tube with the outer doors closed," he said.

After a minute, he looked out over the lagoon, trying to get his bearings. He looked at Mimi. "Where're we headed?"

"To the professor's house," Merith answered. "It's the only place he could have gone."

"Who the hell are you?"

Merith leaned forward and reached out his hand. "Troy Merith, CIA."

Brian looked at Mimi. "You really must have friends in high places to get this kind of support."

"Actually," Merith said as he steered the boat, "I was sent to follow you. You understand, national security and all."

"It was you in Hawaii?"

"No, that was another agent. We found him dead. Someone didn't want you followed to Truk."

Brian rubbed his face, then he remembered. "The orders." His eyes shot to Mimi. "I had the briefcase. I had it in my hands. But I lost it."

From under the center seat, Mimi took out a bundled towel. Wrapped inside was his father's acid-stained briefcase.

Merith brought the small boat ashore a quarter mile down the beach, around the bend and out of sight from the professor's house. The bow hit hard against the coarse sand and the engine gurgled in the surf until he killed it.

As the two men pulled the boat further up onto the beach, the pain in his knees became too much for Brian. He collapsed in the sand.

"Stay with the boat," Merith said.

Brian stood up slowly. "I'm going."

"You got the bends and you know it. Stay here. You're going to get us all killed."

368

"He's got Les and I want him," Brian said, his jaw tight and determined.

Mimi put her hand on Brian's shoulder. "He know what he's doing, Brian. Let him do it."

"This is my territory now," Merith said. He pulled his gun from his trousers.

"I'm going with you." Brian was firm.

Merith could see the pain in Brian's face every time he took a breath. "Give him your gun," he said to Mimi. "At least Wuun won't be expecting us."

Mimi handed Brian her .357 magnum.

"Stay here, Mimi," Merith said. She nodded.

As they turned, she grabbed Brian's wrist. "Be careful."

The two men headed along the beach, veering close to where the jungle reached out to meet the sand. "I'll come from the rear through the jungle near the road," Merith said as they came closer to the house.

Brian followed him a few feet into the mangroves, then stopped to give him time to get in position. After a moment, he moved until he could see the professor's porch. Wuun's police skiff was anchored in the small cove several yards off the beach.

The house was quiet and deserted compared to the sounds of the jungle that now seemed intensified as Brian crept along its floor. Two parakeets fluttered in their nest above him, screeching over a piece of food.

The white curtain that hung in the doorway of the professor's study suddenly lifted. Brian dropped to one knee and aimed at the door. The curtain billowed in the wind and then dropped back down.

He exhaled with relief—then the hand touched him on the shoulder. Spinning, he dropped to the sand, the gun in front of him. It was Mimi. "Jesus Christ." He reached up and pulled her down beside him. "I thought you were going to stay by the boat?"

"Did you really think I was going to stay there?" she asked.

369

Brian shook his head. "Just stay low and do what I tell you."

Brian looked back at the house and watched for movement. There was none. Inching their way closer, he pressed his back against the trunk of the last tree before the clearing. Mimi knelt behind a bush a few feet away. Brian concentrated on slowing his breathing and stopping the hot irons that were piercing into his elbows and knees.

Merith set his shoes under the decomposing log. From his ankle holster, he took the three extra bullets and tucked them into his watchband. Then he moved quickly, almost running through the thick growth of the island. For his size and age, the CIA agent was surprisingly agile.

He stopped twice, waited and listened, then bolted again until he was at the edge of the clearing and twenty feet from the house. He stopped, sucked in a deep breath, and dashed for the back wall. He'd made it. Crouching low, he ducked under the two windows of the workroom and moved to the far side.

Merith was wrong in what he'd told Brian. This wasn't his territory. Washington, D.C., was, as was New York, Los Angeles, Paris, Moscow, or any huge metropolis in the Western world. Although more adept at it in his prime, he could blend in and disappear among the population to fulfill his assignments.

But here, Merith stood out. No matter how well he moved in and out of city crowds, he couldn't apply the techniques to this jungle.

And he was also wrong about Wuun. The police chief was expecting him, and as Merith moved past the third window, he saw him at the edge of the jungle, rising from behind an elephant-eared palm tree. Wuun held his revolver in a firing-line, two-hand stance.

There was no time for reaction. No time to evade the moment and Merith knew it, knew it all too well.

Two quick shots, the first to the throat, the second to the chest half an inch below the heart. Merith fell back against the house and slid slowly to the ground. His body rolled over on his stomach, pushing his face, eyes open, into the sand.

Brian reacted to the shots by moving fast to the kitchen door. He jumped to the porch, skipping the three steps. He stopped, turned, and waved to Mimi to follow.

In ten strides of her small fragile legs, she was beside him.

At the edge of the doorway, Brian waited, then peered in. Empty. He stepped inside, clutching the gun in front of him. He felt Mimi's hand on his back as he moved through the kitchen and into the hallway. It was empty, as was the bathroom. The workroom door was closed. Brian moved cautiously to the professor's study.

There he saw Leslie sitting on one of the chairs, her back to them. Her hands were tied behind her, her mouth gagged, her head slumped forward. The desk had been clear with the sweep of a hand, everything once on the top now scattered across the floor. The encrusted crate sat in the center, saltwater seeping from its cracks.

Tucking the gun into the front of his trunks, he moved to her. Bending down, he gently lifted her face in his hands. The sight made his stomach turn inside out, as the left side of her face was swollen to twice its normal size, her one eye closed off completely, the other filled with tears.

Without looking up, she tried to pull her head away.

"Leslie." he said softly.

She turned and stared at him, unsure whether it was his voice or just her mind wanting it to be. She began to cry.

"It's okay, I'm going to get you out of here," he said, reaching for the knots of the gag at the back of her neck.

"If you move, Commander, you die," Wuun's voice came from the doorway leading into the hall.

Brian froze; his hands were in front of him, the gun, in his trunks. Slowly he looked up and saw himself in the sights of the revolver. Wuun had his left arm around Mimi's throat. She was clawing furiously at him, but the police chief barely noticed.

"Please, Commander, do as I say," Wuun smiled. "I'd hate to have to kill you so soon. Now stand up very slowly."

Brian stood.

"With the left hand, using only your first finger and thumb, take the gun out and lay it on top of the crate. Be very slow, Commander."

Brian drew the gun and set on the moist wooden lid.

"Step back."

Brian did as he was told, moving back against the high bookshelves. Wuun released Mimi and pushed her toward him. He took the gun from the crate, then stepped around Leslie and put her between himself and them. With a smile, he pressed the gun hard to the back of her head.

"Open the crate," he said, his voice harsh.

Brian hesitated as the anger built inside him. Now his body ached not from the decompression sickness but from the yearning to rip Wuun apart.

Mimi grabbed Brian's wrist. Her eyes were suddenly wide with terror but it wasn't from Wuun. She shook her head.

"Aren't you curious what's inside?" Wuun asked.

Brian looked at him. "I know what's inside. A bunch of worthless bones."

"No." Wuun shook his head. "This one has the diamonds."

"If you say so."

Wuun's eyes narrowed on him. "Open it!"

"You open it."

Wuun pushed the gun hard into Leslie's neck. Brian heard her muffled cry as she looked up at him. "Tell you what, Commander. I'll blow her head off while you watch. Then I'll kill the old lady and you and open the crate myself."

"Stop it," the heavy voice said from behind Wuun. The large-framed man stepped in through the doorway. Brian felt suddenly weak as his eyes met the man's. Then anger crept up inside him.

Admiral Mills stepped around Wuun; under his left arm was the black leather briefcase. He looked straight at Brian. "I'm sorry, son. I warned you to let it go, but you had to dig everything up."

"You son of a bitch." Brian took a step toward the admiral.

"No, Brian," Mimi stopped him. "He's going to let us go. He's safe. Without the briefcase or the crate, it's our word against this." She looked at the admiral. "You came because of Tendrey, didn't you?"

Mills stared at her, his eyes trying to bore into the old Chinese woman's, but they couldn't. "Believe me, this is no favor to the old guy. I had to come. My name is on these orders right under his."

"You set them up. You sent my father into this lagoon knowing what was going to happen."

Mills looked hard at Brian, his finger pointing at the center of his chest. "He knew the chances. He was going to back out and I wouldn't have blamed him, but the OSS pushed him. And she pushed him." He turned to Mimi. "Fucking whore tricked him more than Tendrey or me. He knew about the attack, he knew when the Hellcats were coming. But he chose to be inside Truk. He did it for her, that's how he was."

Mimi felt Brian clutch his fists. "No, Brian," she said again, touching his arm. He pulled away from her. "You know the truth, that's all that matters."

Brian's eyes didn't leave Mills. "You think you can just walk away from this?"

Mills stepped closer to him. "Son, that's exactly what I'm going to do. It's what we're all going to do. You can't change what happened, Brian. It was finished before you were born."

Mills looked down at Leslie. She had been so pretty in the photographs. She'd be pretty again. He nodded at

Wuun. "Let's tie them up and get the crate into the boat. We'll drop it off outside the reef and bury it once and for all." He turned back to Brian. "I'm sorry. I really am." He grabbed one of the desk chairs and pushed it toward him. "Now sit down."

Wuun looked at Mills and a grin came to his face. "You don't understand, Admiral," he said in a monotone. "I already have my orders from Admiral Tendrey." Wuun swung the barrel of the revolver to the center of Mills's stomach and fired point-blank.

The briefcase dropped from Mills's hand as he stared at the police chief in disbelief. His face grimaced and he stepped toward him. Wuun fired again and Mills fell heavily at his feet.

Before Wuun's second shot, Brian moved at him, grabbing the empty chair. And as Wuun turned, he hit him with it across the chest, sending him backward. The revolver skidded across the floor and into the hallway.

They fell at Leslie's feet with Brian landing full-force on top of him. But Wuun lifted him off as if he were a paper doll, and suddenly, Brian was face down on the floor, Wuun on top of his back. He struck Brian three times in the back of the head with his fists. Then, from nowhere, he had his knife in his hand.

Wuun hadn't bothered to tie Leslie's legs, and with all her strength, she kicked Wuun in the face, shattering his front teeth. Stunned, he lost his hold on Brian for an instant.

It was all Brian needed. He pushed himself up and turned back to the Trukese. Wuun was already on his feet, the knife in his right hand. "Come on, Commander." He coaxed him with his left. "Your turn to die." He stepped back around the desk until it was between Brian and him.

"Put it down." Mimi's voice was strong and direct. Her eyes ran down the unmoving barrel and at her target.

Wuun looked at her. He balanced the knife between his

thumb and forefinger and looked at the crate. He ran his hand along the edge.

"I said, put it down." She cocked back the hammer.

Wuun smiled. He inserted the knife in the crack of the lid and ran it down the length, breaking the latch free from the rotten wood.

"No!" Mimi screamed. "Brian!" She dropped to the floor.

The instant Wuun opened it, Brian threw himself on top of Leslie. The chair she was in crumbled from their combined weight, splintered as they hit the floor.

The booby-trapped crate was designed to rip open the hull of a Maru-class freighter. But forty years in saltwater had eaten through the connecting wires and stripped most of the power from the Americans' crude plastic explosives. Only the small detonating charge went off, shattering the windows of the room and shaking the books from the shelves.

Before the room cleared of smoke and dust, Brian moved to the other side of what was left of the desk. The walls of the study were riddled with the diamonds. Wuun's body was thrown against the bookshelf and ripped open as if hit by a shotgun blast, the priceless gems blown through him.

Brian lifted Leslie. He could feel her shaking as he untied her hands and took the gag from her mouth. She began to cry, and wrapping her arms around him, she pulled herself to his chest.

"You two okay?" Mimi asked as she stood up and wiped her face with the back of her hand.

"Fine," Brian said as he held Leslie tight. "We're both fine."

THIRTY-SEVEN

Kaimu, Hawaii, 1986

The sun was warm in its last rays, and it seemed to hold itself only a few inches off the horizon, trying to keep the day. The rush of the waves from the distant reef came up the cliff on the breeze.

Admiral Tendrey watched a lone seagull climb on the wind, gliding ever so close to the jagged rocks; it disappeared below and then reappeared a moment later further down the ridge.

"Admiral," Marks said as he walked down the cement path and across to the dense grass lawn where Tendrey had parked himself.

The admiral was expecting his secretary, and without looking up, he put his hand out over his shoulder to receive the phone. But instead, Marks stepped in front of him.

"Admiral," Marks said, his voice stressed again.

"What?" Tendrey said impatiently, looking up at the young man from under his long-billed hat. It was a silly thing with painted red sailboats on the brim. A gift from Miss Swanson, but it kept the sun off his head.

"There are two men to see you."

"Who?"

"They're from the naval office in Honolulu. Internal Affairs, sir," he said, his voice at its highest peak.

Tendrey looked away and out at the reefs. "Tell them I don't want any visitors."

"I told them you weren't to be disturbed, but they're being insistent. Very insistent, Admiral. They said they're here on official business and have several questions to ask you about some lagoon in the Pacific."

Tendrey pulled his green terry-cloth robe tighter around himself. He coughed and then was silent for a moment. Marks waited, though his nerves were frazzled. The two men had been more than insistent, they had been threatening.

"Go in the study and take my memoirs from the safe," the admiral instructed. "Give the gentlemen chapter seventeen. Tell them it will answer their questions completely," Tendrey said. For the first time, his voice was weak and old.

"Yes, sir," Marks turned.

"And, Marks."

"Yes, Admiral?"

Tendrey cleared his throat. "Be sure to ask them to return it when they're finished. And when they do, take it and the rest of my memoirs and burn them."

"Sir?"

"Do it," Tendrey looked hard at him, his red-rimmed eyes stone-cold. "Make sure you burn all of them."

"Yes, Admiral," Marks said, and then hesitantly stepped away.

The admiral watched over his shoulder as his secretary disappeared past the garden and into the house. Then he turned back and stared out at the sea. It was a beautiful royal blue, laced on the tips with whitecaps.

Tendrey turned the collar of his robe up and straightened the silly hat Swanson had given him. Then he reached down and unlatched the wheel lock of his chair.

The wheelchair began to roll forward down the slope, but stopped, the front caster held by the thick grass. Tendrey pushed himself further until he was past the grass and on the solid rocky soil of the cliff.

Then the wheelchair was free and began to roll with its own momentum toward the edge.

The papers will call it an accident, he thought to himself. And the last thing his eyes took in was the wonderful blue color of the sea.

POSTSCRIPT

Moen Island, Truk Lagoon, 1986

Brian felt her squeezing his right hand. Leslie didn't realize she was holding it so tight. He turned his head and smiled up at her. She stared at him, her beautiful almond eye unblinking, the other still swollen closed. Her long hair dancing in the strong wind blown around them by the navy's white Seasprite helicopter.

"I'll be all right," he said, his voice muffled under the clear plastic face-cup that fed him oxygen.

She nodded and tired to smile.

"How're you doing, Commander?" the medic with the baby face and pencil-thin blond mustache asked as he rolled him on the stretcher across the runway toward the chopper. The awkward-looking machine would take them to Ewiwetok Atoll where a decompression chamber was waiting. Brian would be inside in a matter of hours.

Brian nodded and motioned he was okay, but the effort shot pain through his shoulder and elbow. He tried not to show it. Leslie didn't understand the bends could be cured. She was too frightened to listen to the medic's explanation.

"He'll be in the chamber a lot of hours, ma'am, but he'll come out of it, you'll see," the medic reassured her.

Leslie brushed a strand of hair from Brian's forehead. "I know," she said, and forced a small smile.

"I'll give you an ice pack in the transport. It'll help the swelling in that cheek."

"Thank you," Leslie said with a nod, her eyes not leaving Brian.

Magun ran from the airport building and caught up to them. "You're forgetting something," he said.

Brian stopped the medic and sat up the best he could, and Magun handed him the black leather briefcase wrapped in a towel. "I believe this is yours."

Brian took it from him slowly, gently, as if it would crumble in his hands. "Where's Mimi?"

Magun shrugged. "She made a phone call from the office and then gave me the briefcase, and she said to tell you thank you."

"That's it?" Brian asked.

"That's it."

"Who'd she call?" Leslie asked.

"I don't know, but two minutes later, my phone was ringing off the hook from Naval Department in Washington, the CIA, State Department, Department of Records— you name it, they're calling. Suddenly, I'm up to my ears in work."

Brian smiled.

"Here," Magun said to Leslie. "This is yours." He took a small envelope from his breast pocket and gave it to her. "It's a receipt. The value of the diamonds still has to be determined and they'll go to a historical fund. But your father's permits entitled him to a substantial finder's fee. Now it goes to you," he said with a smile.

The medic saw the hand signal from the helicopter pilot. "We've got go, Commander."

"Thanks, Fumio," he said, and then leaned back on the stretcher.

Leslie leaned over and kissed the police officer on the cheek. "For everything," she said softly.

"Come back for a vacation next time," he said with a smile. "Truk is really a beautiful place."

The medic pushed Brian toward the chopper with Leslie staying beside him, not letting go of his hand.

Magun watched as a second man helped lift Brian into the doorway and then helped Leslie. Then the huge four blades of the Seasprite began to spin faster and faster until it forced him to back away.

The engine roared and the chopper rose gently from the ground, hovered a moment, dipped its nose, and climbed into the blue sky over Truk Lagoon.

Magun stood on the runway until they were out of sight, then he turned and headed back to the small one-story buildings that made up the airport. He had his work cut out for him, he knew. But as the new police chief, he would be more than helpful to the U.S. authorities that were coming to his islands.

Mimi walked the narrow path that began at the furthest end of the town and snaked up into the mountains. It wasn't well worn, but was covered and choked off in places by the heavy tropical foliage that blanketed the island. She managed, though, to push her way through.

At the very top, the path veered to the right and became even smaller until it was no path at all, just tall, sweet-smelling grass pushed down by a single passerby. The small lone house in the distance sat almost hidden by a thicket of breadfruit and banana trees. It was partly built of palm-tree logs and partly of scrapped sheet metal, each of different sizes and all set against a four-foot-thick wall that had once made up a Japanese gunnery position.

Perched on this high hill, the precarious little house with its strange angles gave the vision that it was about to slide down into the sea.

But Mimi had come to know this place well over the years. She stepped through the small cleared area in front, the yard as she called it, though the whole of the mountain could be called the yard of this house. Tools and fishing gear cluttered and edges, old nets hung from rusting nails or bent corners of the sheet metal, all to be mended sometime in the future.

A three-legged table rested next to a chair with no back near the open door. Mimi wondered if the canvas she had hung to keep the rain out was ever pulled closed. Probably not. At least never when she had stayed here. A cluster of shells hanging on fishing line chimed in the breeze.

She stepped into the hut as quietly as she could.

"Tea?" the man asked in a hoarse voice. He was standing next to the stove, his back toward her.

"No." Mimi said. She saw he was wearing the same worn khaki-colored shorts he always did.

"Has he gone?" he asked, adjusting the flame under the tea pot.

"Yes," she said softly. "He found the briefcase." She waited for some kind of response but there was none. "I'm sure he'll be back, maybe then . . ."

"No," he said in a whisper. He knew what she wanted him to do, but that, he had decided, was too much to ask of Brian.

Mimi moved closer to him and touched his shoulder. The deep spiderweb scars that completely covered his back and ran up the right side of his neck were dark red from the sun. "Mills is dead and so is Wuun."

He nodded. "And the diamonds?"

"He found those too. Officer Magun said some money will go to the professor's daughter."

"Good," he said.

"I think the two of them will be seeing more of each other," Mimi said.

"Is she nice?"

"Very nice," she said, running her hands up along his back, tracing the scars from the intense heat that molted his skin. Gently she turned him and took his face into her hands.

Soft, thick layers of pink tissue covered where his eyes had once been. Dark, beautiful eyes that used to look deep into hers and make her tremble. She slipped her arms around his waist and held him. "She looks at him like I look at you."

The man smiled at that, then he asked, "Do you want the fossils now?"

"No," she said. "Not now."

"Are you sure?" he asked.

"I'm sure. They can wait a little while longer," she said.

"Come here." He took his cup of tea and stepped away from the stove, counting the exact number of steps to the couch.

He sat down and pulled her next to him. She giggled like a little girl as she snuggled close beside him, putting her cheek against his chest. She could feel his heart beat.

He kissed the top of her head. "You're so beautiful."

"You only remember how I was forty years ago," she said, trying to pull away from him, but he was still strong and he held her. "I'm an old woman. A wrinkled old woman."

"And I'm a blind old man and yet you are still here." He ran his hand along her arm, to her shoulder and through her long soft hair. Then he touched her face. "Do you really think you can see me any better than I see you?"

Mimi smiled and kissed him on the mouth.

He leaned forward and set his cup on the old footlockers stacked to make a coffee table for his home. "You're sure you don't want to take them now?" he asked, tapping the lid of the one on top.

"Are you trying to get rid of me?" She laughed.

"Never."

"It's over," she said, sitting up and looking at his face. "It's finally over. The orders will prove everything."

He took her hand in his and caressed it. "It doesn't bring them back."

"No, nothing can do that," she said softly.

"They were good men, all of them."

"Their names will be cleared. So will yours."

He nodded and then reached up and touched her cheek. "Thank you, Mimi."

She placed her finger over his lips. "Shhh," she said. "All that matters to me is you, Douglas. I loved you from the first."

Gently, he leaned down and kissed her hand. Then he pulled her close and they sat there in the small hut, listening to the shell chimes playing in the warm wind that came up the mountainside of the peaceful blue waters of Truk Lagoon.